TEEN TITANS GO!

Weirder Things

**MATTHEW K. MANNING   DEREK FRIDOLFS   AMANDA DEIBERT
J. TORRES   P.C. MORRISSEY   HEATHER NUHFER
SHOLLY FISCH   IVAN COHEN   LEA H. SEIDMAN**
Writers

**AGNES GARBOWSKA   DEREK FRIDOLFS   ERICH OWEN
SANDY JARRELL   SARAH LEUVER   PHILIP MURPHY**
Artists

**FRANCO RIESCO   PAMELA LOVAS   ERICH OWEN
JEREMY LAWSON   SARAH LEUVER**
Colorists

WES ABBOTT
Letterer

**DARIO BRIZUELA
and FRANCO RIESCO**
Collection Cover Artists

SUPERMAN created by Jerry Siegel and Joe Shuster
By special arrangement with the Jerry Siegel family

KRISTY QUINN Editor – Original Series
JEB WOODARD Group Editor – Collected Editions
ERIKA ROTHBERG Editor – Collected Edition
STEVE COOK Design Director – Books
AMIE BROCKWAY-METCALF Publication Design
CHRISTY SAWYER Publication Production

BOB HARRAS Senior VP – Editor-in-Chief, DC Comics
PAT McCALLUM Executive Editor, DC Comics

DAN DiDIO Publisher
JIM LEE Publisher & Chief Creative Officer
BOBBIE CHASE VP – New Publishing Initiatives & Talent Development
DON FALLETTI VP – Manufacturing Operations & Workflow Management
LAWRENCE GANEM VP – Talent Services
ALISON GILL Senior VP – Manufacturing & Operations
HANK KANALZ Senior VP – Publishing Strategy & Support Services
DAN MIRON VP – Publishing Operations
NICK J. NAPOLITANO VP – Manufacturing Administration & Design
NANCY SPEARS VP – Sales
MICHELE R. WELLS VP & Executive Editor, Young Reader

TEEN TITANS GO!: WEIRDER THINGS

Published by DC Comics. Compilation and all new material Copyright © 2019 DC Comics. All Rights Reserved.
Originally published in single magazine form in TEEN TITANS GO! 31-36 and online as TEEN TITANS GO! Digital Chapters 61-72.
Copyright © 2019 DC Comics. All Rights Reserved. All characters, their distinctive likenesses and related elements featured in this
publication are trademarks of DC Comics. The stories, characters and incidents featured in this publication are entirely fictional.
DC Comics does not read or accept unsolicited submissions of ideas, stories or artwork. DC – a WarnerMedia Company.

DC Comics, 2900 West Alameda Ave., Burbank, CA 91505
Printed by LSC Communications, Kendallville, IN, USA. 10/11/19. First Printing.
ISBN: 978-1-4012-9497-7

Library of Congress Cataloging-in-Publication Data is available.

PEFC Certified

This product is from
sustainably managed
forests and controlled
sources

PEFC/29-31-337 www.pefc.org

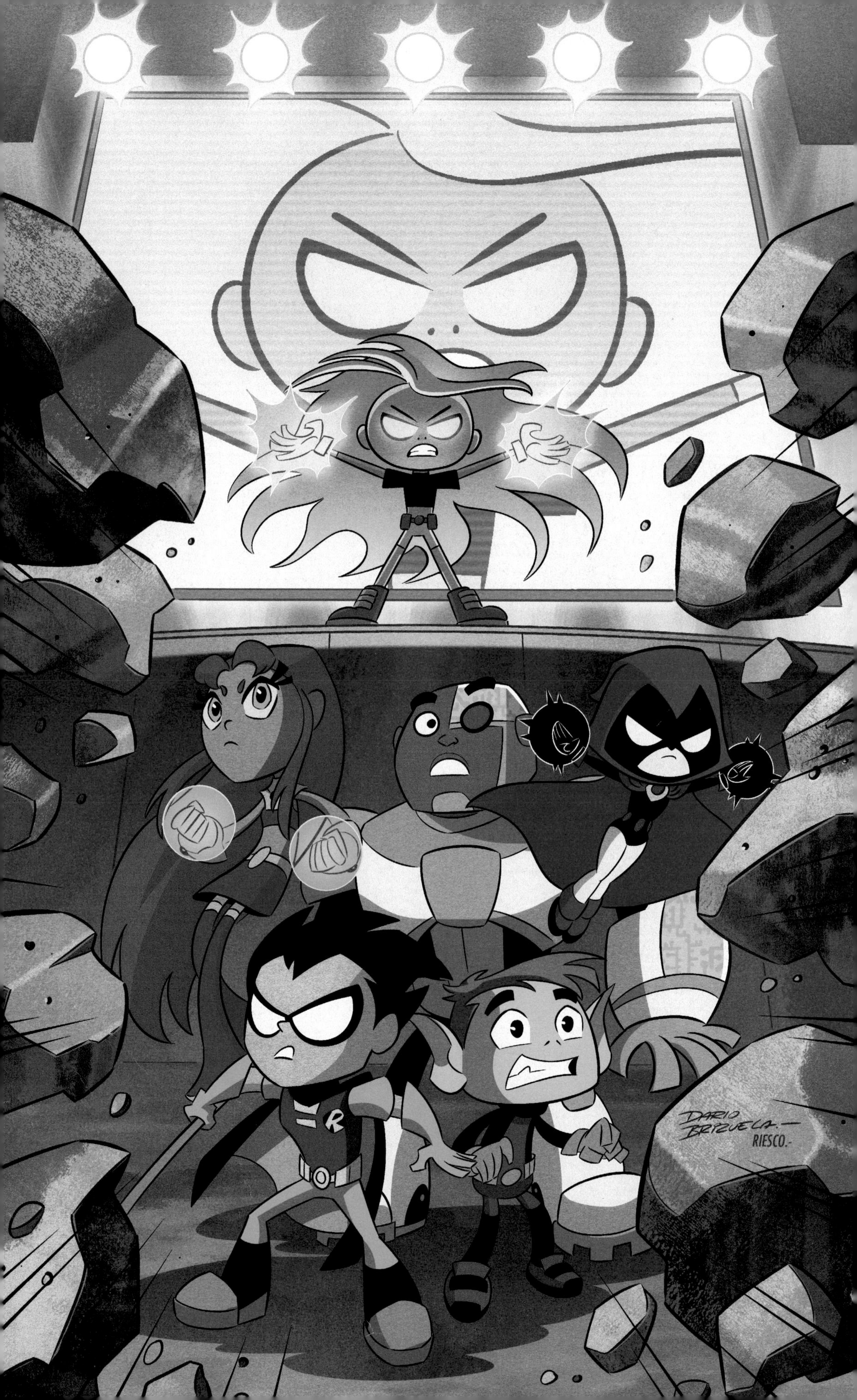
DARIO BRIZUELA
RIESCO.-

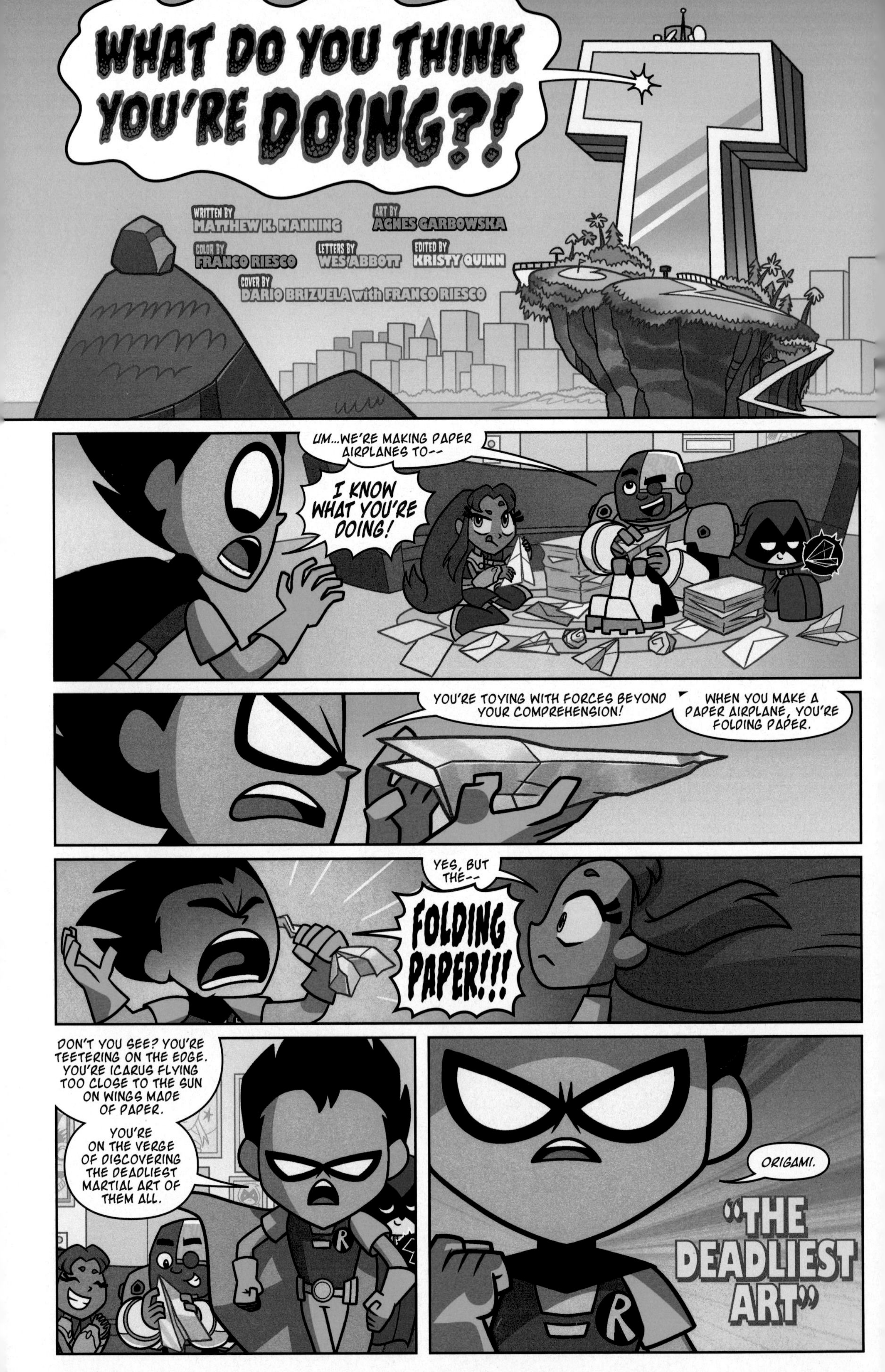
WHAT DO YOU THINK YOU'RE DOING?!
WRITTEN BY MATTHEW K. MANNING
ART BY AGNES GARBOWSKA
COLOR BY FRANCO RIESCO
LETTERS BY WES ABBOTT
EDITED BY KRISTY QUINN
COVER BY DARIO BRIZUELA with FRANCO RIESCO
UM...WE'RE MAKING PAPER AIRPLANES TO--
I KNOW WHAT YOU'RE DOING!
YOU'RE TOYING WITH FORCES BEYOND YOUR COMPREHENSION!
WHEN YOU MAKE A PAPER AIRPLANE, YOU'RE FOLDING PAPER.
YES, BUT THE--
FOLDING PAPER!!!
DON'T YOU SEE? YOU'RE TEETERING ON THE EDGE. YOU'RE ICARUS FLYING TOO CLOSE TO THE SUN ON WINGS MADE OF PAPER.
YOU'RE ON THE VERGE OF DISCOVERING THE DEADLIEST MARTIAL ART OF THEM ALL.
ORIGAMI.
"THE DEADLIEST ART"

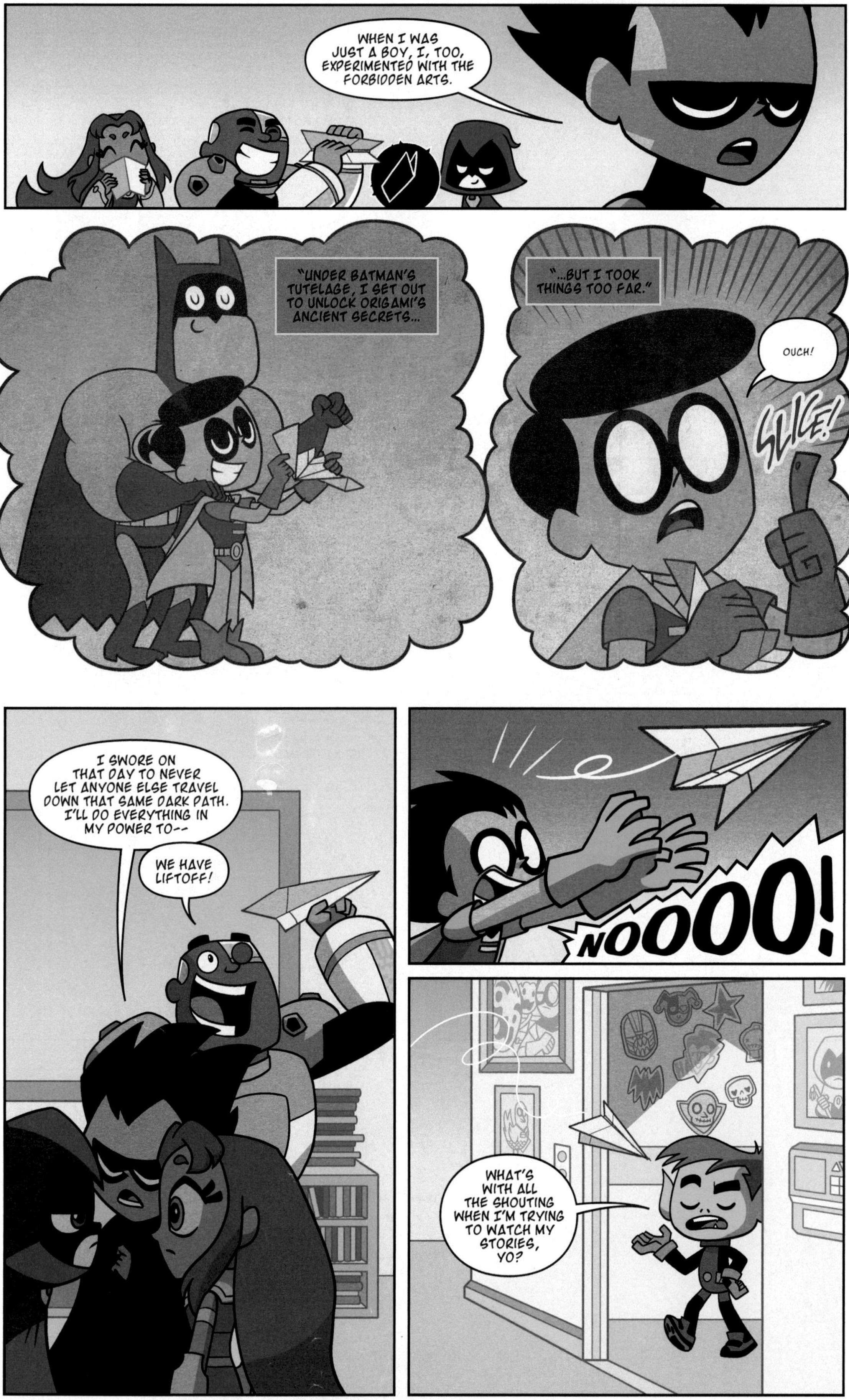
WHEN I WAS JUST A BOY, I, TOO, EXPERIMENTED WITH THE FORBIDDEN ARTS.
"UNDER BATMAN'S TUTELAGE, I SET OUT TO UNLOCK ORIGAMI'S ANCIENT SECRETS...
"...BUT I TOOK THINGS TOO FAR."
OUCH!
SLICE!
I SWORE ON THAT DAY TO NEVER LET ANYONE ELSE TRAVEL DOWN THAT SAME DARK PATH. I'LL DO EVERYTHING IN MY POWER TO--
WE HAVE LIFTOFF!
NOOOO!
WHAT'S WITH ALL THE SHOUTING WHEN I'M TRYING TO WATCH MY STORIES, YO?

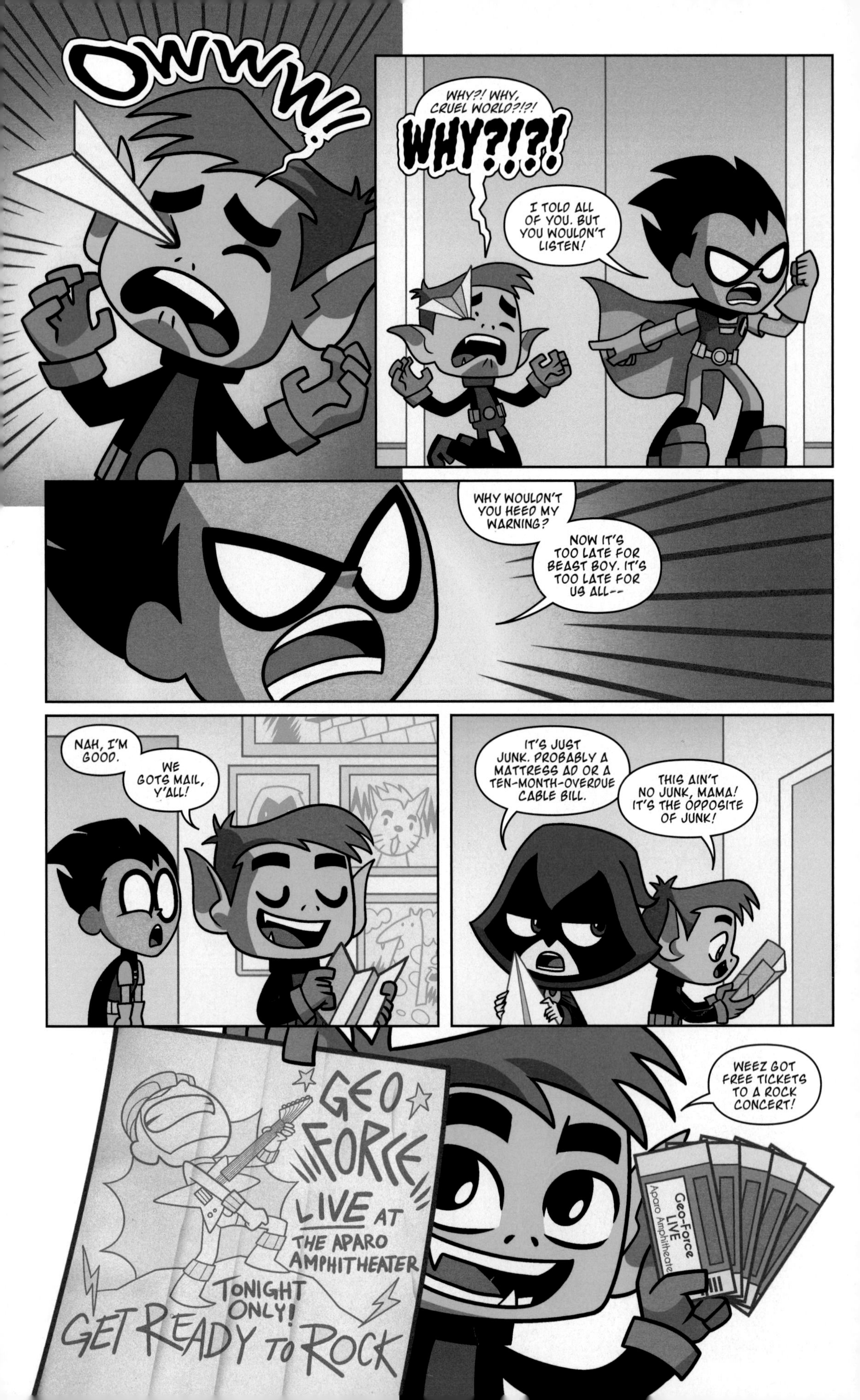
OWWW!
WHY?! WHY, CRUEL WORLD?!?!
WHY?!?!
I TOLD ALL OF YOU. BUT YOU WOULDN'T LISTEN!
WHY WOULDN'T YOU HEED MY WARNING?
NOW IT'S TOO LATE FOR BEAST BOY. IT'S TOO LATE FOR US ALL--
NAH, I'M GOOD.
WE GOTS MAIL, Y'ALL!
IT'S JUST JUNK. PROBABLY A MATTRESS AD OR A TEN-MONTH-OVERDUE CABLE BILL.
THIS AIN'T NO JUNK, MAMA! IT'S THE OPPOSITE OF JUNK!
GEO FORCE LIVE AT THE APARO AMPHITHEATER
TONIGHT ONLY!
GET READY TO ROCK
WEEZ GOT FREE TICKETS TO A ROCK CONCERT!
Geo-Force LIVE
Aparo Amphitheater

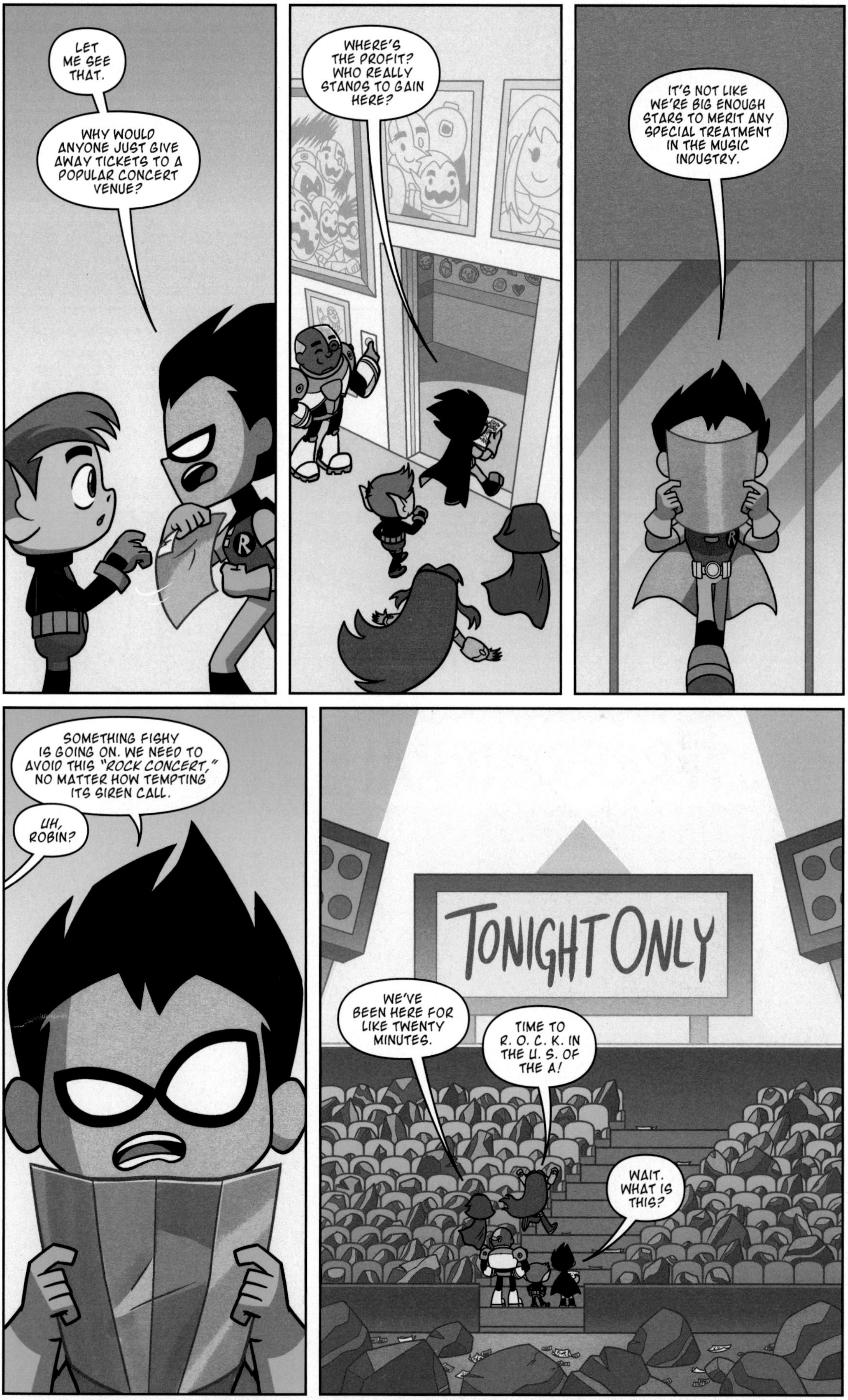
LET ME SEE THAT.
WHY WOULD ANYONE JUST GIVE AWAY TICKETS TO A POPULAR CONCERT VENUE?
WHERE'S THE PROFIT? WHO REALLY STANDS TO GAIN HERE?
IT'S NOT LIKE WE'RE BIG ENOUGH STARS TO MERIT ANY SPECIAL TREATMENT IN THE MUSIC INDUSTRY.
SOMETHING FISHY IS GOING ON. WE NEED TO AVOID THIS "ROCK CONCERT," NO MATTER HOW TEMPTING ITS SIREN CALL.
UH, ROBIN?
TONIGHT ONLY
WE'VE BEEN HERE FOR LIKE TWENTY MINUTES.
TIME TO R. O. C. K. IN THE U. S. OF THE A!
WAIT. WHAT IS THIS?

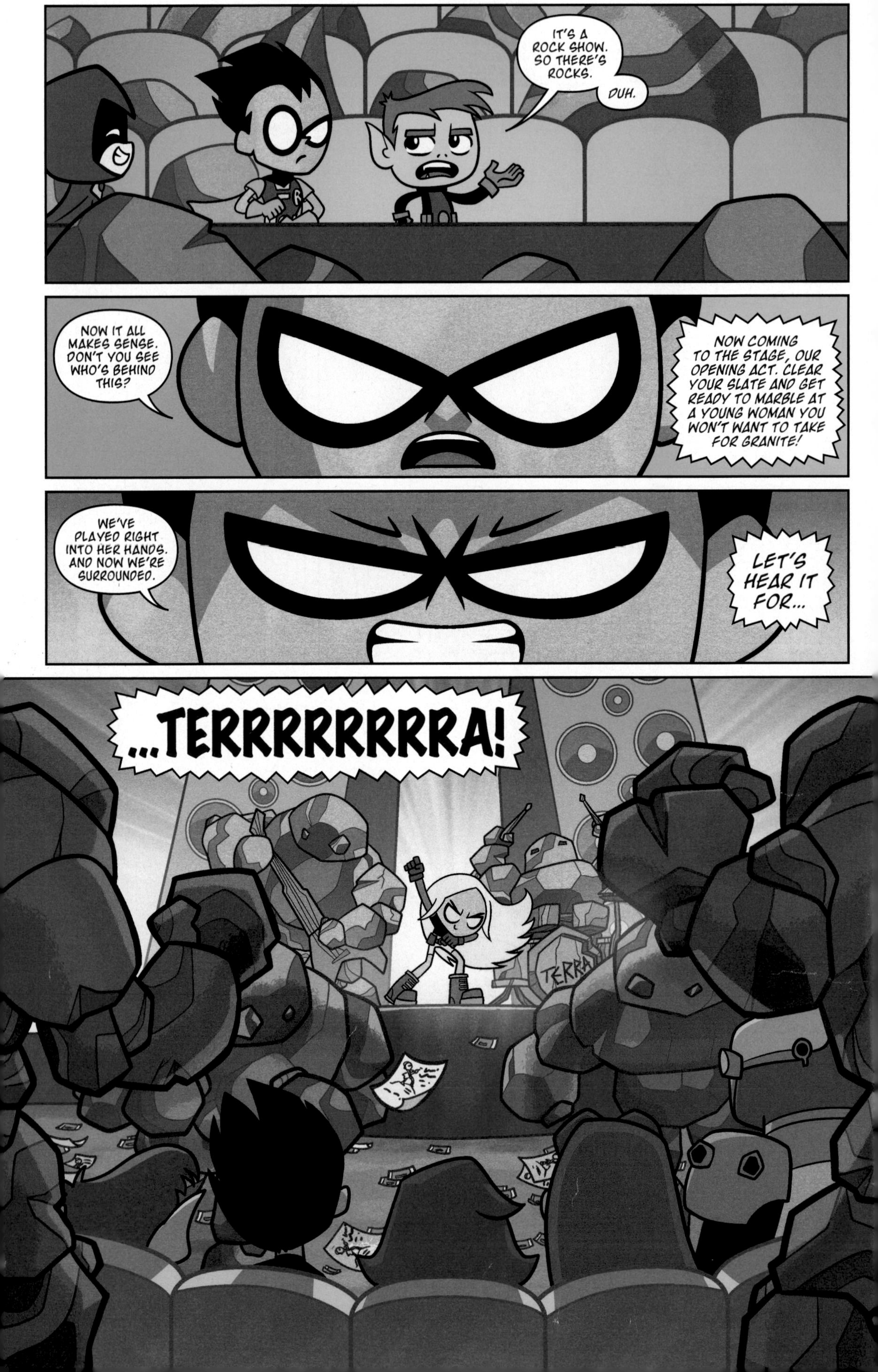
IT'S A ROCK SHOW. SO THERE'S ROCKS.
DUH.
NOW IT ALL MAKES SENSE. DON'T YOU SEE WHO'S BEHIND THIS?
NOW COMING TO THE STAGE, OUR OPENING ACT. CLEAR YOUR SLATE AND GET READY TO MARBLE AT A YOUNG WOMAN YOU WON'T WANT TO TAKE FOR GRANITE!
WE'VE PLAYED RIGHT INTO HER HANDS. AND NOW WE'RE SURROUNDED.
LET'S HEAR IT FOR...
...TERRRRRRRRA!
TERRA

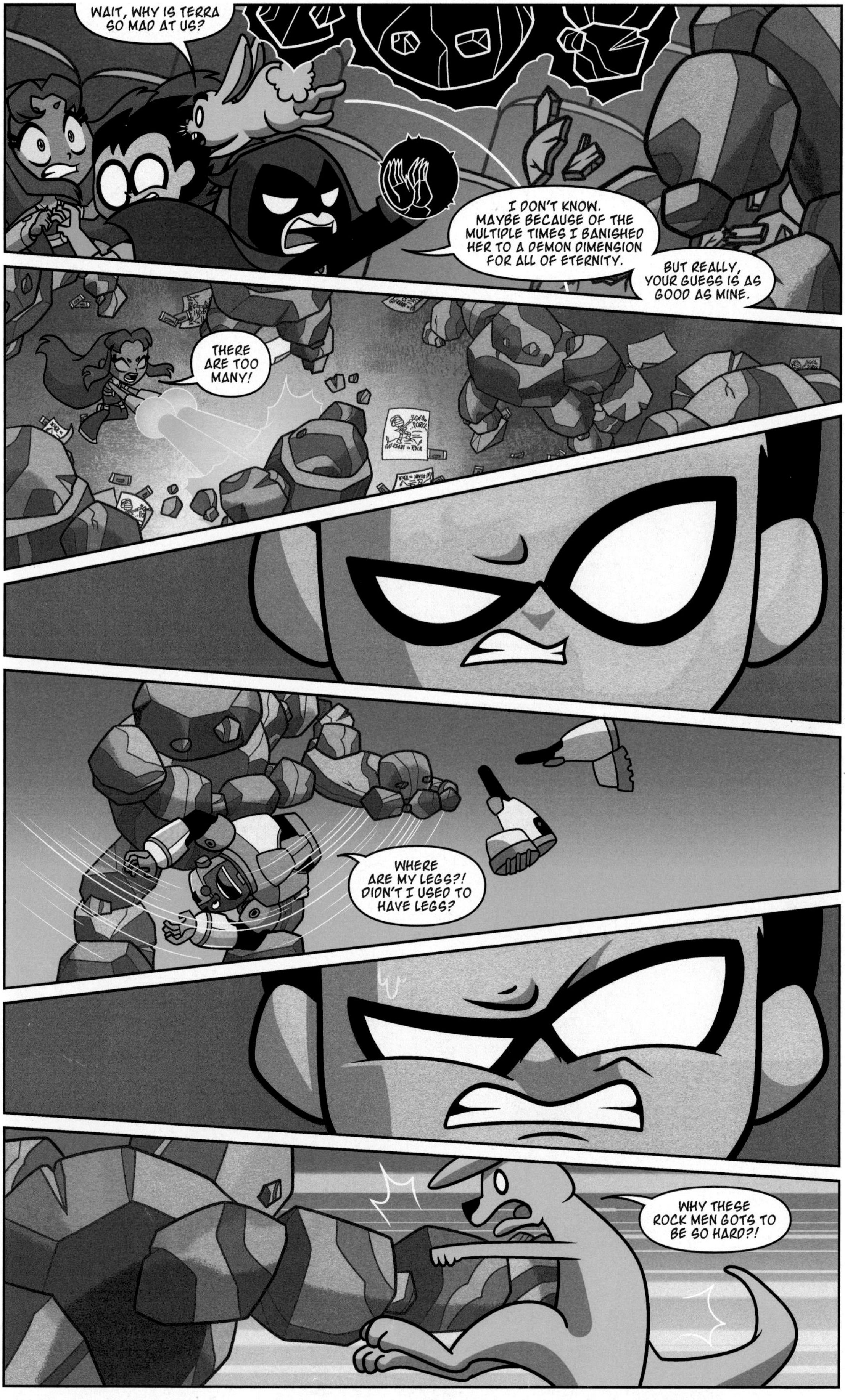
WAIT, WHY IS TERRA SO MAD AT US?
I DON'T KNOW. MAYBE BECAUSE OF THE MULTIPLE TIMES I BANISHED HER TO A DEMON DIMENSION FOR ALL OF ETERNITY.
BUT REALLY, YOUR GUESS IS AS GOOD AS MINE.
THERE ARE TOO MANY!
WHERE ARE MY LEGS?! DIDN'T I USED TO HAVE LEGS?
WHY THESE ROCK MEN GOTS TO BE SO HARD?!

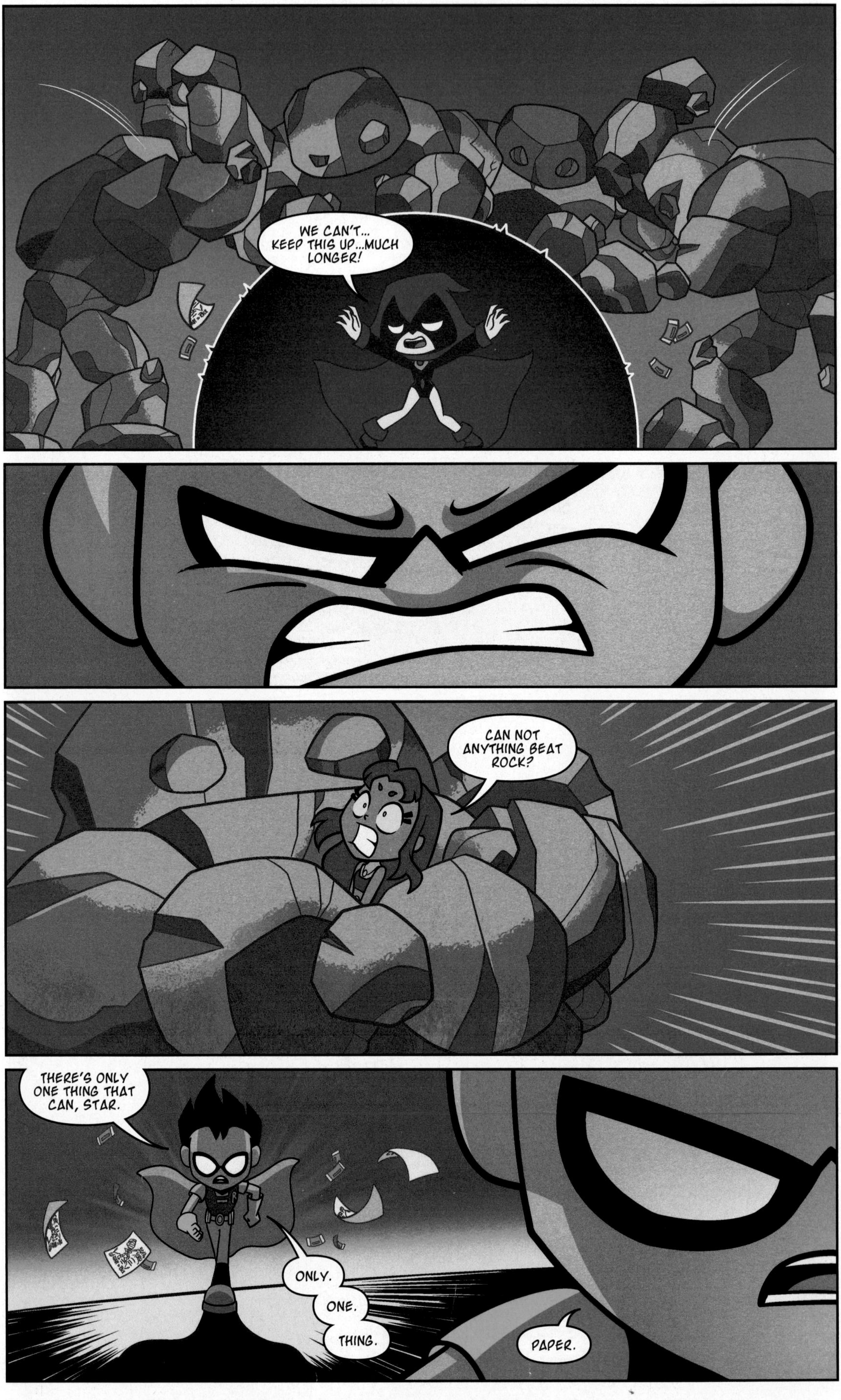
WE CAN'T... KEEP THIS UP...MUCH LONGER!
CAN NOT ANYTHING BEAT ROCK?
THERE'S ONLY ONE THING THAT CAN, STAR.
ONLY.
ONE.
THING.
PAPER.

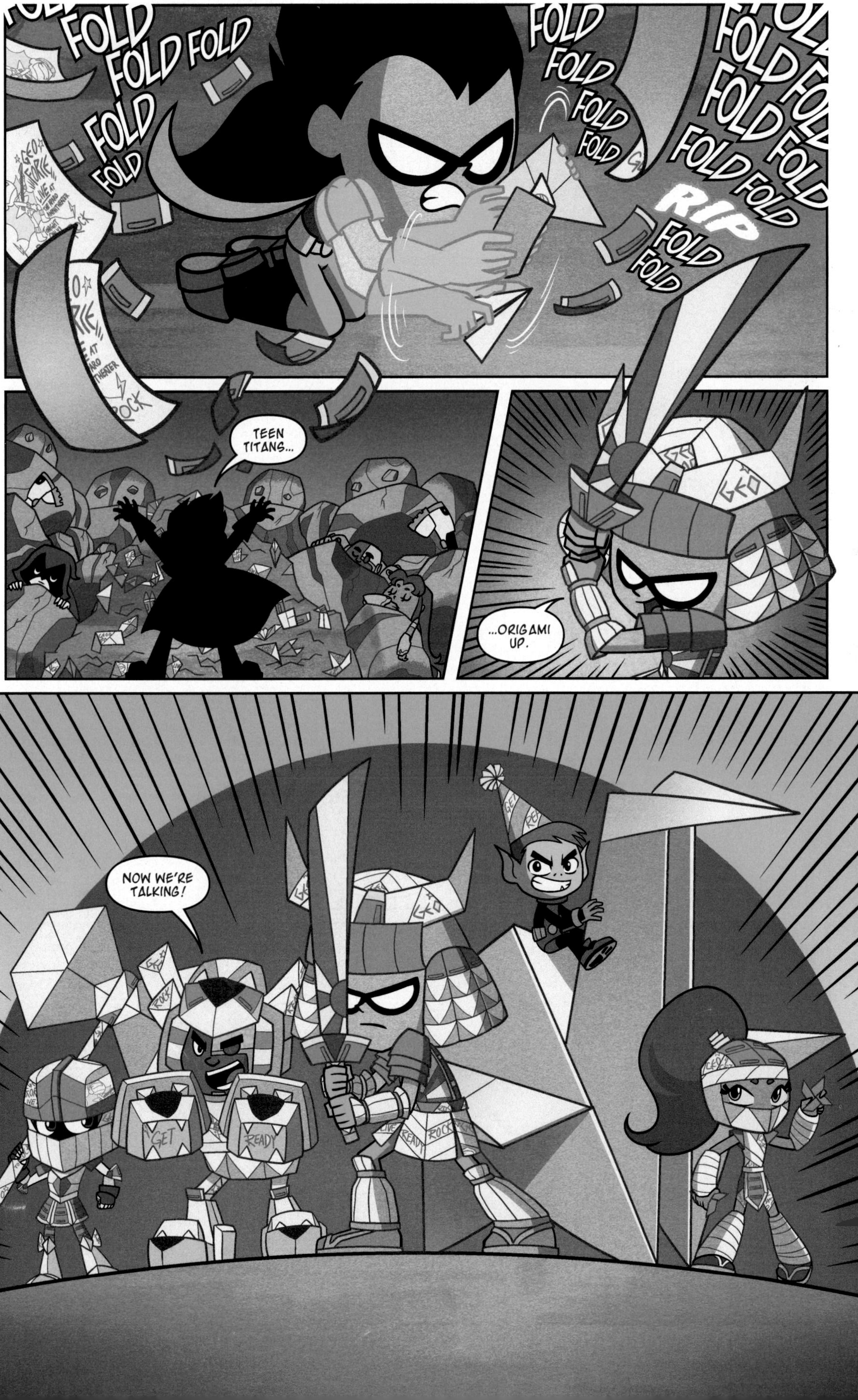
FOLD
FOLD FOLD FOLD
FOLD
FOLD
FOLD
FOLD
FOLD
FOLD
FOLD
FOLD
FOLD FOLD
FOLD FOLD
FOLD FOLD
FOLD FOLD
RIP
FOLD
FOLD
TEEN TITANS...
...ORIGAMI UP.
NOW WE'RE TALKING!

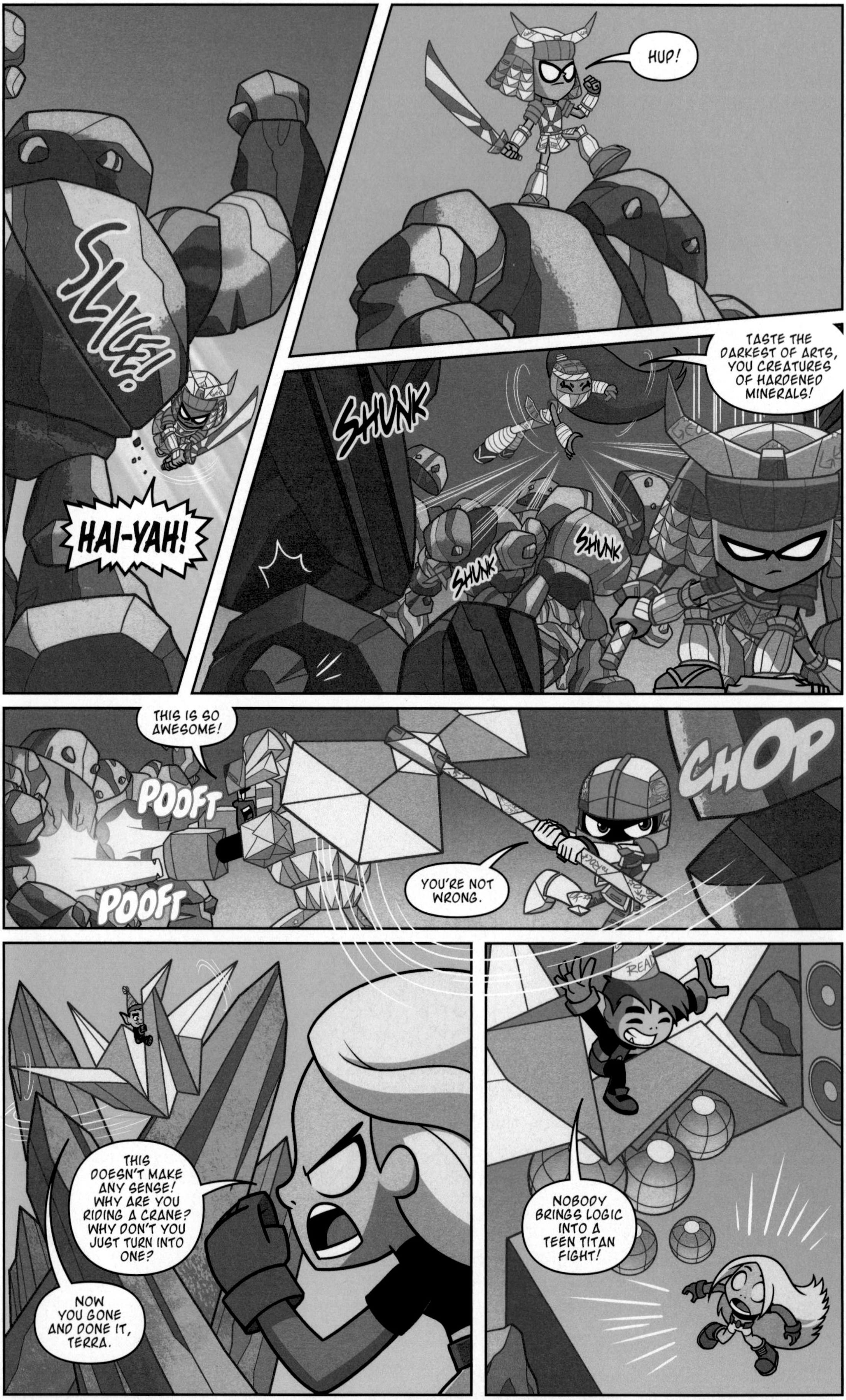
SLICE!
HAI-YAH!
HUP!
SHUNK
TASTE THE DARKEST OF ARTS, YOU CREATURES OF HARDENED MINERALS!
SHUNK
SHUNK
THIS IS SO AWESOME!
POOFT
POOFT
CHOP
YOU'RE NOT WRONG.
THIS DOESN'T MAKE ANY SENSE! WHY ARE YOU RIDING A CRANE? WHY DON'T YOU JUST TURN INTO ONE?
NOW YOU GONE AND DONE IT, TERRA.
NOBODY BRINGS LOGIC INTO A TEEN TITAN FIGHT!

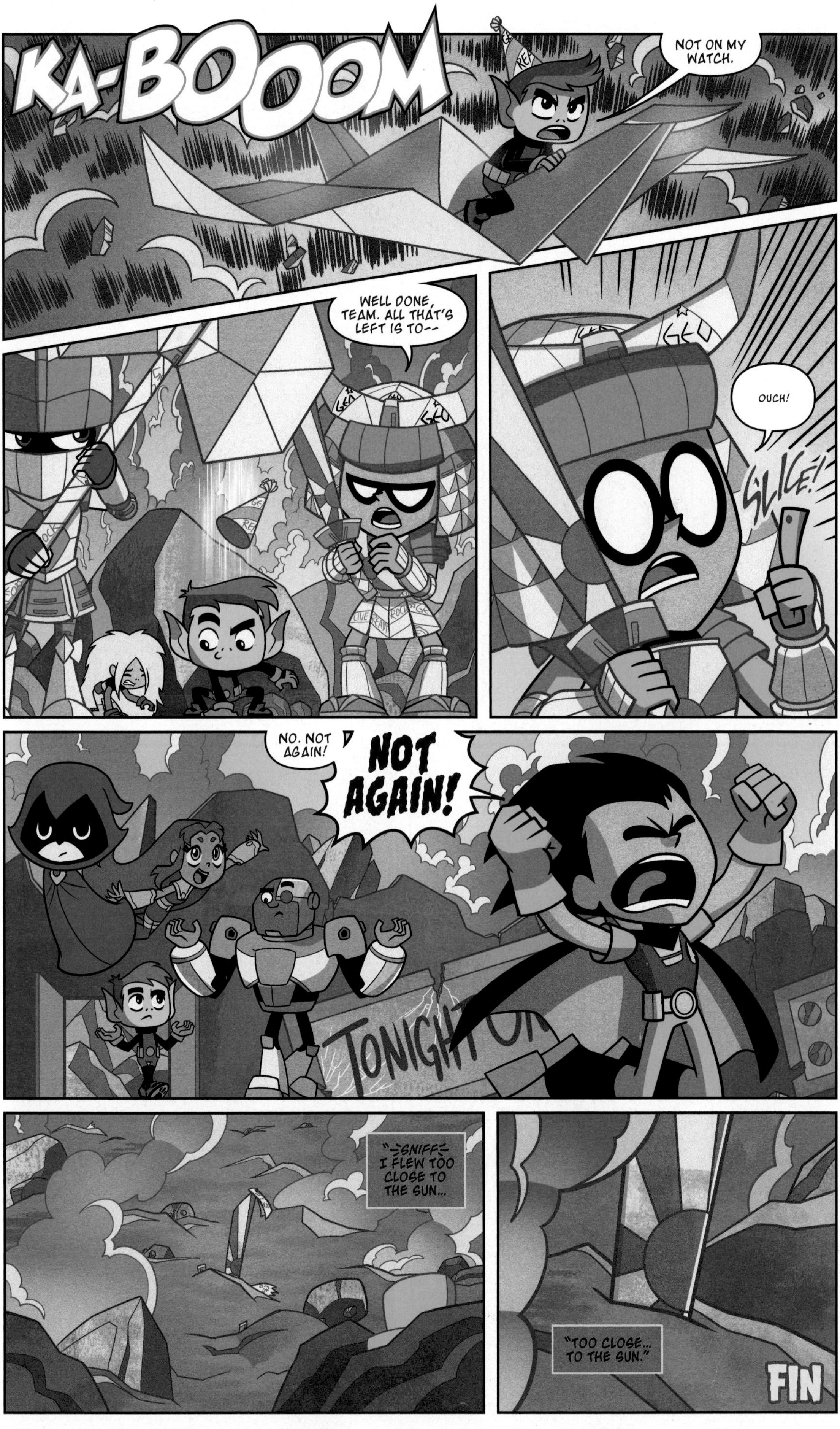
KA-BOOOOM
NOT ON MY WATCH.
WELL DONE, TEAM. ALL THAT'S LEFT IS TO--
OUCH!
SLICE!
NO. NOT AGAIN!
NOT AGAIN!
TONIGHT
SNIFF I FLEW TOO CLOSE TO THE SUN...
"TOO CLOSE... TO THE SUN."
FIN

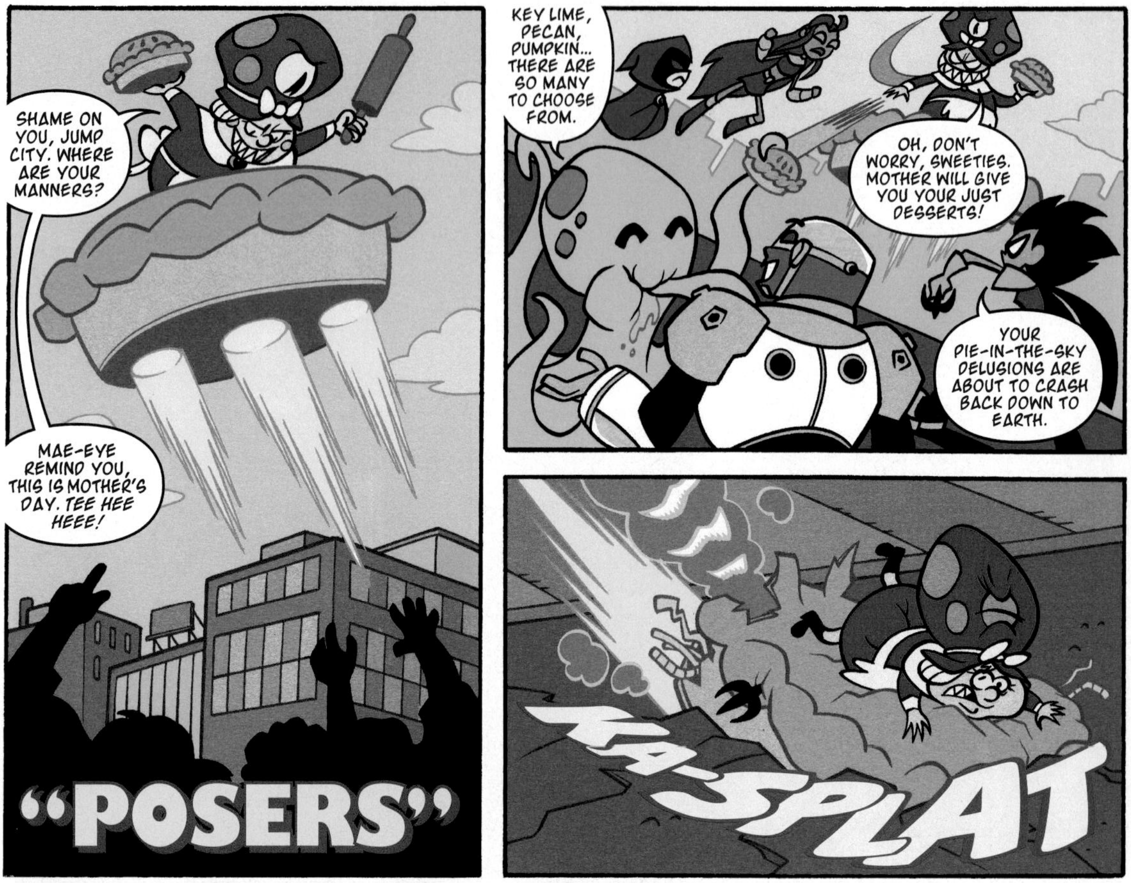
SHAME ON YOU, JUMP CITY. WHERE ARE YOUR MANNERS?
MAE-EYE REMIND YOU, THIS IS MOTHER'S DAY. TEE HEE HEEE!
"POSERS"
KEY LIME, PECAN, PUMPKIN... THERE ARE SO MANY TO CHOOSE FROM.
OH, DON'T WORRY, SWEETIES. MOTHER WILL GIVE YOU YOUR JUST DESSERTS!
YOUR PIE-IN-THE-SKY DELUSIONS ARE ABOUT TO CRASH BACK DOWN TO EARTH.
KA-SPLAT

WRITTEN & DRAWN BY DEREK FRIDOLFS   COLOR BY PAMELA LOVAS   LETTERS BY WES ABBOTT   EDITED BY KRISTY QUINN

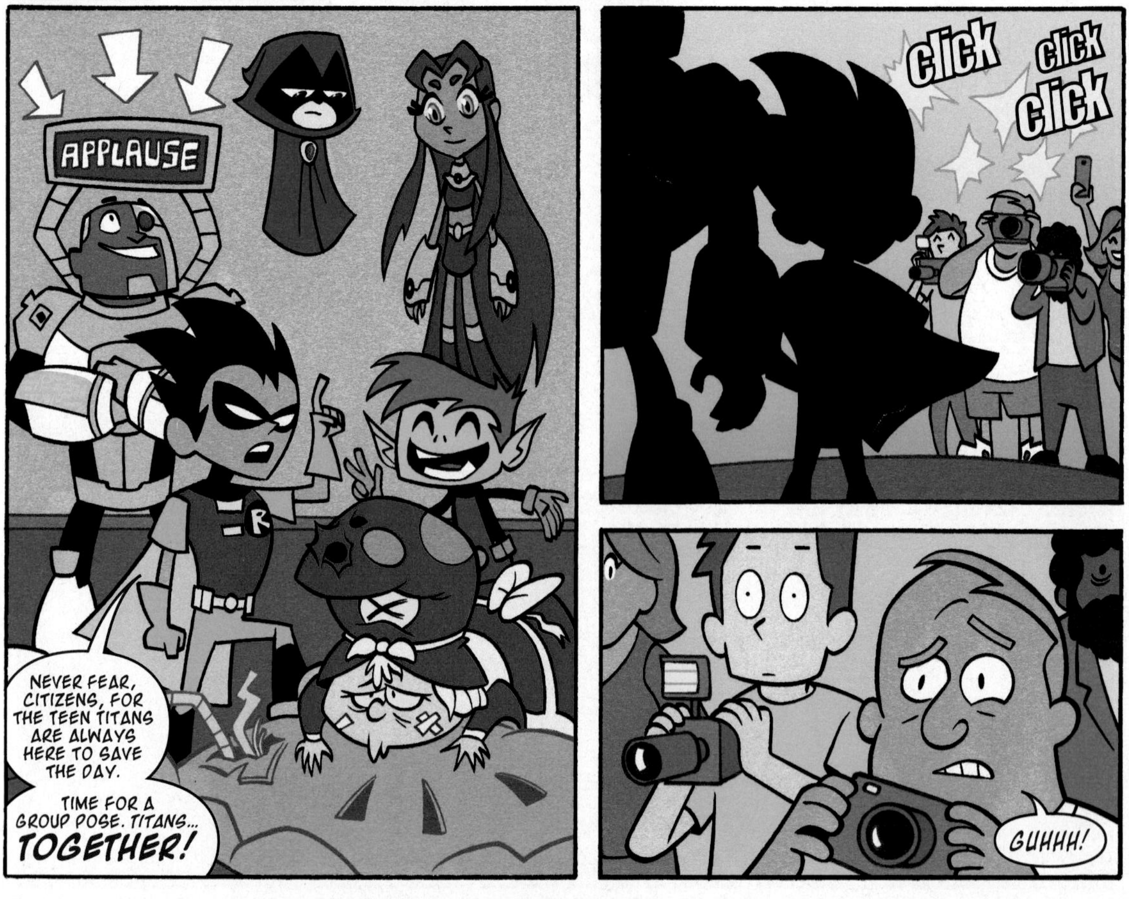
APPLAUSE
NEVER FEAR, CITIZENS, FOR THE TEEN TITANS ARE ALWAYS HERE TO SAVE THE DAY.
TIME FOR A GROUP POSE. TITANS... TOGETHER!
click
click
click
GUHHH!

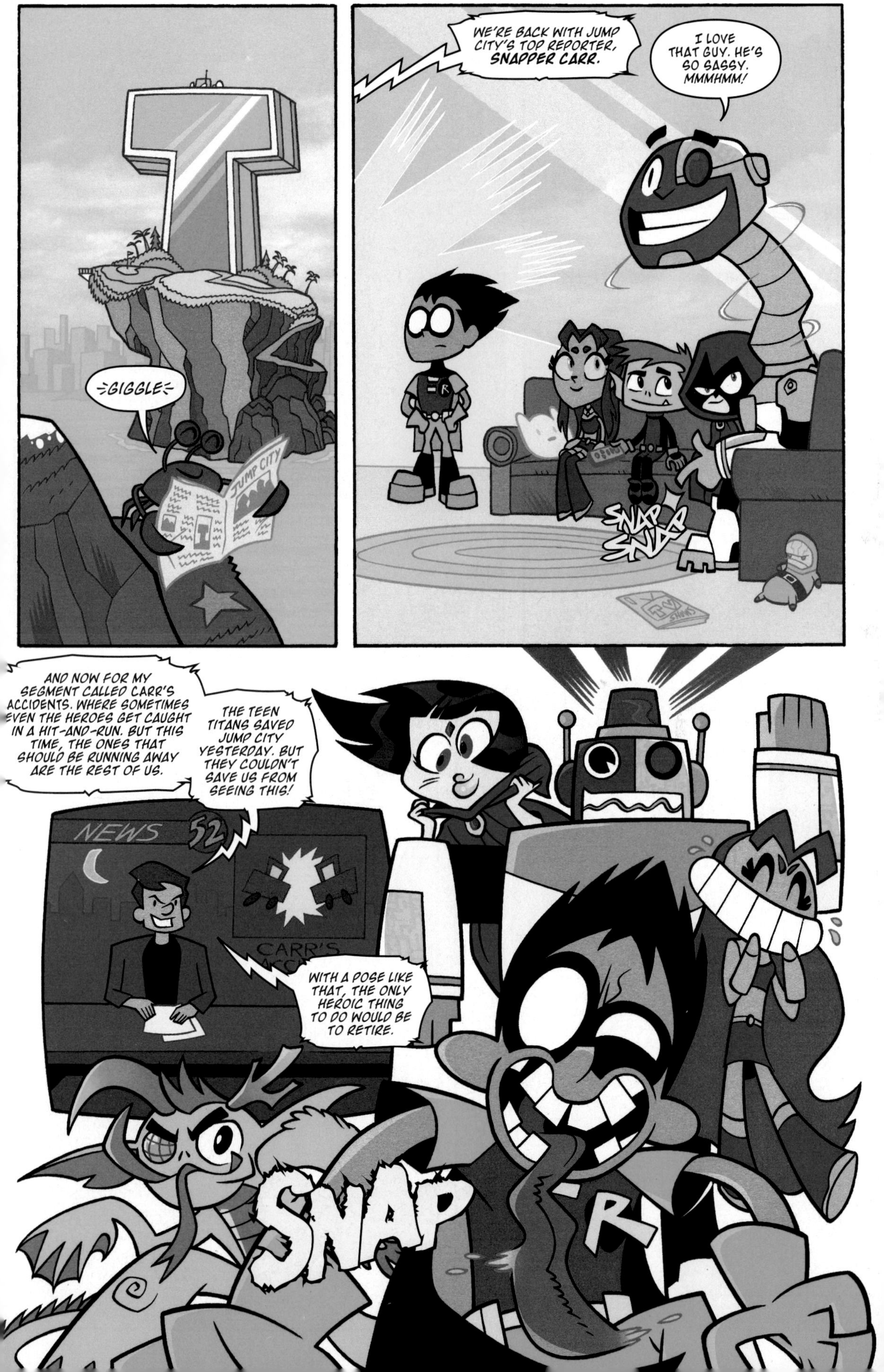

GIGGLE
JUMP CITY
WE'RE BACK WITH JUMP CITY'S TOP REPORTER, SNAPPER CARR.
I LOVE THAT GUY. HE'S SO SASSY. MMMHMM!
SNAP SNAP
AND NOW FOR MY SEGMENT CALLED CARR'S ACCIDENTS. WHERE SOMETIMES EVEN THE HEROES GET CAUGHT IN A HIT-AND-RUN. BUT THIS TIME, THE ONES THAT SHOULD BE RUNNING AWAY ARE THE REST OF US.
THE TEEN TITANS SAVED JUMP CITY YESTERDAY. BUT THEY COULDN'T SAVE US FROM SEEING THIS!
NEWS 52
CARR'S
WITH A POSE LIKE THAT, THE ONLY HEROIC THING TO DO WOULD BE TO RETIRE.
SNAP

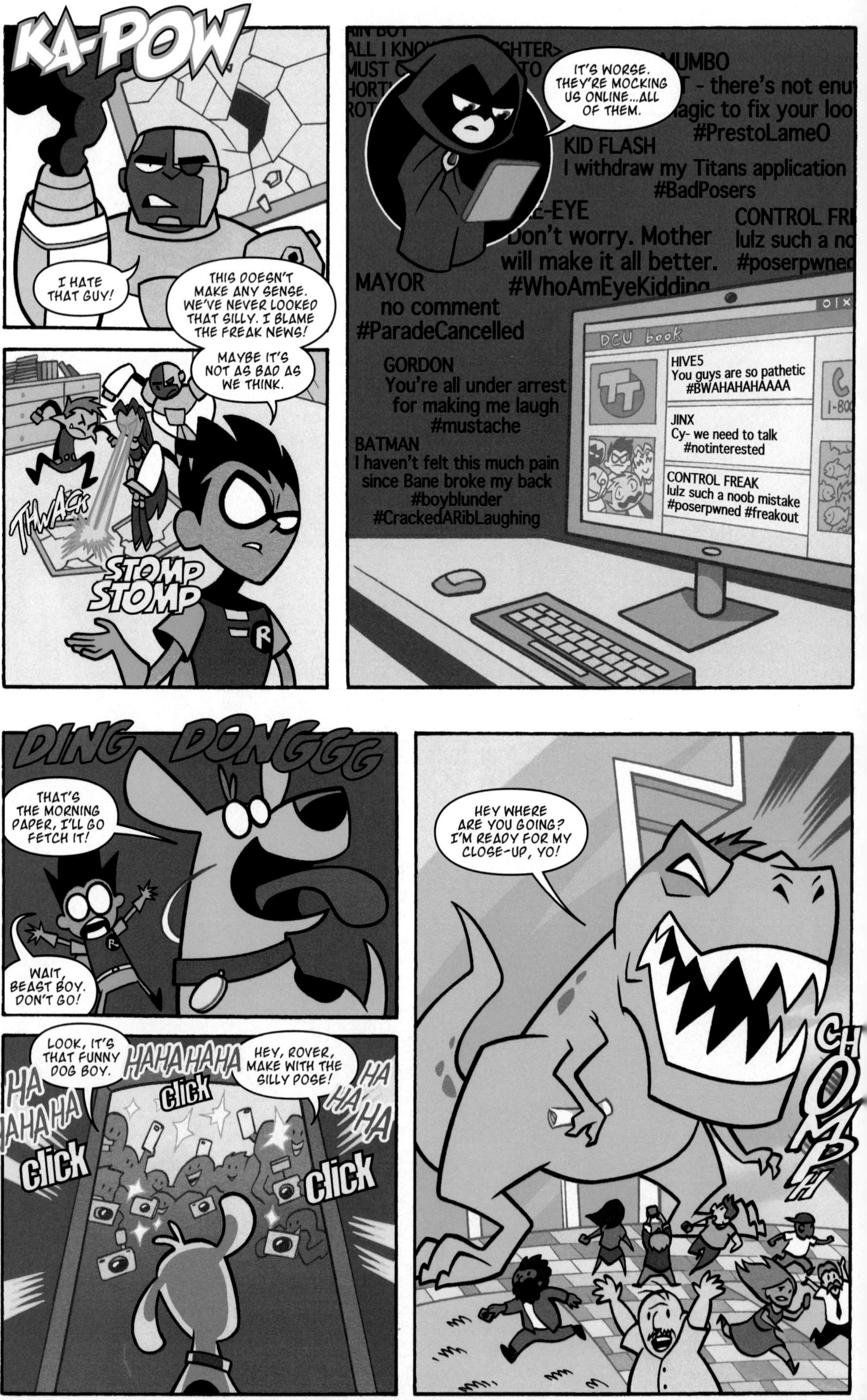
KA-POW
I HATE THAT GUY!
THIS DOESN'T MAKE ANY SENSE. WE'VE NEVER LOOKED THAT SILLY. I BLAME THE FREAK NEWS!
MAYBE IT'S NOT AS BAD AS WE THINK.
THWACK
STOMP STOMP
IT'S WORSE. THEY'RE MOCKING US ONLINE...ALL OF THEM.
MUMBO
- there's not enu
agic to fix your loo
#PrestoLameO
KID FLASH
I withdraw my Titans application
#BadPosers
CONTROL FR
lulz such a no
#poserpwned
E-EYE
Don't worry. Mother will make it all better.
MAYOR
no comment
#ParadeCancelled
GORDON
You're all under arrest for making me laugh
#mustache
BATMAN
I haven't felt this much pain since Bane broke my back
#boyblunder
#CrackedARibLaughing
DCU book
HIVE5
You guys are so pathetic
#BWAHAHAHAAAA
JINX
Cy- we need to talk
#notinterested
CONTROL FREAK
lulz such a noob mistake
#poserpwned #freakout
DING DONGGG
THAT'S THE MORNING PAPER, I'LL GO FETCH IT!
WAIT, BEAST BOY. DON'T GO!
LOOK, IT'S THAT FUNNY DOG BOY.
HAHAHAHA
HEY, ROVER, MAKE WITH THE SILLY POSE!
HA HAHAHA
HA HA HA
click
click
click
HEY WHERE ARE YOU GOING? I'M READY FOR MY CLOSE-UP, YO!
CHOMP

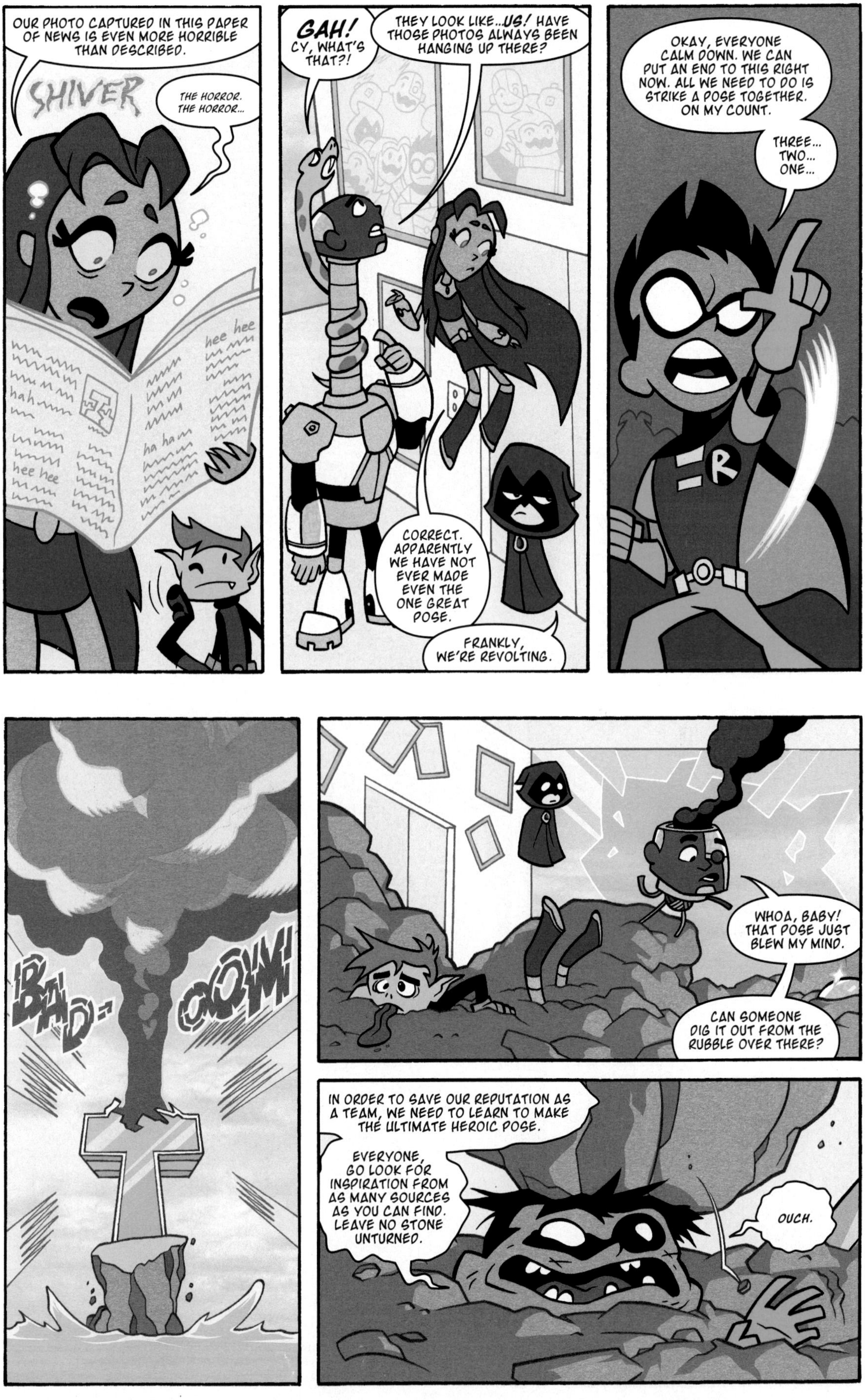
OUR PHOTO CAPTURED IN THIS PAPER OF NEWS IS EVEN MORE HORRIBLE THAN DESCRIBED.
SHIVER
THE HORROR. THE HORROR...
hee hee
hah
ha ha
hee hee
GAH! CY, WHAT'S THAT?!
THEY LOOK LIKE...US! HAVE THOSE PHOTOS ALWAYS BEEN HANGING UP THERE?
CORRECT. APPARENTLY WE HAVE NOT EVER MADE EVEN THE ONE GREAT POSE.
FRANKLY, WE'RE REVOLTING.
OKAY, EVERYONE CALM DOWN. WE CAN PUT AN END TO THIS RIGHT NOW. ALL WE NEED TO DO IS STRIKE A POSE TOGETHER. ON MY COUNT.
THREE... TWO... ONE...
BA-DOOM!
WHOA, BABY! THAT POSE JUST BLEW MY MIND.
CAN SOMEONE DIG IT OUT FROM THE RUBBLE OVER THERE?
IN ORDER TO SAVE OUR REPUTATION AS A TEAM, WE NEED TO LEARN TO MAKE THE ULTIMATE HEROIC POSE.
EVERYONE, GO LOOK FOR INSPIRATION FROM AS MANY SOURCES AS YOU CAN FIND. LEAVE NO STONE UNTURNED.
OUCH.

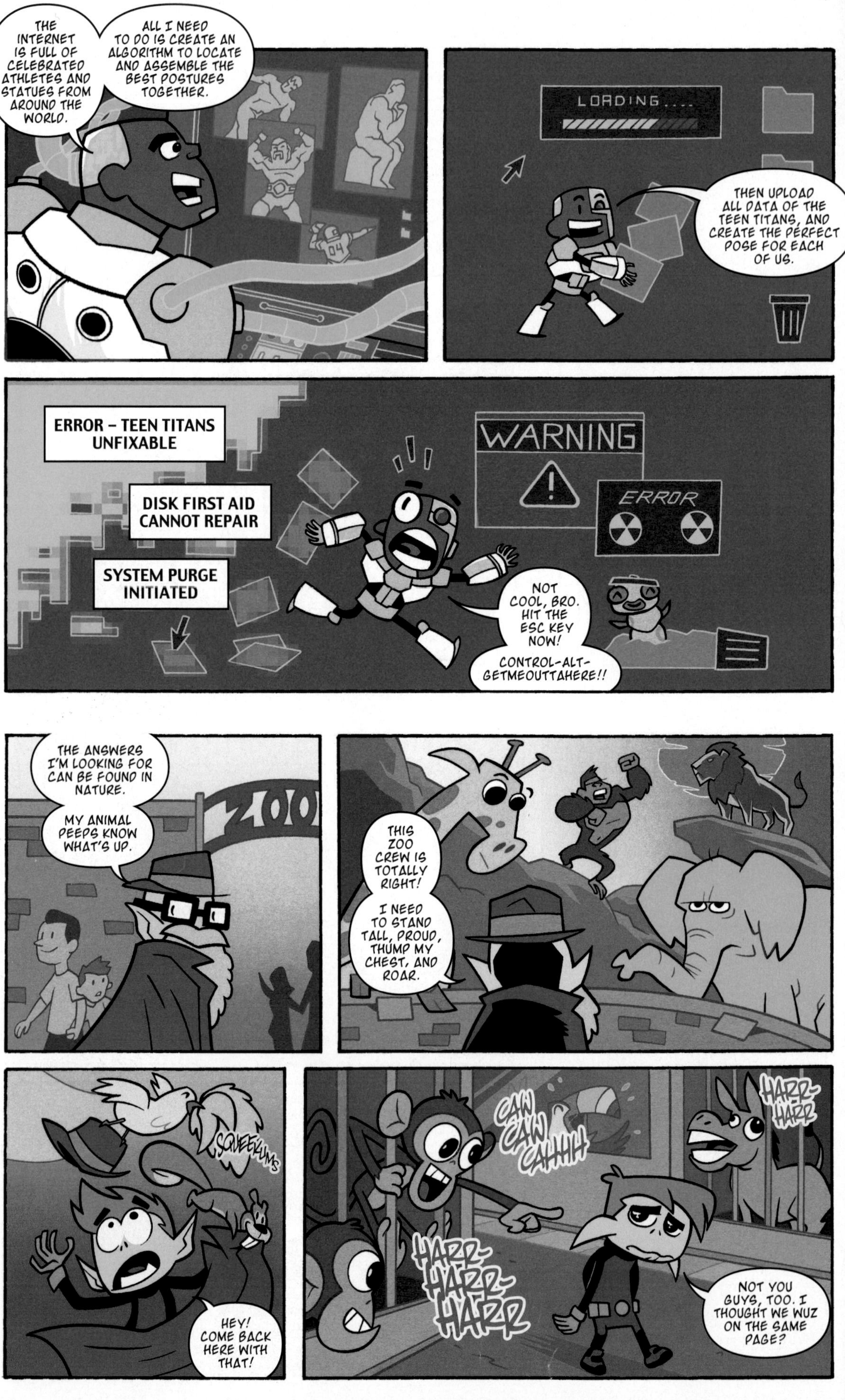
THE INTERNET IS FULL OF CELEBRATED ATHLETES AND STATUES FROM AROUND THE WORLD.
ALL I NEED TO DO IS CREATE AN ALGORITHM TO LOCATE AND ASSEMBLE THE BEST POSTURES TOGETHER.
LOADING....
THEN UPLOAD ALL DATA OF THE TEEN TITANS, AND CREATE THE PERFECT POSE FOR EACH OF US.
ERROR – TEEN TITANS UNFIXABLE
DISK FIRST AID CANNOT REPAIR
SYSTEM PURGE INITIATED
WARNING
ERROR
NOT COOL, BRO. HIT THE ESC KEY NOW!
CONTROL-ALT-GETMEOUTTAHERE!!
THE ANSWERS I'M LOOKING FOR CAN BE FOUND IN NATURE.
MY ANIMAL PEEPS KNOW WHAT'S UP.
ZOO
THIS ZOO CREW IS TOTALLY RIGHT!
I NEED TO STAND TALL, PROUD, THUMP MY CHEST, AND ROAR.
SQUEEKUMS
HEY! COME BACK HERE WITH THAT!
CAW CAW CAHHH
HARR-HARR
HARR-HARR-HARR
NOT YOU GUYS, TOO. I THOUGHT WE WUZ ON THE SAME PAGE?

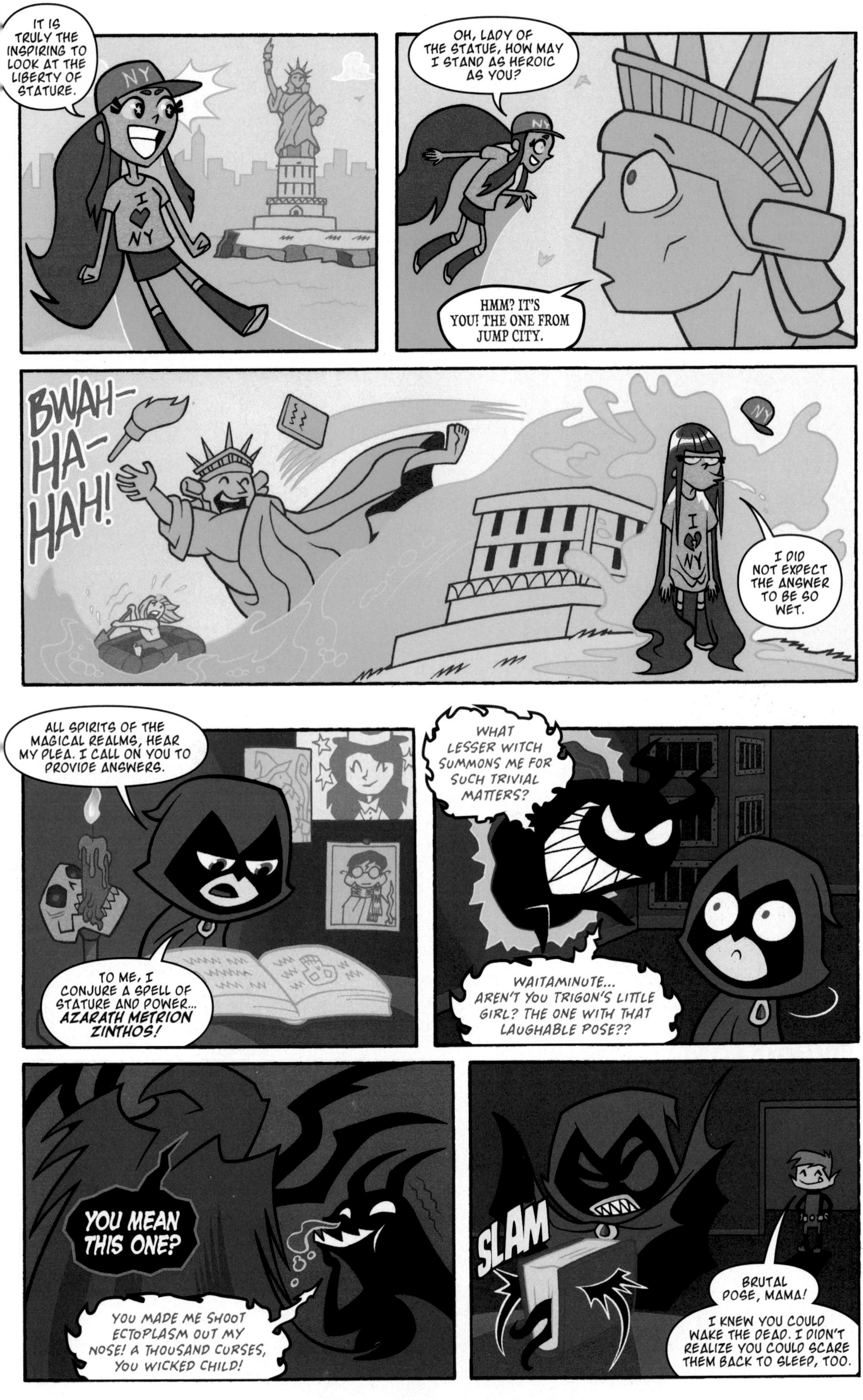

IT IS TRULY THE INSPIRING TO LOOK AT THE LIBERTY OF STATURE.
NY
I ♥ NY
OH, LADY OF THE STATUE, HOW MAY I STAND AS HEROIC AS YOU?
NY
HMM? IT'S YOU! THE ONE FROM JUMP CITY.
BWAH-HA-HAH!
NY
I DID NOT EXPECT THE ANSWER TO BE SO WET.
ALL SPIRITS OF THE MAGICAL REALMS, HEAR MY PLEA. I CALL ON YOU TO PROVIDE ANSWERS.
TO ME, I CONJURE A SPELL OF STATURE AND POWER... AZARATH METRION ZINTHOS!
WHAT LESSER WITCH SUMMONS ME FOR SUCH TRIVIAL MATTERS?
WAITAMINUTE... AREN'T YOU TRIGON'S LITTLE GIRL? THE ONE WITH THAT LAUGHABLE POSE??
YOU MEAN THIS ONE?
YOU MADE ME SHOOT ECTOPLASM OUT MY NOSE! A THOUSAND CURSES, YOU WICKED CHILD!
SLAM
BRUTAL POSE, MAMA!
I KNEW YOU COULD WAKE THE DEAD. I DIDN'T REALIZE YOU COULD SCARE THEM BACK TO SLEEP, TOO.

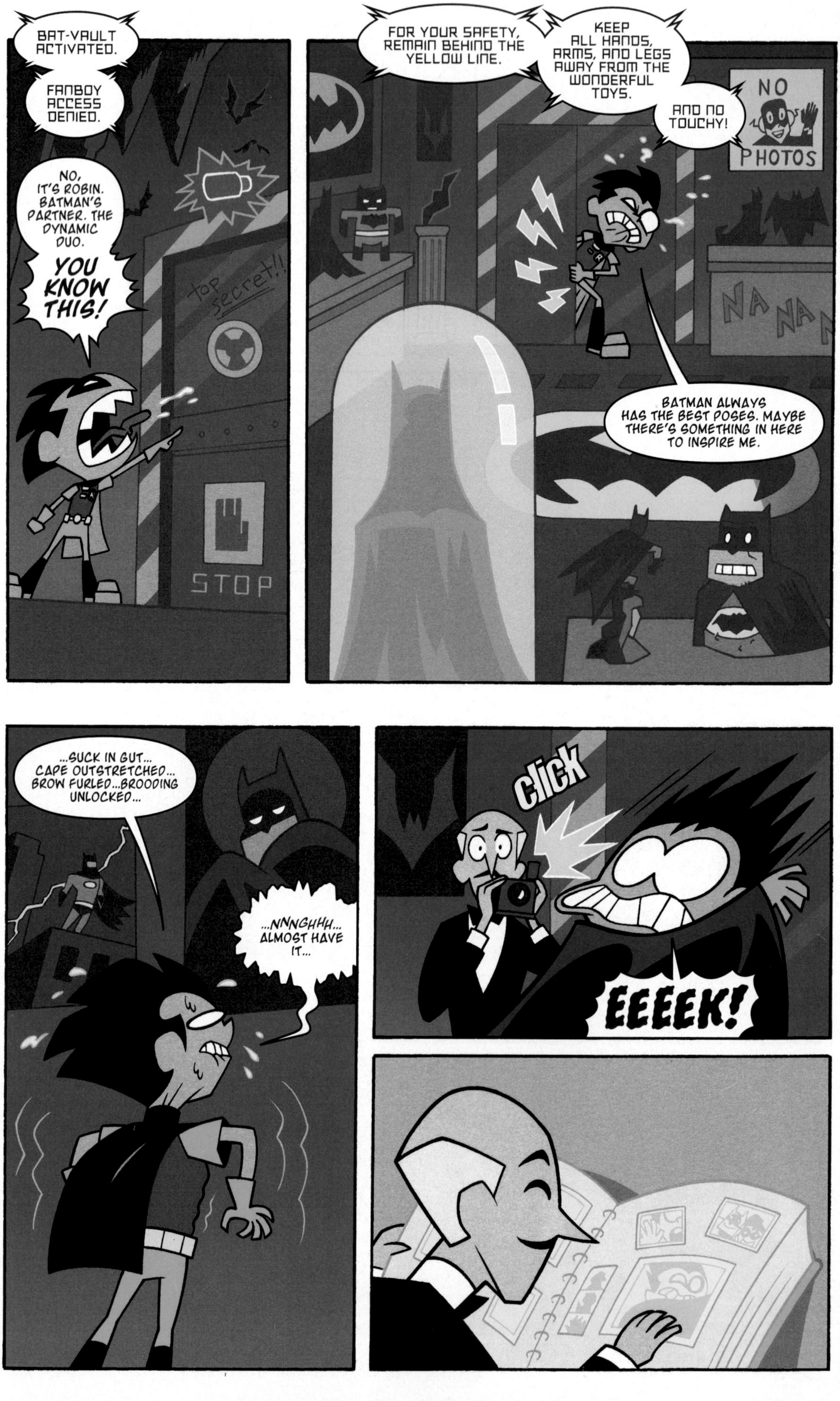
BAT-VAULT ACTIVATED.
FANBOY ACCESS DENIED.
NO, IT'S ROBIN. BATMAN'S PARTNER. THE DYNAMIC DUO.
YOU KNOW THIS!
top secret!!
STOP
FOR YOUR SAFETY, REMAIN BEHIND THE YELLOW LINE.
KEEP ALL HANDS, ARMS, AND LEGS AWAY FROM THE WONDERFUL TOYS.
AND NO TOUCHY!
NO PHOTOS
BATMAN ALWAYS HAS THE BEST POSES. MAYBE THERE'S SOMETHING IN HERE TO INSPIRE ME.
...SUCK IN GUT... CAPE OUTSTRETCHED... BROW FURLED...BROODING UNLOCKED...
...NNNGHHH... ALMOST HAVE IT...
click
EEEEK!

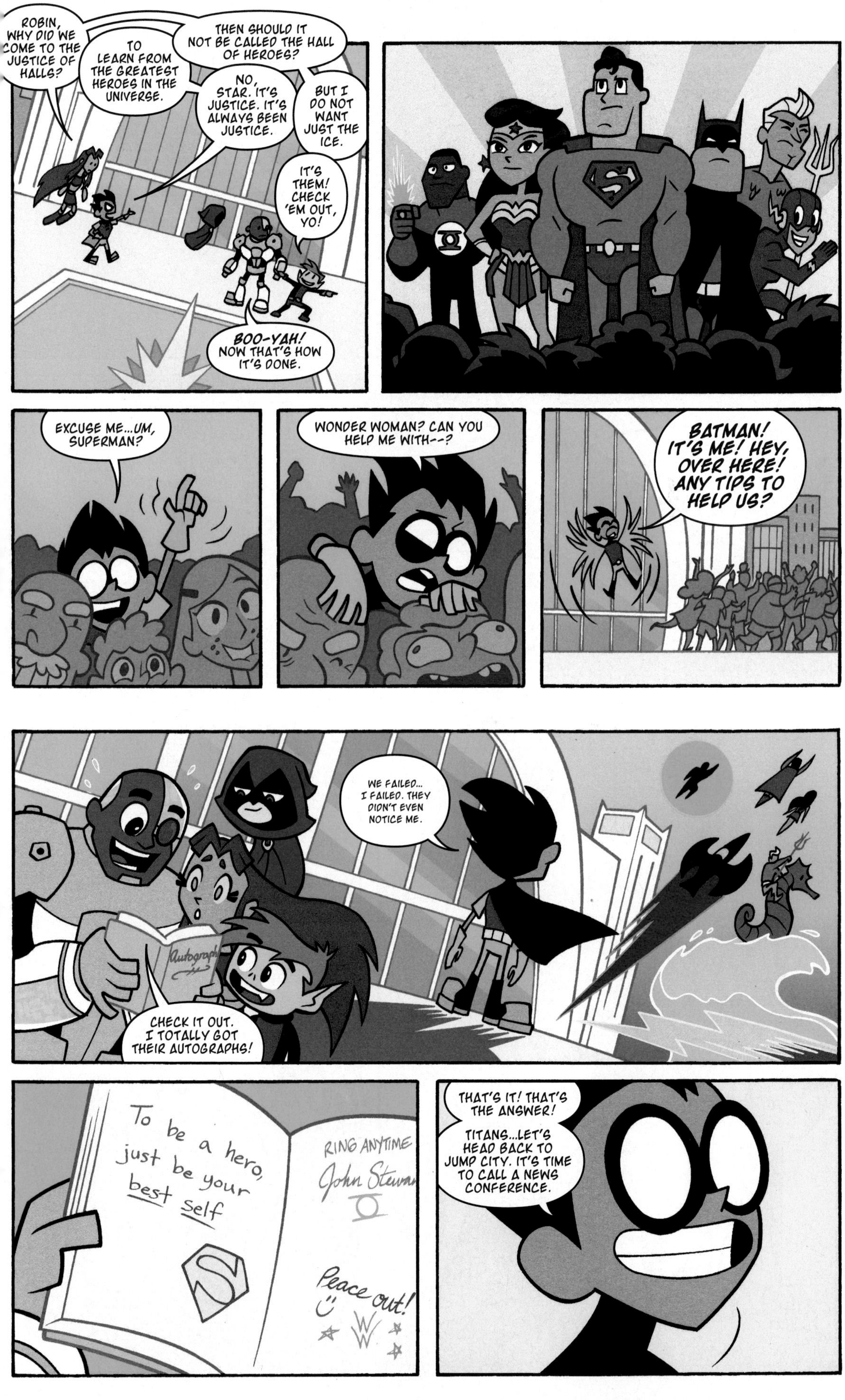
ROBIN, WHY DID WE COME TO THE JUSTICE OF HALLS?
TO LEARN FROM THE GREATEST HEROES IN THE UNIVERSE.
THEN SHOULD IT NOT BE CALLED THE HALL OF HEROES?
NO, STAR. IT'S JUSTICE. IT'S ALWAYS BEEN JUSTICE.
BUT I DO NOT WANT JUST THE ICE.
IT'S THEM! CHECK 'EM OUT, YO!
BOO-YAH! NOW THAT'S HOW IT'S DONE.
EXCUSE ME...UM, SUPERMAN?
WONDER WOMAN? CAN YOU HELP ME WITH--?
BATMAN! IT'S ME! HEY, OVER HERE! ANY TIPS TO HELP US?
WE FAILED... I FAILED. THEY DIDN'T EVEN NOTICE ME.
CHECK IT OUT. I TOTALLY GOT THEIR AUTOGRAPHS!
Autographs
To be a hero, just be your best self
RING ANYTIME
John Stewart
Peace out!
THAT'S IT! THAT'S THE ANSWER!
TITANS...LET'S HEAD BACK TO JUMP CITY. IT'S TIME TO CALL A NEWS CONFERENCE.

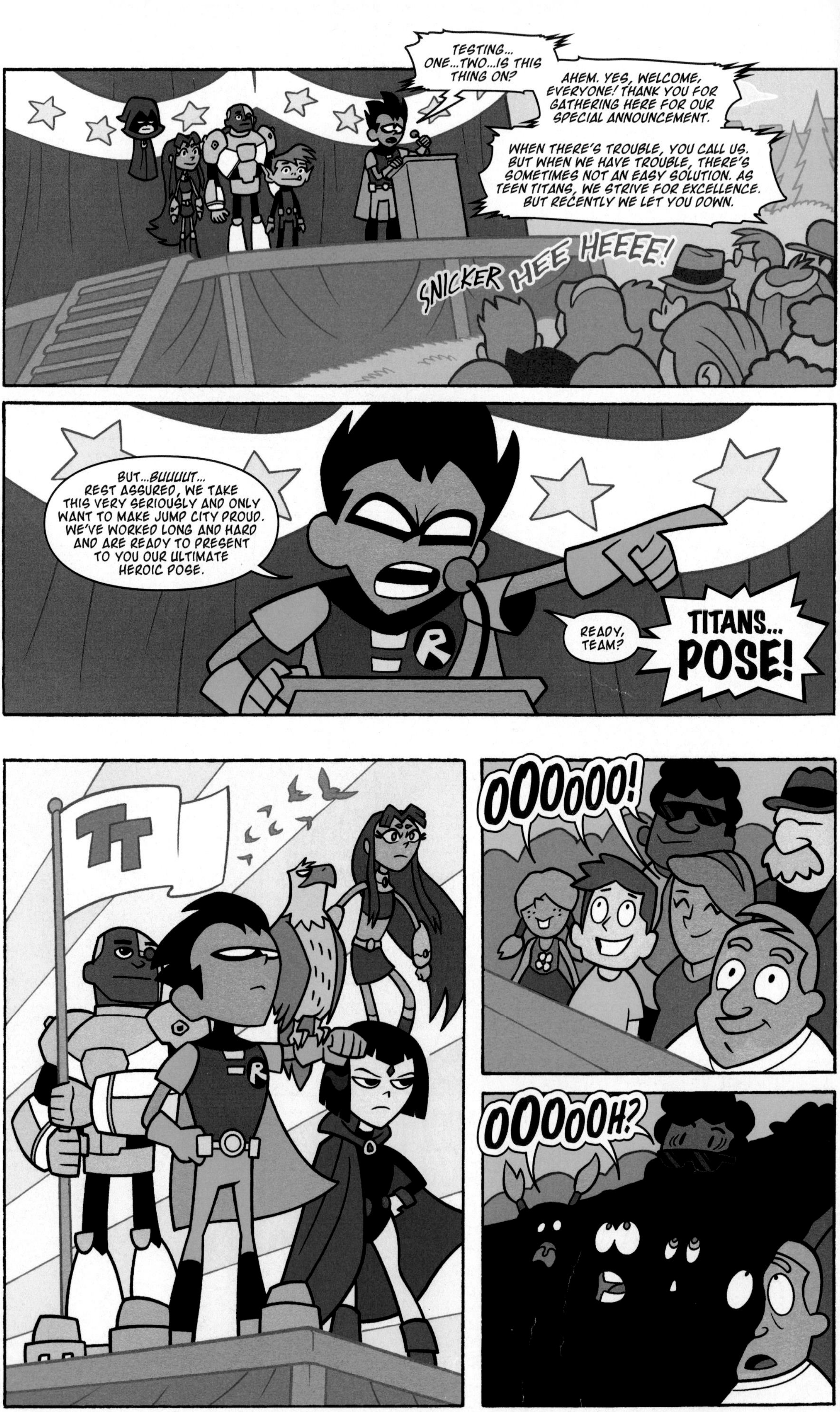
TESTING... ONE...TWO...IS THIS THING ON?
AHEM. YES, WELCOME, EVERYONE! THANK YOU FOR GATHERING HERE FOR OUR SPECIAL ANNOUNCEMENT.
WHEN THERE'S TROUBLE, YOU CALL US. BUT WHEN WE HAVE TROUBLE, THERE'S SOMETIMES NOT AN EASY SOLUTION. AS TEEN TITANS, WE STRIVE FOR EXCELLENCE. BUT RECENTLY WE LET YOU DOWN.
SNICKER
HEE HEEEE!
BUT...BUUUUT... REST ASSURED, WE TAKE THIS VERY SERIOUSLY AND ONLY WANT TO MAKE JUMP CITY PROUD. WE'VE WORKED LONG AND HARD AND ARE READY TO PRESENT TO YOU OUR ULTIMATE HEROIC POSE.
READY, TEAM?
TITANS... POSE!
TT
OOOOOO!
OOOOOH?

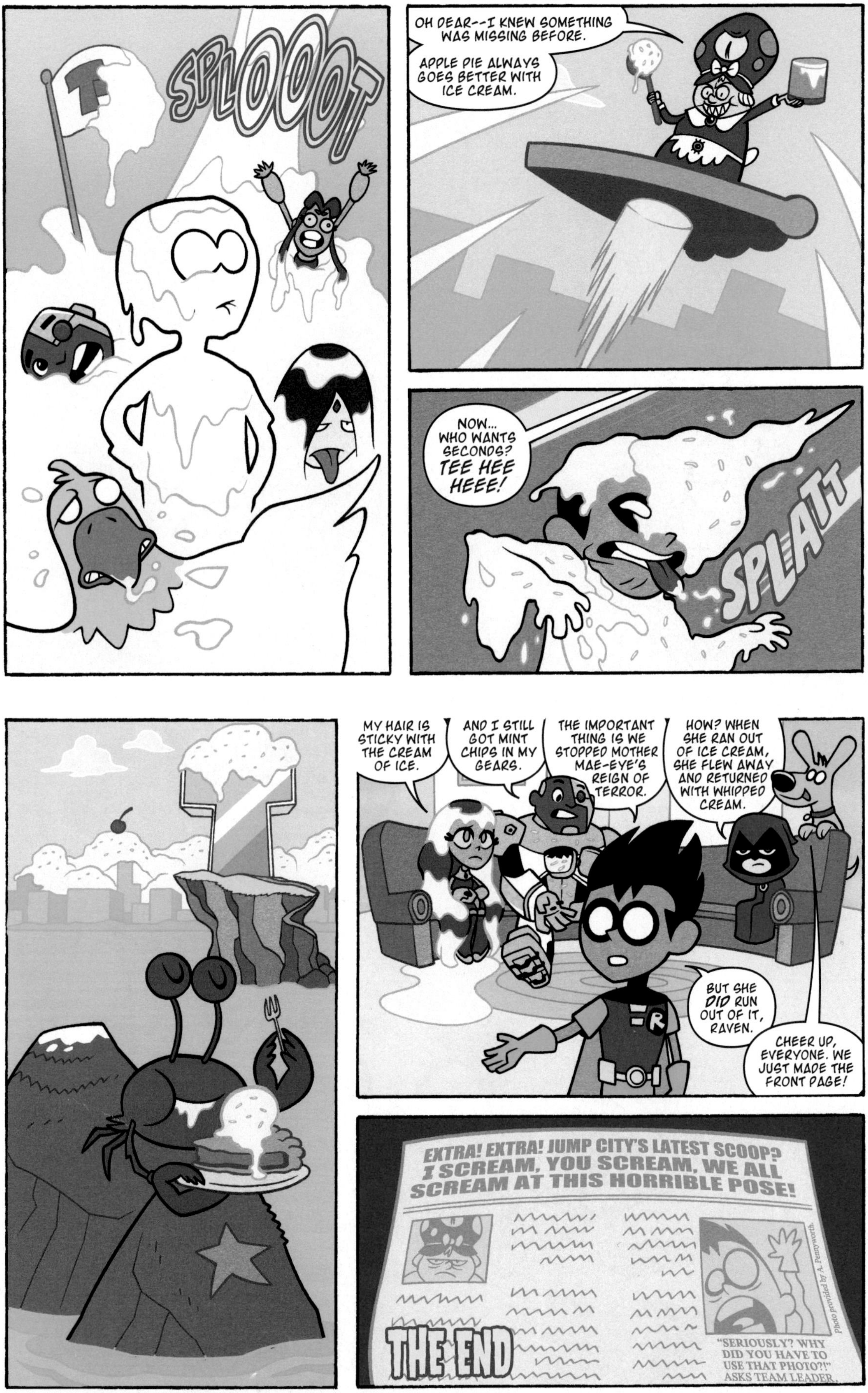
SPLOOOT
OH DEAR--I KNEW SOMETHING WAS MISSING BEFORE.
APPLE PIE ALWAYS GOES BETTER WITH ICE CREAM.
NOW... WHO WANTS SECONDS? TEE HEE HEEE!
SPLATT
MY HAIR IS STICKY WITH THE CREAM OF ICE.
AND I STILL GOT MINT CHIPS IN MY GEARS.
THE IMPORTANT THING IS WE STOPPED MOTHER MAE-EYE'S REIGN OF TERROR.
HOW? WHEN SHE RAN OUT OF ICE CREAM, SHE FLEW AWAY AND RETURNED WITH WHIPPED CREAM.
BUT SHE DID RUN OUT OF IT, RAVEN.
CHEER UP, EVERYONE. WE JUST MADE THE FRONT PAGE!
EXTRA! EXTRA! JUMP CITY'S LATEST SCOOP? I SCREAM, YOU SCREAM, WE ALL SCREAM AT THIS HORRIBLE POSE!
Photo provided by A. Pennyworth.
"SERIOUSLY? WHY DID YOU HAVE TO USE THAT PHOTO?!" ASKS TEAM LEADER.
THE END

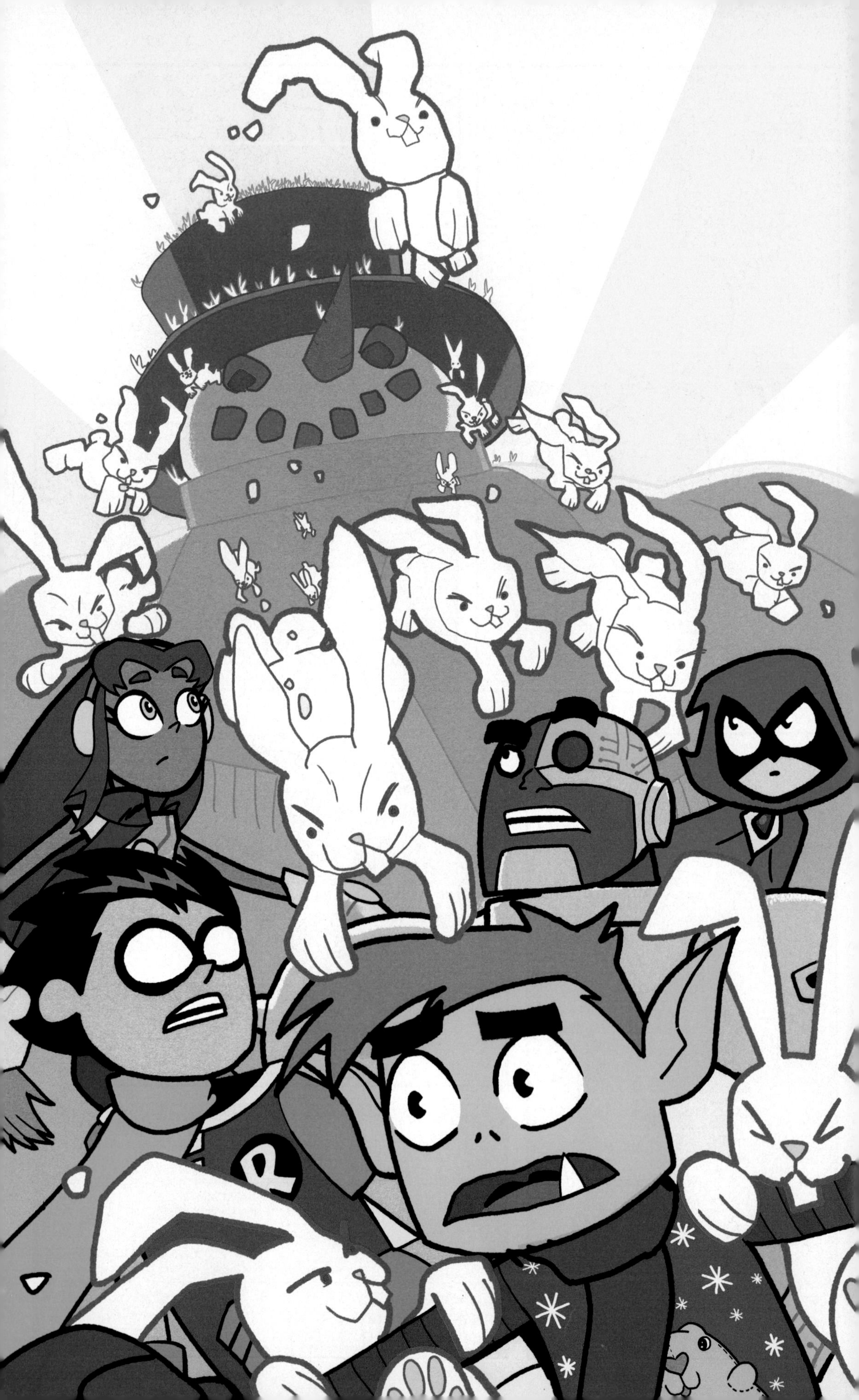

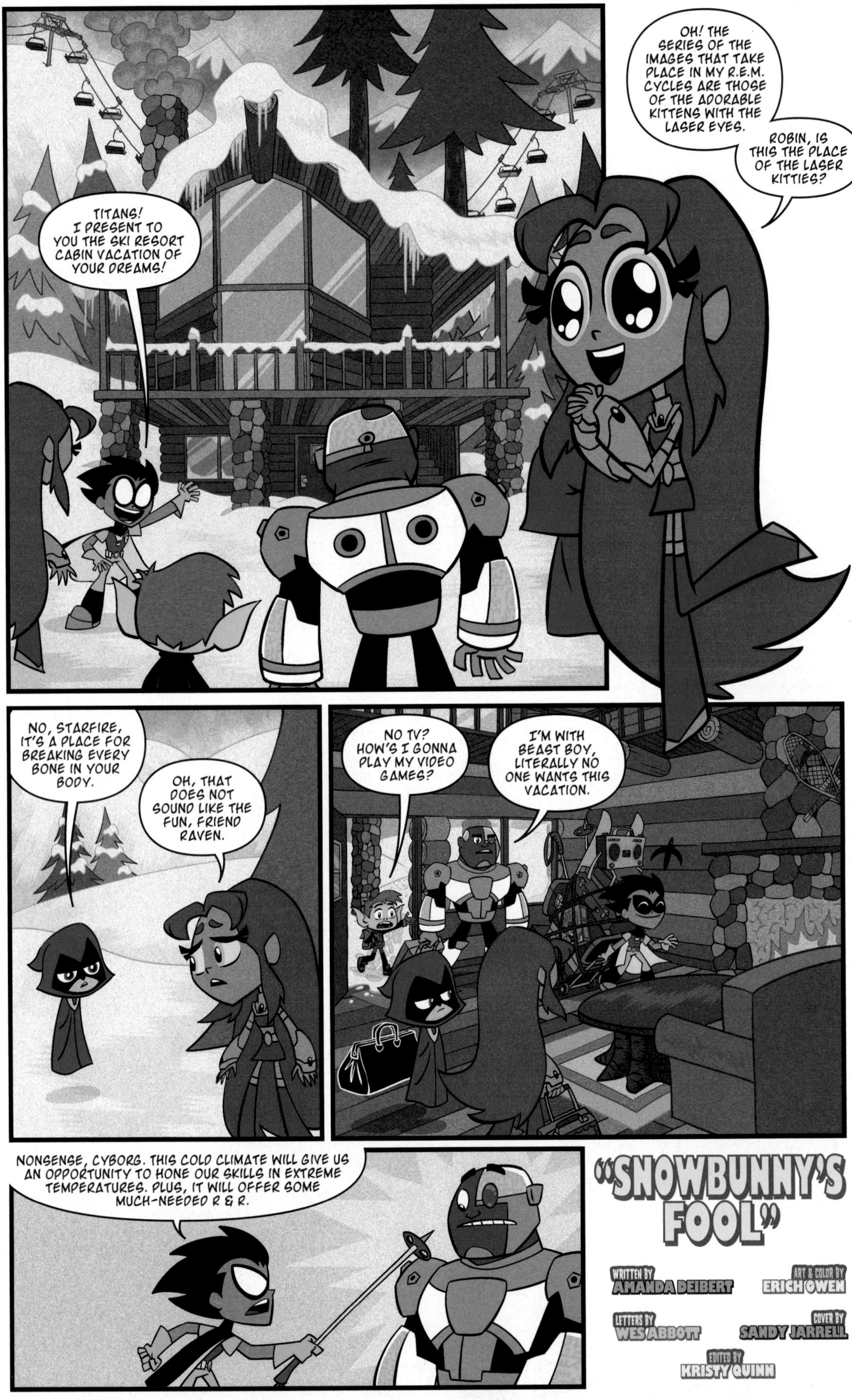

TITANS! I PRESENT TO YOU THE SKI RESORT CABIN VACATION OF YOUR DREAMS!
OH! THE SERIES OF THE IMAGES THAT TAKE PLACE IN MY R.E.M. CYCLES ARE THOSE OF THE ADORABLE KITTENS WITH THE LASER EYES.
ROBIN, IS THIS THE PLACE OF THE LASER KITTIES?
NO, STARFIRE, IT'S A PLACE FOR BREAKING EVERY BONE IN YOUR BODY.
OH, THAT DOES NOT SOUND LIKE THE FUN, FRIEND RAVEN.
NO TV? HOW'S I GONNA PLAY MY VIDEO GAMES?
I'M WITH BEAST BOY, LITERALLY NO ONE WANTS THIS VACATION.
NONSENSE, CYBORG. THIS COLD CLIMATE WILL GIVE US AN OPPORTUNITY TO HONE OUR SKILLS IN EXTREME TEMPERATURES. PLUS, IT WILL OFFER SOME MUCH-NEEDED R & R.
"SNOWBUNNY'S FOOL"
WRITTEN BY AMANDA DEIBERT
ART & COLOR BY ERICH OWEN
LETTERS BY WES ABBOTT
COVER BY SANDY JARRELL
EDITED BY KRISTY QUINN

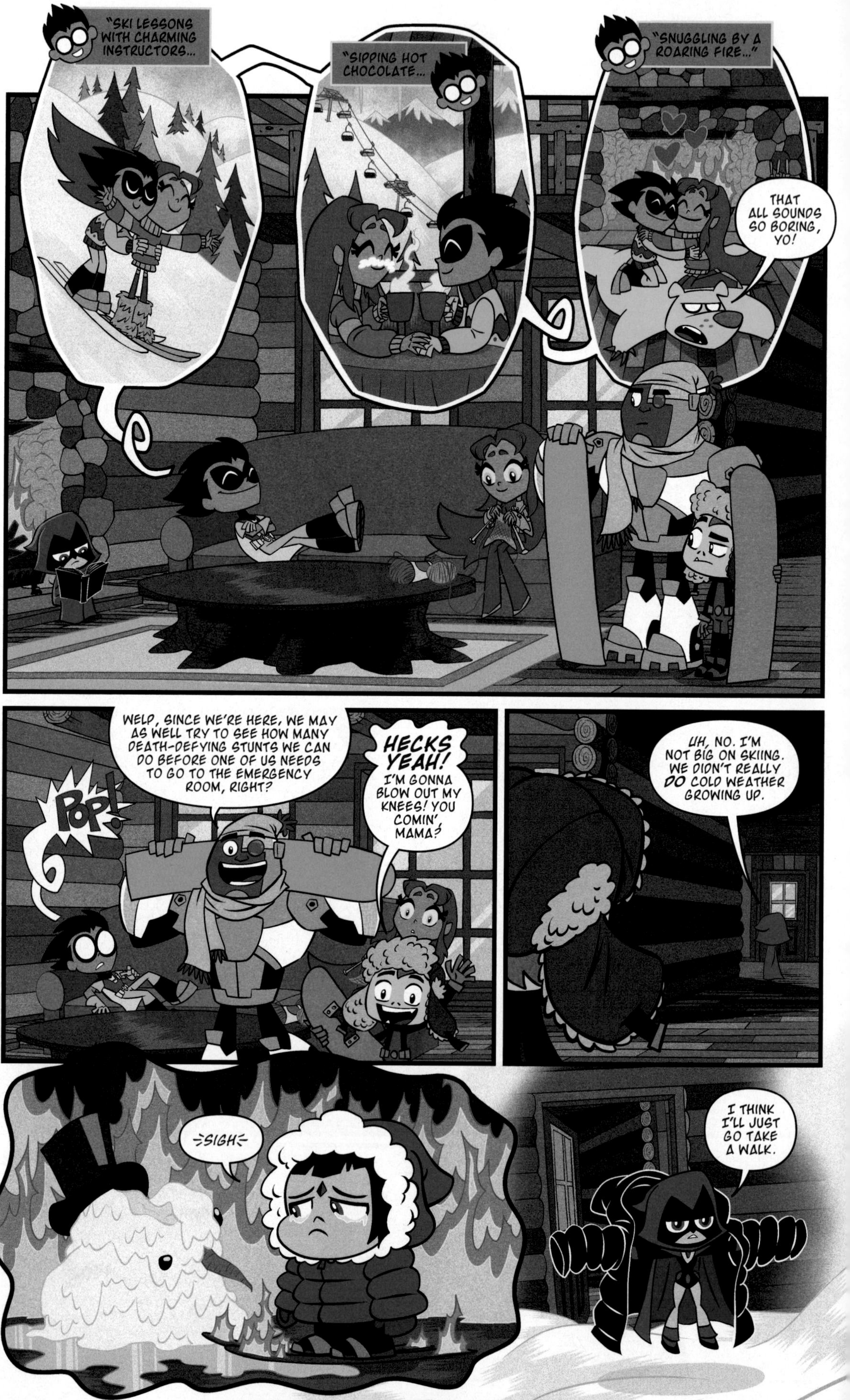
"SKI LESSONS WITH CHARMING INSTRUCTORS...
"SIPPING HOT CHOCOLATE...
"SNUGGLING BY A ROARING FIRE..."
THAT ALL SOUNDS SO BORING, YO!
WELP, SINCE WE'RE HERE, WE MAY AS WELL TRY TO SEE HOW MANY DEATH-DEFYING STUNTS WE CAN DO BEFORE ONE OF US NEEDS TO GO TO THE EMERGENCY ROOM, RIGHT?
POP!
HECKS YEAH!
I'M GONNA BLOW OUT MY KNEES! YOU COMIN', MAMA?
UH, NO. I'M NOT BIG ON SKIING. WE DIDN'T REALLY DO COLD WEATHER GROWING UP.
=SIGH=
I THINK I'LL JUST GO TAKE A WALK.

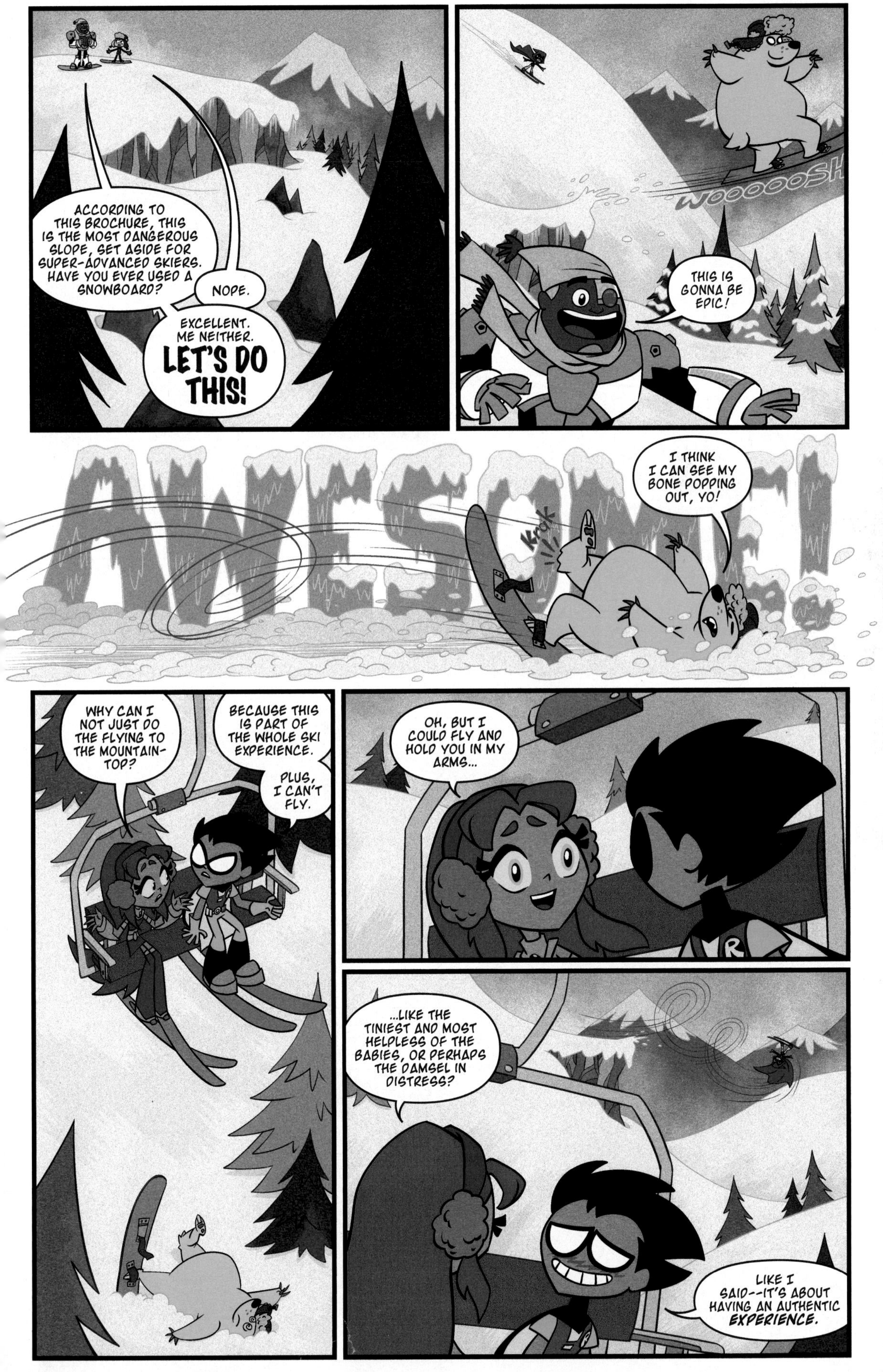
ACCORDING TO THIS BROCHURE, THIS IS THE MOST DANGEROUS SLOPE, SET ASIDE FOR SUPER-ADVANCED SKIERS. HAVE YOU EVER USED A SNOWBOARD?
NOPE.
EXCELLENT. ME NEITHER. LET'S DO THIS!
WOOOOOSH
THIS IS GONNA BE EPIC!
AWESOME!
KROK
I THINK I CAN SEE MY BONE POPPING OUT, YO!
WHY CAN I NOT JUST DO THE FLYING TO THE MOUNTAIN-TOP?
BECAUSE THIS IS PART OF THE WHOLE SKI EXPERIENCE.
PLUS, I CAN'T FLY.
OH, BUT I COULD FLY AND HOLD YOU IN MY ARMS...
...LIKE THE TINIEST AND MOST HELPLESS OF THE BABIES, OR PERHAPS THE DAMSEL IN DISTRESS?
LIKE I SAID--IT'S ABOUT HAVING AN AUTHENTIC EXPERIENCE.

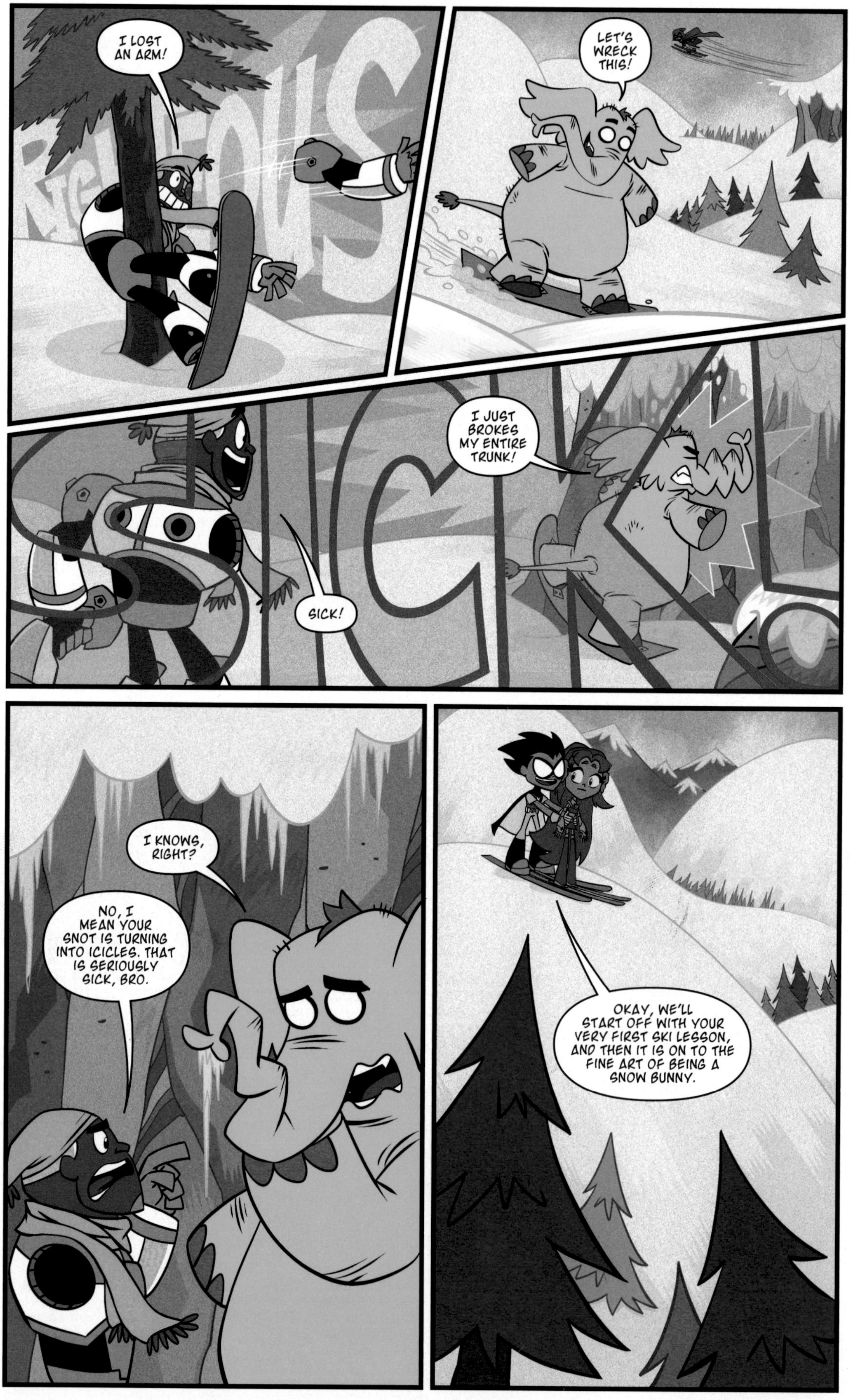
I LOST AN ARM!
LET'S WRECK THIS!
I JUST BROKES MY ENTIRE TRUNK!
SICK!
I KNOWS, RIGHT?
NO, I MEAN YOUR SNOT IS TURNING INTO ICICLES. THAT IS SERIOUSLY SICK, BRO.
OKAY, WE'LL START OFF WITH YOUR VERY FIRST SKI LESSON, AND THEN IT IS ON TO THE FINE ART OF BEING A SNOW BUNNY.

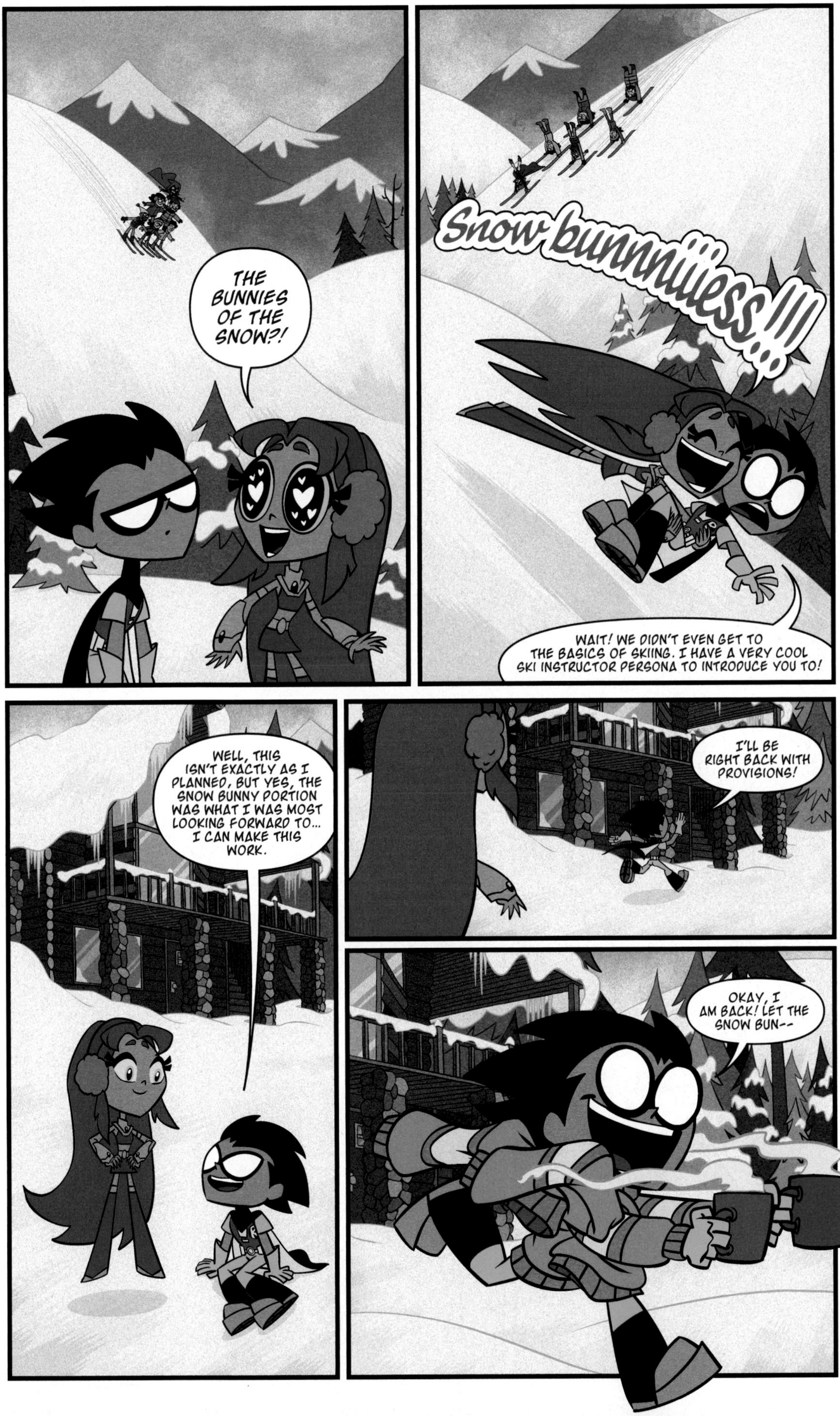
THE BUNNIES OF THE SNOW?!
Snow bunnniiess!!!
WAIT! WE DIDN'T EVEN GET TO THE BASICS OF SKIING. I HAVE A VERY COOL SKI INSTRUCTOR PERSONA TO INTRODUCE YOU TO!
WELL, THIS ISN'T EXACTLY AS I PLANNED, BUT YES, THE SNOW BUNNY PORTION WAS WHAT I WAS MOST LOOKING FORWARD TO... I CAN MAKE THIS WORK.
I'LL BE RIGHT BACK WITH PROVISIONS!
OKAY, I AM BACK! LET THE SNOW BUN--

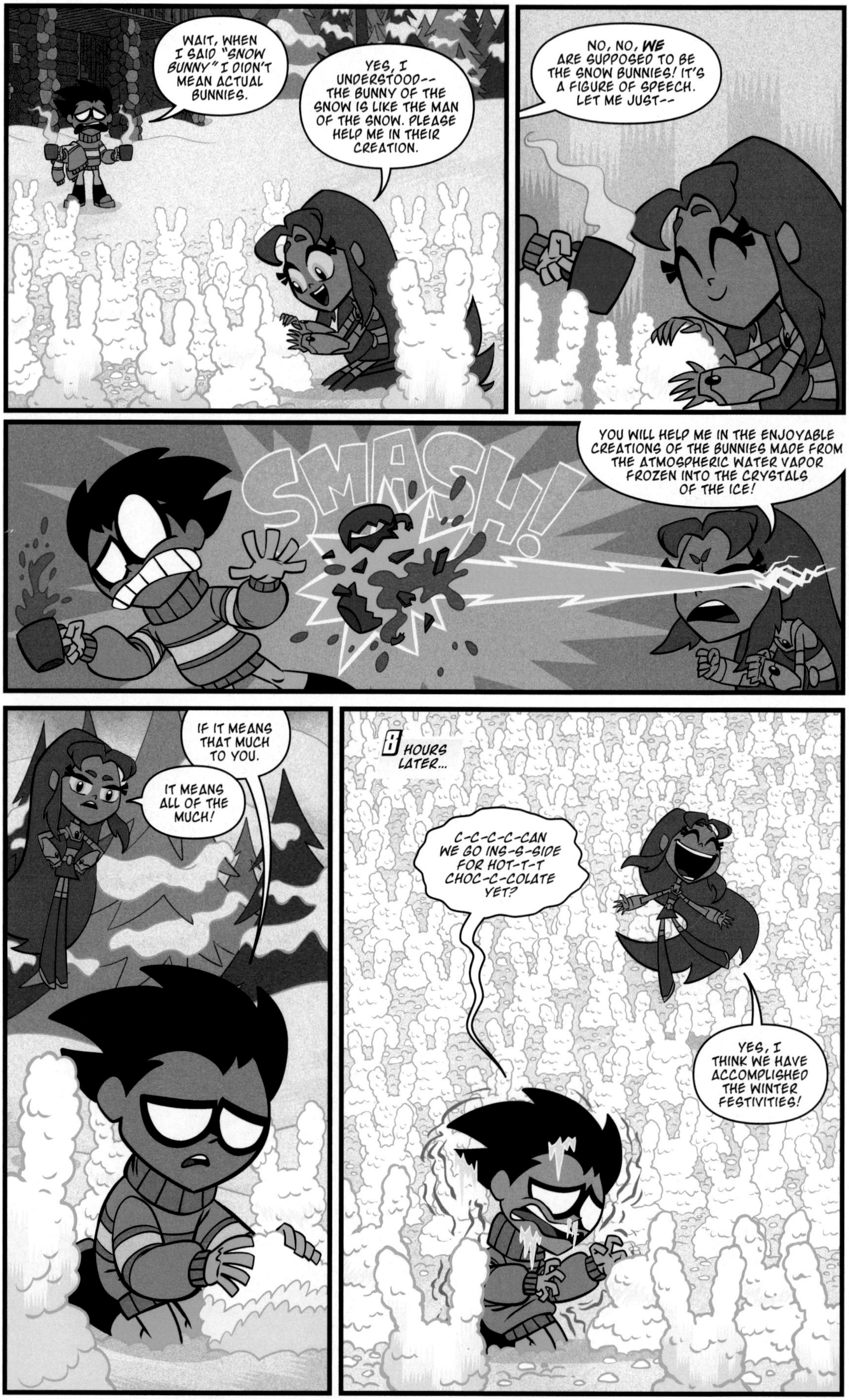

WAIT, WHEN I SAID "SNOW BUNNY" I DIDN'T MEAN ACTUAL BUNNIES.
YES, I UNDERSTOOD-- THE BUNNY OF THE SNOW IS LIKE THE MAN OF THE SNOW. PLEASE HELP ME IN THEIR CREATION.
NO, NO, WE ARE SUPPOSED TO BE THE SNOW BUNNIES! IT'S A FIGURE OF SPEECH. LET ME JUST--
SMASH!
YOU WILL HELP ME IN THE ENJOYABLE CREATIONS OF THE BUNNIES MADE FROM THE ATMOSPHERIC WATER VAPOR FROZEN INTO THE CRYSTALS OF THE ICE!
IF IT MEANS THAT MUCH TO YOU.
IT MEANS ALL OF THE MUCH!
8 HOURS LATER...
C-C-C-C-CAN WE GO INS-S-SIDE FOR HOT-T-T CHOC-C-COLATE YET?
YES, I THINK WE HAVE ACCOMPLISHED THE WINTER FESTIVITIES!

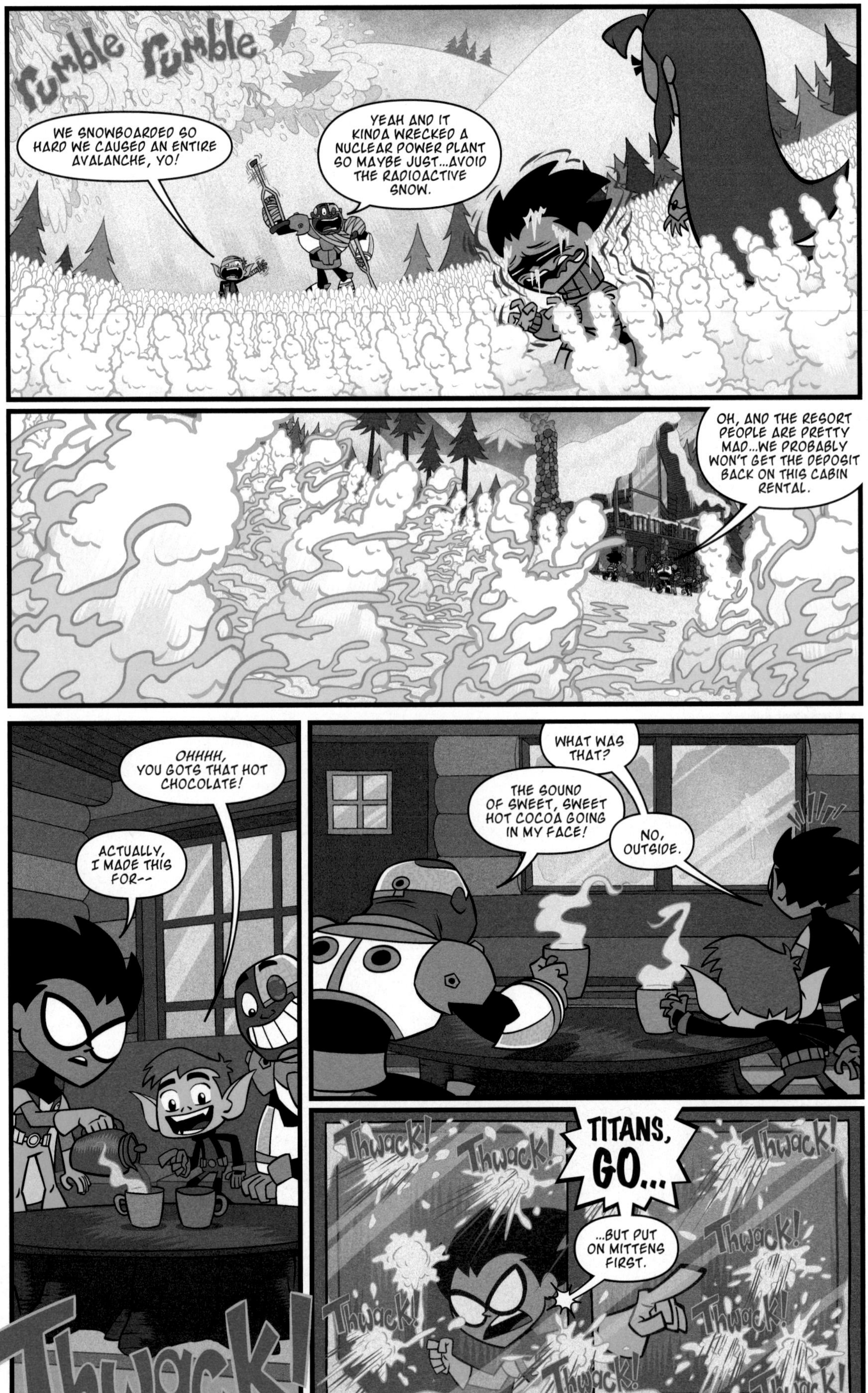
rumble rumble
WE SNOWBOARDED SO HARD WE CAUSED AN ENTIRE AVALANCHE, YO!
YEAH AND IT KINDA WRECKED A NUCLEAR POWER PLANT SO MAYBE JUST...AVOID THE RADIOACTIVE SNOW.
OH, AND THE RESORT PEOPLE ARE PRETTY MAD...WE PROBABLY WON'T GET THE DEPOSIT BACK ON THIS CABIN RENTAL.
OHHHH, YOU GOTS THAT HOT CHOCOLATE!
ACTUALLY, I MADE THIS FOR--
THWACK!
WHAT WAS THAT?
THE SOUND OF SWEET, SWEET HOT COCOA GOING IN MY FACE!
NO, OUTSIDE.
THWACK! THWACK! THWACK!
TITANS, GO...
...BUT PUT ON MITTENS FIRST.
THWACK! THWACK! THWACK! THWACK! THWACK!

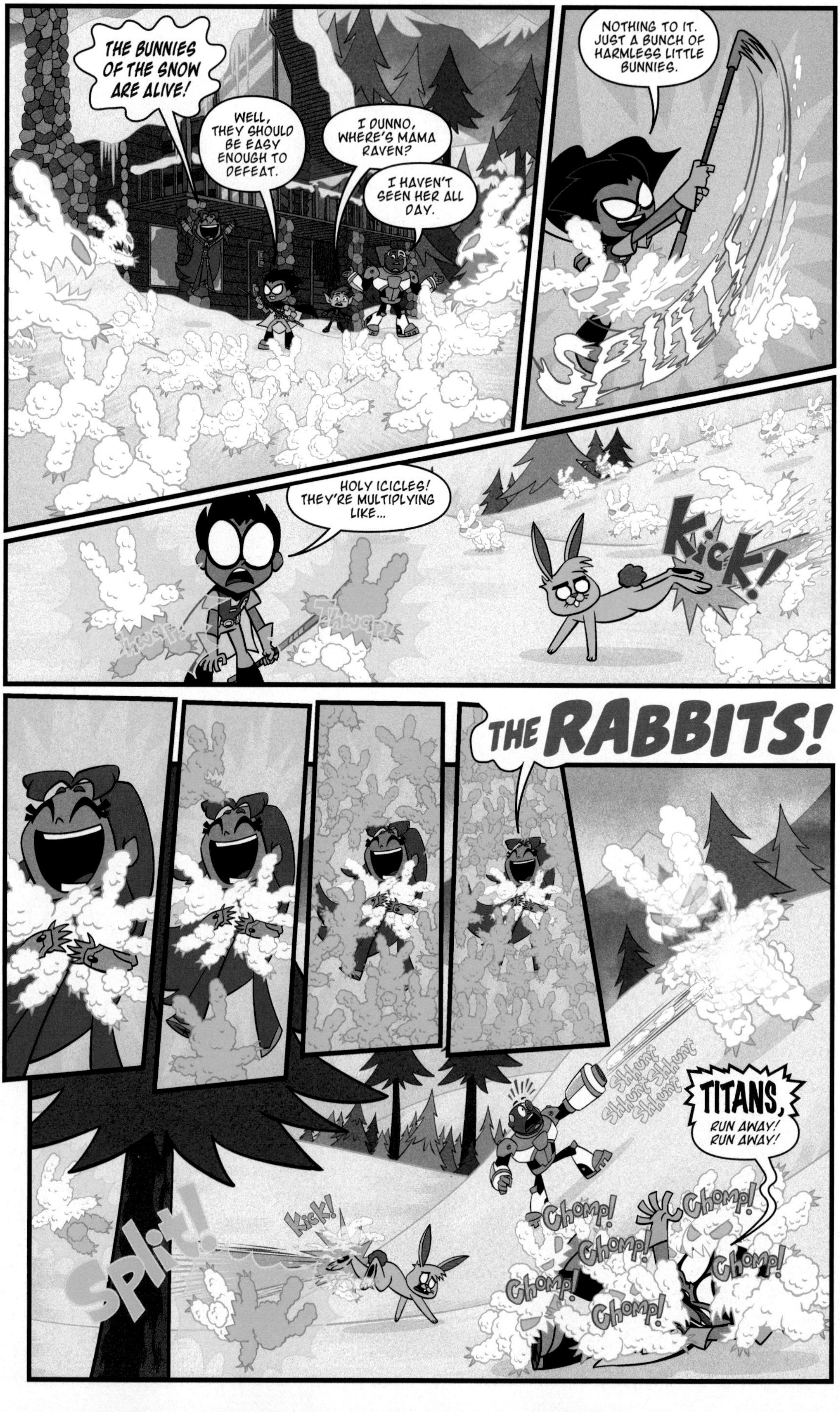
THE BUNNIES OF THE SNOW ARE ALIVE!
WELL, THEY SHOULD BE EASY ENOUGH TO DEFEAT.
I DUNNO, WHERE'S MAMA RAVEN?
I HAVEN'T SEEN HER ALL DAY.
NOTHING TO IT. JUST A BUNCH OF HARMLESS LITTLE BUNNIES.
SPLAT
HOLY ICICLES! THEY'RE MULTIPLYING LIKE...
Thwap!
Thwap!
Kick!
THE RABBITS!
Shhunt Shhunt Shhunt Shhunt
TITANS, RUN AWAY! RUN AWAY!
Kick!
Split!
Chomp!
Chomp!
Chomp!
Chomp!
Chomp!
Chomp!

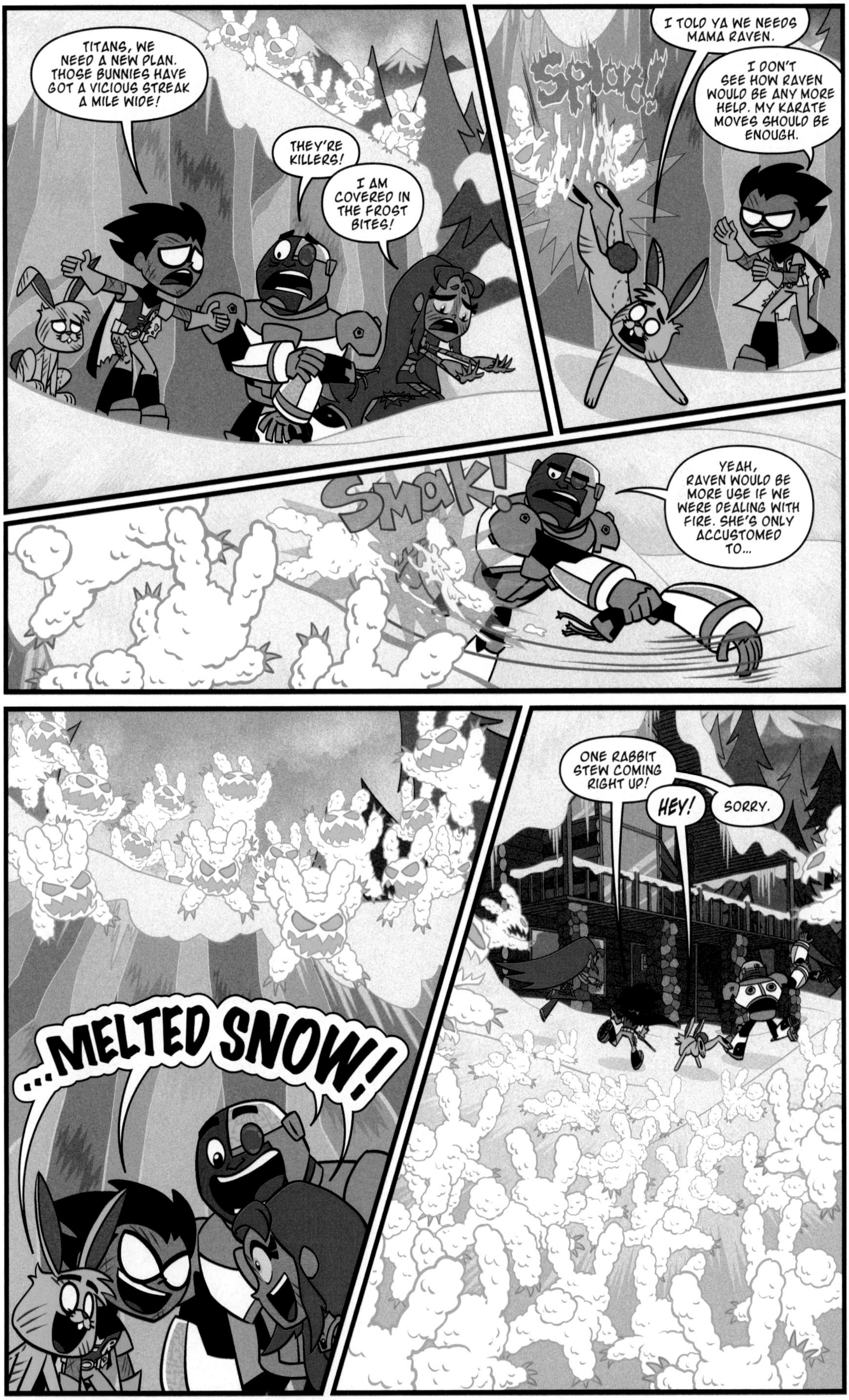
TITANS, WE NEED A NEW PLAN. THOSE BUNNIES HAVE GOT A VICIOUS STREAK A MILE WIDE!
THEY'RE KILLERS!
I AM COVERED IN THE FROST BITES!
SPLAT!
I TOLD YA WE NEEDS MAMA RAVEN.
I DON'T SEE HOW RAVEN WOULD BE ANY MORE HELP. MY KARATE MOVES SHOULD BE ENOUGH.
SMAK!
YEAH, RAVEN WOULD BE MORE USE IF WE WERE DEALING WITH FIRE. SHE'S ONLY ACCUSTOMED TO...
...MELTED SNOW!
ONE RABBIT STEW COMING RIGHT UP!
HEY!
SORRY.

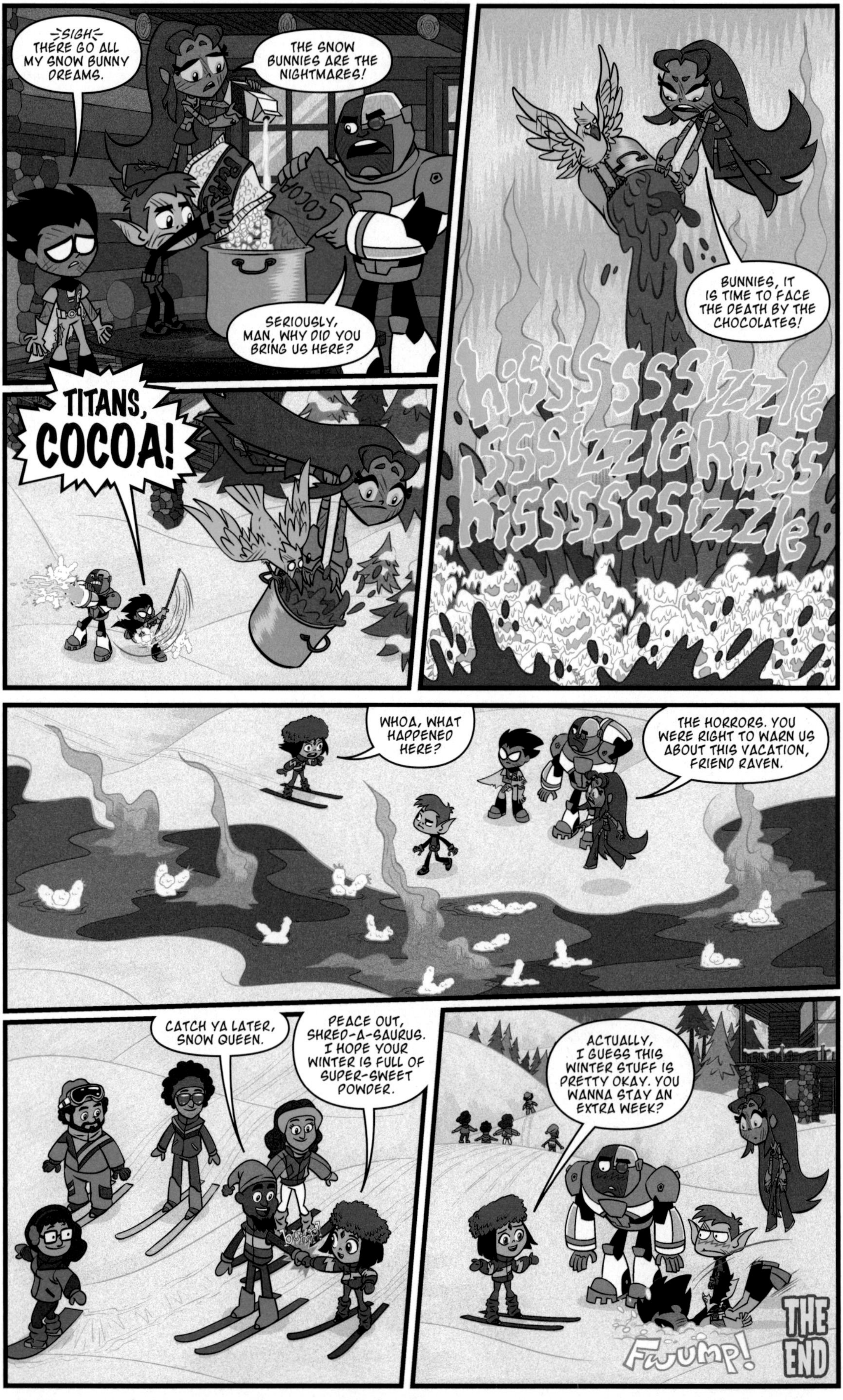

SIGH
THERE GO ALL MY SNOW BUNNY DREAMS.
THE SNOW BUNNIES ARE THE NIGHTMARES!
COCOA
SERIOUSLY, MAN, WHY DID YOU BRING US HERE?
BUNNIES, IT IS TIME TO FACE THE DEATH BY THE CHOCOLATES!
TITANS, COCOA!
hisssssssizzle
sssizzlehisss
hisssssssizzle
WHOA, WHAT HAPPENED HERE?
THE HORRORS. YOU WERE RIGHT TO WARN US ABOUT THIS VACATION, FRIEND RAVEN.
CATCH YA LATER, SNOW QUEEN.
PEACE OUT, SHRED-A-SAURUS. I HOPE YOUR WINTER IS FULL OF SUPER-SWEET POWDER.
ACTUALLY, I GUESS THIS WINTER STUFF IS PRETTY OKAY. YOU WANNA STAY AN EXTRA WEEK?
FWUMP!
THE END

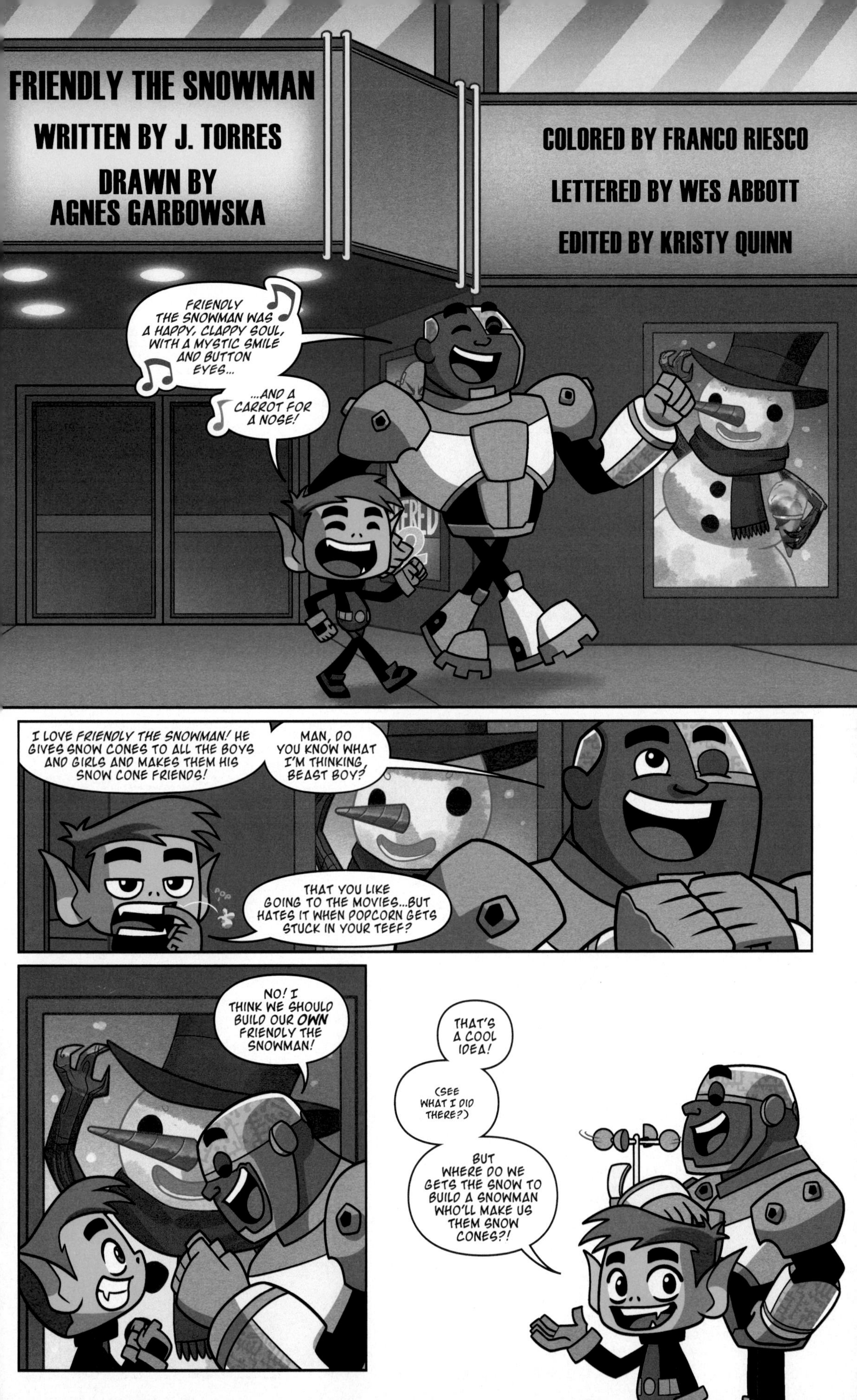
FRIENDLY THE SNOWMAN
WRITTEN BY J. TORRES
DRAWN BY AGNES GARBOWSKA
COLORED BY FRANCO RIESCO
LETTERED BY WES ABBOTT
EDITED BY KRISTY QUINN
FRIENDLY THE SNOWMAN WAS A HAPPY, CLAPPY SOUL, WITH A MYSTIC SMILE AND BUTTON EYES...
...AND A CARROT FOR A NOSE!
I LOVE FRIENDLY THE SNOWMAN! HE GIVES SNOW CONES TO ALL THE BOYS AND GIRLS AND MAKES THEM HIS SNOW CONE FRIENDS!
MAN, DO YOU KNOW WHAT I'M THINKING, BEAST BOY?
POP
THAT YOU LIKE GOING TO THE MOVIES...BUT HATES IT WHEN POPCORN GETS STUCK IN YOUR TEEF?
NO! I THINK WE SHOULD BUILD OUR OWN FRIENDLY THE SNOWMAN!
THAT'S A COOL IDEA!
(SEE WHAT I DID THERE?)
BUT WHERE DO WE GETS THE SNOW TO BUILD A SNOWMAN WHO'LL MAKE US THEM SNOW CONES?!

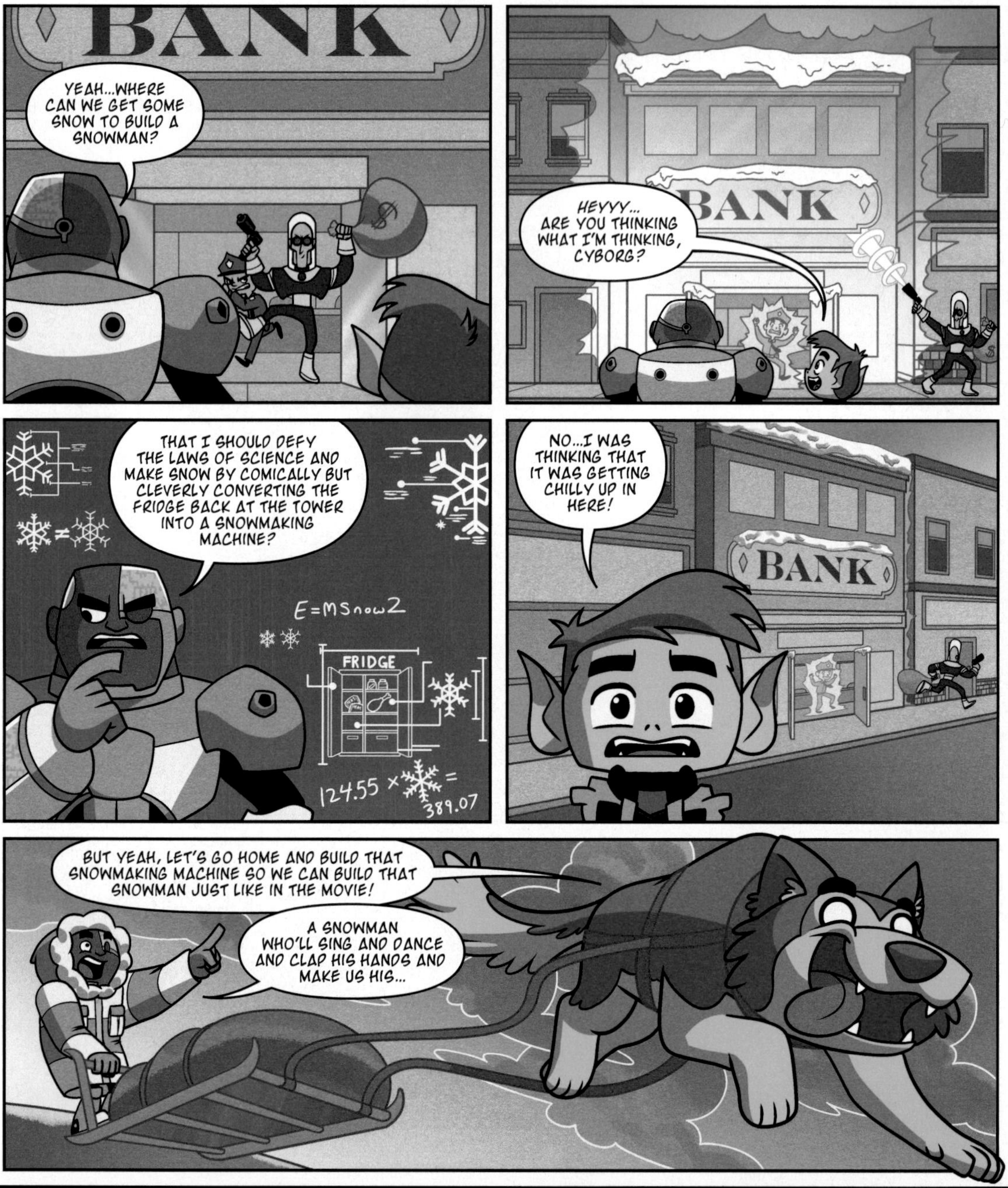
BANK
YEAH...WHERE CAN WE GET SOME SNOW TO BUILD A SNOWMAN?
BANK
HEYYY... ARE YOU THINKING WHAT I'M THINKING, CYBORG?
THAT I SHOULD DEFY THE LAWS OF SCIENCE AND MAKE SNOW BY COMICALLY BUT CLEVERLY CONVERTING THE FRIDGE BACK AT THE TOWER INTO A SNOWMAKING MACHINE?
E=MSnow2
FRIDGE
124.55 × = 389.07
NO...I WAS THINKING THAT IT WAS GETTING CHILLY UP IN HERE!
BANK
BUT YEAH, LET'S GO HOME AND BUILD THAT SNOWMAKING MACHINE SO WE CAN BUILD THAT SNOWMAN JUST LIKE IN THE MOVIE!
A SNOWMAN WHO'LL SING AND DANCE AND CLAP HIS HANDS AND MAKE US HIS...

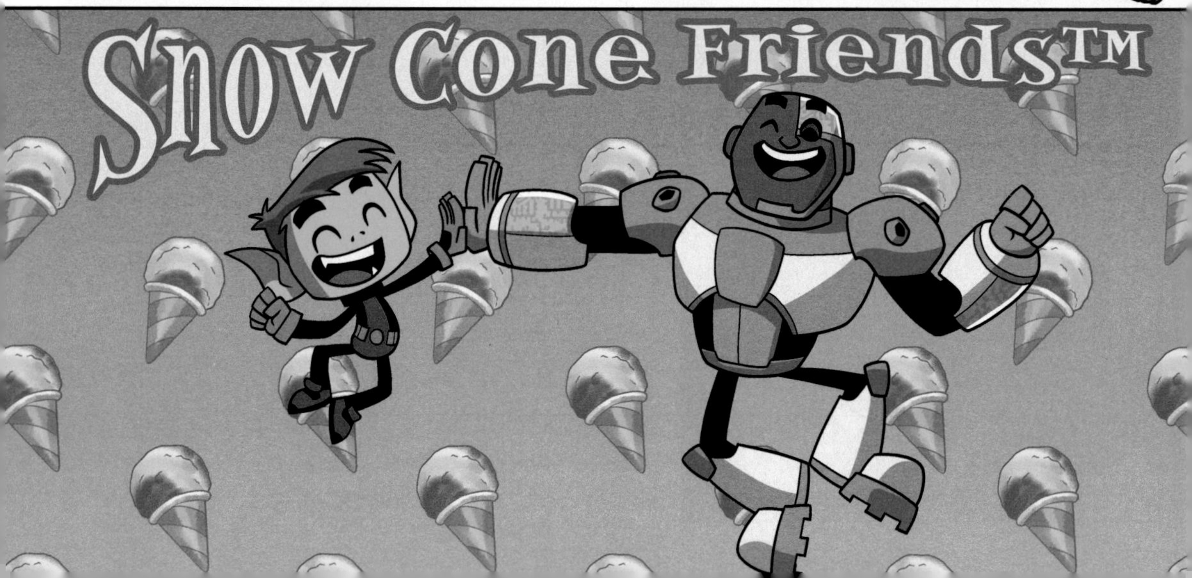
Snow Cone Friends™

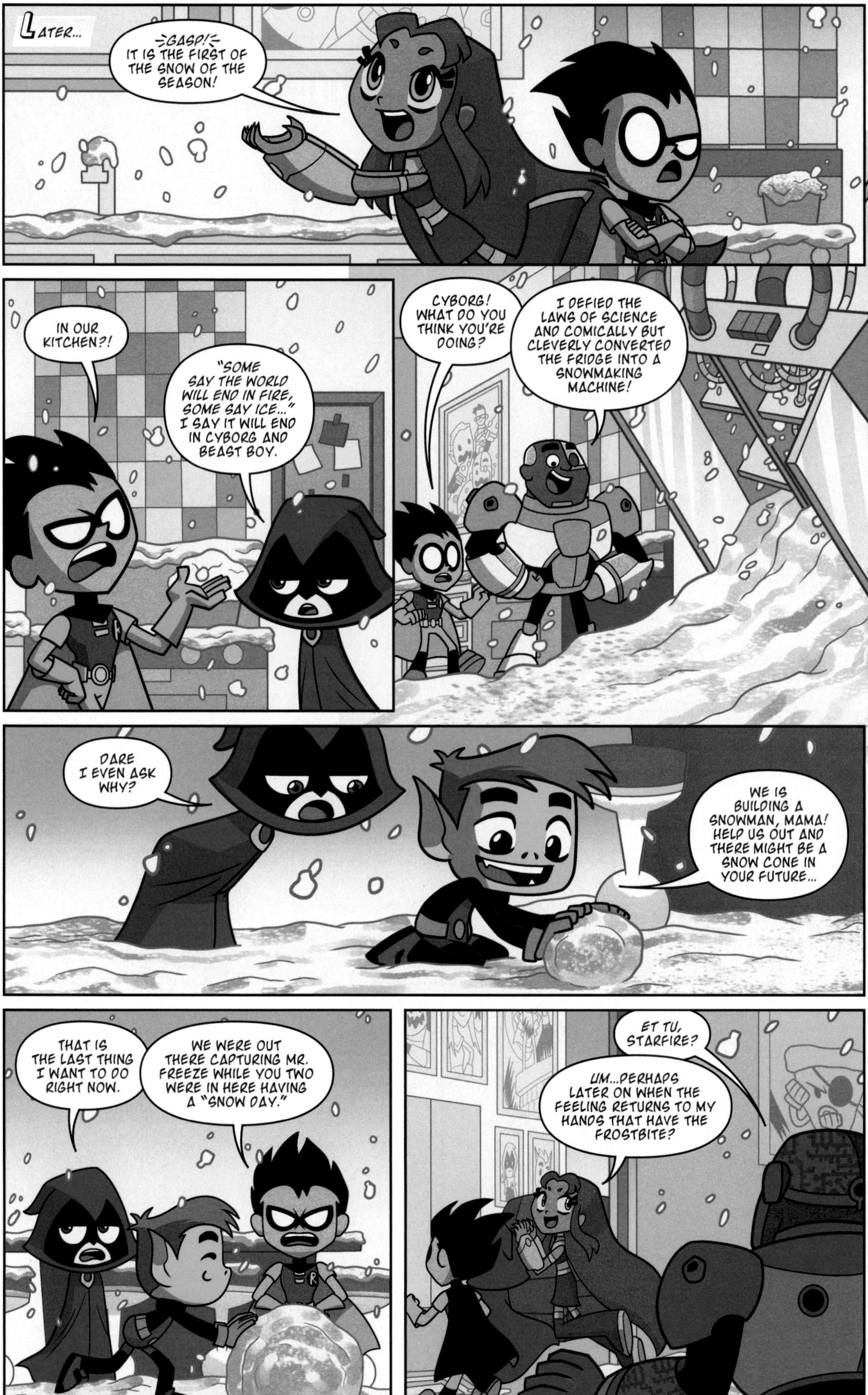
LATER...
GASP! IT IS THE FIRST OF THE SNOW OF THE SEASON!
IN OUR KITCHEN?!
"SOME SAY THE WORLD WILL END IN FIRE, SOME SAY ICE..." I SAY IT WILL END IN CYBORG AND BEAST BOY.
CYBORG! WHAT DO YOU THINK YOU'RE DOING?
I DEFIED THE LAWS OF SCIENCE AND COMICALLY BUT CLEVERLY CONVERTED THE FRIDGE INTO A SNOWMAKING MACHINE!
DARE I EVEN ASK WHY?
WE IS BUILDING A SNOWMAN, MAMA! HELP US OUT AND THERE MIGHT BE A SNOW CONE IN YOUR FUTURE...
THAT IS THE LAST THING I WANT TO DO RIGHT NOW.
WE WERE OUT THERE CAPTURING MR. FREEZE WHILE YOU TWO WERE IN HERE HAVING A "SNOW DAY."
ET TU, STARFIRE?
UM...PERHAPS LATER ON WHEN THE FEELING RETURNS TO MY HANDS THAT HAVE THE FROSTBITE?

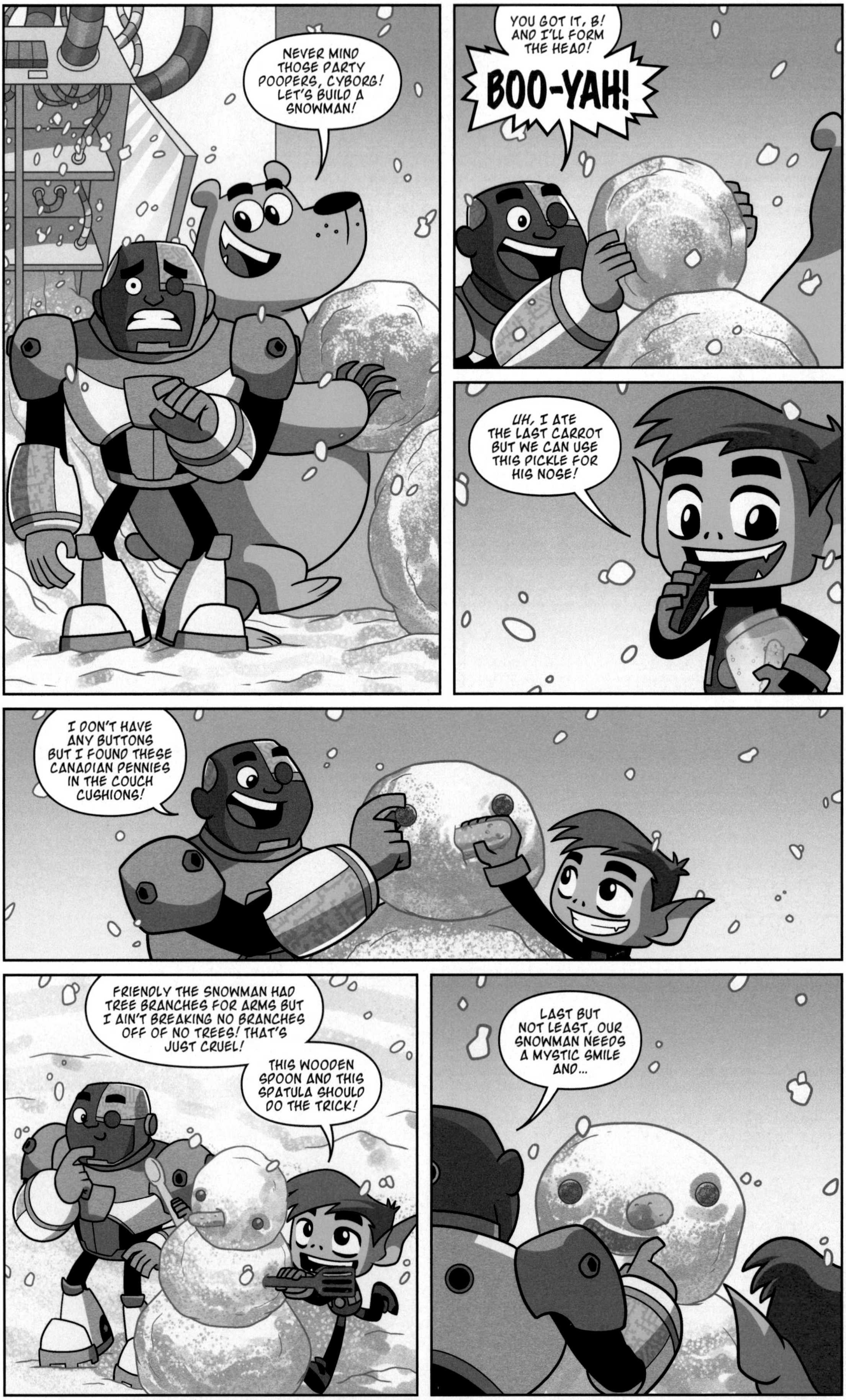
NEVER MIND THOSE PARTY POOPERS, CYBORG! LET'S BUILD A SNOWMAN!
YOU GOT IT, B! AND I'LL FORM THE HEAD!
BOO-YAH!
UH, I ATE THE LAST CARROT BUT WE CAN USE THIS PICKLE FOR HIS NOSE!
I DON'T HAVE ANY BUTTONS BUT I FOUND THESE CANADIAN PENNIES IN THE COUCH CUSHIONS!
FRIENDLY THE SNOWMAN HAD TREE BRANCHES FOR ARMS BUT I AIN'T BREAKING NO BRANCHES OFF OF NO TREES! THAT'S JUST CRUEL!
THIS WOODEN SPOON AND THIS SPATULA SHOULD DO THE TRICK!
LAST BUT NOT LEAST, OUR SNOWMAN NEEDS A MYSTIC SMILE AND...

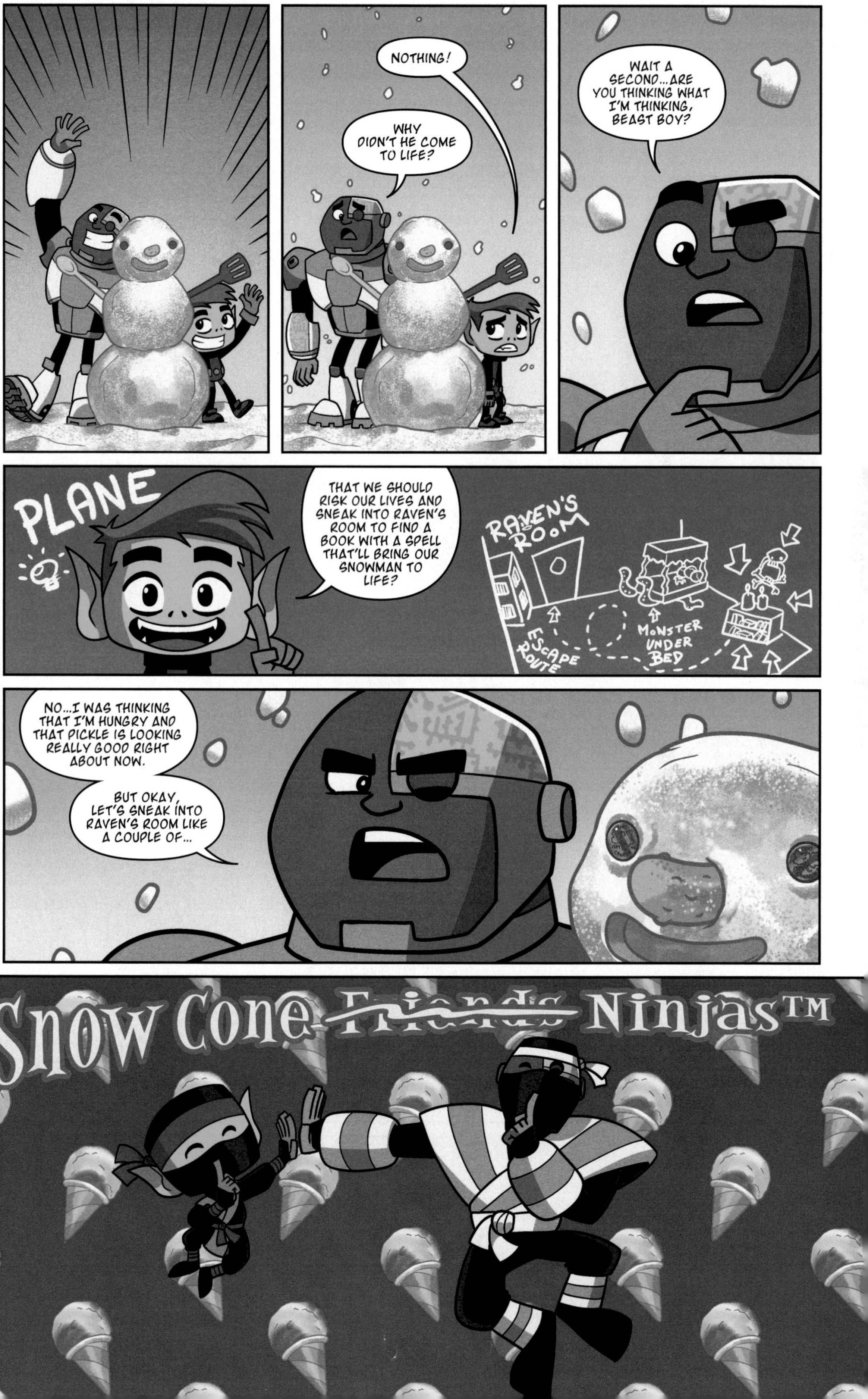
NOTHING!
WHY DIDN'T HE COME TO LIFE?
WAIT A SECOND...ARE YOU THINKING WHAT I'M THINKING, BEAST BOY?
PLANE
THAT WE SHOULD RISK OUR LIVES AND SNEAK INTO RAVEN'S ROOM TO FIND A BOOK WITH A SPELL THAT'LL BRING OUR SNOWMAN TO LIFE?
RAVEN'S ROOM
ESCAPE ROUTE
MONSTER UNDER BED
NO...I WAS THINKING THAT I'M HUNGRY AND THAT PICKLE IS LOOKING REALLY GOOD RIGHT ABOUT NOW.
BUT OKAY, LET'S SNEAK INTO RAVEN'S ROOM LIKE A COUPLE OF...
Snow Cone ~~Friends~~ Ninjas™

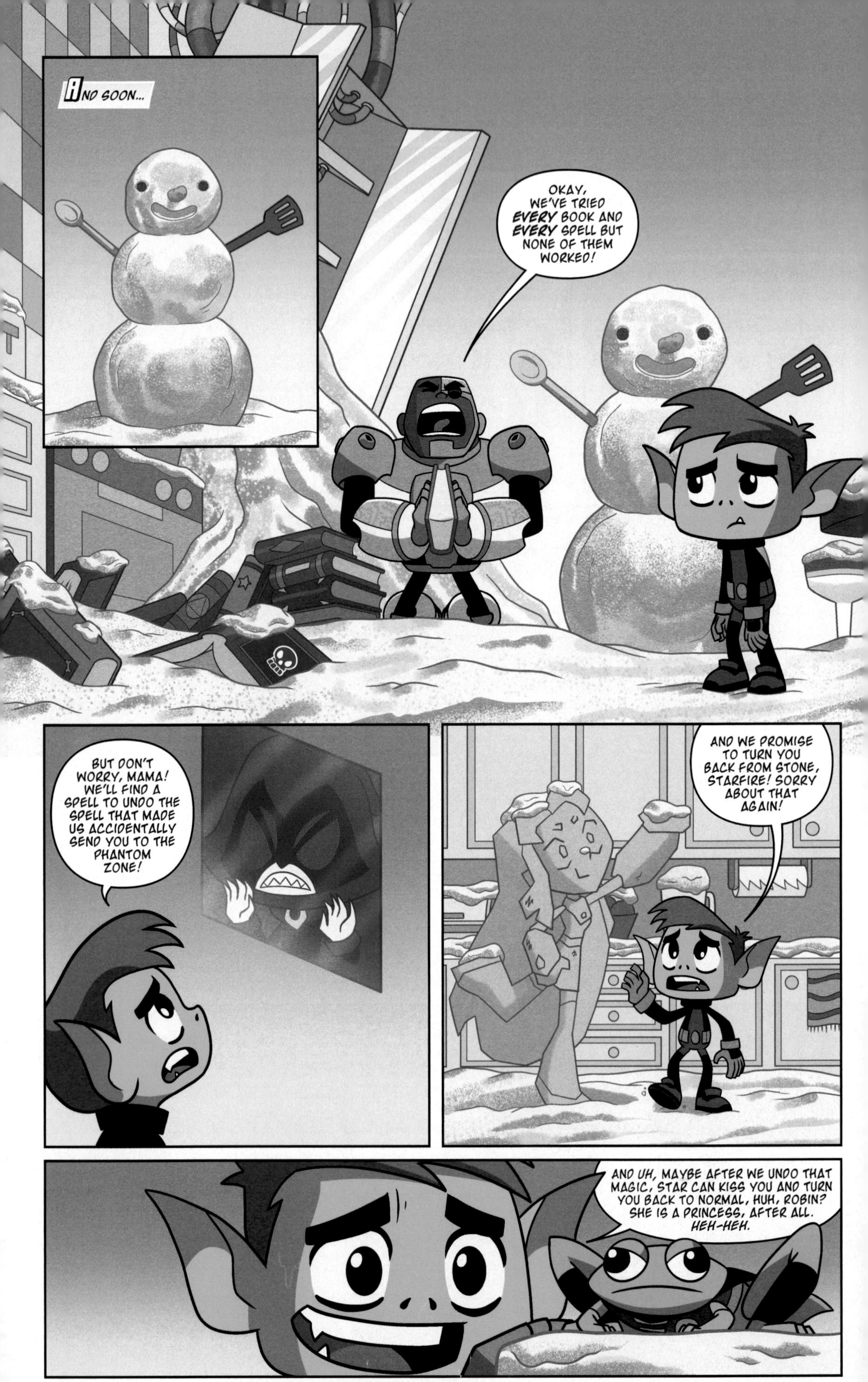
AND SOON...
OKAY, WE'VE TRIED EVERY BOOK AND EVERY SPELL BUT NONE OF THEM WORKED!
BUT DON'T WORRY, MAMA! WE'LL FIND A SPELL TO UNDO THE SPELL THAT MADE US ACCIDENTALLY SEND YOU TO THE PHANTOM ZONE!
AND WE PROMISE TO TURN YOU BACK FROM STONE, STARFIRE! SORRY ABOUT THAT AGAIN!
AND UH, MAYBE AFTER WE UNDO THAT MAGIC, STAR CAN KISS YOU AND TURN YOU BACK TO NORMAL, HUH, ROBIN? SHE IS A PRINCESS, AFTER ALL. HEH-HEH.

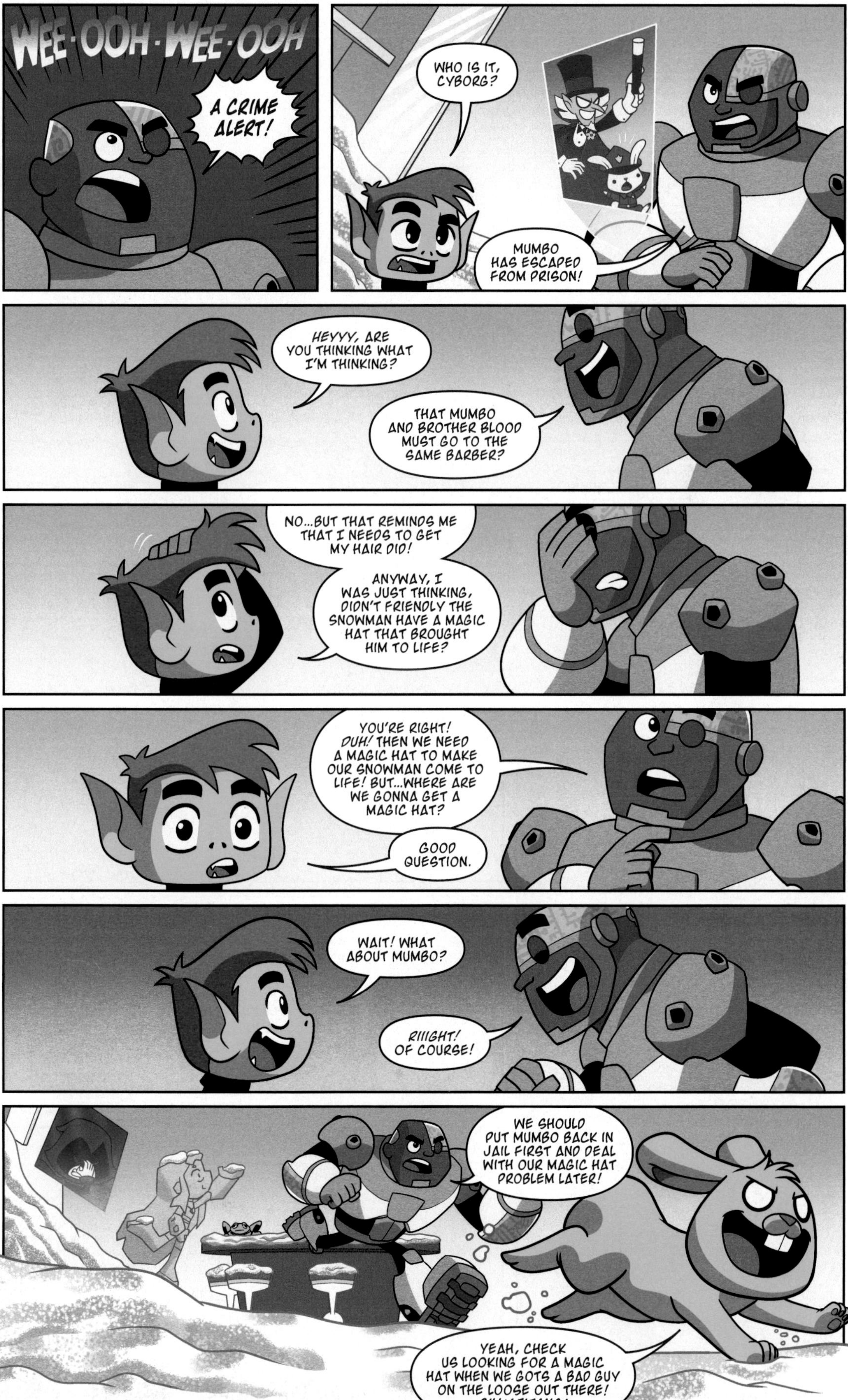
WEE-OOH-WEE-OOH
A CRIME ALERT!
WHO IS IT, CYBORG?
MUMBO HAS ESCAPED FROM PRISON!
HEYYY, ARE YOU THINKING WHAT I'M THINKING?
THAT MUMBO AND BROTHER BLOOD MUST GO TO THE SAME BARBER?
NO...BUT THAT REMINDS ME THAT I NEEDS TO GET MY HAIR DID!
ANYWAY, I WAS JUST THINKING, DIDN'T FRIENDLY THE SNOWMAN HAVE A MAGIC HAT THAT BROUGHT HIM TO LIFE?
YOU'RE RIGHT! DUH! THEN WE NEED A MAGIC HAT TO MAKE OUR SNOWMAN COME TO LIFE! BUT...WHERE ARE WE GONNA GET A MAGIC HAT?
GOOD QUESTION.
WAIT! WHAT ABOUT MUMBO?
RIIIGHT! OF COURSE!
WE SHOULD PUT MUMBO BACK IN JAIL FIRST AND DEAL WITH OUR MAGIC HAT PROBLEM LATER!
YEAH, CHECK US LOOKING FOR A MAGIC HAT WHEN WE GOTS A BAD GUY ON THE LOOSE OUT THERE! SILLY TITANS!

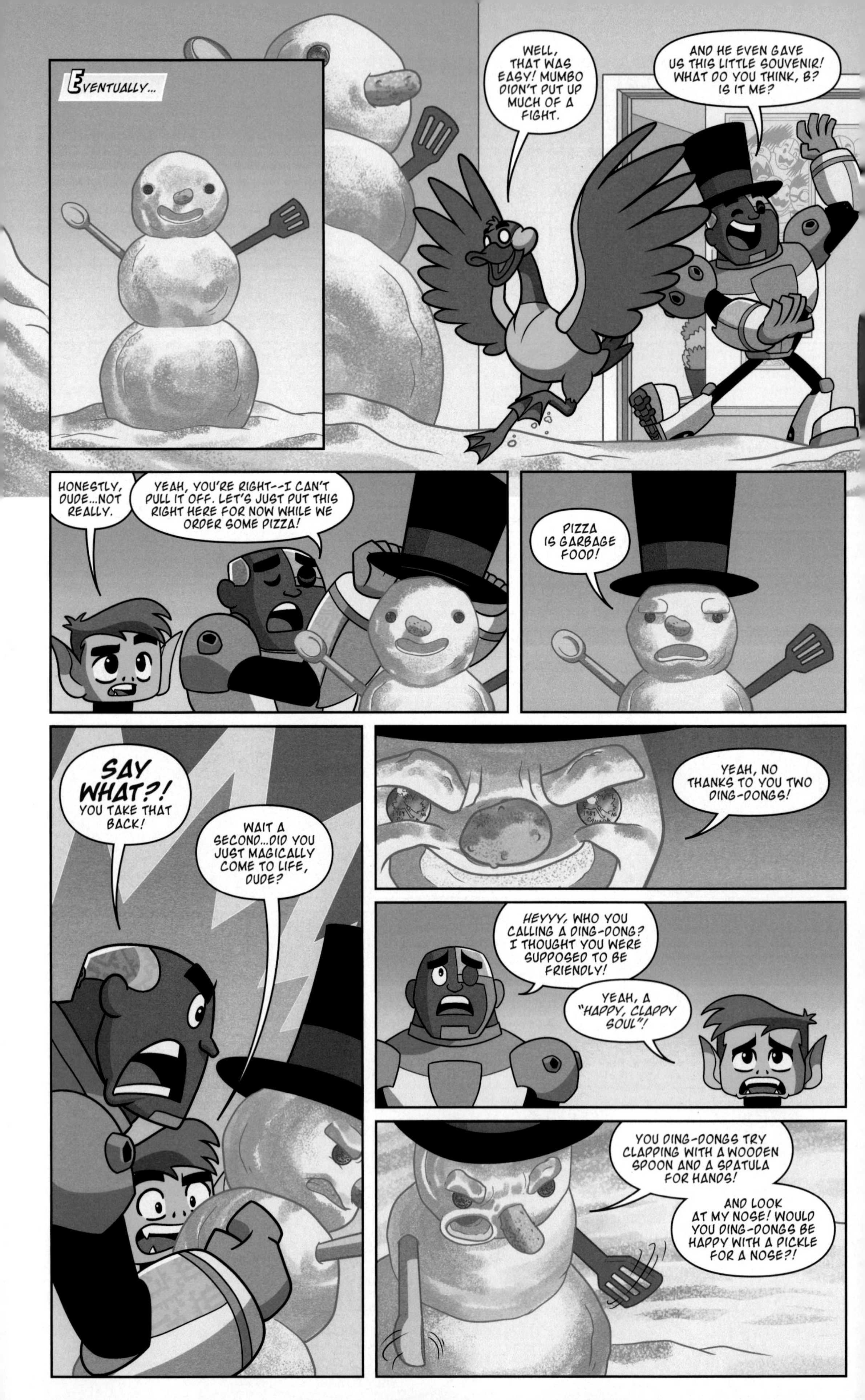
EVENTUALLY...
WELL, THAT WAS EASY! MUMBO DIDN'T PUT UP MUCH OF A FIGHT.
AND HE EVEN GAVE US THIS LITTLE SOUVENIR! WHAT DO YOU THINK, B? IS IT ME?
HONESTLY, DUDE...NOT REALLY.
YEAH, YOU'RE RIGHT--I CAN'T PULL IT OFF. LET'S JUST PUT THIS RIGHT HERE FOR NOW WHILE WE ORDER SOME PIZZA!
PIZZA IS GARBAGE FOOD!
SAY WHAT?! YOU TAKE THAT BACK!
WAIT A SECOND...DID YOU JUST MAGICALLY COME TO LIFE, DUDE?
YEAH, NO THANKS TO YOU TWO DING-DONGS!
HEYYY, WHO YOU CALLING A DING-DONG? I THOUGHT YOU WERE SUPPOSED TO BE FRIENDLY!
YEAH, A "HAPPY, CLAPPY SOUL"!
YOU DING-DONGS TRY CLAPPING WITH A WOODEN SPOON AND A SPATULA FOR HANDS!
AND LOOK AT MY NOSE! WOULD YOU DING-DONGS BE HAPPY WITH A PICKLE FOR A NOSE?!

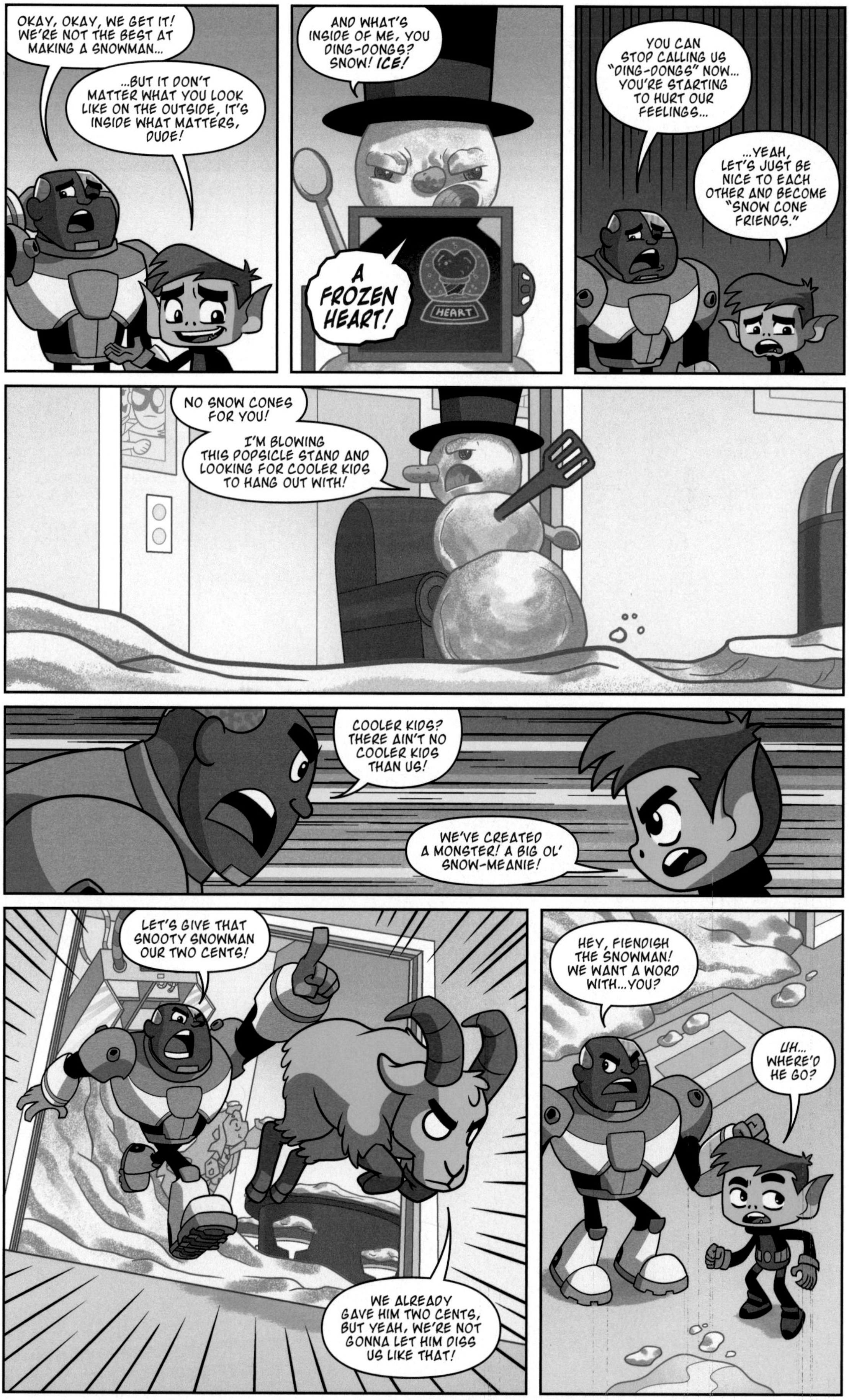
OKAY, OKAY, WE GET IT! WE'RE NOT THE BEST AT MAKING A SNOWMAN...
...BUT IT DON'T MATTER WHAT YOU LOOK LIKE ON THE OUTSIDE, IT'S INSIDE WHAT MATTERS, DUDE!
AND WHAT'S INSIDE OF ME, YOU DING-DONGS? SNOW! ICE!
A FROZEN HEART!
HEART
YOU CAN STOP CALLING US "DING-DONGS" NOW... YOU'RE STARTING TO HURT OUR FEELINGS...
...YEAH, LET'S JUST BE NICE TO EACH OTHER AND BECOME "SNOW CONE FRIENDS."
NO SNOW CONES FOR YOU!
I'M BLOWING THIS POPSICLE STAND AND LOOKING FOR COOLER KIDS TO HANG OUT WITH!
COOLER KIDS? THERE AIN'T NO COOLER KIDS THAN US!
WE'VE CREATED A MONSTER! A BIG OL' SNOW-MEANIE!
LET'S GIVE THAT SNOOTY SNOWMAN OUR TWO CENTS!
WE ALREADY GAVE HIM TWO CENTS, BUT YEAH, WE'RE NOT GONNA LET HIM DISS US LIKE THAT!
HEY, FIENDISH THE SNOWMAN! WE WANT A WORD WITH...YOU?
UH... WHERE'D HE GO?

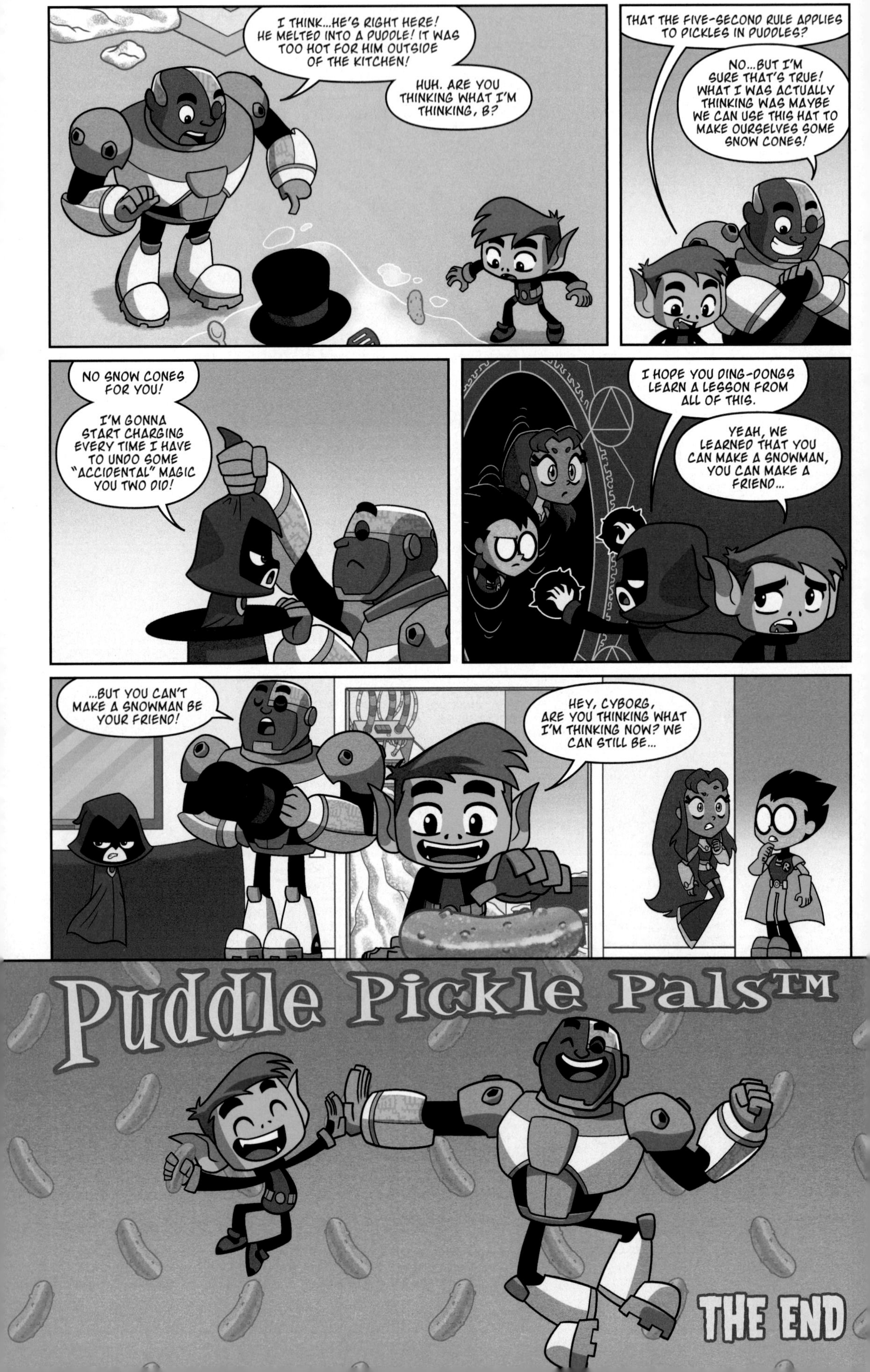
I THINK...HE'S RIGHT HERE! HE MELTED INTO A PUDDLE! IT WAS TOO HOT FOR HIM OUTSIDE OF THE KITCHEN!
HUH. ARE YOU THINKING WHAT I'M THINKING, B?
THAT THE FIVE-SECOND RULE APPLIES TO PICKLES IN PUDDLES?
NO...BUT I'M SURE THAT'S TRUE! WHAT I WAS ACTUALLY THINKING WAS MAYBE WE CAN USE THIS HAT TO MAKE OURSELVES SOME SNOW CONES!
NO SNOW CONES FOR YOU!
I'M GONNA START CHARGING EVERY TIME I HAVE TO UNDO SOME "ACCIDENTAL" MAGIC YOU TWO DID!
I HOPE YOU DING-DONGS LEARN A LESSON FROM ALL OF THIS.
YEAH, WE LEARNED THAT YOU CAN MAKE A SNOWMAN, YOU CAN MAKE A FRIEND...
...BUT YOU CAN'T MAKE A SNOWMAN BE YOUR FRIEND!
HEY, CYBORG, ARE YOU THINKING WHAT I'M THINKING NOW? WE CAN STILL BE...
Puddle Pickle Pals™
THE END

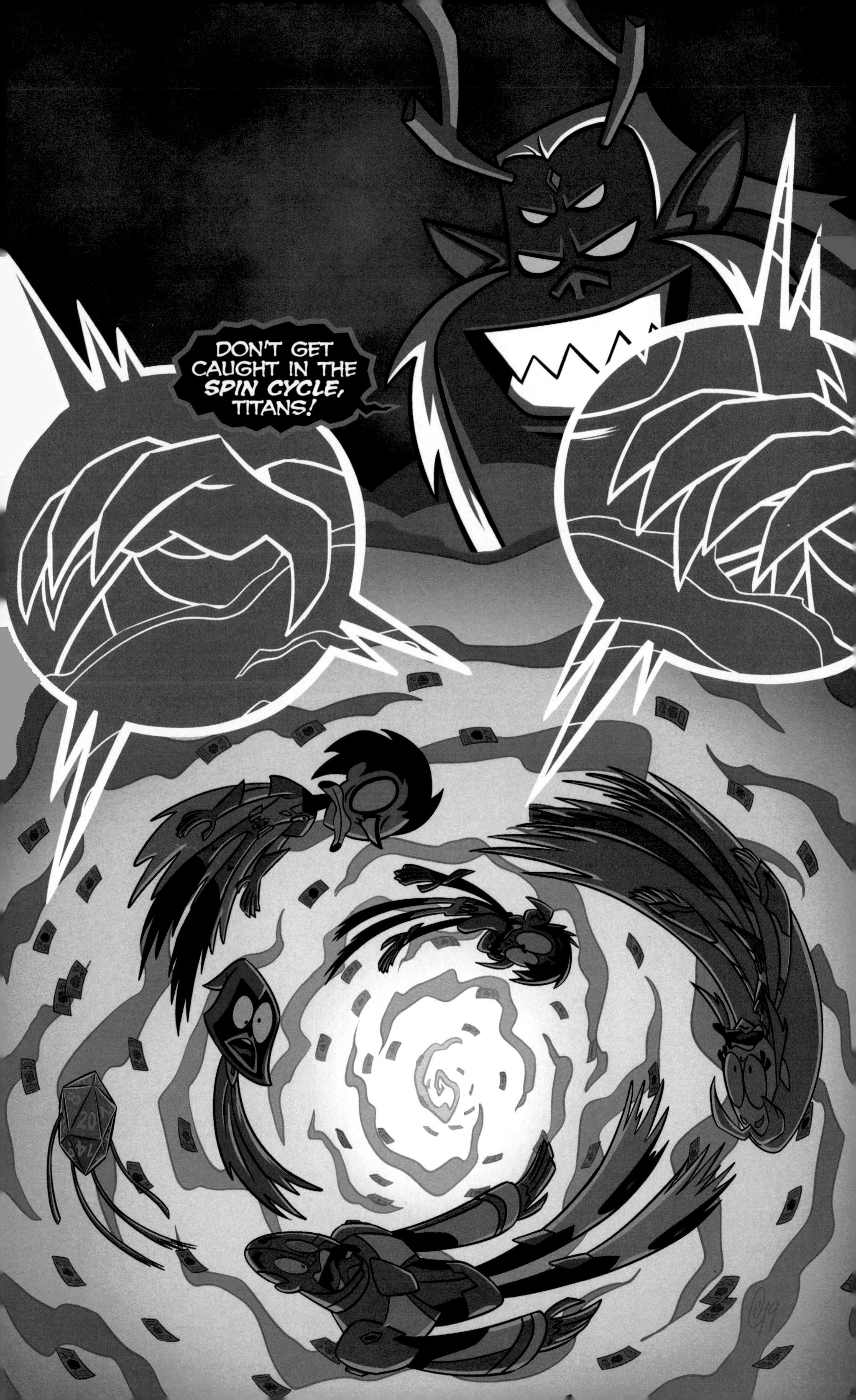
DON'T GET CAUGHT IN THE *SPIN CYCLE,* TITANS!

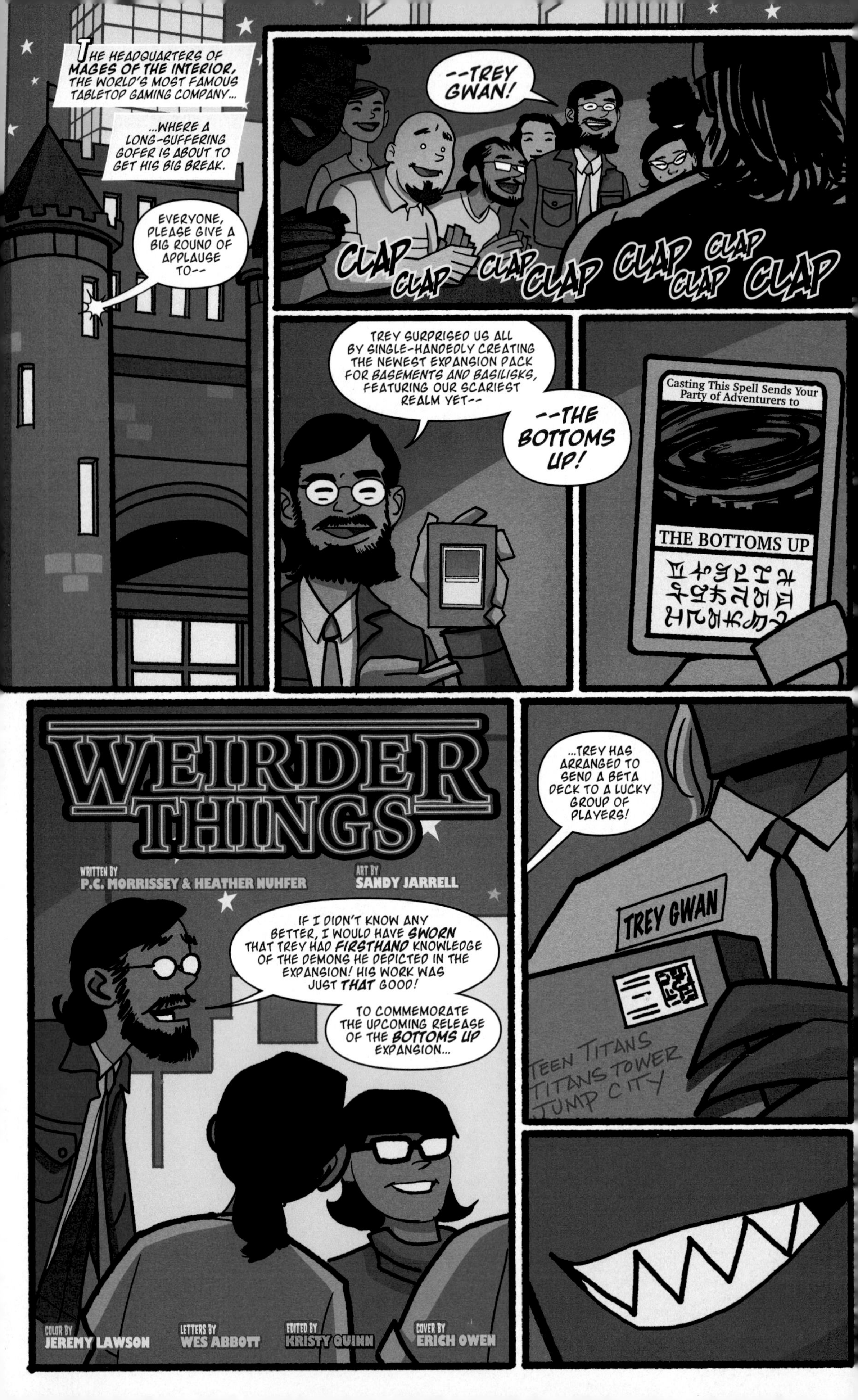
THE HEADQUARTERS OF MAGES OF THE INTERIOR, THE WORLD'S MOST FAMOUS TABLETOP GAMING COMPANY...
...WHERE A LONG-SUFFERING GOFER IS ABOUT TO GET HIS BIG BREAK.
EVERYONE, PLEASE GIVE A BIG ROUND OF APPLAUSE TO--
--TREY GWAN!
CLAP CLAP CLAP CLAP CLAP CLAP CLAP CLAP
TREY SURPRISED US ALL BY SINGLE-HANDEDLY CREATING THE NEWEST EXPANSION PACK FOR BASEMENTS AND BASILISKS, FEATURING OUR SCARIEST REALM YET--
--THE BOTTOMS UP!
Casting This Spell Sends Your Party of Adventurers to
THE BOTTOMS UP
WEIRDER THINGS
WRITTEN BY P.C. MORRISSEY & HEATHER NUHFER
ART BY SANDY JARRELL
IF I DIDN'T KNOW ANY BETTER, I WOULD HAVE SWORN THAT TREY HAD FIRSTHAND KNOWLEDGE OF THE DEMONS HE DEPICTED IN THE EXPANSION! HIS WORK WAS JUST THAT GOOD!
TO COMMEMORATE THE UPCOMING RELEASE OF THE BOTTOMS UP EXPANSION...
...TREY HAS ARRANGED TO SEND A BETA DECK TO A LUCKY GROUP OF PLAYERS!
TREY GWAN
TEEN TITANS TITANS TOWER JUMP CITY
COLOR BY JEREMY LAWSON
LETTERS BY WES ABBOTT
EDITED BY KRISTY QUINN
COVER BY ERICH OWEN

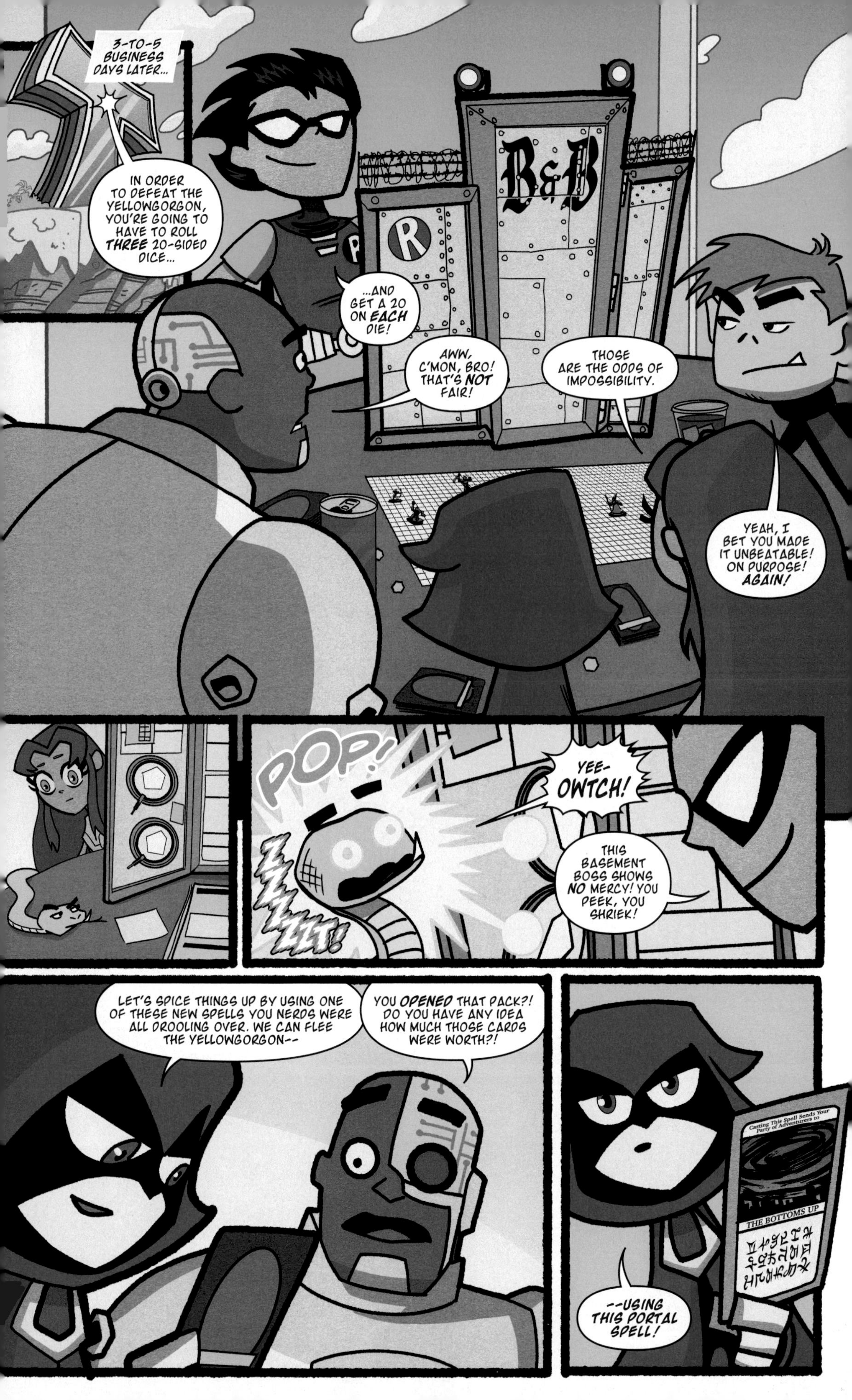
3-TO-5 BUSINESS DAYS LATER...
IN ORDER TO DEFEAT THE YELLOWGORGON, YOU'RE GOING TO HAVE TO ROLL **THREE** 20-SIDED DICE...
...AND GET A 20 ON **EACH** DIE!
AWW, C'MON, BRO! THAT'S **NOT** FAIR!
THOSE ARE THE ODDS OF IMPOSSIBILITY.
YEAH, I BET YOU MADE IT UNBEATABLE! ON PURPOSE! **AGAIN!**
B&B
POP!
ZZZZZT!
YEE-OWTCH!
THIS BASEMENT BOSS SHOWS **NO** MERCY! YOU PEEK, YOU SHRIEK!
LET'S SPICE THINGS UP BY USING ONE OF THESE NEW SPELLS YOU NERDS WERE ALL DROOLING OVER. WE CAN FLEE THE YELLOWGORGON--
YOU **OPENED** THAT PACK?! DO YOU HAVE ANY IDEA HOW MUCH THOSE CARDS WERE WORTH?!
Casting This Spell Sends Your Party of Adventurers to
THE BOTTOMS UP
--USING THIS PORTAL SPELL!

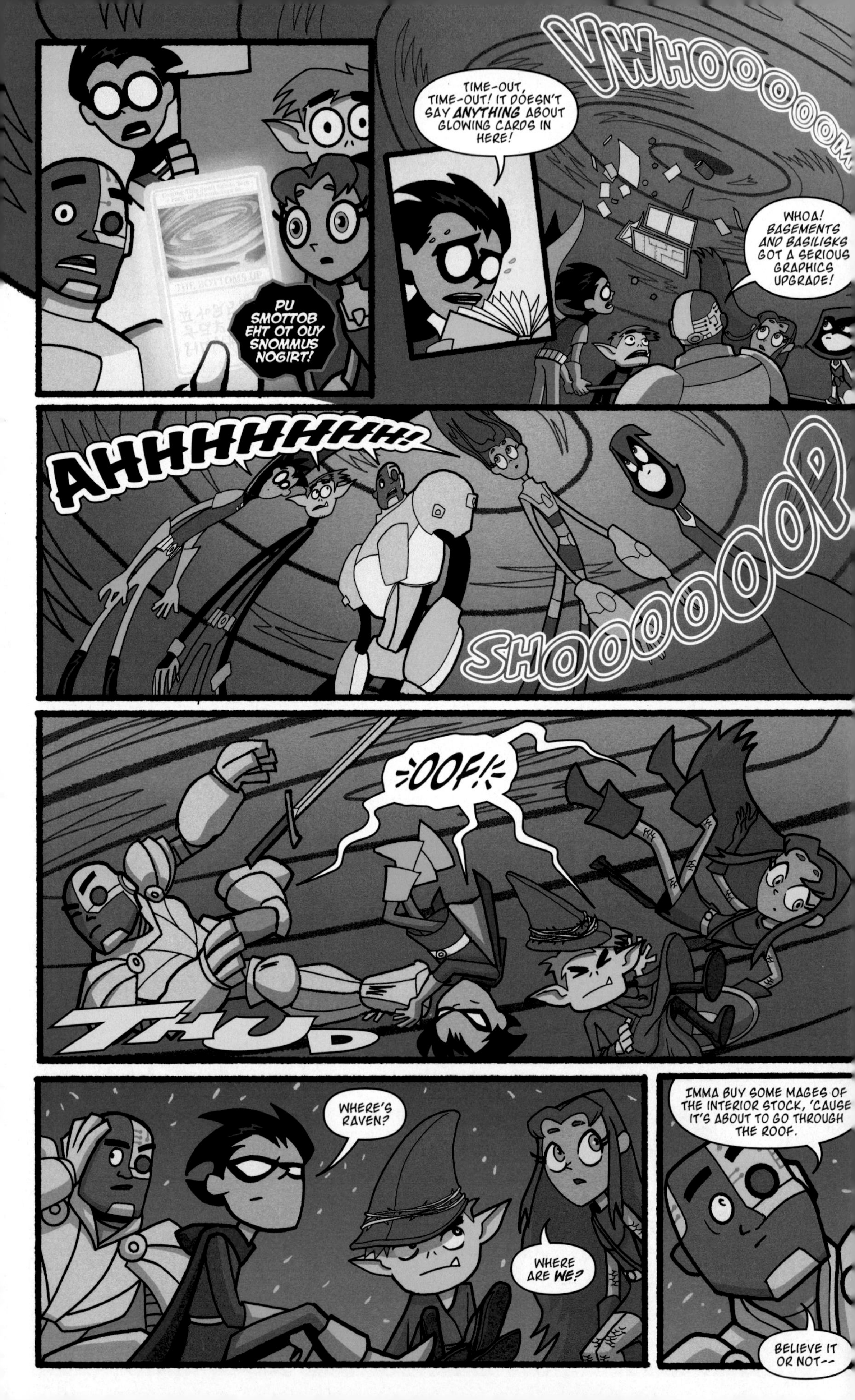
THE BOTTOMS UP
PU SMOTTOB EHT OT OUY SNOMMUS NOGIRT!
TIME-OUT, TIME-OUT! IT DOESN'T SAY ANYTHING ABOUT GLOWING CARDS IN HERE!
VWHOOOOOOM
WHOA! BASEMENTS AND BASILISKS GOT A SERIOUS GRAPHICS UPGRADE!
AHHHHHHHH!
SHOOOOOOOP
OOF!
THUD
WHERE'S RAVEN?
WHERE ARE WE?
IMMA BUY SOME MAGES OF THE INTERIOR STOCK, 'CAUSE IT'S ABOUT TO GO THROUGH THE ROOF.
BELIEVE IT OR NOT--

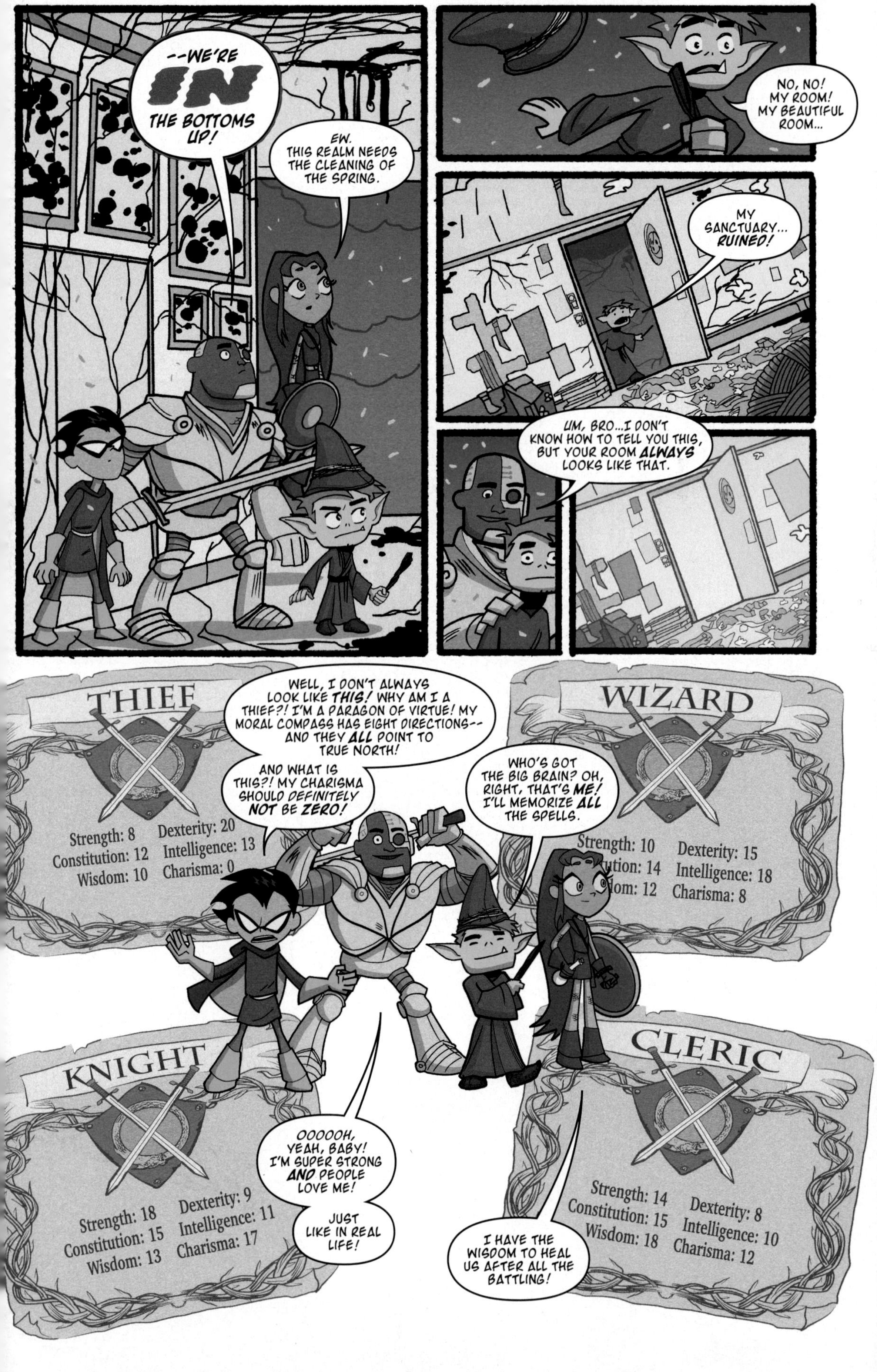
--WE'RE IN THE BOTTOMS UP!
EW. THIS REALM NEEDS THE CLEANING OF THE SPRING.
NO, NO! MY ROOM! MY BEAUTIFUL ROOM...
MY SANCTUARY... RUINED!
UM, BRO...I DON'T KNOW HOW TO TELL YOU THIS, BUT YOUR ROOM ALWAYS LOOKS LIKE THAT.
THIEF
Strength: 8 Dexterity: 20
Constitution: 12 Intelligence: 13
Wisdom: 10 Charisma: 0
WELL, I DON'T ALWAYS LOOK LIKE THIS! WHY AM I A THIEF?! I'M A PARAGON OF VIRTUE! MY MORAL COMPASS HAS EIGHT DIRECTIONS--AND THEY ALL POINT TO TRUE NORTH!
AND WHAT IS THIS?! MY CHARISMA SHOULD DEFINITELY NOT BE ZERO!
WIZARD
WHO'S GOT THE BIG BRAIN? OH, RIGHT, THAT'S ME! I'LL MEMORIZE ALL THE SPELLS.
Strength: 10 Dexterity: 15
Intelligence: 18
Charisma: 8
KNIGHT
Strength: 18 Dexterity: 9
Constitution: 15 Intelligence: 11
Wisdom: 13 Charisma: 17
OOOOOH, YEAH, BABY! I'M SUPER STRONG AND PEOPLE LOVE ME!
JUST LIKE IN REAL LIFE!
CLERIC
Strength: 14 Dexterity: 8
Constitution: 15 Intelligence: 10
Wisdom: 18 Charisma: 12
I HAVE THE WISDOM TO HEAL US AFTER ALL THE BATTLING!

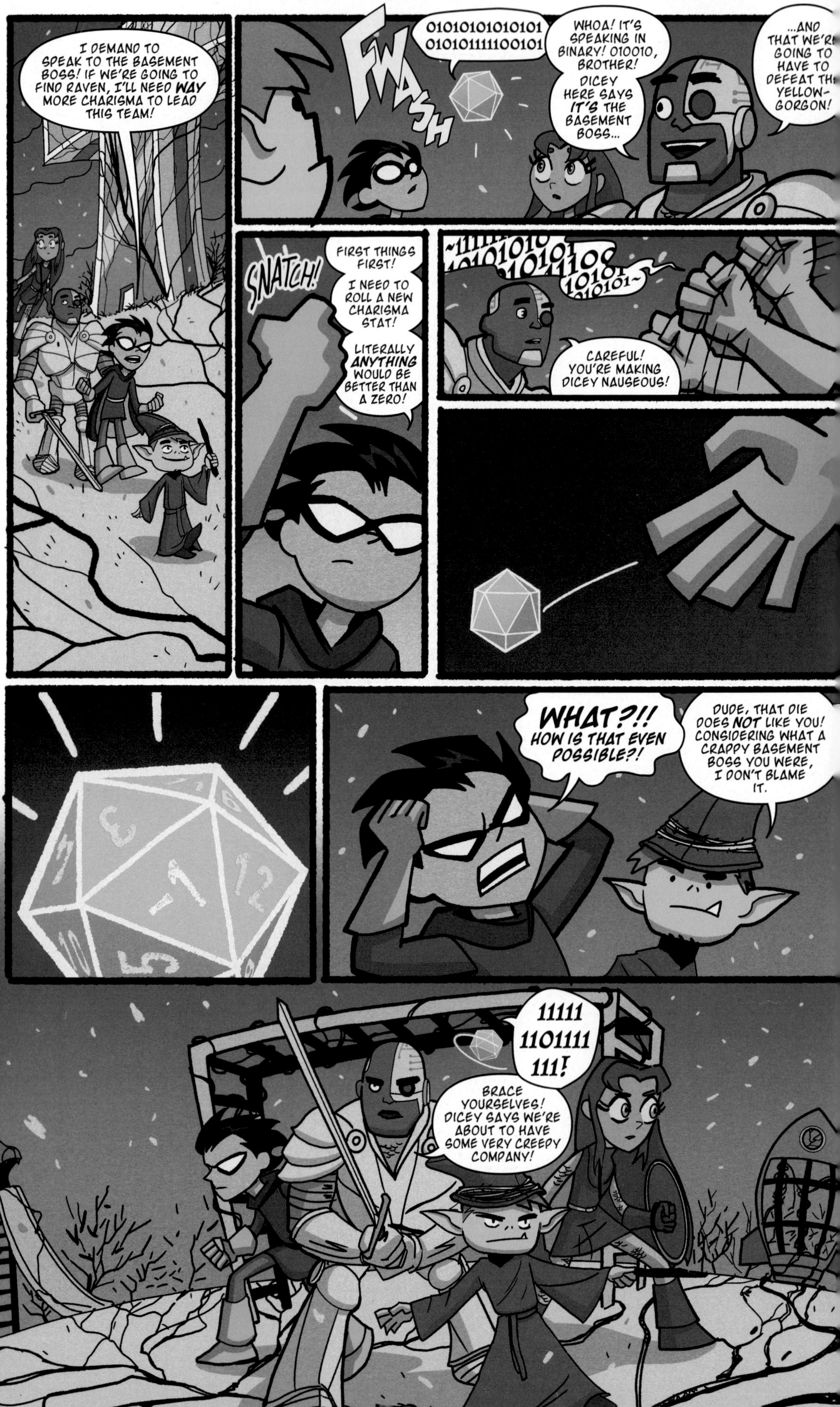
I DEMAND TO SPEAK TO THE BASEMENT BOSS! IF WE'RE GOING TO FIND RAVEN, I'LL NEED **WAY** MORE CHARISMA TO LEAD THIS TEAM!
FWASH
0101010101010101 010101111100101
WHOA! IT'S SPEAKING IN BINARY! 010010, BROTHER!
DICEY HERE SAYS **IT'S** THE BASEMENT BOSS...
...AND THAT WE'RE GOING TO HAVE TO DEFEAT THE YELLOW-GORGON!
SNATCH!
FIRST THINGS FIRST!
I NEED TO ROLL A NEW CHARISMA STAT!
LITERALLY **ANYTHING** WOULD BE BETTER THAN A ZERO!
CAREFUL! YOU'RE MAKING DICEY NAUSEOUS!
WHAT?!! HOW IS THAT EVEN POSSIBLE?!
DUDE, THAT DIE DOES **NOT** LIKE YOU! CONSIDERING WHAT A CRAPPY BASEMENT BOSS YOU WERE, I DON'T BLAME IT.
11111 1101111 111!
BRACE YOURSELVES! DICEY SAYS WE'RE ABOUT TO HAVE SOME VERY CREEPY COMPANY!

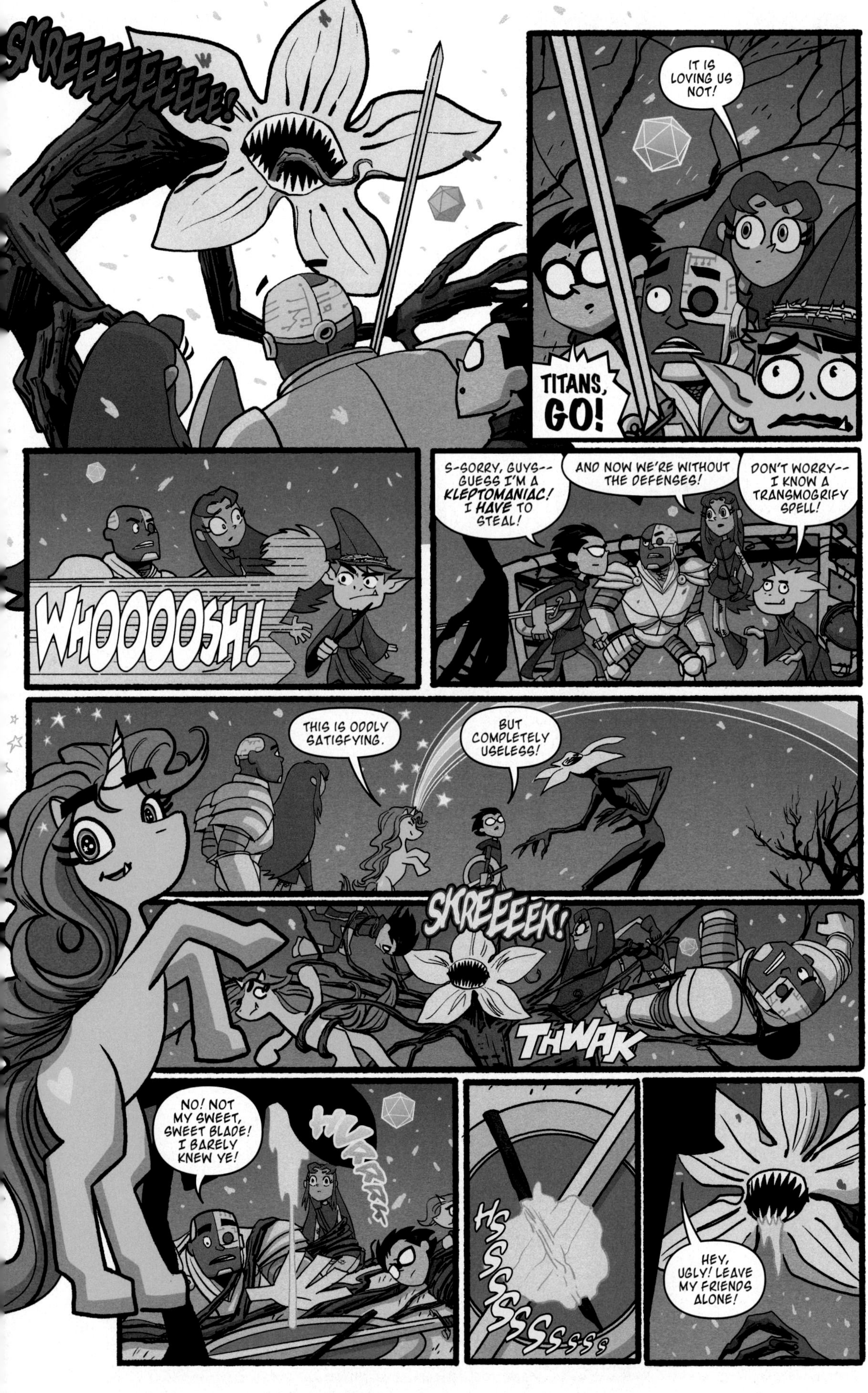
SKREEEEEEEEEE!
IT IS LOVING US NOT!
TITANS, GO!
WHOOOOSH!
S-SORRY, GUYS--GUESS I'M A KLEPTOMANIAC! I HAVE TO STEAL!
AND NOW WE'RE WITHOUT THE DEFENSES!
DON'T WORRY--I KNOW A TRANSMOGRIFY SPELL!
THIS IS ODDLY SATISFYING.
BUT COMPLETELY USELESS!
SKREEEEK!
THWAK
NO! NOT MY SWEET, SWEET BLADE! I BARELY KNEW YE!
HSSSSSSSSSS
HEY, UGLY! LEAVE MY FRIENDS ALONE!

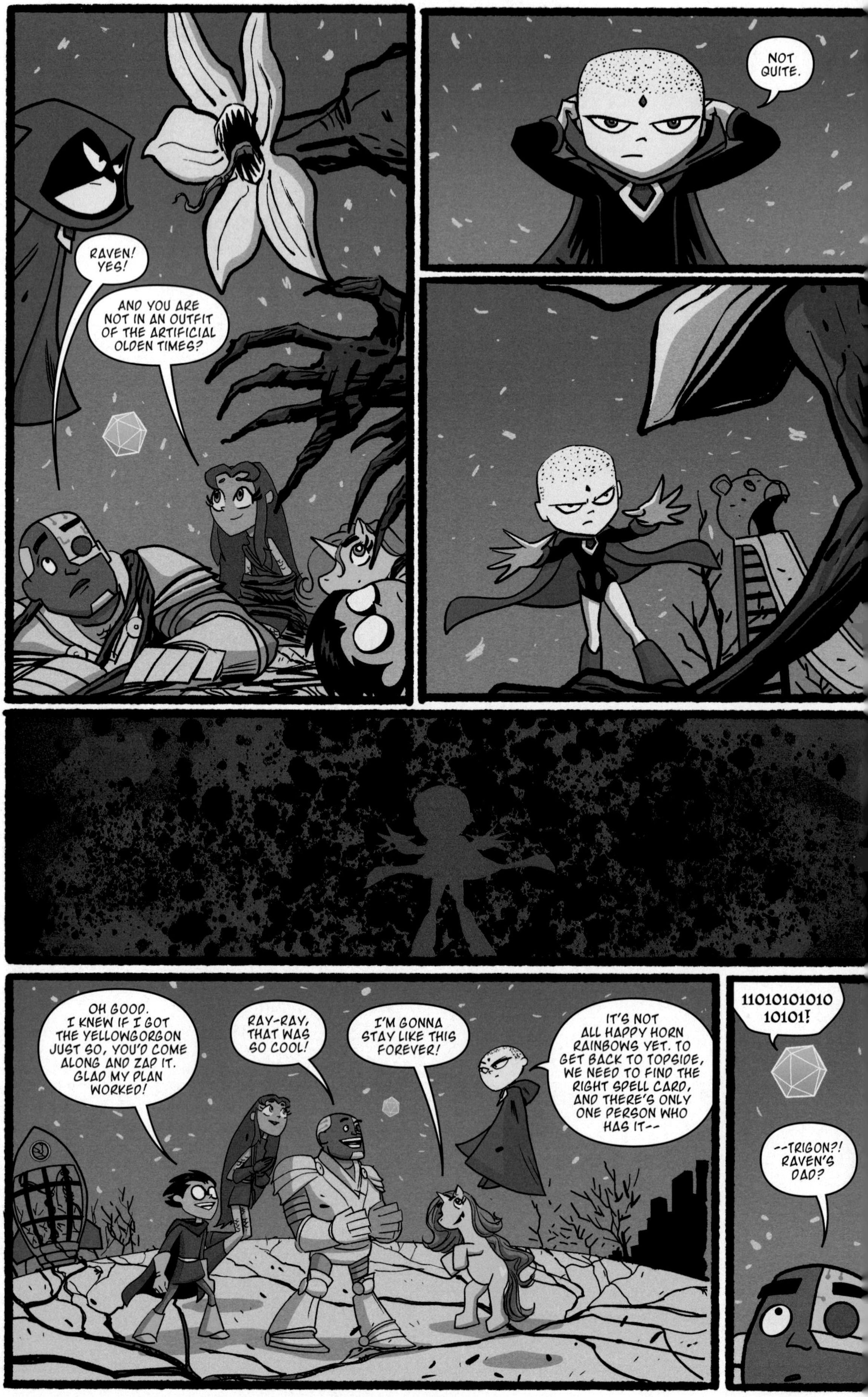
RAVEN! YES!
AND YOU ARE NOT IN AN OUTFIT OF THE ARTIFICIAL OLDEN TIMES?
NOT QUITE.
OH GOOD. I KNEW IF I GOT THE YELLOWGORGON JUST SO, YOU'D COME ALONG AND ZAP IT. GLAD MY PLAN WORKED!
RAY-RAY, THAT WAS SO COOL!
I'M GONNA STAY LIKE THIS FOREVER!
IT'S NOT ALL HAPPY HORN RAINBOWS YET. TO GET BACK TO TOPSIDE, WE NEED TO FIND THE RIGHT SPELL CARD, AND THERE'S ONLY ONE PERSON WHO HAS IT--
11010101010 10101!
--TRIGON?! RAVEN'S DAD?

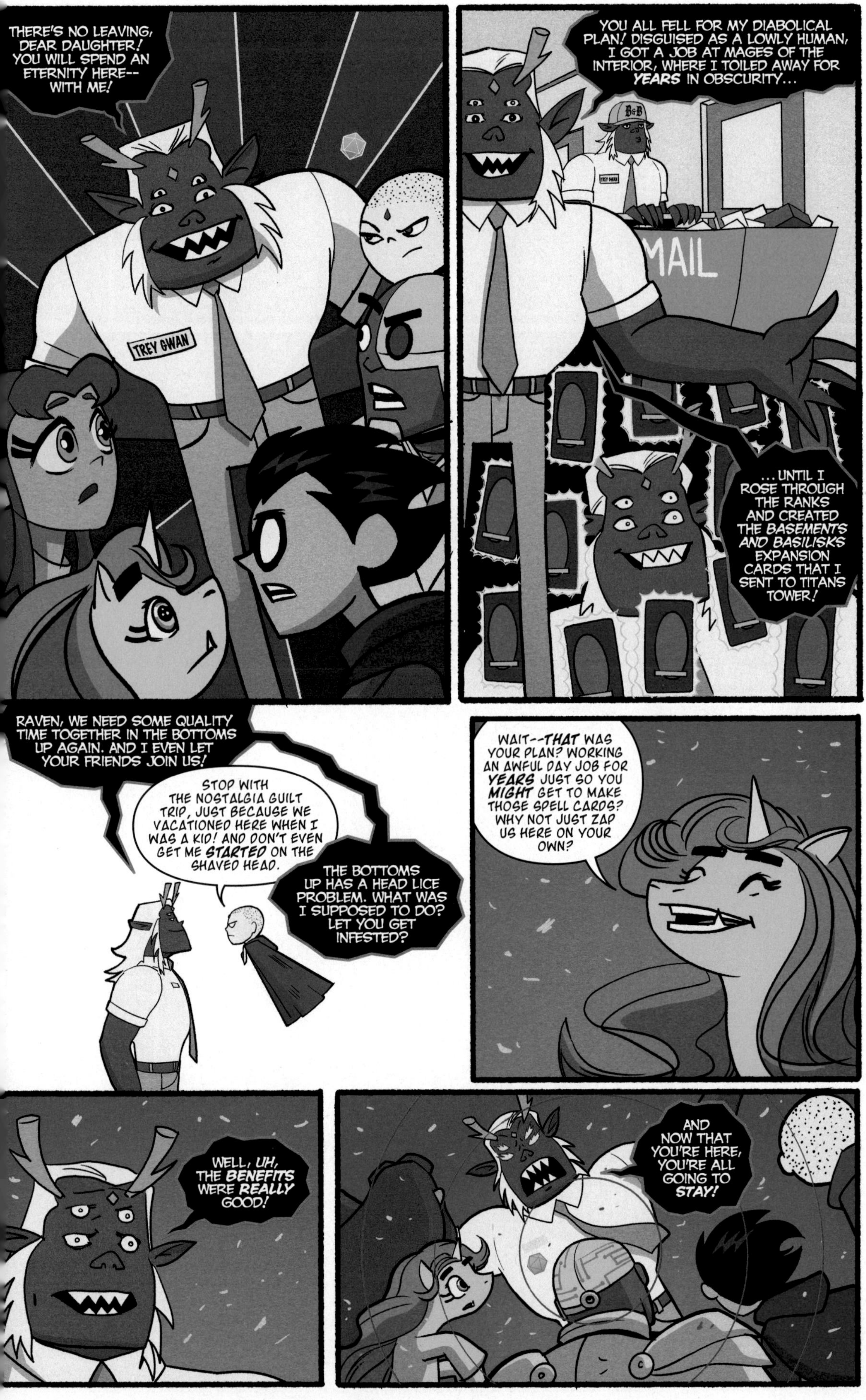
THERE'S NO LEAVING, DEAR DAUGHTER! YOU WILL SPEND AN ETERNITY HERE-- WITH ME!
TREY GWAN
YOU ALL FELL FOR MY DIABOLICAL PLAN! DISGUISED AS A LOWLY HUMAN, I GOT A JOB AT MAGES OF THE INTERIOR, WHERE I TOILED AWAY FOR YEARS IN OBSCURITY...
B&B
TREY GWAN
MAIL
...UNTIL I ROSE THROUGH THE RANKS AND CREATED THE BASEMENTS AND BASILISKS EXPANSION CARDS THAT I SENT TO TITANS TOWER!
RAVEN, WE NEED SOME QUALITY TIME TOGETHER IN THE BOTTOMS UP AGAIN. AND I EVEN LET YOUR FRIENDS JOIN US!
STOP WITH THE NOSTALGIA GUILT TRIP, JUST BECAUSE WE VACATIONED HERE WHEN I WAS A KID! AND DON'T EVEN GET ME STARTED ON THE SHAVED HEAD.
THE BOTTOMS UP HAS A HEAD LICE PROBLEM. WHAT WAS I SUPPOSED TO DO? LET YOU GET INFESTED?
WAIT--THAT WAS YOUR PLAN? WORKING AN AWFUL DAY JOB FOR YEARS JUST SO YOU MIGHT GET TO MAKE THOSE SPELL CARDS? WHY NOT JUST ZAP US HERE ON YOUR OWN?
WELL, UH, THE BENEFITS WERE REALLY GOOD!
AND NOW THAT YOU'RE HERE, YOU'RE ALL GOING TO STAY!

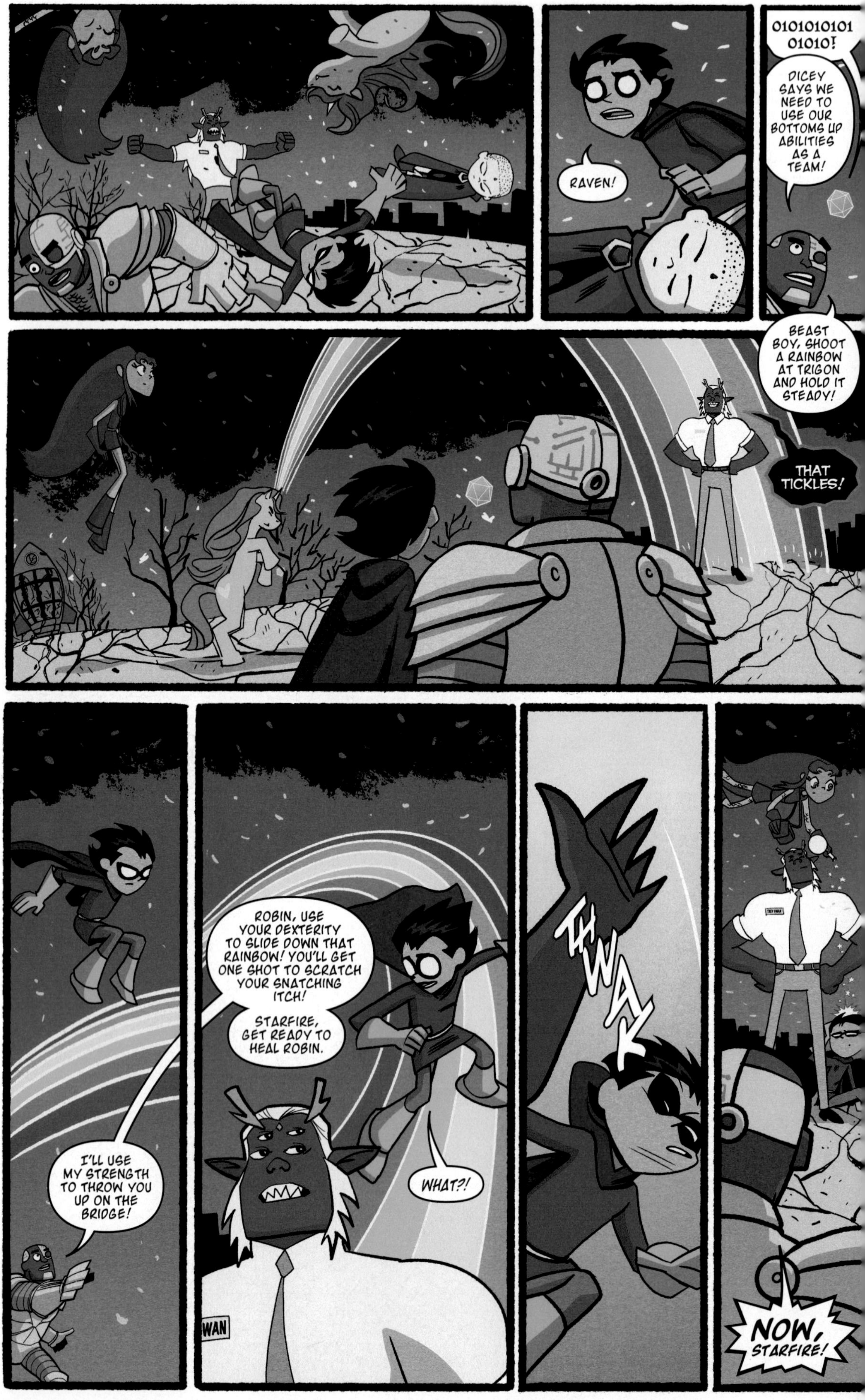
RAVEN!
0101010101 01010!
DICEY SAYS WE NEED TO USE OUR BOTTOMS UP ABILITIES AS A TEAM!
BEAST BOY, SHOOT A RAINBOW AT TRIGON AND HOLD IT STEADY!
THAT TICKLES!
I'LL USE MY STRENGTH TO THROW YOU UP ON THE BRIDGE!
ROBIN, USE YOUR DEXTERITY TO SLIDE DOWN THAT RAINBOW! YOU'LL GET ONE SHOT TO SCRATCH YOUR SNATCHING ITCH!
STARFIRE, GET READY TO HEAL ROBIN.
WHAT?!
THWAK
NOW, STARFIRE!

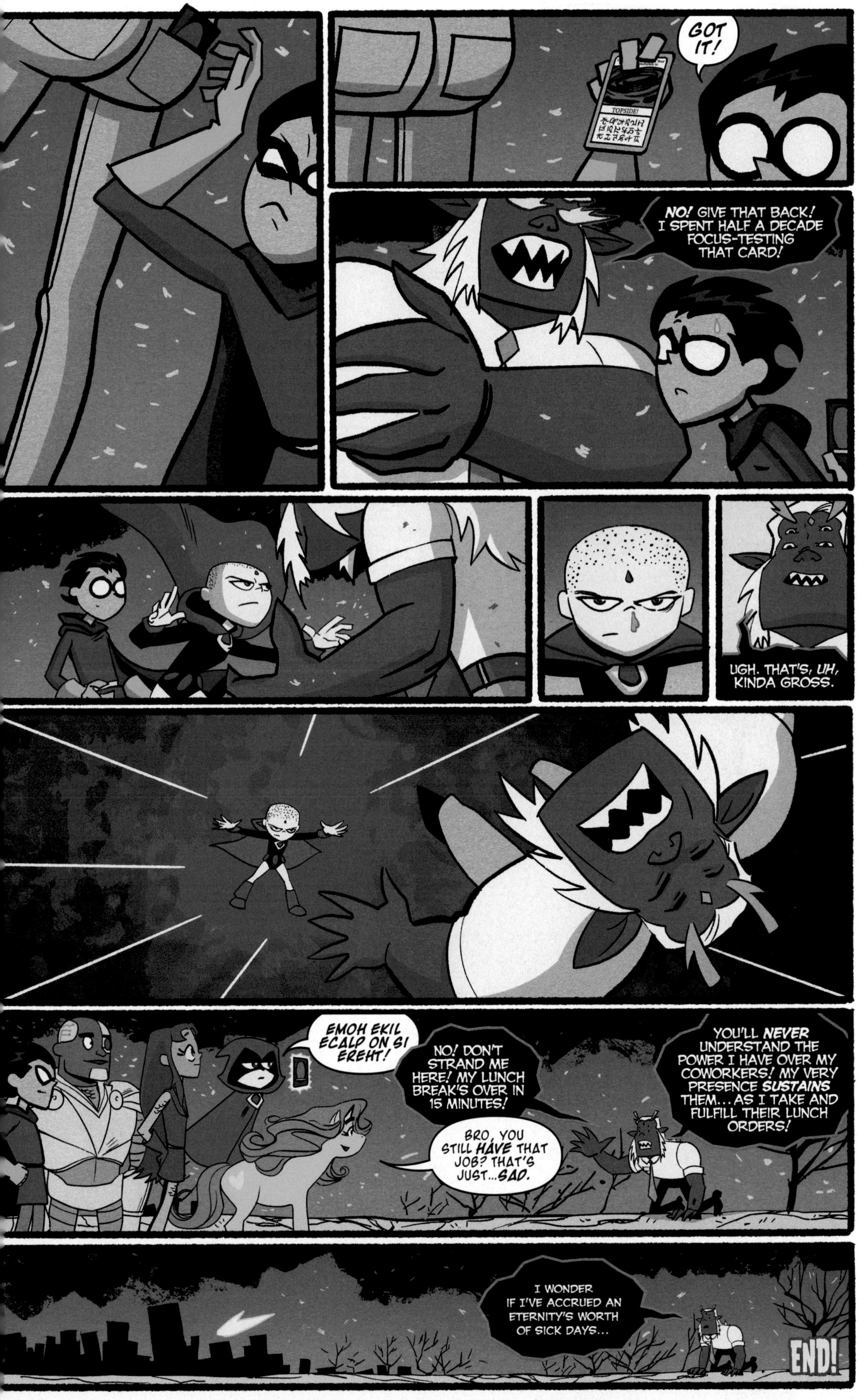
GOT IT!
TOPSIDE!
NO! GIVE THAT BACK! I SPENT HALF A DECADE FOCUS-TESTING THAT CARD!
UGH. THAT'S, UH, KINDA GROSS.
EMOH EKIL ECALP ON SI EREHT!
NO! DON'T STRAND ME HERE! MY LUNCH BREAK'S OVER IN 15 MINUTES!
BRO, YOU STILL HAVE THAT JOB? THAT'S JUST...SAD.
YOU'LL NEVER UNDERSTAND THE POWER I HAVE OVER MY COWORKERS! MY VERY PRESENCE SUSTAINS THEM...AS I TAKE AND FULFILL THEIR LUNCH ORDERS!
I WONDER IF I'VE ACCRUED AN ETERNITY'S WORTH OF SICK DAYS...
END!

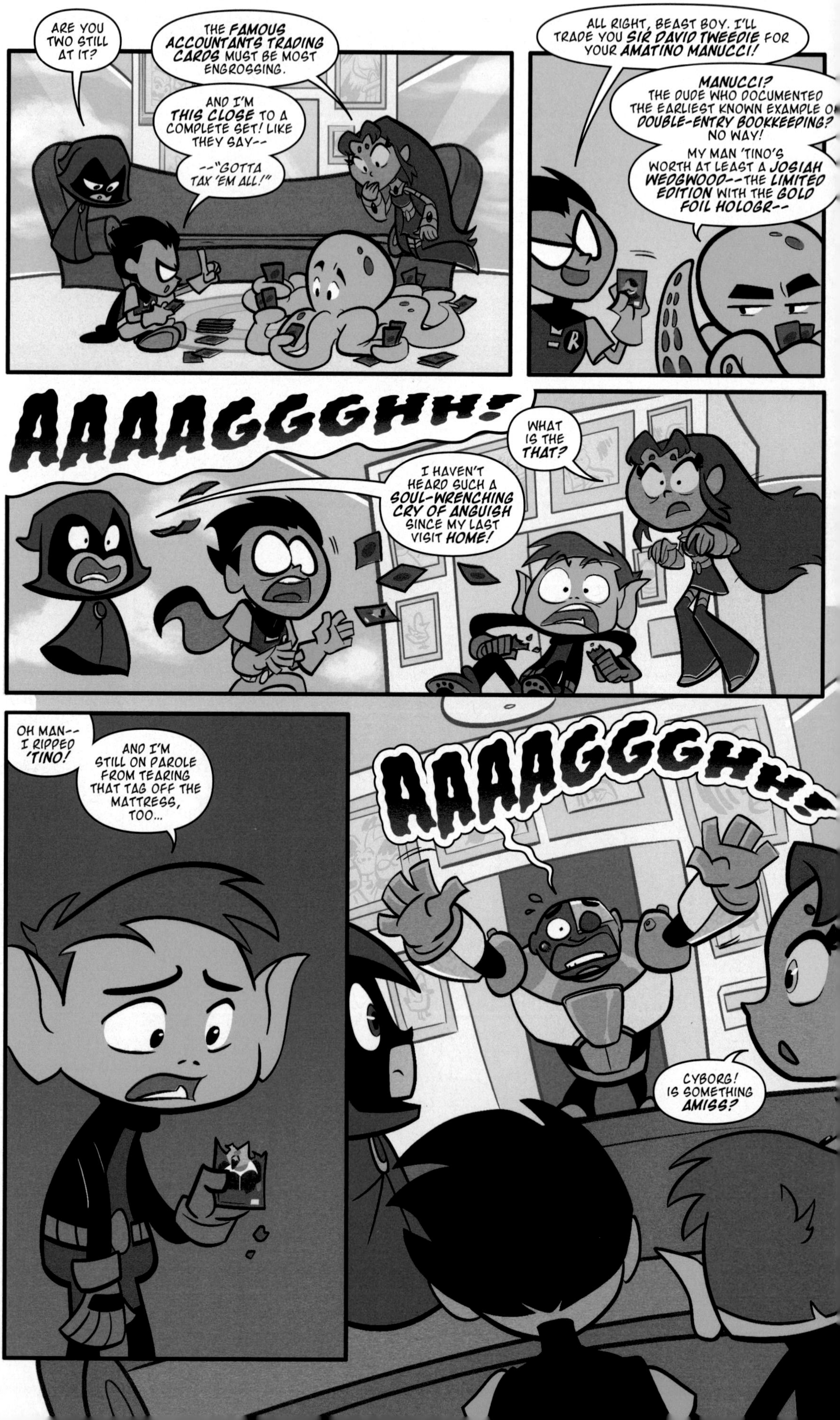
ARE YOU TWO STILL AT IT?
THE FAMOUS ACCOUNTANTS TRADING CARDS MUST BE MOST ENGROSSING.
AND I'M THIS CLOSE TO A COMPLETE SET! LIKE THEY SAY--
--"GOTTA TAX 'EM ALL!"
ALL RIGHT, BEAST BOY. I'LL TRADE YOU SIR DAVID TWEEDIE FOR YOUR AMATINO MANUCCI!
MANUCCI? THE DUDE WHO DOCUMENTED THE EARLIEST KNOWN EXAMPLE OF DOUBLE-ENTRY BOOKKEEPING? NO WAY!
MY MAN 'TINO'S WORTH AT LEAST A JOSIAH WEDGWOOD--THE LIMITED EDITION WITH THE GOLD FOIL HOLOGR--
AAAAGGGHH!
WHAT IS THE THAT?
I HAVEN'T HEARD SUCH A SOUL-WRENCHING CRY OF ANGUISH SINCE MY LAST VISIT HOME!
OH MAN-- I RIPPED 'TINO!
AND I'M STILL ON PAROLE FROM TEARING THAT TAG OFF THE MATTRESS, TOO...
AAAAGGGHH!
CYBORG! IS SOMETHING AMISS?

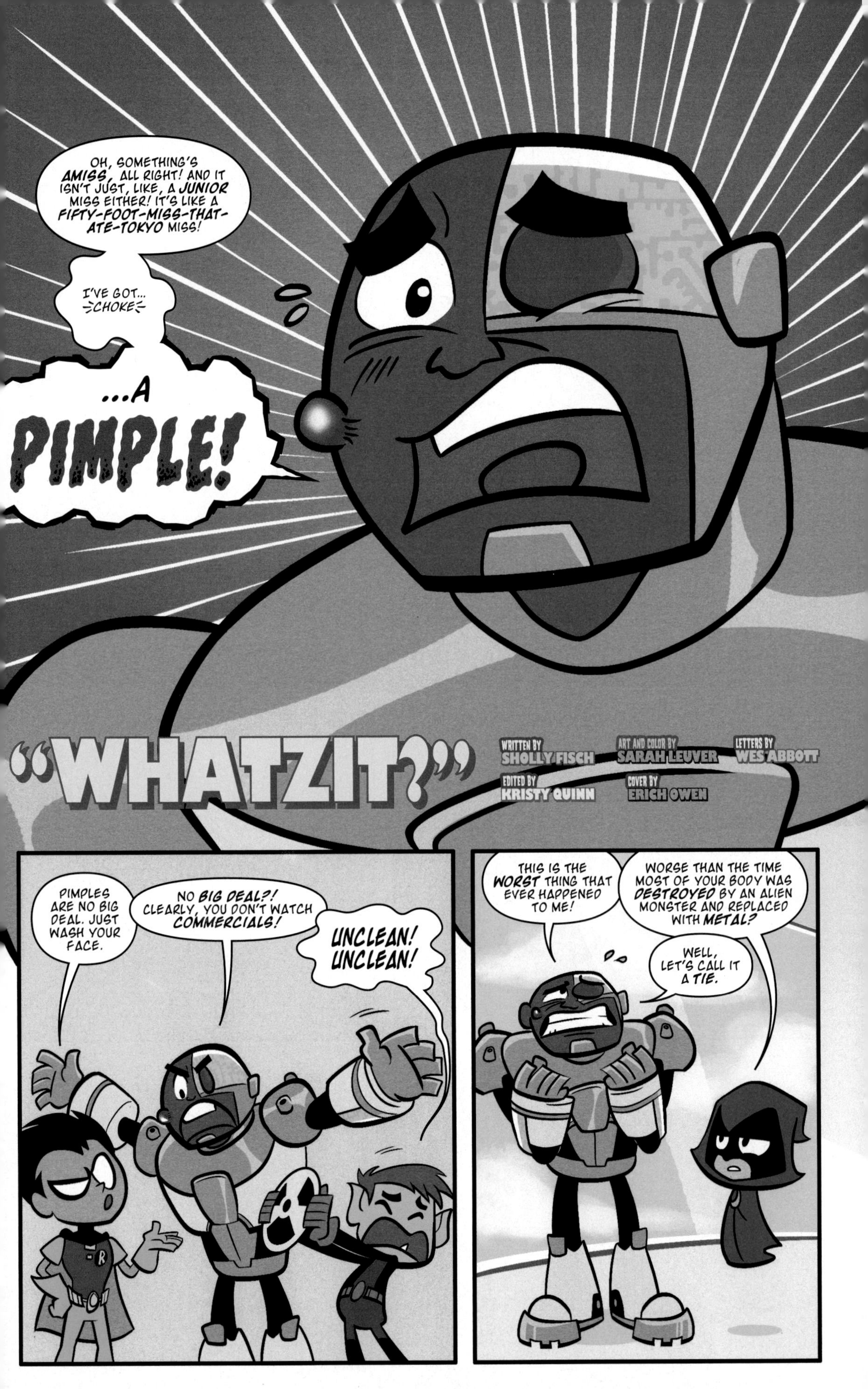
OH, SOMETHING'S AMISS, ALL RIGHT! AND IT ISN'T JUST, LIKE, A JUNIOR MISS EITHER! IT'S LIKE A FIFTY-FOOT-MISS-THAT-ATE-TOKYO MISS!
I'VE GOT... CHOKE
...A PIMPLE!
"WHATZIT?"
WRITTEN BY SHOLLY FISCH
ART AND COLOR BY SARAH LEUVER
LETTERS BY WES ABBOTT
EDITED BY KRISTY QUINN
COVER BY ERICH OWEN
PIMPLES ARE NO BIG DEAL. JUST WASH YOUR FACE.
NO BIG DEAL?! CLEARLY, YOU DON'T WATCH COMMERCIALS!
UNCLEAN! UNCLEAN!
THIS IS THE WORST THING THAT EVER HAPPENED TO ME!
WORSE THAN THE TIME MOST OF YOUR BODY WAS DESTROYED BY AN ALIEN MONSTER AND REPLACED WITH METAL?
WELL, LET'S CALL IT A TIE.

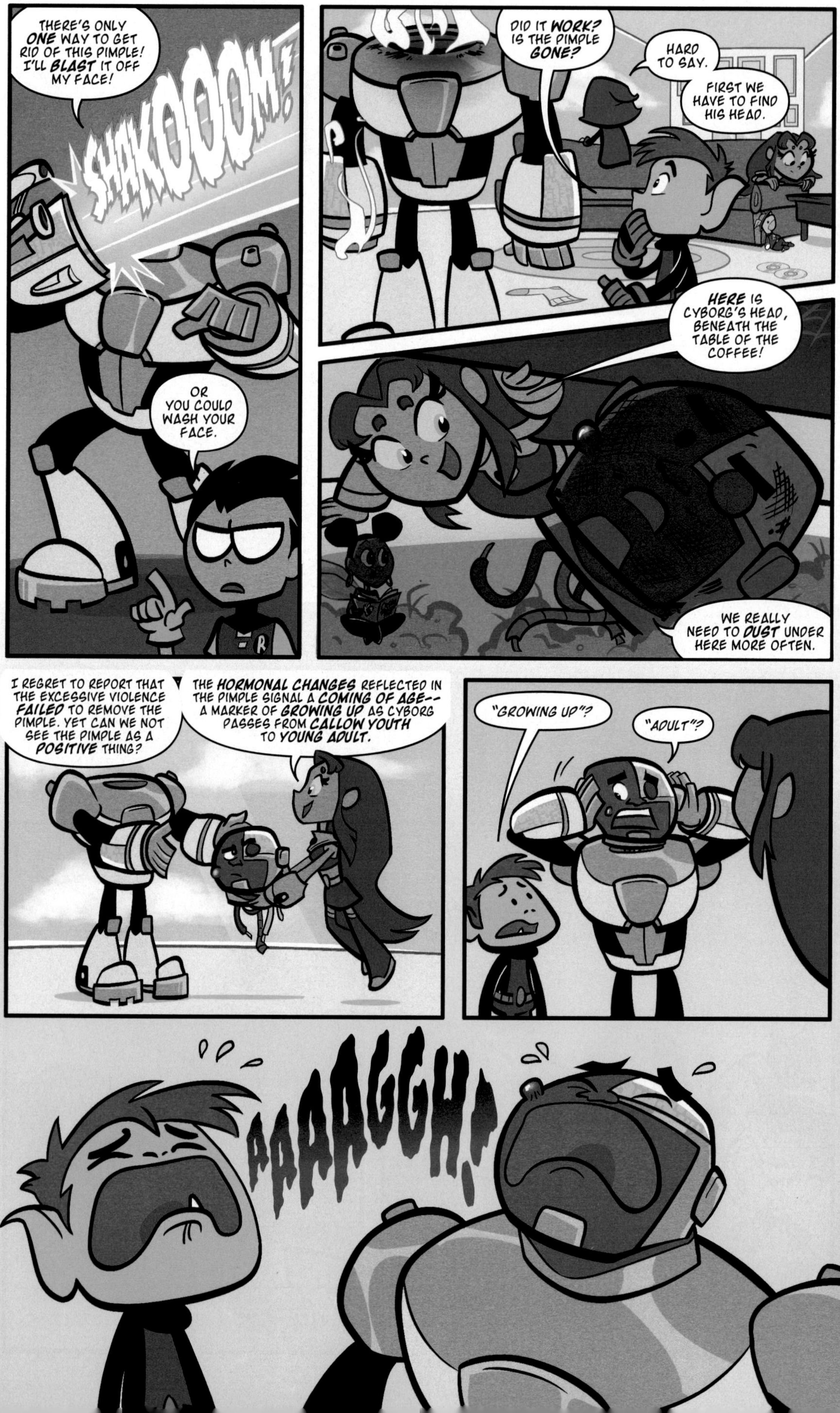
THERE'S ONLY ONE WAY TO GET RID OF THIS PIMPLE! I'LL BLAST IT OFF MY FACE!
SHAKOOOM!
OR YOU COULD WASH YOUR FACE.
DID IT WORK? IS THE PIMPLE GONE?
HARD TO SAY.
FIRST WE HAVE TO FIND HIS HEAD.
HERE IS CYBORG'S HEAD, BENEATH THE TABLE OF THE COFFEE!
WE REALLY NEED TO DUST UNDER HERE MORE OFTEN.
I REGRET TO REPORT THAT THE EXCESSIVE VIOLENCE FAILED TO REMOVE THE PIMPLE. YET CAN WE NOT SEE THE PIMPLE AS A POSITIVE THING?
THE HORMONAL CHANGES REFLECTED IN THE PIMPLE SIGNAL A COMING OF AGE-- A MARKER OF GROWING UP AS CYBORG PASSES FROM CALLOW YOUTH TO YOUNG ADULT.
"GROWING UP"?
"ADULT"?
AAAAGGH!

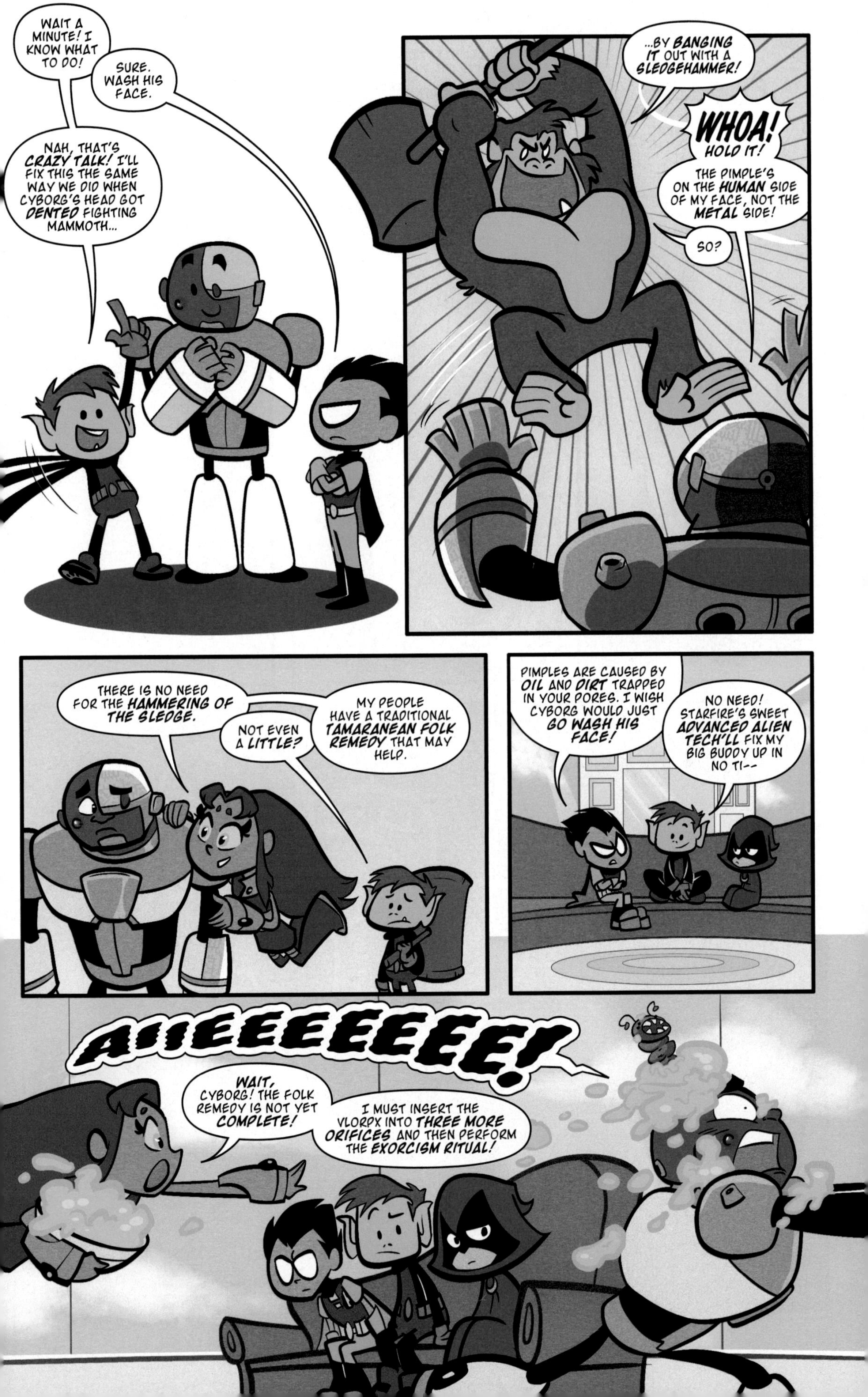

WAIT A MINUTE! I KNOW WHAT TO DO!
SURE. WASH HIS FACE.
NAH, THAT'S CRAZY TALK! I'LL FIX THIS THE SAME WAY WE DID WHEN CYBORG'S HEAD GOT DENTED FIGHTING MAMMOTH...
...BY BANGING IT OUT WITH A SLEDGEHAMMER!
WHOA! HOLD IT!
THE PIMPLE'S ON THE HUMAN SIDE OF MY FACE, NOT THE METAL SIDE!
SO?
THERE IS NO NEED FOR THE HAMMERING OF THE SLEDGE.
NOT EVEN A LITTLE?
MY PEOPLE HAVE A TRADITIONAL TAMARANEAN FOLK REMEDY THAT MAY HELP.
PIMPLES ARE CAUSED BY OIL AND DIRT TRAPPED IN YOUR PORES. I WISH CYBORG WOULD JUST GO WASH HIS FACE!
NO NEED! STARFIRE'S SWEET ADVANCED ALIEN TECH'LL FIX MY BIG BUDDY UP IN NO TI--
AIIEEEEEEEEE!
WAIT, CYBORG! THE FOLK REMEDY IS NOT YET COMPLETE!
I MUST INSERT THE VLORPX INTO THREE MORE ORIFICES AND THEN PERFORM THE EXORCISM RITUAL!

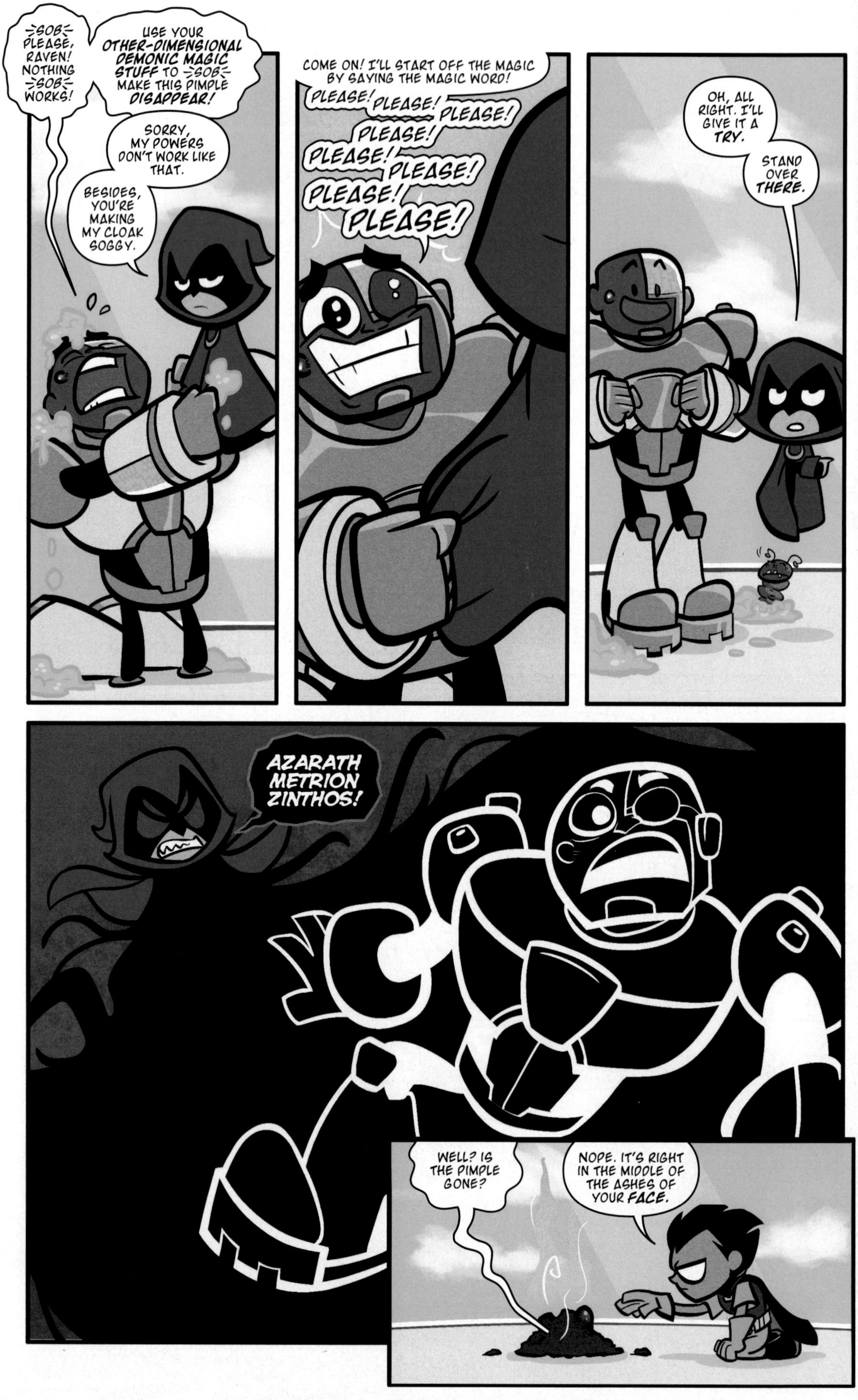

-SOB- PLEASE, RAVEN! NOTHING -SOB- WORKS!
USE YOUR OTHER-DIMENSIONAL DEMONIC MAGIC STUFF TO -SOB- MAKE THIS PIMPLE DISAPPEAR!
SORRY, MY POWERS DON'T WORK LIKE THAT.
BESIDES, YOU'RE MAKING MY CLOAK SOGGY.
COME ON! I'LL START OFF THE MAGIC BY SAYING THE MAGIC WORD!
PLEASE! PLEASE! PLEASE! PLEASE! PLEASE! PLEASE! PLEASE! PLEASE!
OH, ALL RIGHT. I'LL GIVE IT A TRY.
STAND OVER THERE.
AZARATH METRION ZINTHOS!
WELL? IS THE PIMPLE GONE?
NOPE. IT'S RIGHT IN THE MIDDLE OF THE ASHES OF YOUR FACE.

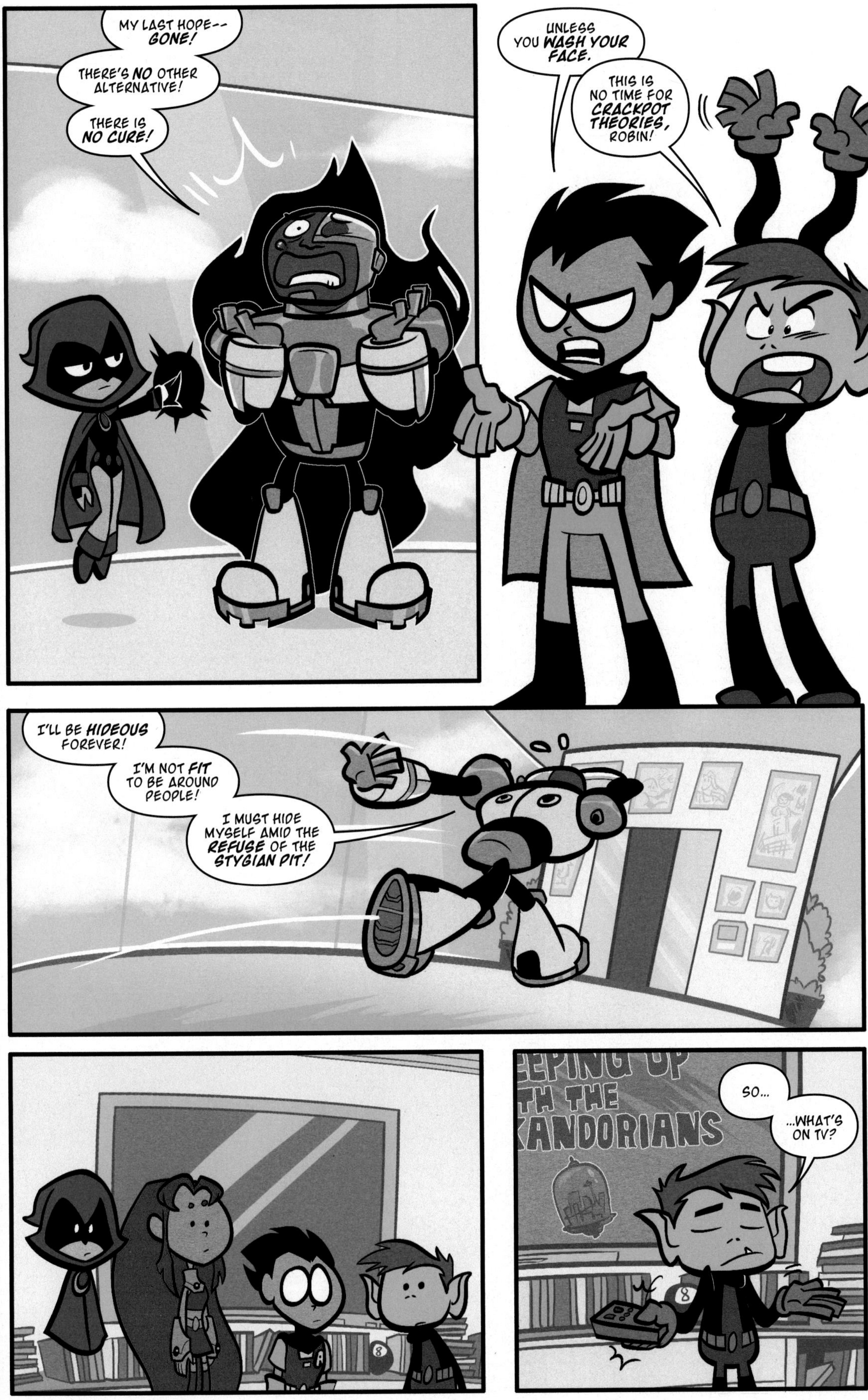
MY LAST HOPE--
GONE!
THERE'S NO OTHER ALTERNATIVE!
THERE IS NO CURE!
UNLESS YOU WASH YOUR FACE.
THIS IS NO TIME FOR CRACKPOT THEORIES, ROBIN!
I'LL BE HIDEOUS FOREVER!
I'M NOT FIT TO BE AROUND PEOPLE!
I MUST HIDE MYSELF AMID THE REFUSE OF THE STYGIAN PIT!
EEPING UP
TH THE
KANDORIANS
SO...
...WHAT'S ON TV?

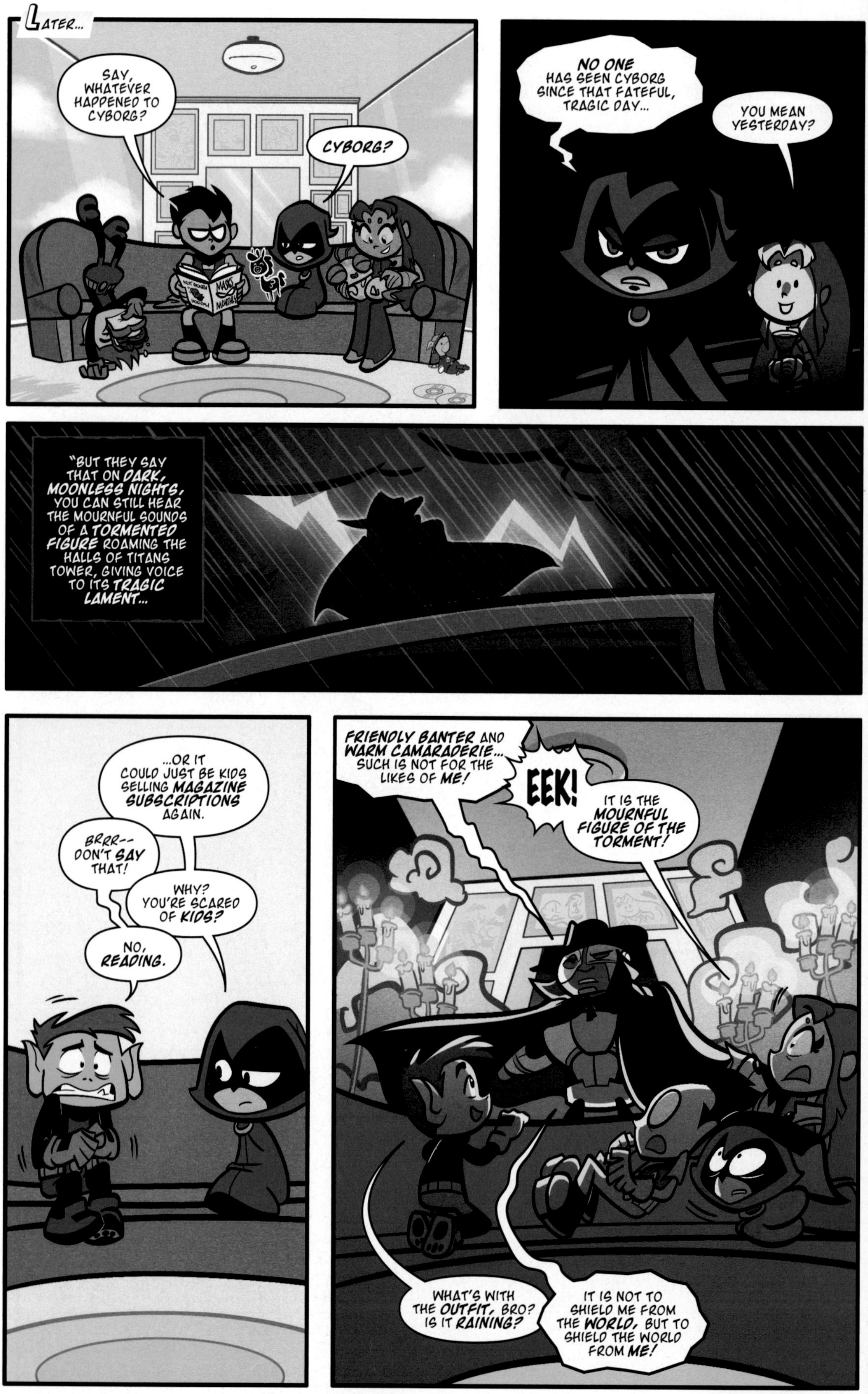
LATER...
SAY, WHATEVER HAPPENED TO CYBORG?
CYBORG?
NO ONE HAS SEEN CYBORG SINCE THAT FATEFUL, TRAGIC DAY...
YOU MEAN YESTERDAY?
"BUT THEY SAY THAT ON DARK, MOONLESS NIGHTS, YOU CAN STILL HEAR THE MOURNFUL SOUNDS OF A TORMENTED FIGURE ROAMING THE HALLS OF TITANS TOWER, GIVING VOICE TO ITS TRAGIC LAMENT...
...OR IT COULD JUST BE KIDS SELLING MAGAZINE SUBSCRIPTIONS AGAIN.
BRRR-- DON'T SAY THAT!
WHY? YOU'RE SCARED OF KIDS?
NO, READING.
FRIENDLY BANTER AND WARM CAMARADERIE... SUCH IS NOT FOR THE LIKES OF ME!
EEK!
IT IS THE MOURNFUL FIGURE OF THE TORMENT!
WHAT'S WITH THE OUTFIT, BRO? IS IT RAINING?
IT IS NOT TO SHIELD ME FROM THE WORLD, BUT TO SHIELD THE WORLD FROM ME!

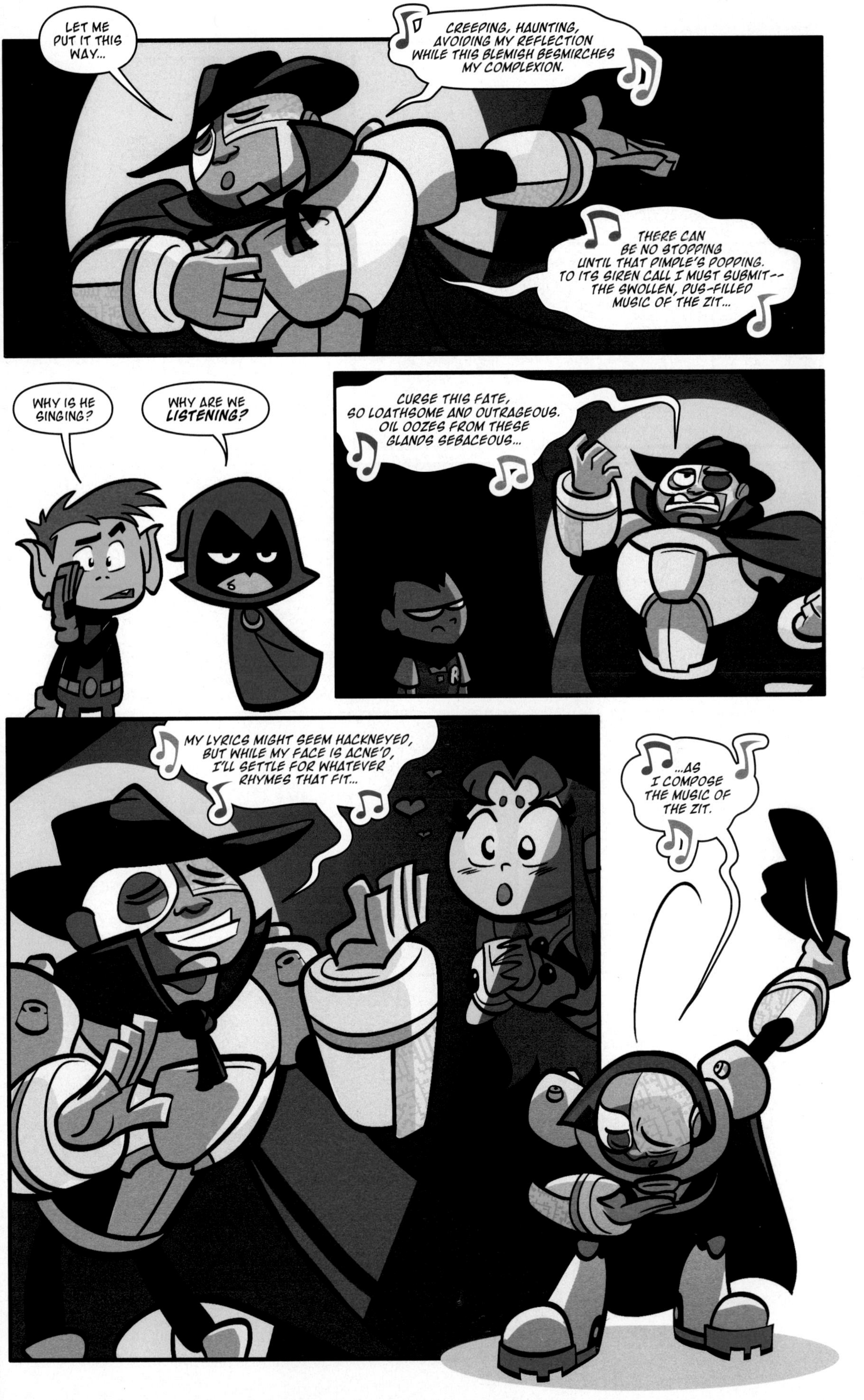
LET ME PUT IT THIS WAY...
CREEPING, HAUNTING, AVOIDING MY REFLECTION WHILE THIS BLEMISH BESMIRCHES MY COMPLEXION.
THERE CAN BE NO STOPPING UNTIL THAT PIMPLE'S POPPING. TO ITS SIREN CALL I MUST SUBMIT-- THE SWOLLEN, PUS-FILLED MUSIC OF THE ZIT...
WHY IS HE SINGING?
WHY ARE WE **LISTENING?**
CURSE THIS FATE, SO LOATHSOME AND OUTRAGEOUS. OIL OOZES FROM THESE GLANDS SEBACEOUS...
MY LYRICS MIGHT SEEM HACKNEYED, BUT WHILE MY FACE IS ACNE'D, I'LL SETTLE FOR WHATEVER RHYMES THAT FIT...
...AS I COMPOSE THE MUSIC OF THE ZIT.

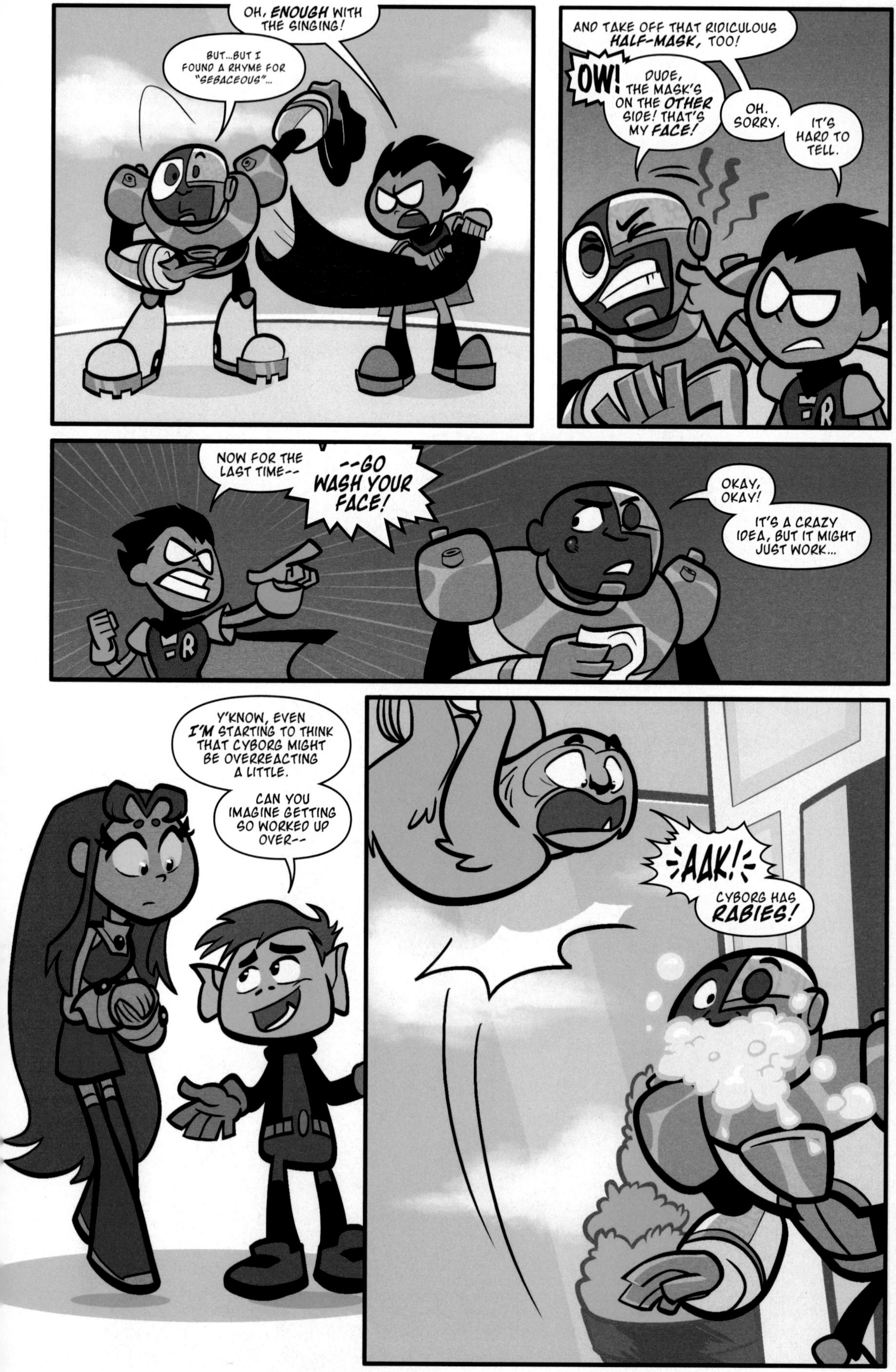
OH, ENOUGH WITH THE SINGING!
BUT...BUT I FOUND A RHYME FOR "SEBACEOUS"...
AND TAKE OFF THAT RIDICULOUS HALF-MASK, TOO!
OW!
DUDE, THE MASK'S ON THE OTHER SIDE! THAT'S MY FACE!
OH. SORRY.
IT'S HARD TO TELL.
NOW FOR THE LAST TIME--
--GO WASH YOUR FACE!
OKAY, OKAY!
IT'S A CRAZY IDEA, BUT IT MIGHT JUST WORK...
Y'KNOW, EVEN I'M STARTING TO THINK THAT CYBORG MIGHT BE OVERREACTING A LITTLE.
CAN YOU IMAGINE GETTING SO WORKED UP OVER--
AAK!
CYBORG HAS RABIES!

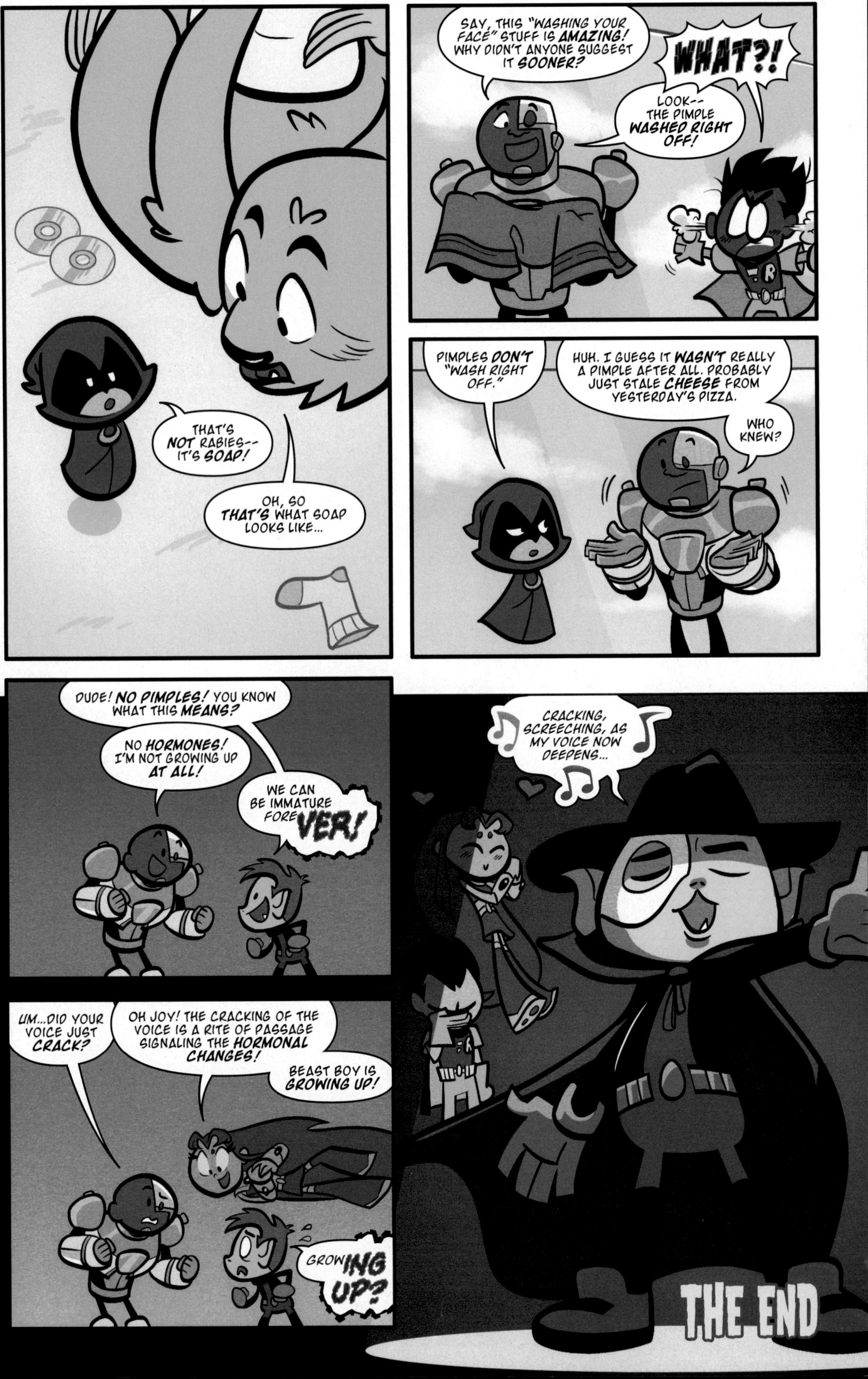
THAT'S NOT RABIES--IT'S SOAP!
OH, SO THAT'S WHAT SOAP LOOKS LIKE...
SAY, THIS "WASHING YOUR FACE" STUFF IS AMAZING! WHY DIDN'T ANYONE SUGGEST IT SOONER?
WHAT?!
LOOK-- THE PIMPLE WASHED RIGHT OFF!
PIMPLES DON'T "WASH RIGHT OFF."
HUH. I GUESS IT WASN'T REALLY A PIMPLE AFTER ALL. PROBABLY JUST STALE CHEESE FROM YESTERDAY'S PIZZA.
WHO KNEW?
DUDE! NO PIMPLES! YOU KNOW WHAT THIS MEANS?
NO HORMONES! I'M NOT GROWING UP AT ALL!
WE CAN BE IMMATURE FOREVER!
UM...DID YOUR VOICE JUST CRACK?
OH JOY! THE CRACKING OF THE VOICE IS A RITE OF PASSAGE SIGNALING THE HORMONAL CHANGES!
BEAST BOY IS GROWING UP!
GROWING UP?
CRACKING, SCREECHING, AS MY VOICE NOW DEEPENS...
THE END

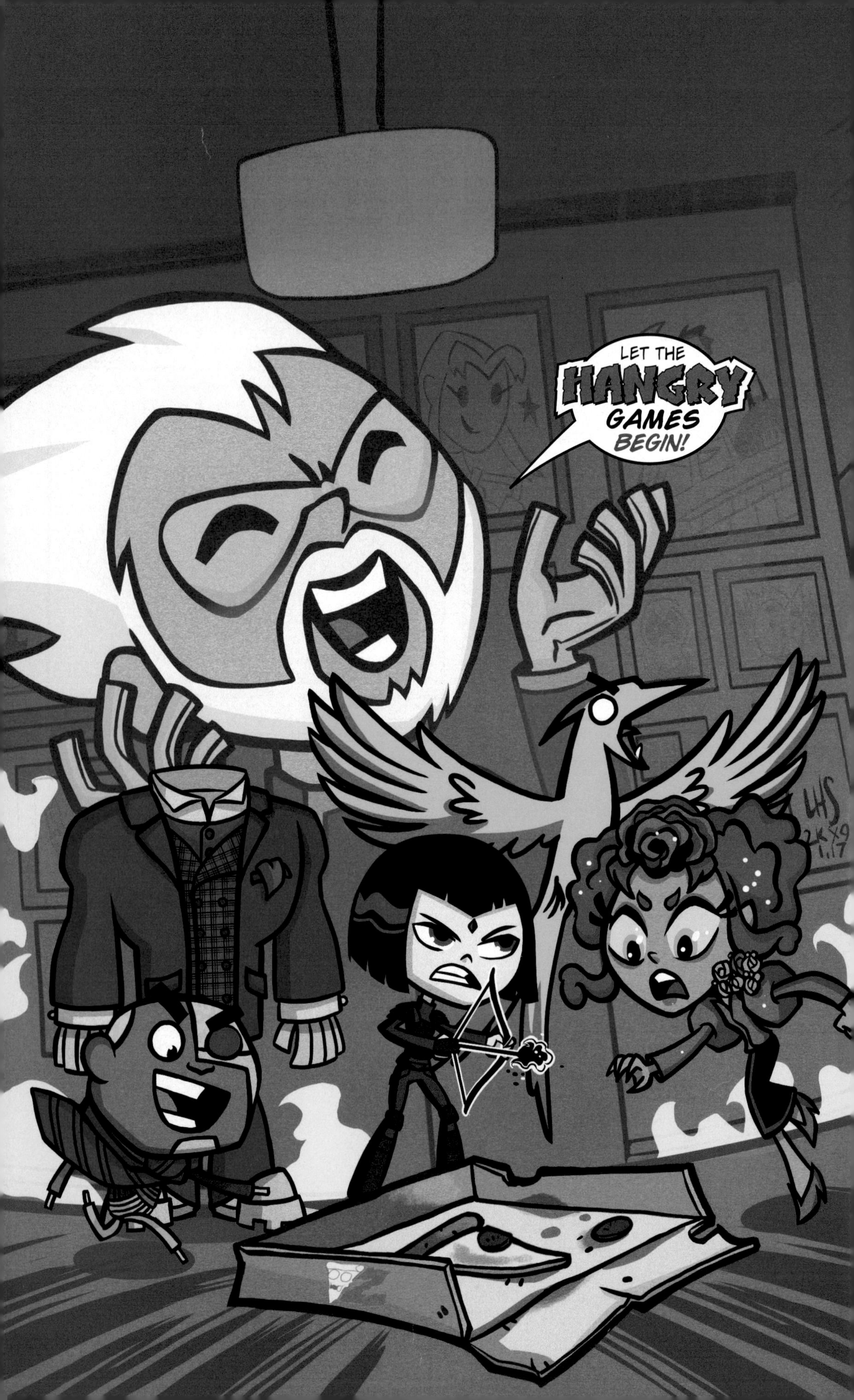
LET THE HANGRY GAMES BEGIN!

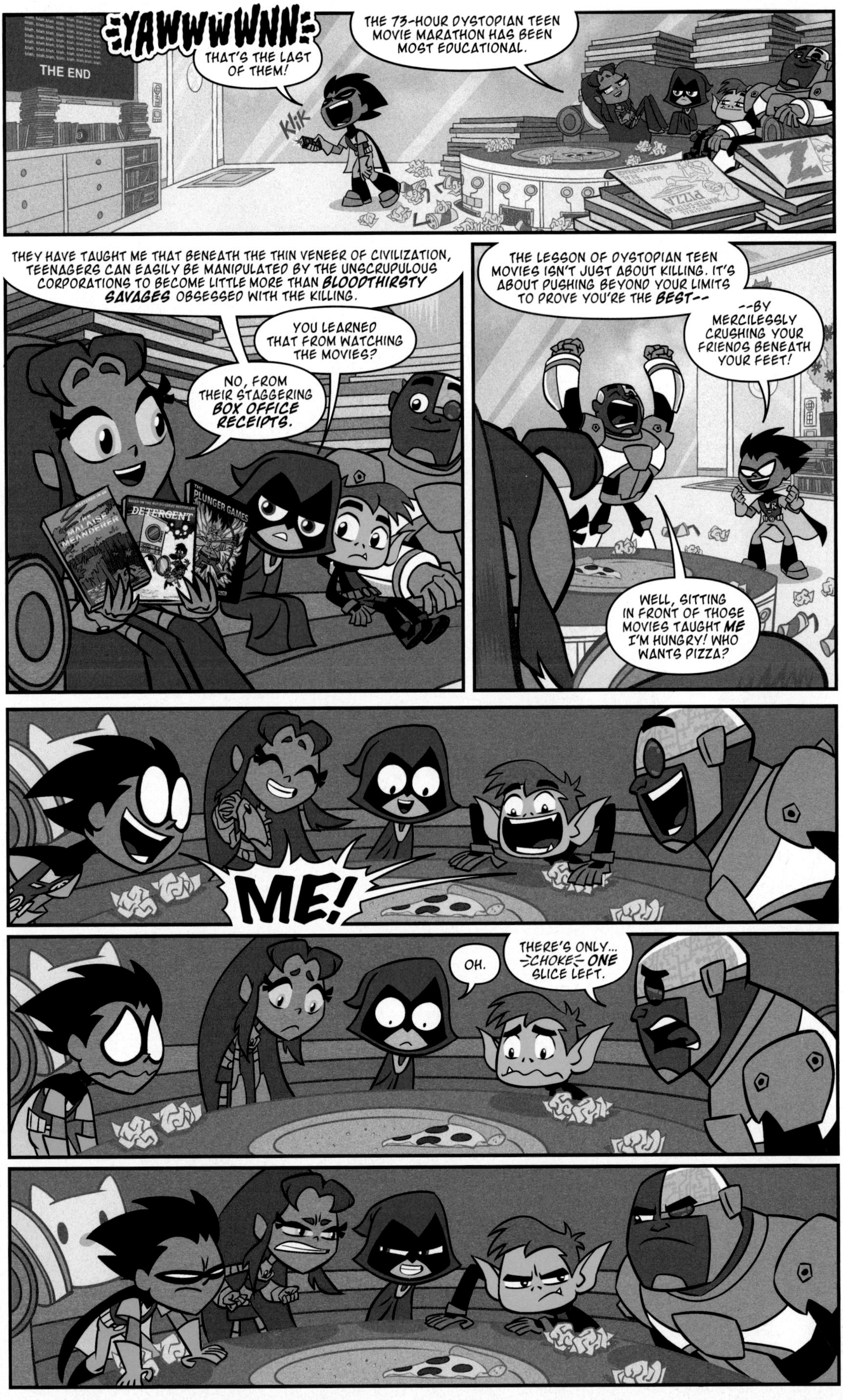

YAWWWWNN
THE END
THAT'S THE LAST OF THEM!
KLIK
THE 73-HOUR DYSTOPIAN TEEN MOVIE MARATHON HAS BEEN MOST EDUCATIONAL.
THEY HAVE TAUGHT ME THAT BENEATH THE THIN VENEER OF CIVILIZATION, TEENAGERS CAN EASILY BE MANIPULATED BY THE UNSCRUPULOUS CORPORATIONS TO BECOME LITTLE MORE THAN BLOODTHIRSTY SAVAGES OBSESSED WITH THE KILLING.
YOU LEARNED THAT FROM WATCHING THE MOVIES?
NO, FROM THEIR STAGGERING BOX OFFICE RECEIPTS.
THE MALAISE MEANDERER
DETERGENT
THE PLUNGER GAMES
THE LESSON OF DYSTOPIAN TEEN MOVIES ISN'T JUST ABOUT KILLING. IT'S ABOUT PUSHING BEYOND YOUR LIMITS TO PROVE YOU'RE THE BEST--
--BY MERCILESSLY CRUSHING YOUR FRIENDS BENEATH YOUR FEET!
WELL, SITTING IN FRONT OF THOSE MOVIES TAUGHT ME I'M HUNGRY! WHO WANTS PIZZA?
ME!
OH.
THERE'S ONLY... CHOKE ONE SLICE LEFT.

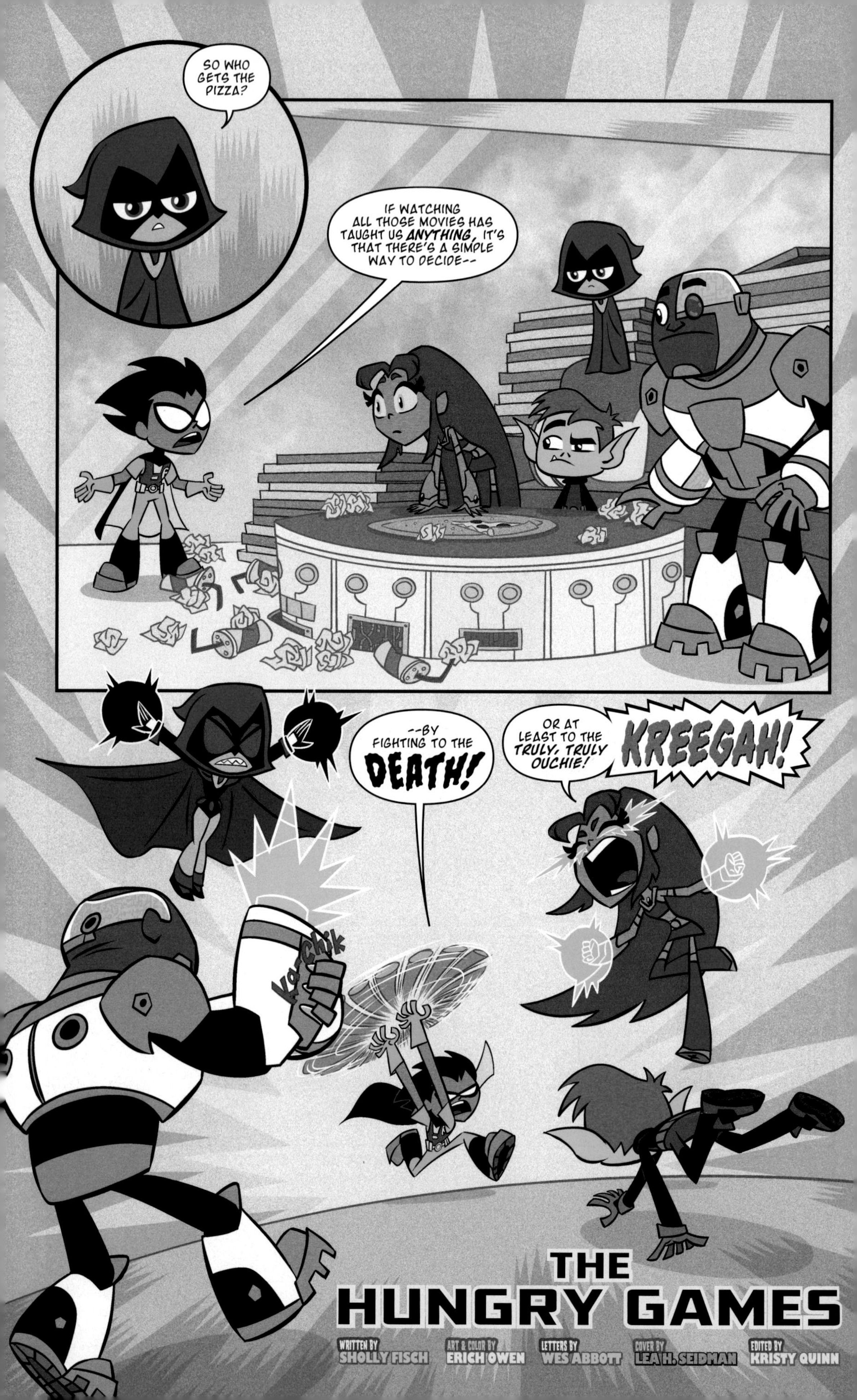
SO WHO GETS THE PIZZA?
IF WATCHING ALL THOSE MOVIES HAS TAUGHT US ANYTHING, IT'S THAT THERE'S A SIMPLE WAY TO DECIDE--
--BY FIGHTING TO THE DEATH!
OR AT LEAST TO THE TRULY, TRULY OUCHIE!
KREEGAH!
Karchik
THE HUNGRY GAMES
WRITTEN BY SHOLLY FISCH
ART & COLOR BY ERICH OWEN
LETTERS BY WES ABBOTT
COVER BY LEA H. SEIDMAN
EDITED BY KRISTY QUINN

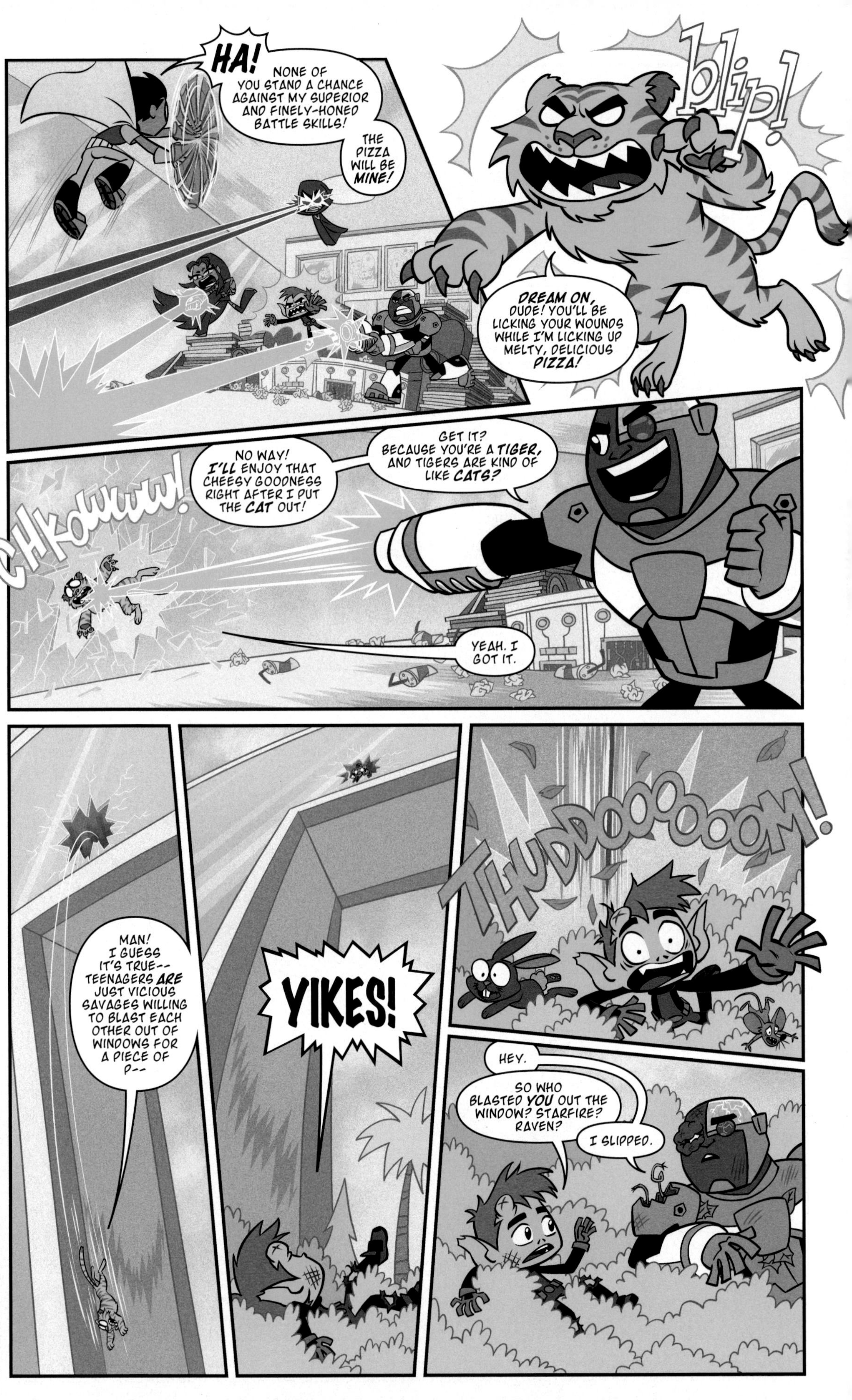

HA!
NONE OF YOU STAND A CHANCE AGAINST MY SUPERIOR AND FINELY-HONED BATTLE SKILLS!
THE PIZZA WILL BE MINE!
blip!
DREAM ON, DUDE! YOU'LL BE LICKING YOUR WOUNDS WHILE I'M LICKING UP MELTY, DELICIOUS PIZZA!
NO WAY! I'LL ENJOY THAT CHEESY GOODNESS RIGHT AFTER I PUT THE CAT OUT!
GET IT? BECAUSE YOU'RE A TIGER, AND TIGERS ARE KIND OF LIKE CATS?
CHKowwww!
YEAH. I GOT IT.
MAN! I GUESS IT'S TRUE--TEENAGERS ARE JUST VICIOUS SAVAGES WILLING TO BLAST EACH OTHER OUT OF WINDOWS FOR A PIECE OF P--
YIKES!
THUDDOOOOOOM!
HEY.
SO WHO BLASTED YOU OUT THE WINDOW? STARFIRE? RAVEN?
I SLIPPED.

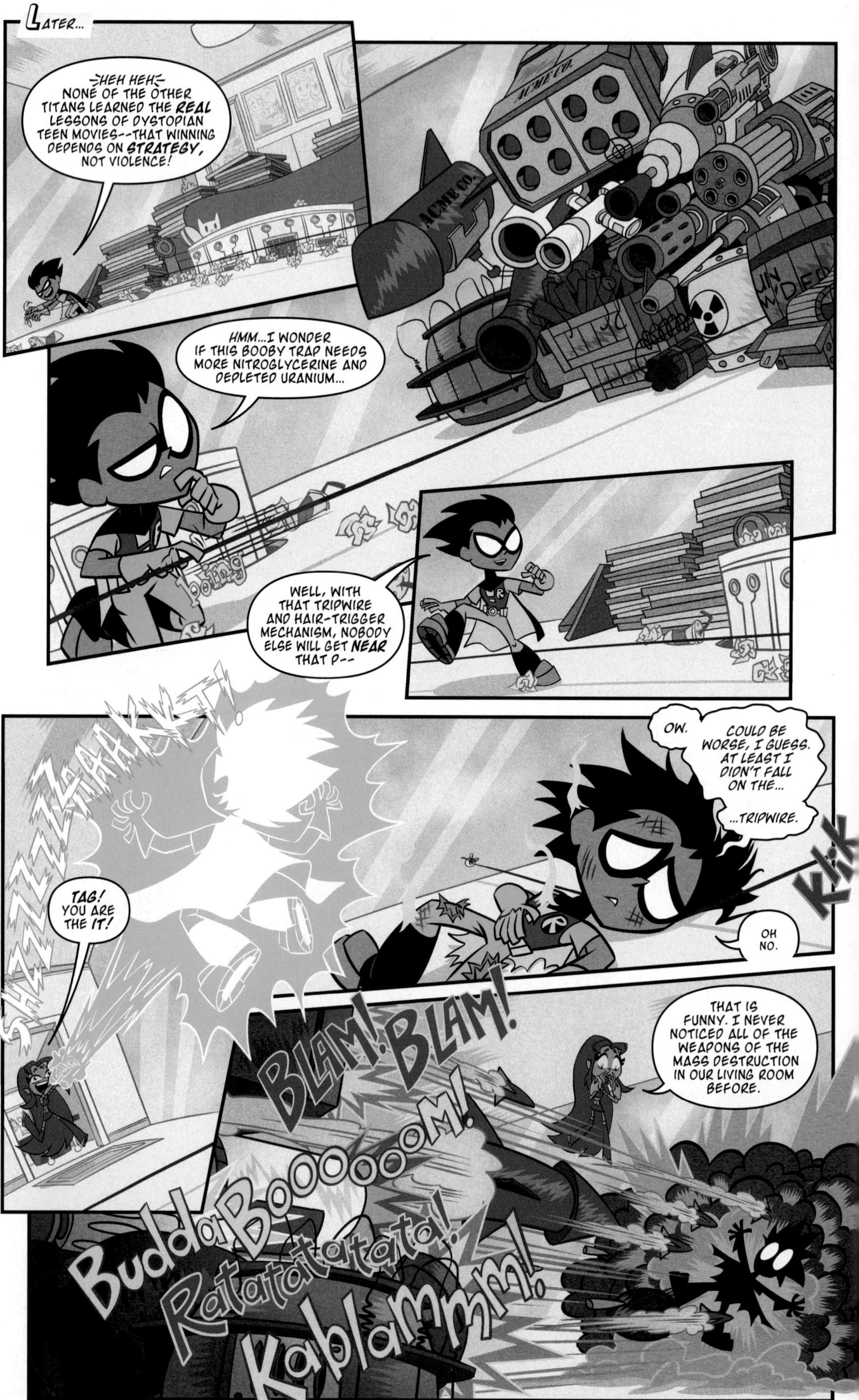
LATER...
HEH HEH NONE OF THE OTHER TITANS LEARNED THE REAL LESSONS OF DYSTOPIAN TEEN MOVIES--THAT WINNING DEPENDS ON STRATEGY, NOT VIOLENCE!
ACME CO.
ACME CO.
HMM...I WONDER IF THIS BOOBY TRAP NEEDS MORE NITROGLYCERINE AND DEPLETED URANIUM...
boing
WELL, WITH THAT TRIPWIRE AND HAIR-TRIGGER MECHANISM, NOBODY ELSE WILL GET NEAR THAT P--
SHZZZZZAKKT!
OW.
COULD BE WORSE, I GUESS. AT LEAST I DIDN'T FALL ON THE...
...TRIPWIRE.
TAG! YOU ARE THE IT!
klik
OH NO.
BLAM! BLAM!
THAT IS FUNNY. I NEVER NOTICED ALL OF THE WEAPONS OF THE MASS DESTRUCTION IN OUR LIVING ROOM BEFORE.
BuddaBoOOOoooM!
Ratatatatata!
Kablammm!

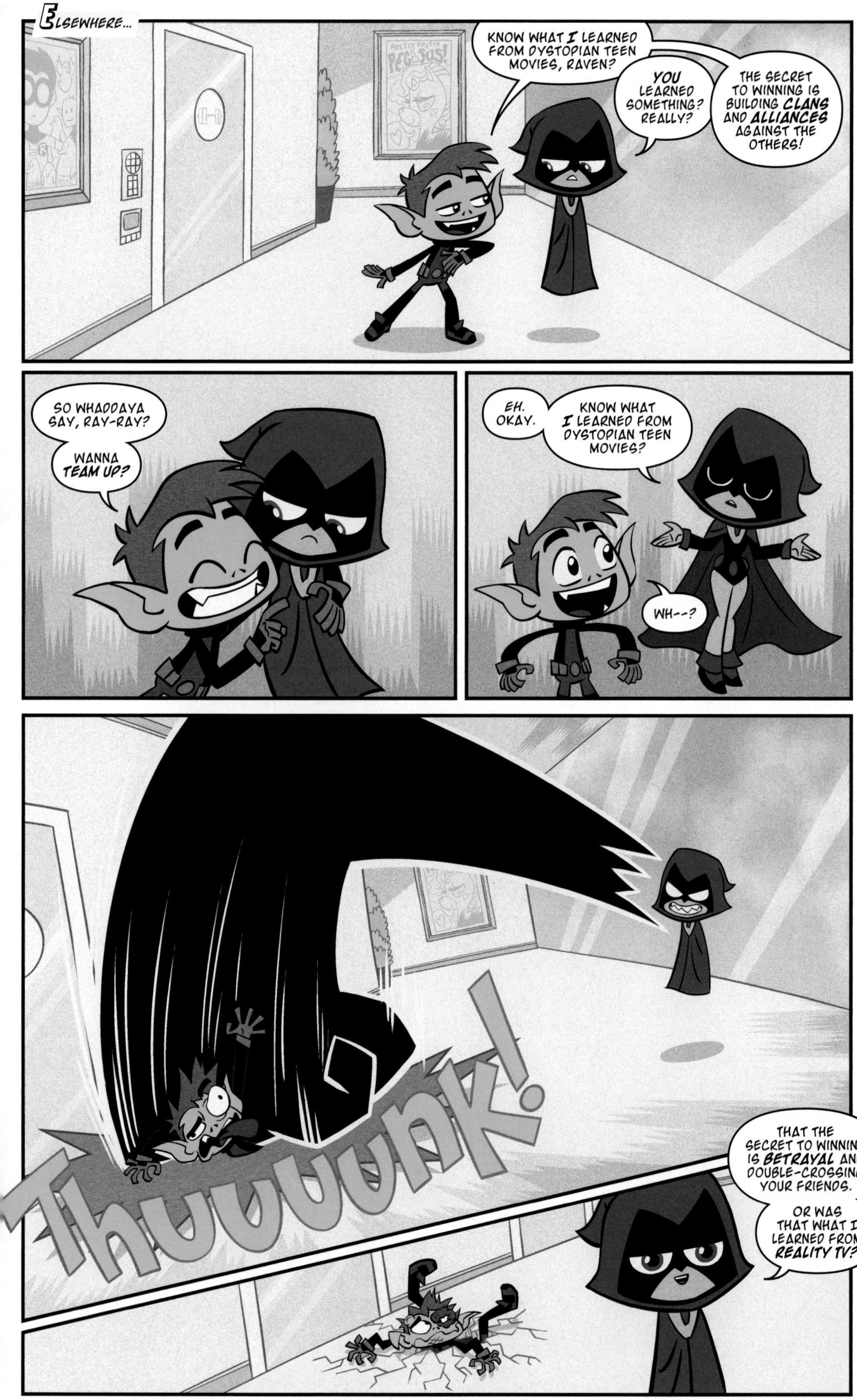
ELSEWHERE...
KNOW WHAT I LEARNED FROM DYSTOPIAN TEEN MOVIES, RAVEN?
YOU LEARNED SOMETHING? REALLY?
THE SECRET TO WINNING IS BUILDING CLANS AND ALLIANCES AGAINST THE OTHERS!
PRETTY PRETTY PEGASUS!
SO WHADDAYA SAY, RAY-RAY?
WANNA TEAM UP?
EH. OKAY.
KNOW WHAT I LEARNED FROM DYSTOPIAN TEEN MOVIES?
WH--?
THUUUUNK!
THAT THE SECRET TO WINNING IS BETRAYAL AND DOUBLE-CROSSING YOUR FRIENDS.
OR WAS THAT WHAT I LEARNED FROM REALITY TV?

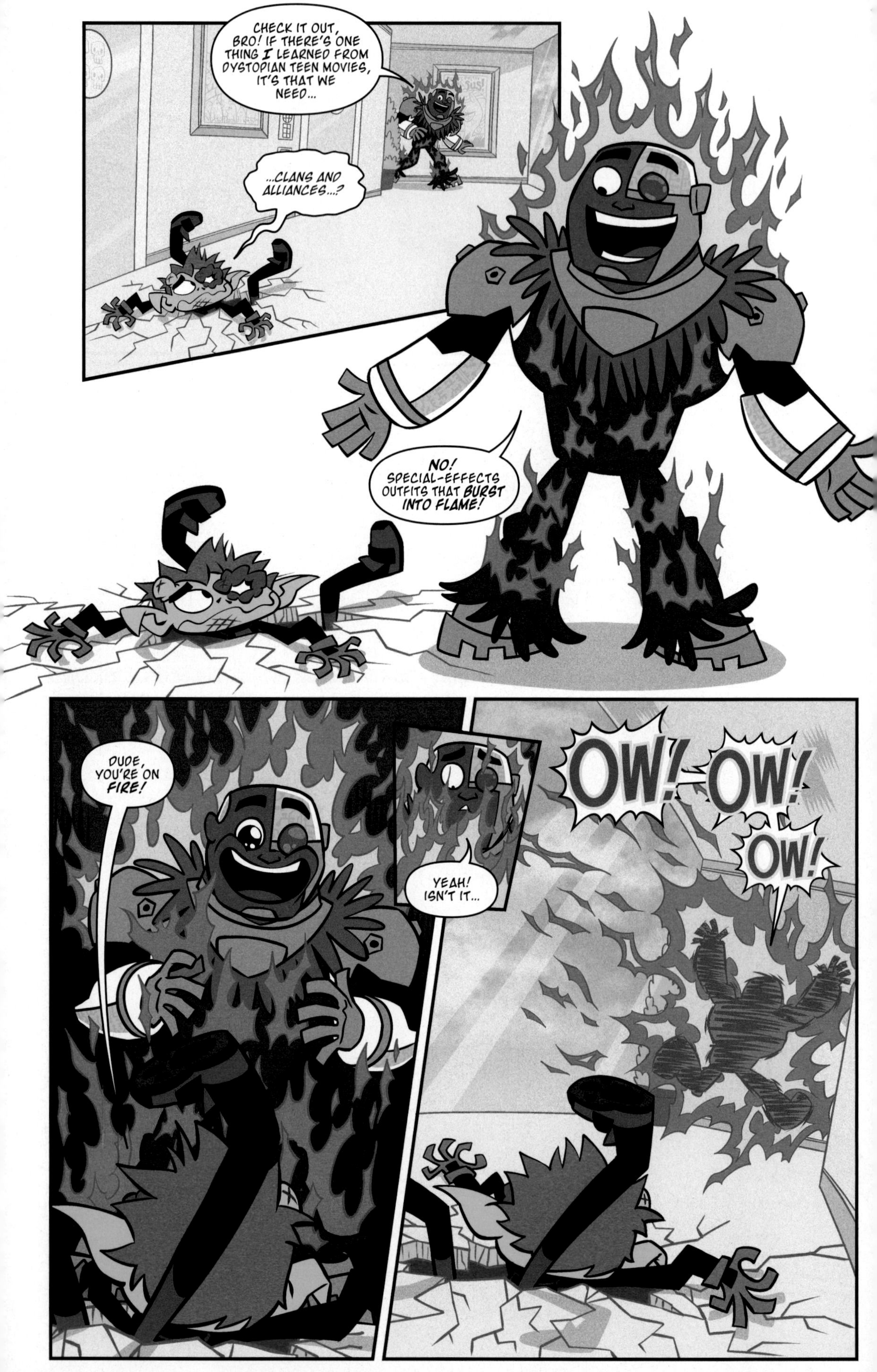
CHECK IT OUT, BRO! IF THERE'S ONE THING I LEARNED FROM DYSTOPIAN TEEN MOVIES, IT'S THAT WE NEED...
...CLANS AND ALLIANCES...?
NO! SPECIAL-EFFECTS OUTFITS THAT BURST INTO FLAME!
DUDE, YOU'RE ON FIRE!
YEAH! ISN'T IT...
OW! OW! OW!

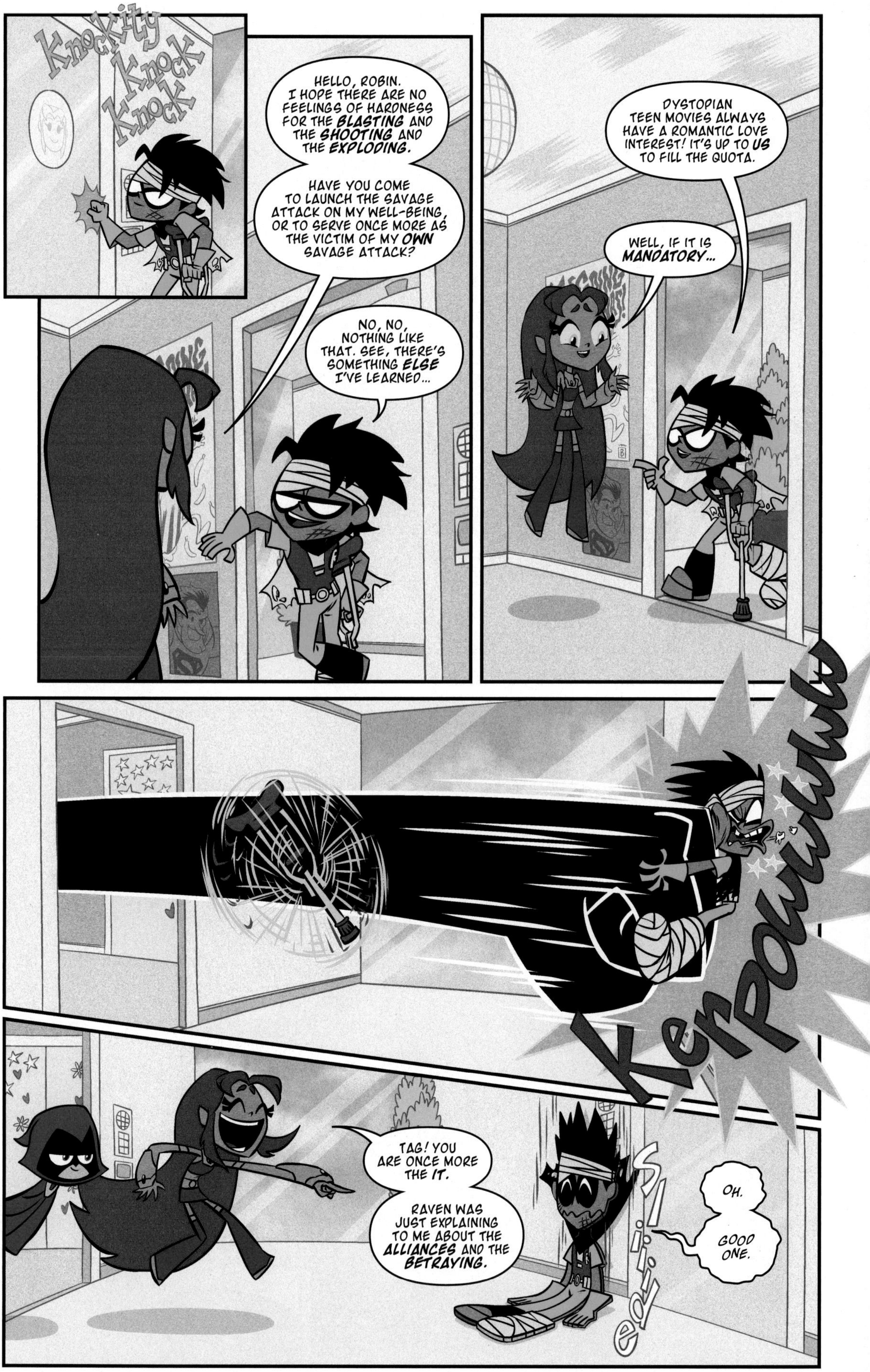

Knockity Knock Knock
HELLO, ROBIN. I HOPE THERE ARE NO FEELINGS OF HARDNESS FOR THE **BLASTING** AND THE **SHOOTING** AND THE **EXPLODING.**
HAVE YOU COME TO LAUNCH THE SAVAGE ATTACK ON MY WELL-BEING, OR TO SERVE ONCE MORE AS THE VICTIM OF MY **OWN** SAVAGE ATTACK?
NO, NO, NOTHING LIKE THAT. SEE, THERE'S SOMETHING **ELSE** I'VE LEARNED...
DYSTOPIAN TEEN MOVIES ALWAYS HAVE A ROMANTIC LOVE INTEREST! IT'S UP TO **US** TO FILL THE QUOTA.
WELL, IF IT IS **MANDATORY**...
Kerpowwww
TAG! YOU ARE ONCE MORE THE *IT.*
RAVEN WAS JUST EXPLAINING TO ME ABOUT THE **ALLIANCES** AND THE **BETRAYING.**
Sliiide
OH.
GOOD ONE.

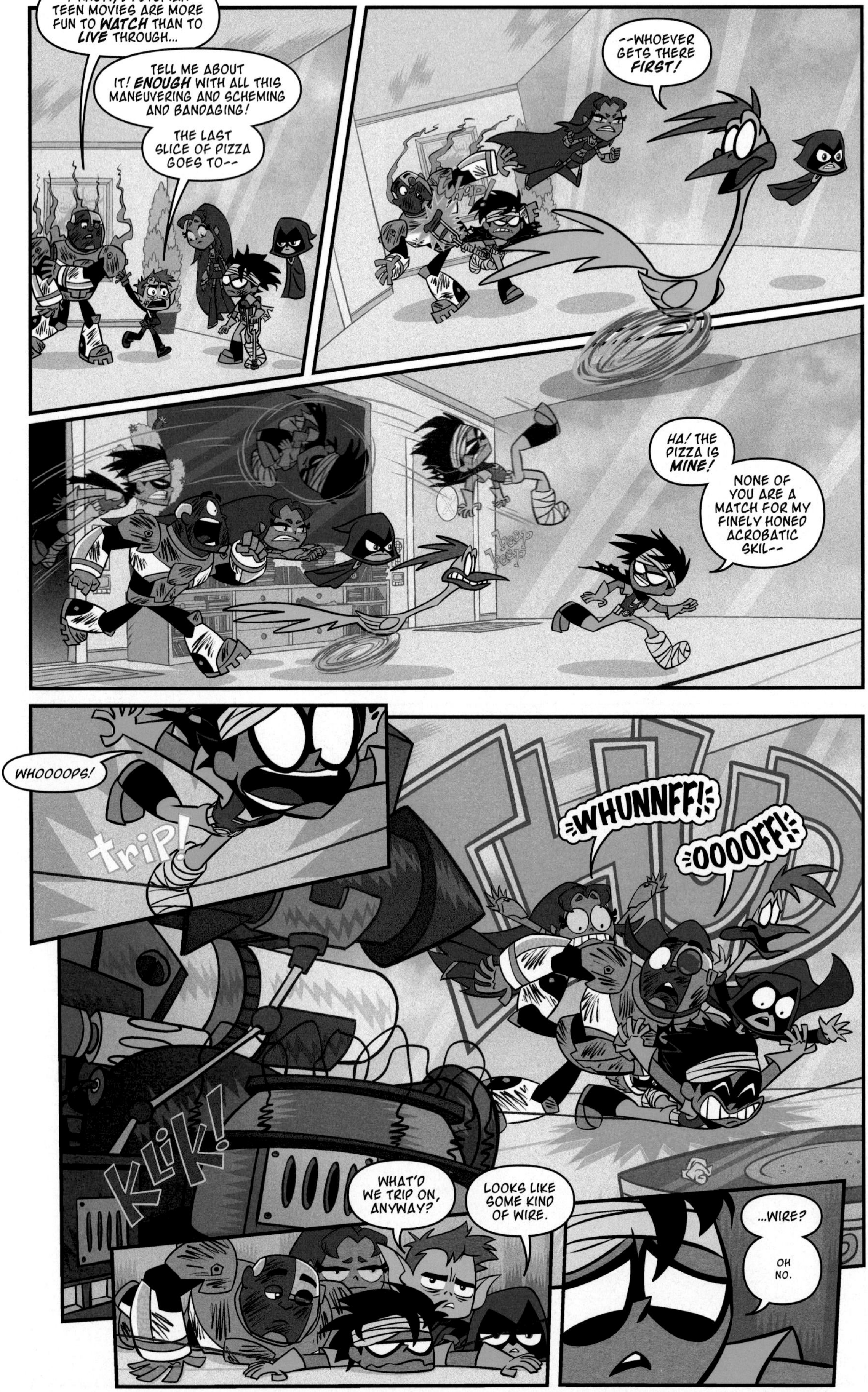
Y'KNOW, DYSTOPIAN TEEN MOVIES ARE MORE FUN TO WATCH THAN TO LIVE THROUGH...
TELL ME ABOUT IT! ENOUGH WITH ALL THIS MANEUVERING AND SCHEMING AND BANDAGING!
THE LAST SLICE OF PIZZA GOES TO--
--WHOEVER GETS THERE FIRST!
beep beep
HA! THE PIZZA IS MINE!
NONE OF YOU ARE A MATCH FOR MY FINELY HONED ACROBATIC SKIL--
WHOOOOPS!
trip!
WHUNNFF!
OOOOFF!
KLIK!
WHAT'D WE TRIP ON, ANYWAY?
LOOKS LIKE SOME KIND OF WIRE.
...WIRE?
OH NO.

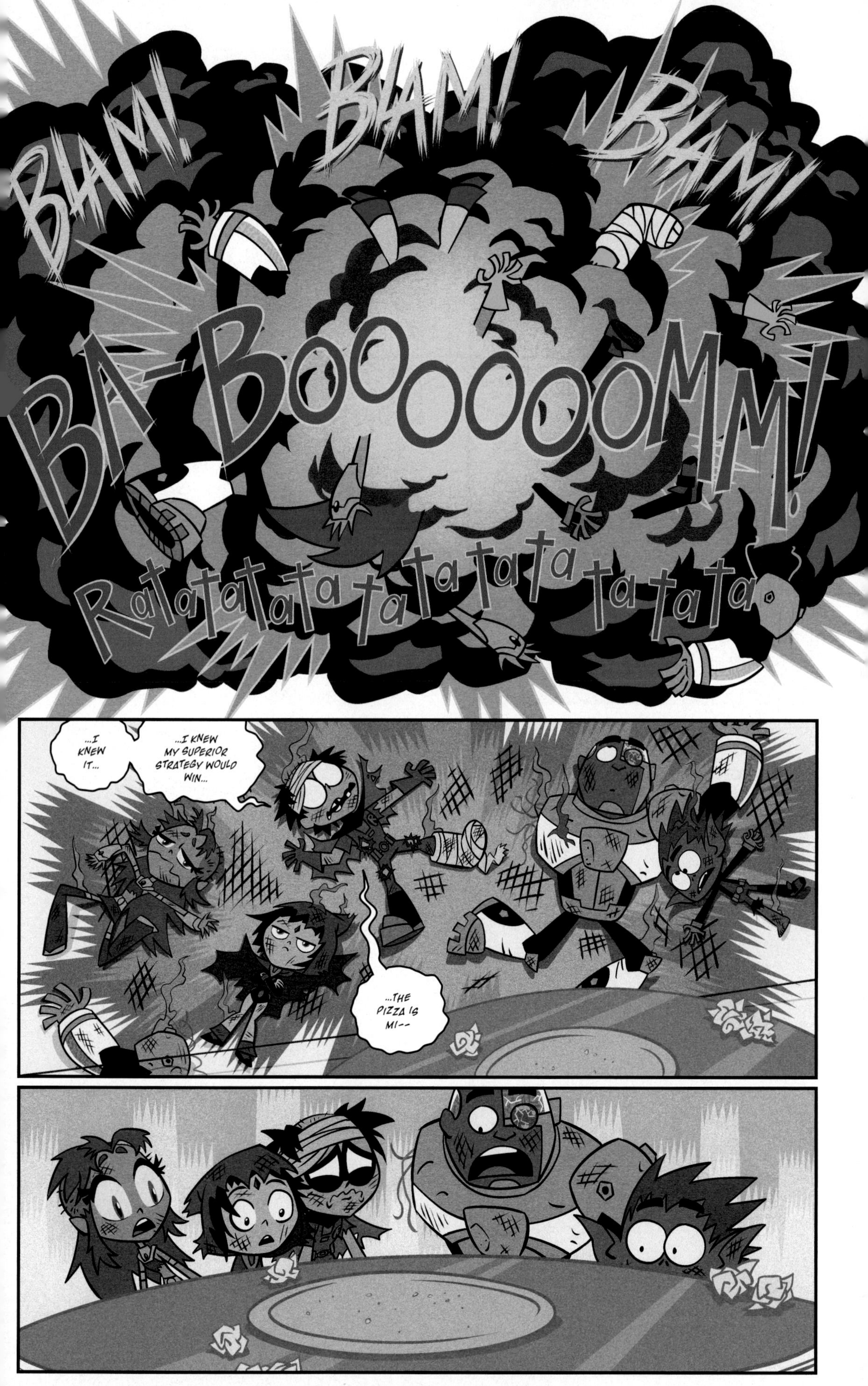
BLAM! BLAM! BLAM!
BA-BOOOOOOMM!
Ratatatata tatatata tatata
...I KNEW IT...
...I KNEW MY SUPERIOR STRATEGY WOULD WIN...
...THE PIZZA IS MI--

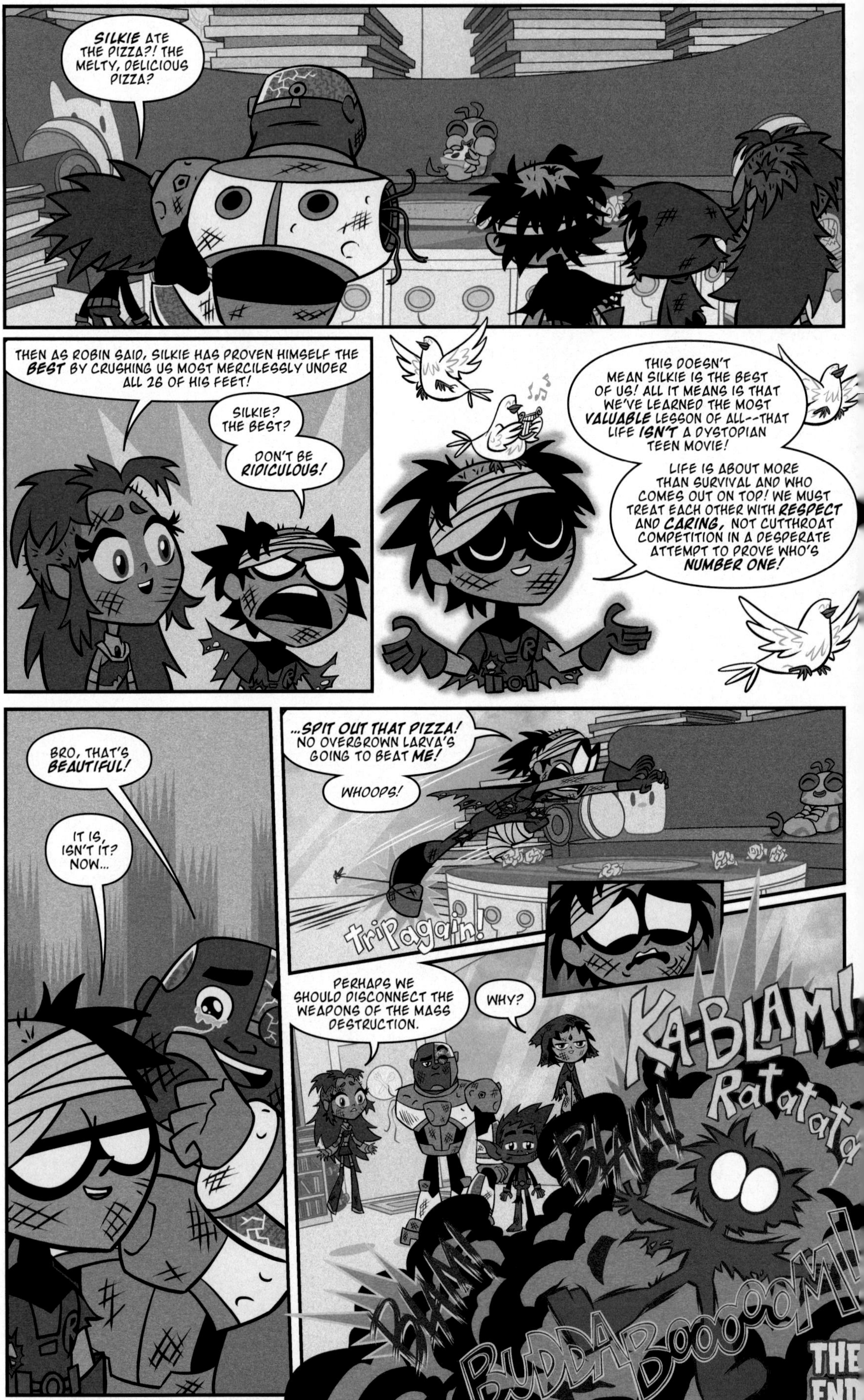
SILKIE ATE THE PIZZA?! THE MELTY, DELICIOUS PIZZA?
THEN AS ROBIN SAID, SILKIE HAS PROVEN HIMSELF THE BEST BY CRUSHING US MOST MERCILESSLY UNDER ALL 26 OF HIS FEET!
SILKIE? THE BEST?
DON'T BE RIDICULOUS!
THIS DOESN'T MEAN SILKIE IS THE BEST OF US! ALL IT MEANS IS THAT WE'VE LEARNED THE MOST VALUABLE LESSON OF ALL--THAT LIFE ISN'T A DYSTOPIAN TEEN MOVIE!
LIFE IS ABOUT MORE THAN SURVIVAL AND WHO COMES OUT ON TOP! WE MUST TREAT EACH OTHER WITH RESPECT AND CARING, NOT CUTTHROAT COMPETITION IN A DESPERATE ATTEMPT TO PROVE WHO'S NUMBER ONE!
BRO, THAT'S BEAUTIFUL!
IT IS, ISN'T IT? NOW...
...SPIT OUT THAT PIZZA! NO OVERGROWN LARVA'S GOING TO BEAT ME!
WHOOPS!
tripagain!
PERHAPS WE SHOULD DISCONNECT THE WEAPONS OF THE MASS DESTRUCTION.
WHY?
KA-BLAM!
Ratatata
BLAM!
BLAM!
BUDDABOOOOOOM!
THE END

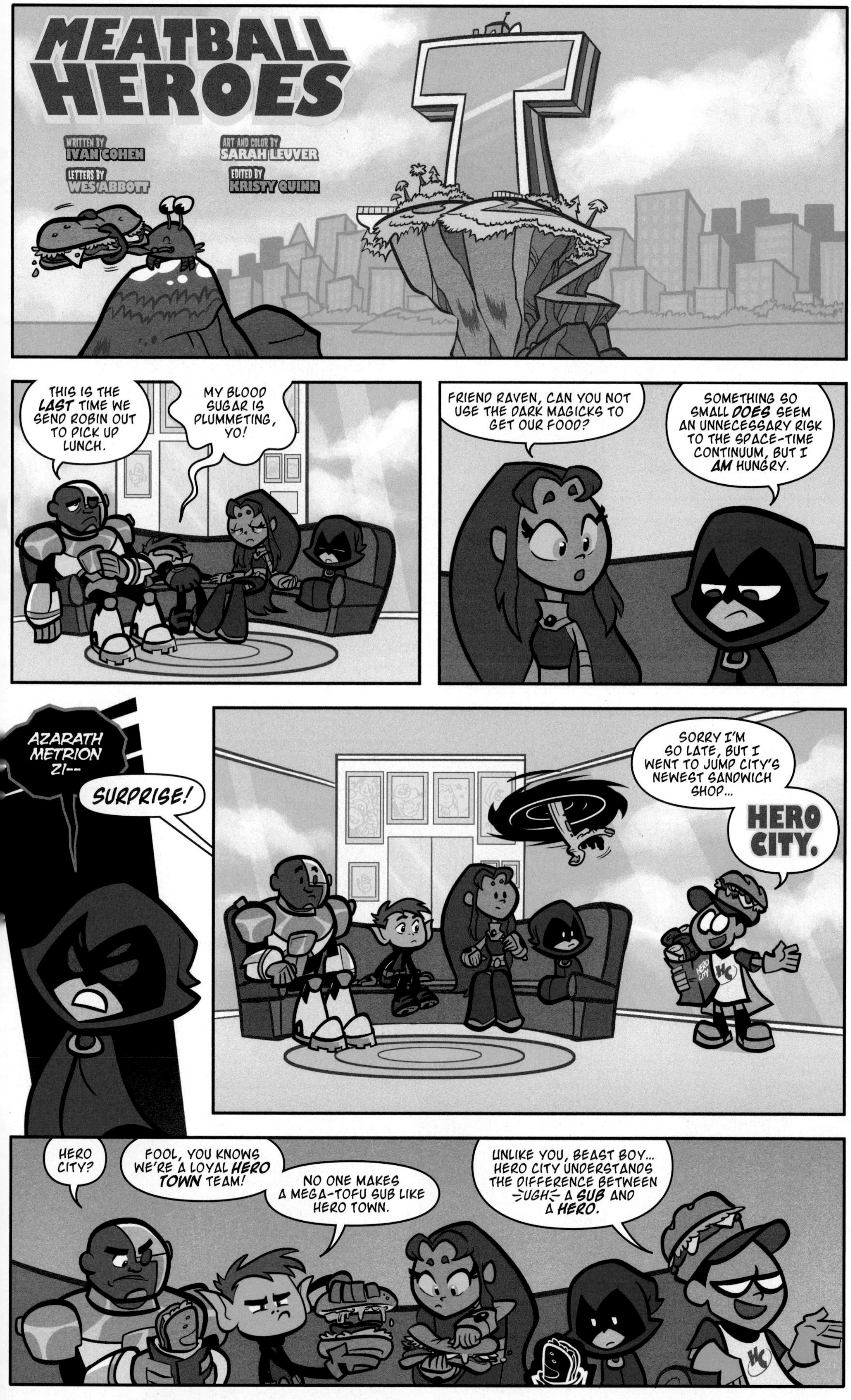
MEATBALL HEROES
WRITTEN BY IVAN COHEN
ART AND COLOR BY SARAH LEUVER
LETTERS BY WES ABBOTT
EDITED BY KRISTY QUINN
THIS IS THE LAST TIME WE SEND ROBIN OUT TO PICK UP LUNCH.
MY BLOOD SUGAR IS PLUMMETING, YO!
FRIEND RAVEN, CAN YOU NOT USE THE DARK MAGICKS TO GET OUR FOOD?
SOMETHING SO SMALL DOES SEEM AN UNNECESSARY RISK TO THE SPACE-TIME CONTINUUM, BUT I AM HUNGRY.
AZARATH METRION ZI--
SURPRISE!
SORRY I'M SO LATE, BUT I WENT TO JUMP CITY'S NEWEST SANDWICH SHOP...
HERO CITY.
HERO CITY
HC
HERO CITY?
FOOL, YOU KNOWS WE'RE A LOYAL HERO TOWN TEAM!
NO ONE MAKES A MEGA-TOFU SUB LIKE HERO TOWN.
UNLIKE YOU, BEAST BOY... HERO CITY UNDERSTANDS THE DIFFERENCE BETWEEN -UGH- A SUB AND A HERO.
HC

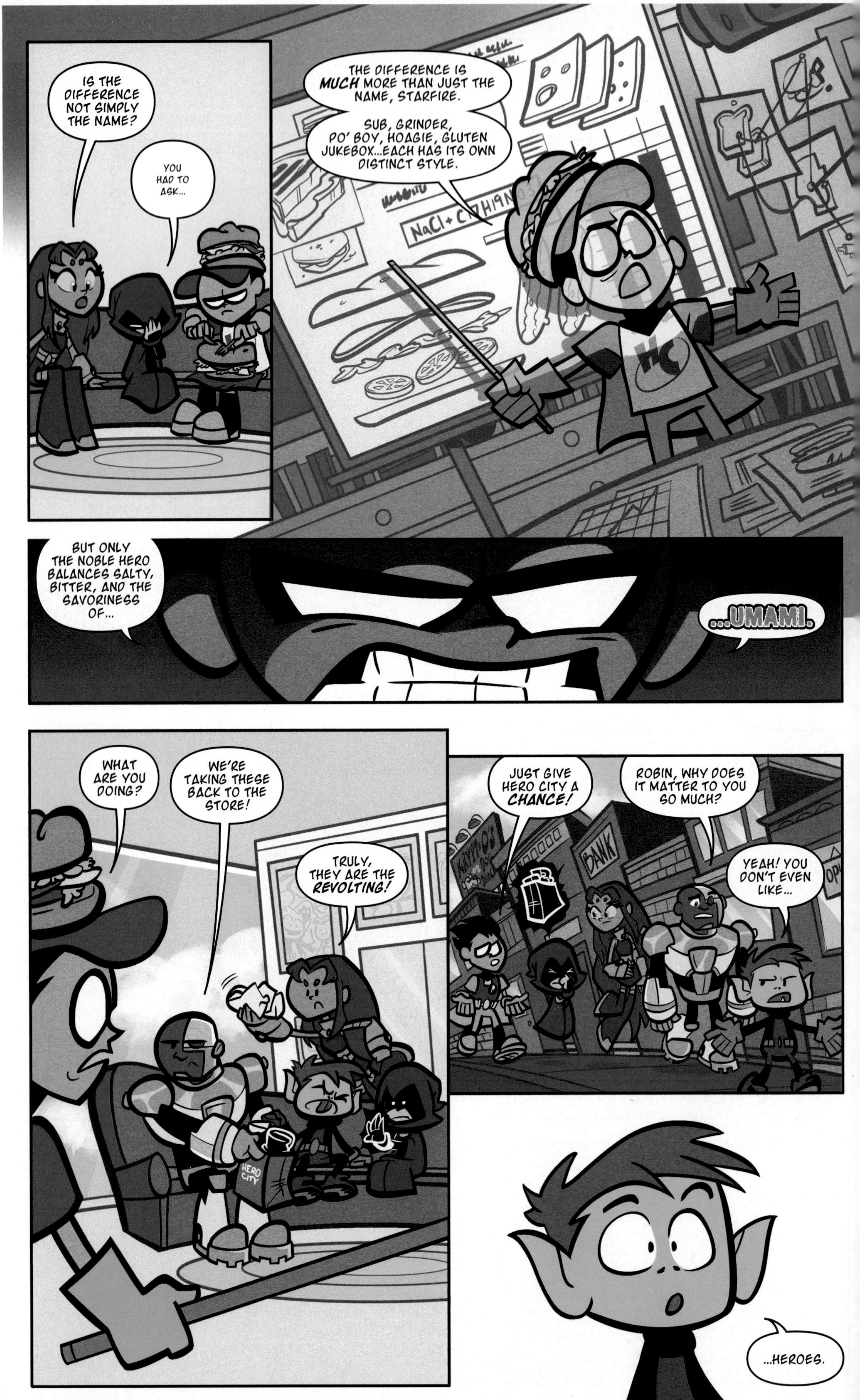
IS THE DIFFERENCE NOT SIMPLY THE NAME?
YOU HAD TO ASK...
THE DIFFERENCE IS MUCH MORE THAN JUST THE NAME, STARFIRE.
SUB, GRINDER, PO' BOY, HOAGIE, GLUTEN JUKEBOX...EACH HAS ITS OWN DISTINCT STYLE.
NaCl + C17H19NO3
BUT ONLY THE NOBLE HERO BALANCES SALTY, BITTER, AND THE SAVORINESS OF...
...UMAMI.
WHAT ARE YOU DOING?
WE'RE TAKING THESE BACK TO THE STORE!
TRULY, THEY ARE THE REVOLTING!
HERO CITY
JUST GIVE HERO CITY A CHANCE!
ROBIN, WHY DOES IT MATTER TO YOU SO MUCH?
BANK
YEAH! YOU DON'T EVEN LIKE...
...HEROES.

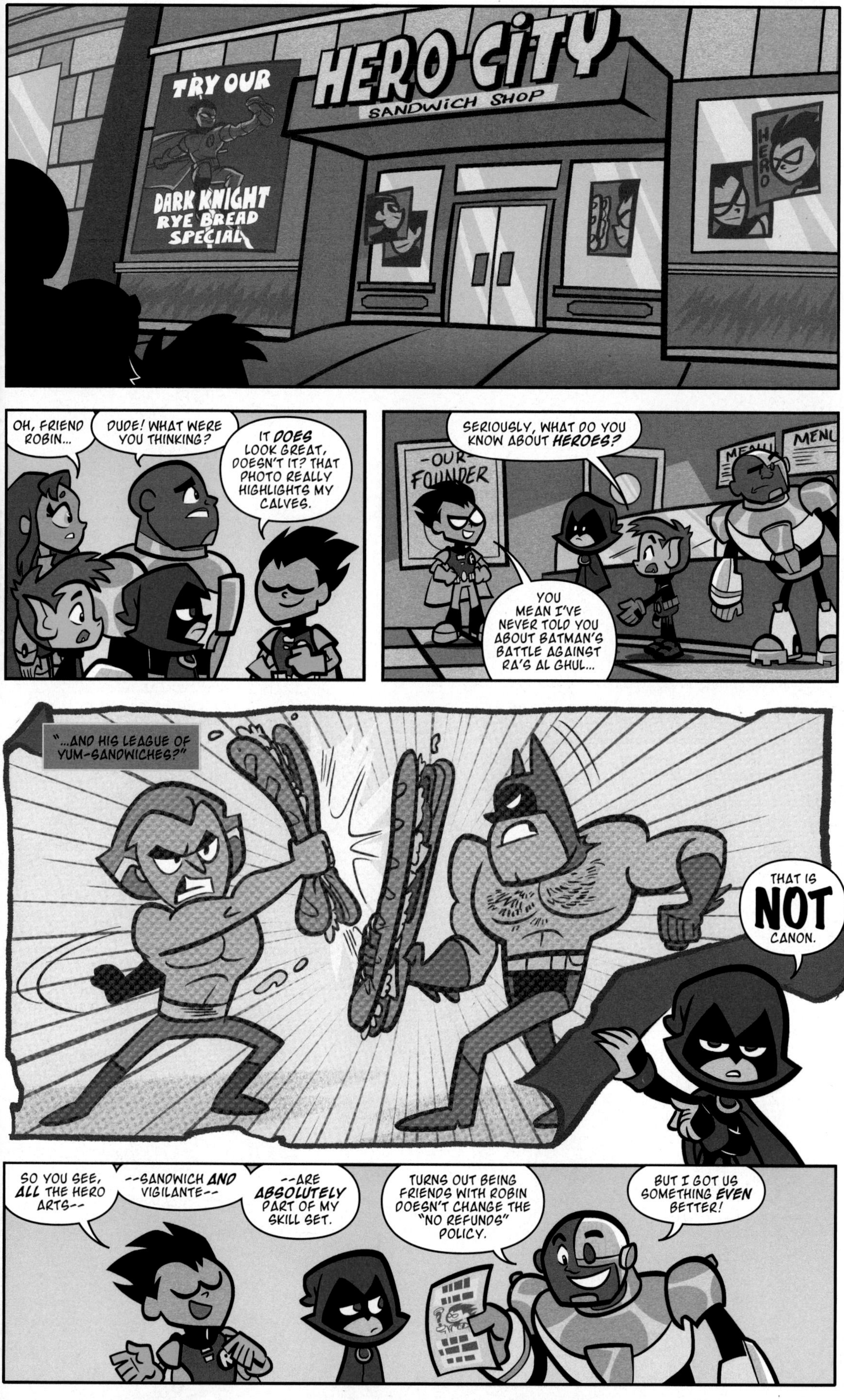
TRY OUR
DARK KNIGHT RYE BREAD SPECIAL
HERO CITY
SANDWICH SHOP
HERO
OH, FRIEND ROBIN...
DUDE! WHAT WERE YOU THINKING?
IT DOES LOOK GREAT, DOESN'T IT? THAT PHOTO REALLY HIGHLIGHTS MY CALVES.
-OUR- FOUNDER
MENU
SERIOUSLY, WHAT DO YOU KNOW ABOUT HEROES?
YOU MEAN I'VE NEVER TOLD YOU ABOUT BATMAN'S BATTLE AGAINST RA'S AL GHUL...
"...AND HIS LEAGUE OF YUM-SANDWICHES?"
THAT IS NOT CANON.
SO YOU SEE, ALL THE HERO ARTS--
--SANDWICH AND VIGILANTE--
--ARE ABSOLUTELY PART OF MY SKILL SET.
TURNS OUT BEING FRIENDS WITH ROBIN DOESN'T CHANGE THE "NO REFUNDS" POLICY.
BUT I GOT US SOMETHING EVEN BETTER!

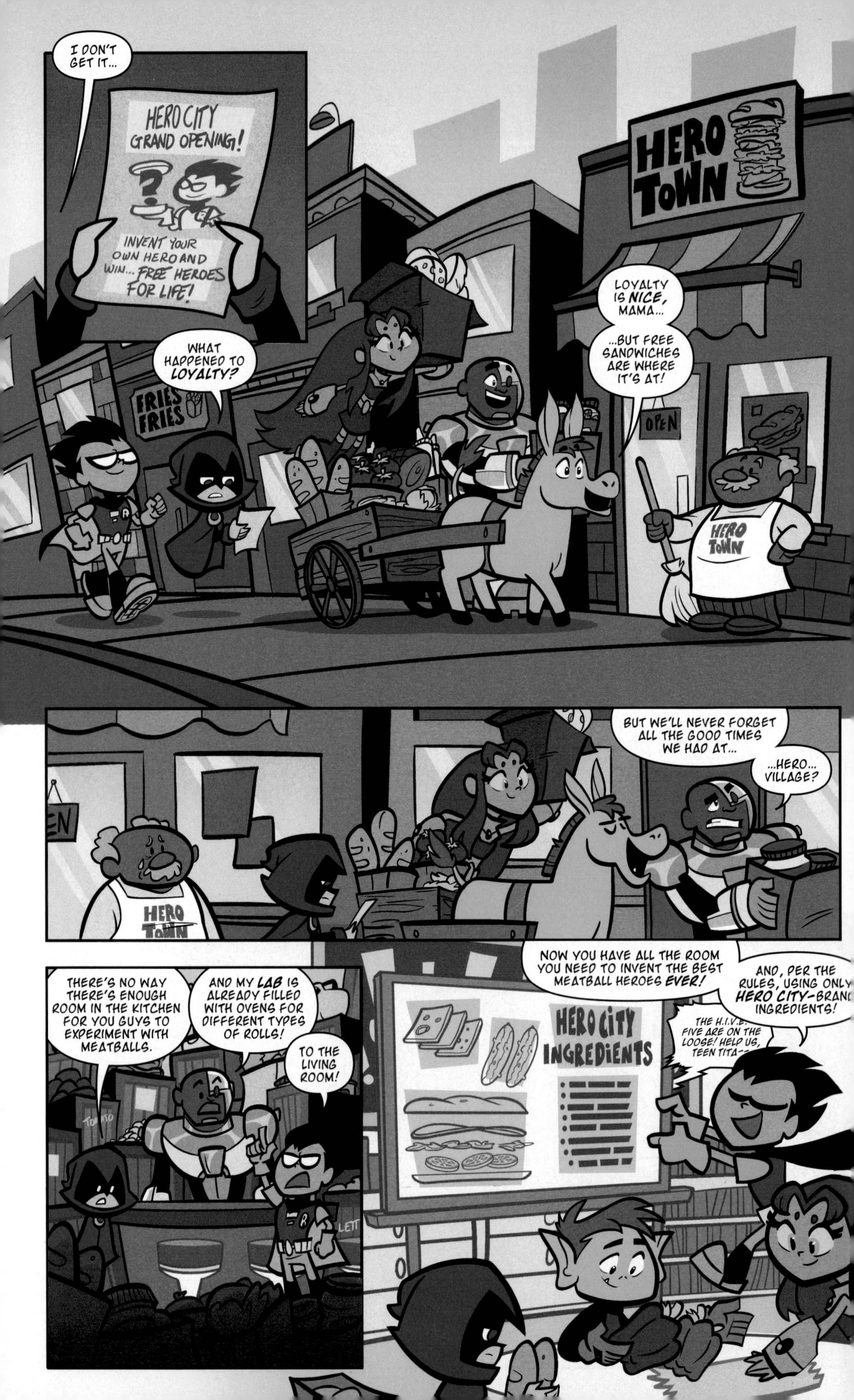
I DON'T GET IT...
HERO CITY GRAND OPENING!
INVENT YOUR OWN HERO AND WIN... FREE HEROES FOR LIFE!
HERO TOWN
WHAT HAPPENED TO LOYALTY?
FRIES FRIES
LOYALTY IS NICE, MAMA...
...BUT FREE SANDWICHES ARE WHERE IT'S AT!
OPEN
HERO TOWN
BUT WE'LL NEVER FORGET ALL THE GOOD TIMES WE HAD AT...
...HERO... VILLAGE?
HERO TOWN
THERE'S NO WAY THERE'S ENOUGH ROOM IN THE KITCHEN FOR YOU GUYS TO EXPERIMENT WITH MEATBALLS.
AND MY LAB IS ALREADY FILLED WITH OVENS FOR DIFFERENT TYPES OF ROLLS!
TO THE LIVING ROOM!
NOW YOU HAVE ALL THE ROOM YOU NEED TO INVENT THE BEST MEATBALL HEROES EVER!
AND, PER THE RULES, USING ONLY HERO CITY-BRAN INGREDIENTS!
HERO CITY INGREDIENTS
THE H.I.V.E. FIVE ARE ON THE LOOSE! HELP US, TEEN TITA--

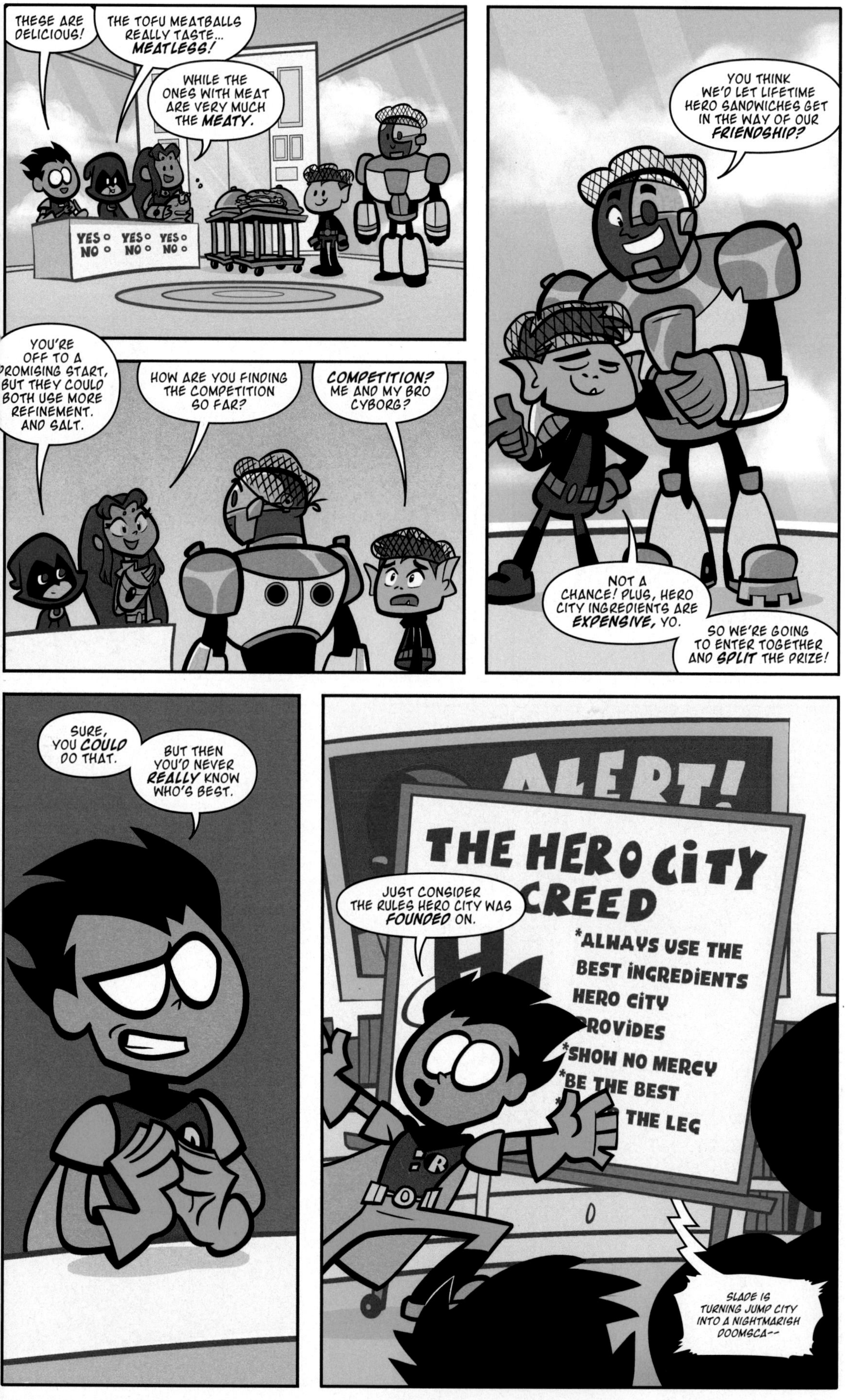

THESE ARE DELICIOUS!
THE TOFU MEATBALLS REALLY TASTE... MEATLESS!
WHILE THE ONES WITH MEAT ARE VERY MUCH THE MEATY.
YES NO YES NO YES NO
YOU'RE OFF TO A PROMISING START, BUT THEY COULD BOTH USE MORE REFINEMENT. AND SALT.
HOW ARE YOU FINDING THE COMPETITION SO FAR?
COMPETITION? ME AND MY BRO CYBORG?
YOU THINK WE'D LET LIFETIME HERO SANDWICHES GET IN THE WAY OF OUR FRIENDSHIP?
NOT A CHANCE! PLUS, HERO CITY INGREDIENTS ARE EXPENSIVE, YO.
SO WE'RE GOING TO ENTER TOGETHER AND SPLIT THE PRIZE!
SURE, YOU COULD DO THAT.
BUT THEN YOU'D NEVER REALLY KNOW WHO'S BEST.
ALERT!
THE HERO CITY CREED
*ALWAYS USE THE BEST INGREDIENTS HERO CITY PROVIDES
*SHOW NO MERCY
*BE THE BEST
THE LEG
JUST CONSIDER THE RULES HERO CITY WAS FOUNDED ON.
SLADE IS TURNING JUMP CITY INTO A NIGHTMARISH DOOMSCA--

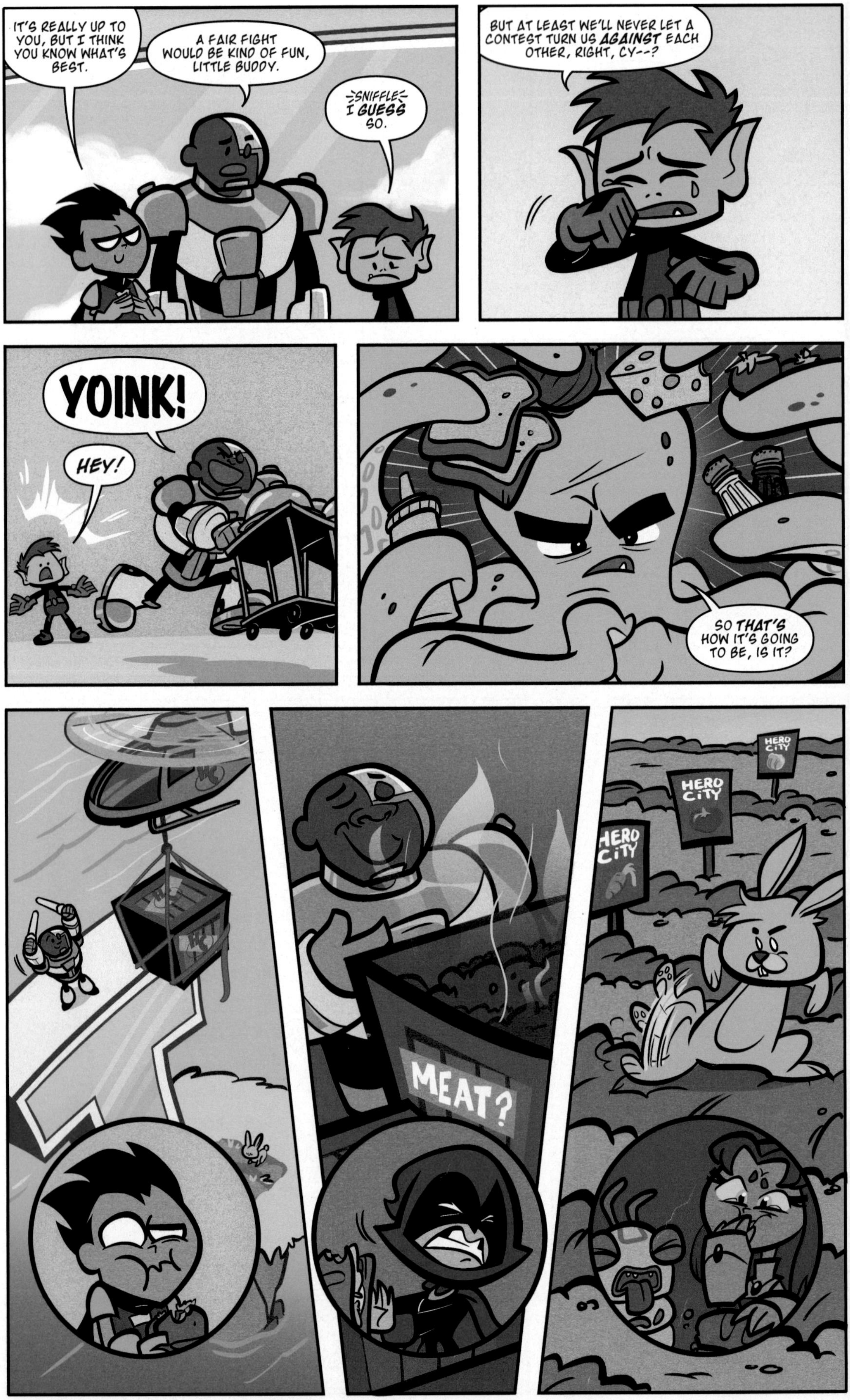
IT'S REALLY UP TO YOU, BUT I THINK YOU KNOW WHAT'S BEST.
A FAIR FIGHT WOULD BE KIND OF FUN, LITTLE BUDDY.
SNIFFLE I GUESS SO.
BUT AT LEAST WE'LL NEVER LET A CONTEST TURN US AGAINST EACH OTHER, RIGHT, CY--?
YOINK!
HEY!
SO THAT'S HOW IT'S GOING TO BE, IS IT?
HERO CITY
HERO CITY
HERO CITY
MEAT?

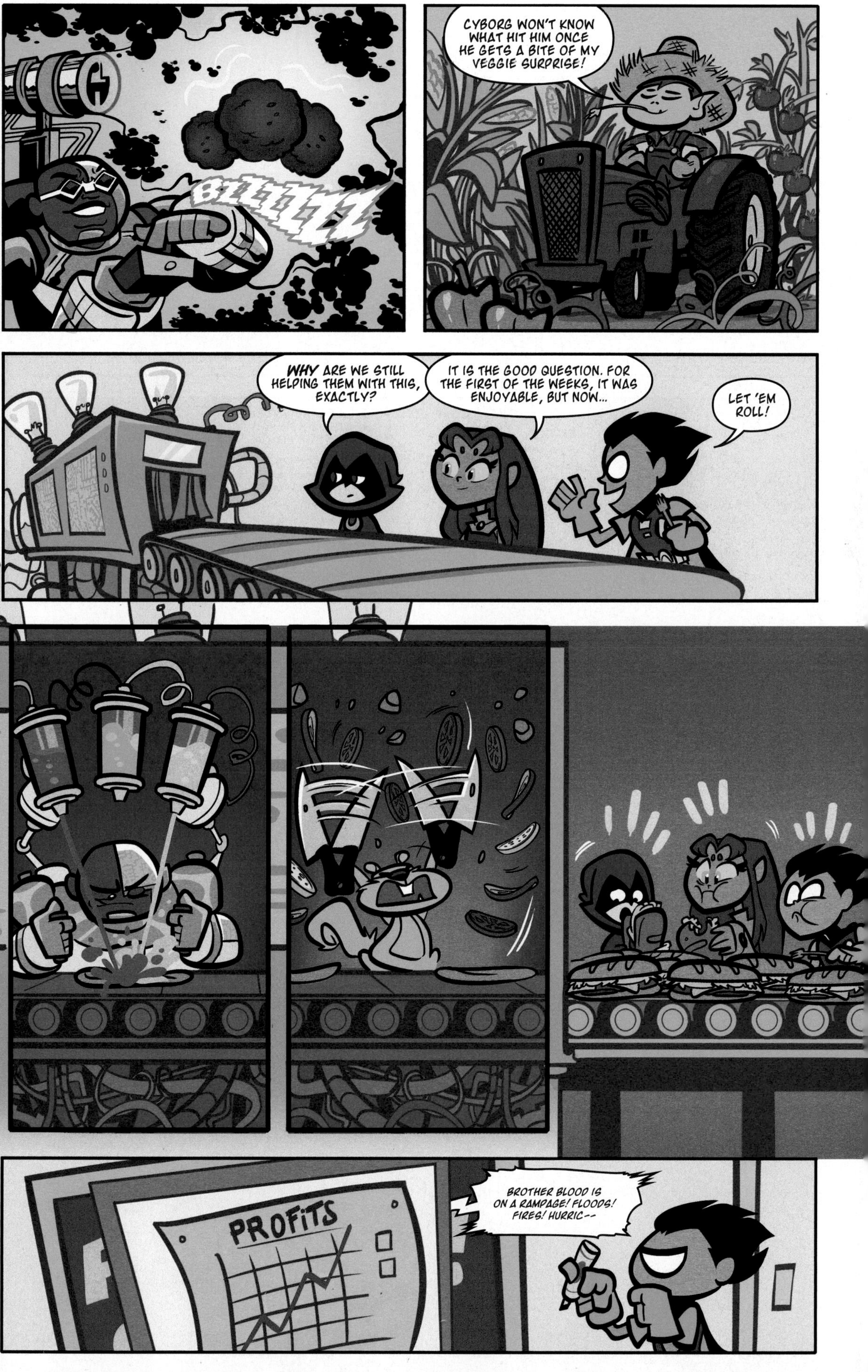
BZZZZZZ
CYBORG WON'T KNOW WHAT HIT HIM ONCE HE GETS A BITE OF MY VEGGIE SURPRISE!
WHY ARE WE STILL HELPING THEM WITH THIS, EXACTLY?
IT IS THE GOOD QUESTION. FOR THE FIRST OF THE WEEKS, IT WAS ENJOYABLE, BUT NOW...
LET 'EM ROLL!
PROFITS
BROTHER BLOOD IS ON A RAMPAGE! FLOODS! FIRES! HURRIC--

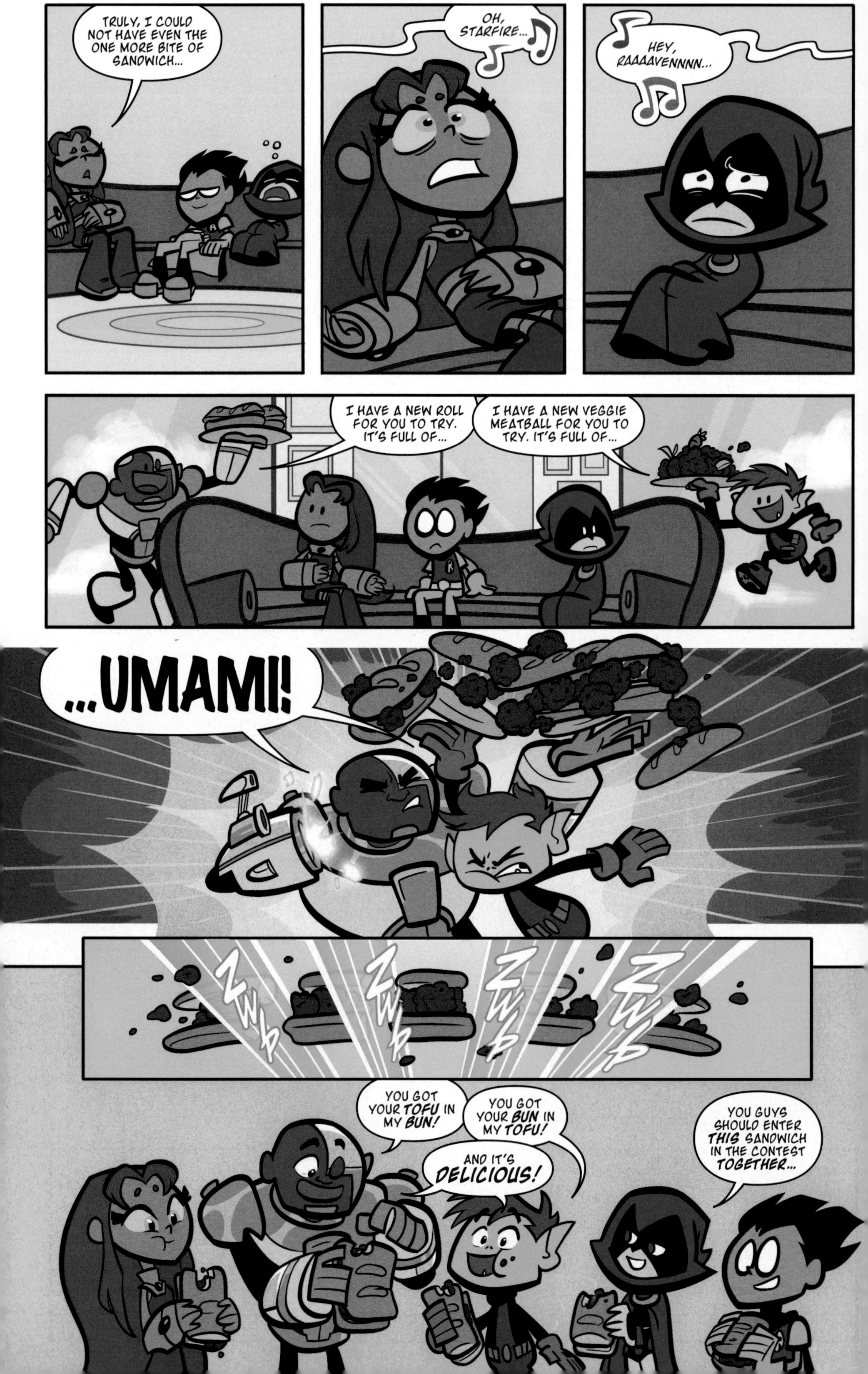
TRULY, I COULD NOT HAVE EVEN THE ONE MORE BITE OF SANDWICH...
OH, STARFIRE...
HEY, RAAAAVENNNN...
I HAVE A NEW ROLL FOR YOU TO TRY. IT'S FULL OF...
I HAVE A NEW VEGGIE MEATBALL FOR YOU TO TRY. IT'S FULL OF...
...UMAMI!
ZWIP
ZWIP
ZWIP
ZWIP
YOU GOT YOUR TOFU IN MY BUN!
YOU GOT YOUR BUN IN MY TOFU!
AND IT'S DELICIOUS!
YOU GUYS SHOULD ENTER THIS SANDWICH IN THE CONTEST TOGETHER...

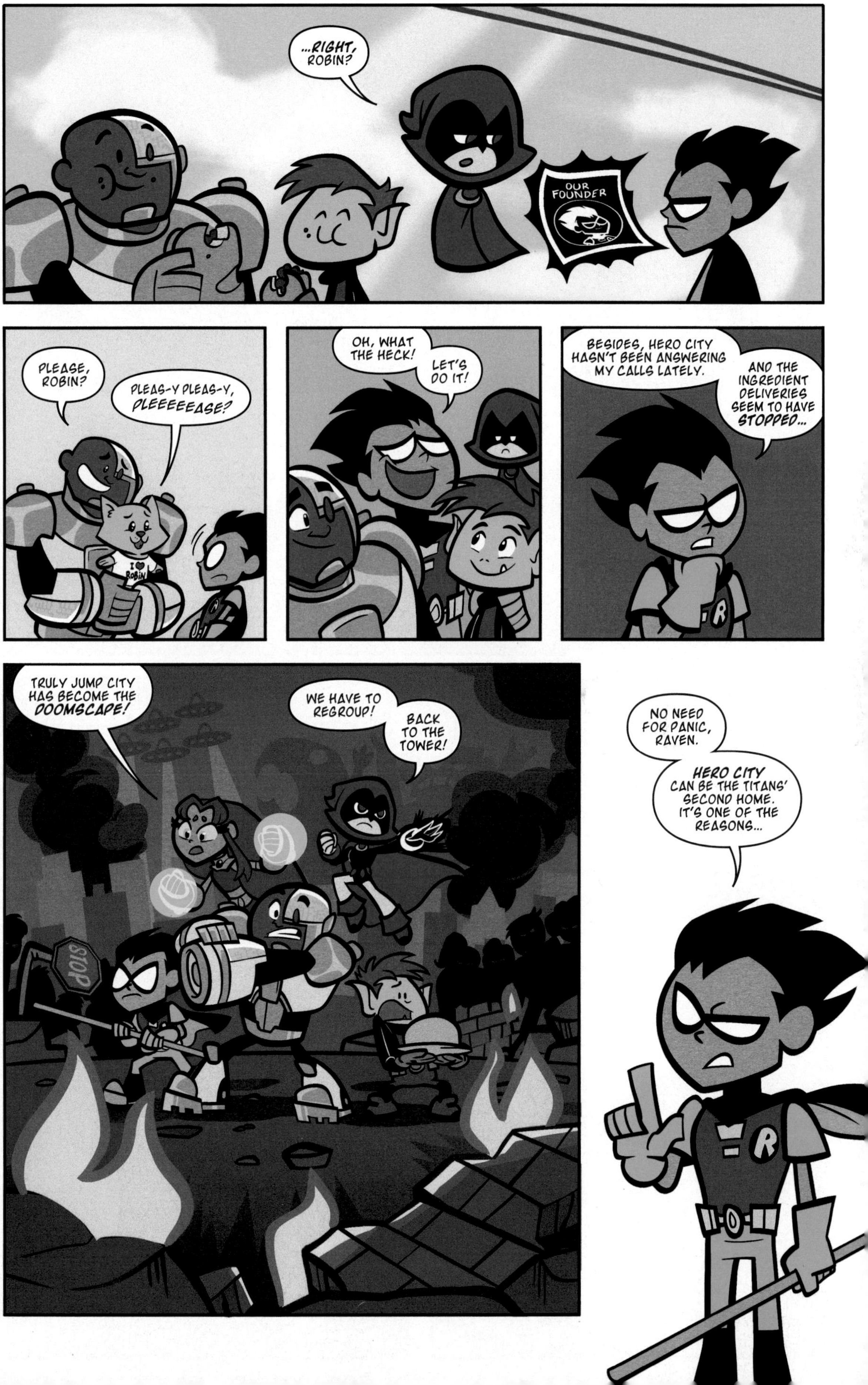
...RIGHT, ROBIN?
OUR FOUNDER
PLEASE, ROBIN?
PLEAS-Y PLEAS-Y, PLEEEEEASE?
OH, WHAT THE HECK!
LET'S DO IT!
BESIDES, HERO CITY HASN'T BEEN ANSWERING MY CALLS LATELY.
AND THE INGREDIENT DELIVERIES SEEM TO HAVE STOPPED...
TRULY JUMP CITY HAS BECOME THE DOOMSCAPE!
WE HAVE TO REGROUP!
BACK TO THE TOWER!
NO NEED FOR PANIC, RAVEN.
HERO CITY CAN BE THE TITANS' SECOND HOME. IT'S ONE OF THE REASONS...

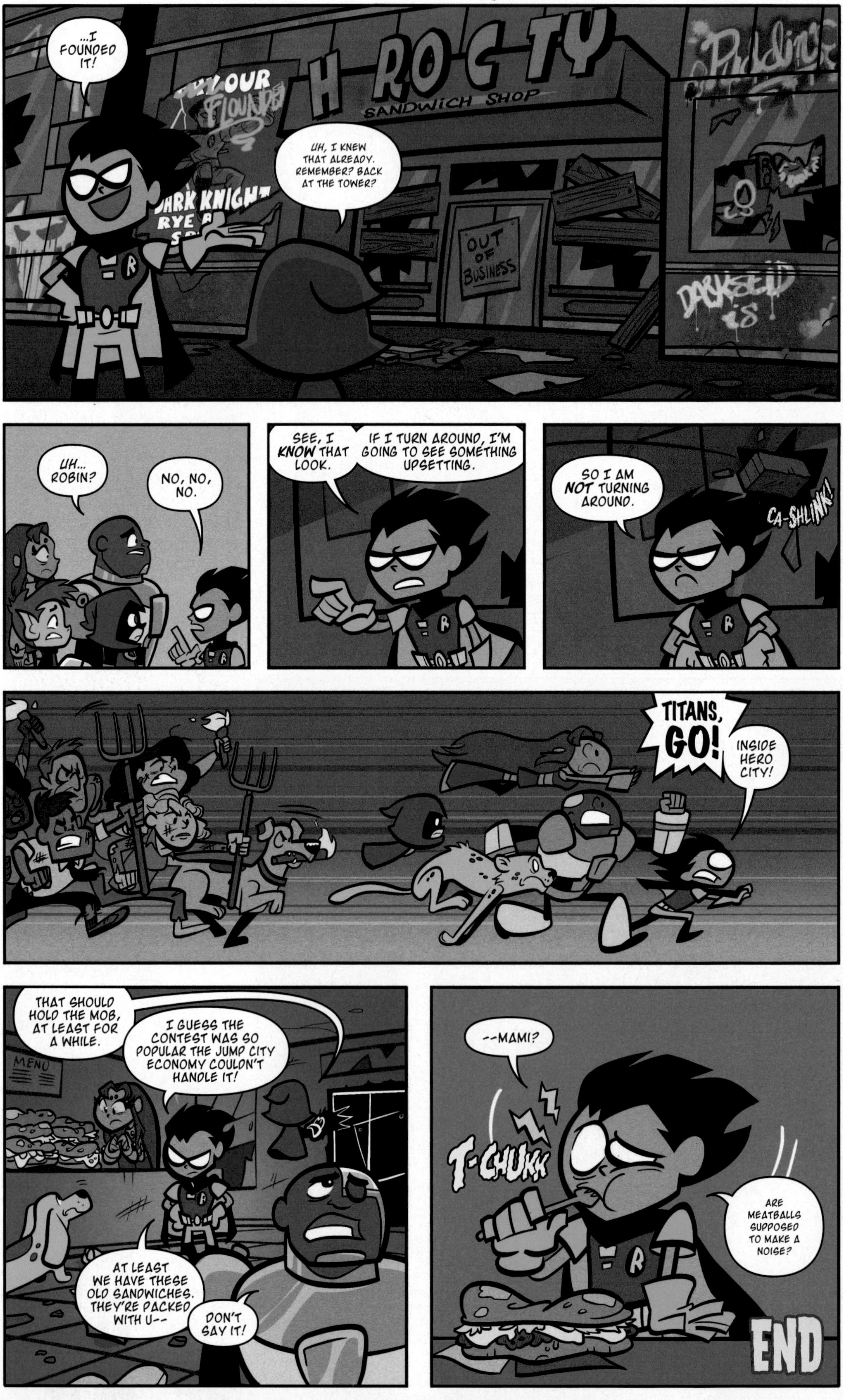

...I FOUNDED IT!
H RO C TY
SANDWICH SHOP
OUR
DARK KNIGHT RYE
UH, I KNEW THAT ALREADY. REMEMBER? BACK AT THE TOWER?
OUT OF BUSINESS
DARKSEID IS
UH... ROBIN?
NO, NO, NO.
SEE, I KNOW THAT LOOK.
IF I TURN AROUND, I'M GOING TO SEE SOMETHING UPSETTING.
SO I AM NOT TURNING AROUND.
CA-SHLINK!
TITANS, GO!
INSIDE HERO CITY!
THAT SHOULD HOLD THE MOB, AT LEAST FOR A WHILE.
I GUESS THE CONTEST WAS SO POPULAR THE JUMP CITY ECONOMY COULDN'T HANDLE IT!
MENU
AT LEAST WE HAVE THESE OLD SANDWICHES. THEY'RE PACKED WITH U--
DON'T SAY IT!
--MAMI?
T-CHUKK
ARE MEATBALLS SUPPOSED TO MAKE A NOISE?
END

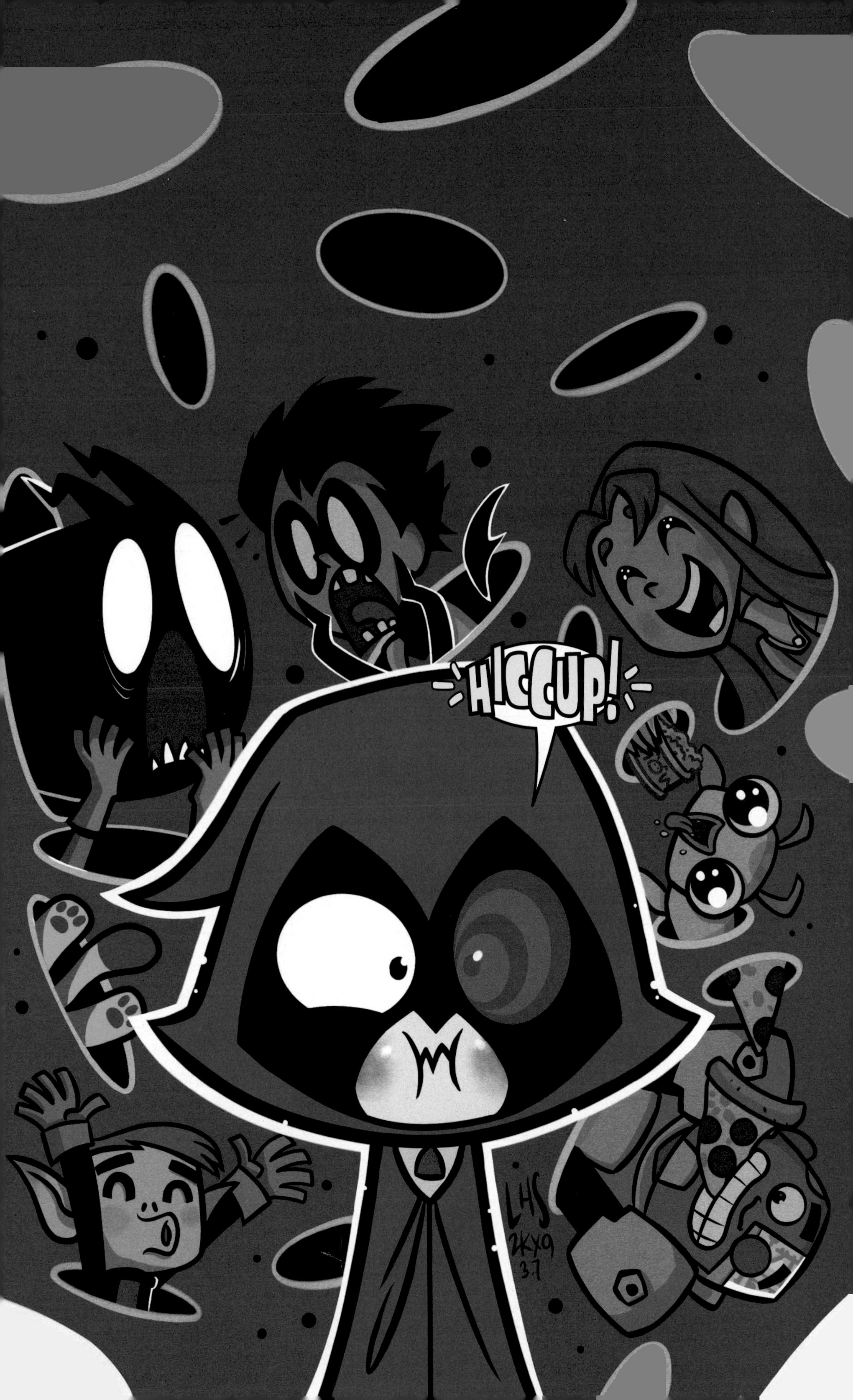
HICCUP!

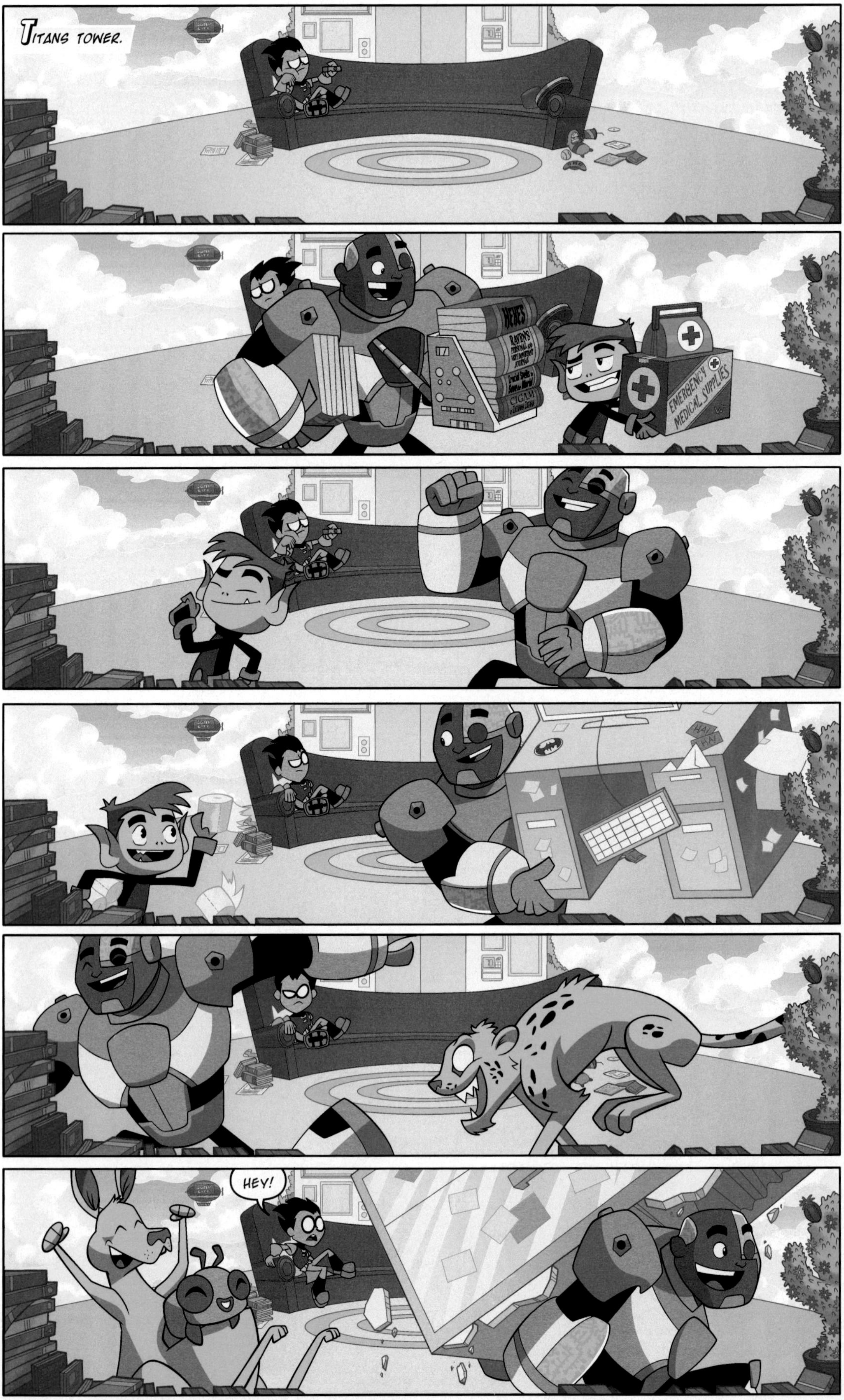
TITANS TOWER.
HEXES
RAVEN'S PERSONAL AND VERY IMPORTANT JOURNAL
Crucial Spells to Save the World
CIGAM
EMERGENCY MEDICAL SUPPLIES
HA! HA!
HEY!

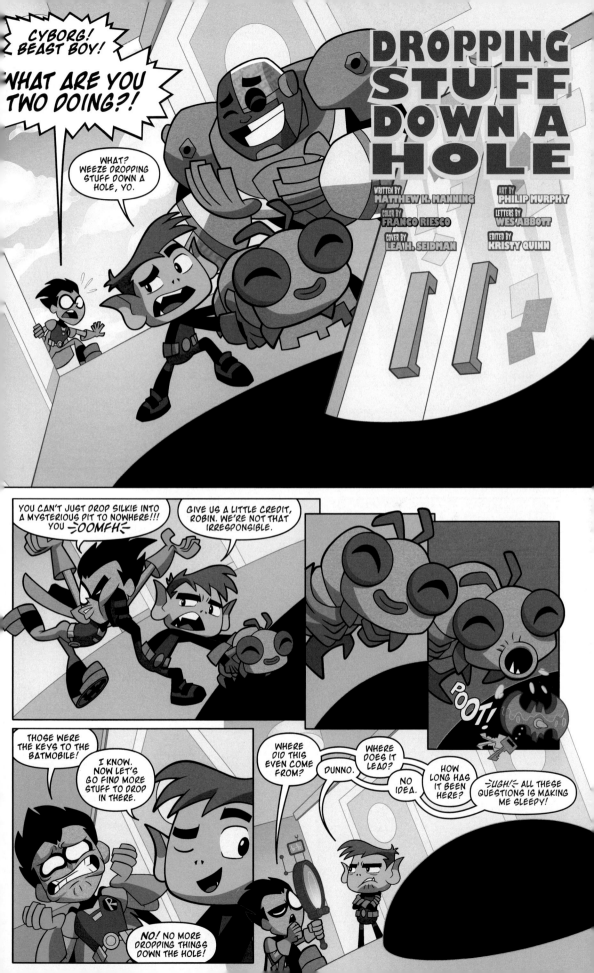

DROPPING STUFF DOWN A HOLE

WRITTEN BY
MATTHEW K. MANNING

ART BY
PHILIP MURPHY

COLOR BY
FRANCO RIESCO

LETTERS BY
WES ABBOTT

COVER BY
LEA H. SEIDMAN

EDITED BY
KRISTY QUINN

CYBORG! BEAST BOY! WHAT ARE YOU TWO DOING?!

WHAT? WEEZE DROPPING STUFF DOWN A HOLE, YO.

YOU CAN'T JUST DROP SILKIE INTO A MYSTERIOUS PIT TO NOWHERE!!! YOU =OOMFH=

GIVE US A LITTLE CREDIT, ROBIN. WE'RE NOT THAT IRRESPONSIBLE.

POOT!

THOSE WERE THE KEYS TO THE BATMOBILE!

I KNOW. NOW LET'S GO FIND MORE STUFF TO DROP IN THERE.

WHERE DID THIS EVEN COME FROM?

DUNNO.

WHERE DOES IT LEAD?

NO IDEA.

HOW LONG HAS IT BEEN HERE?

=UGH!= ALL THESE QUESTIONS IS MAKING ME SLEEPY!

NO! NO MORE DROPPING THINGS DOWN THE HOLE!

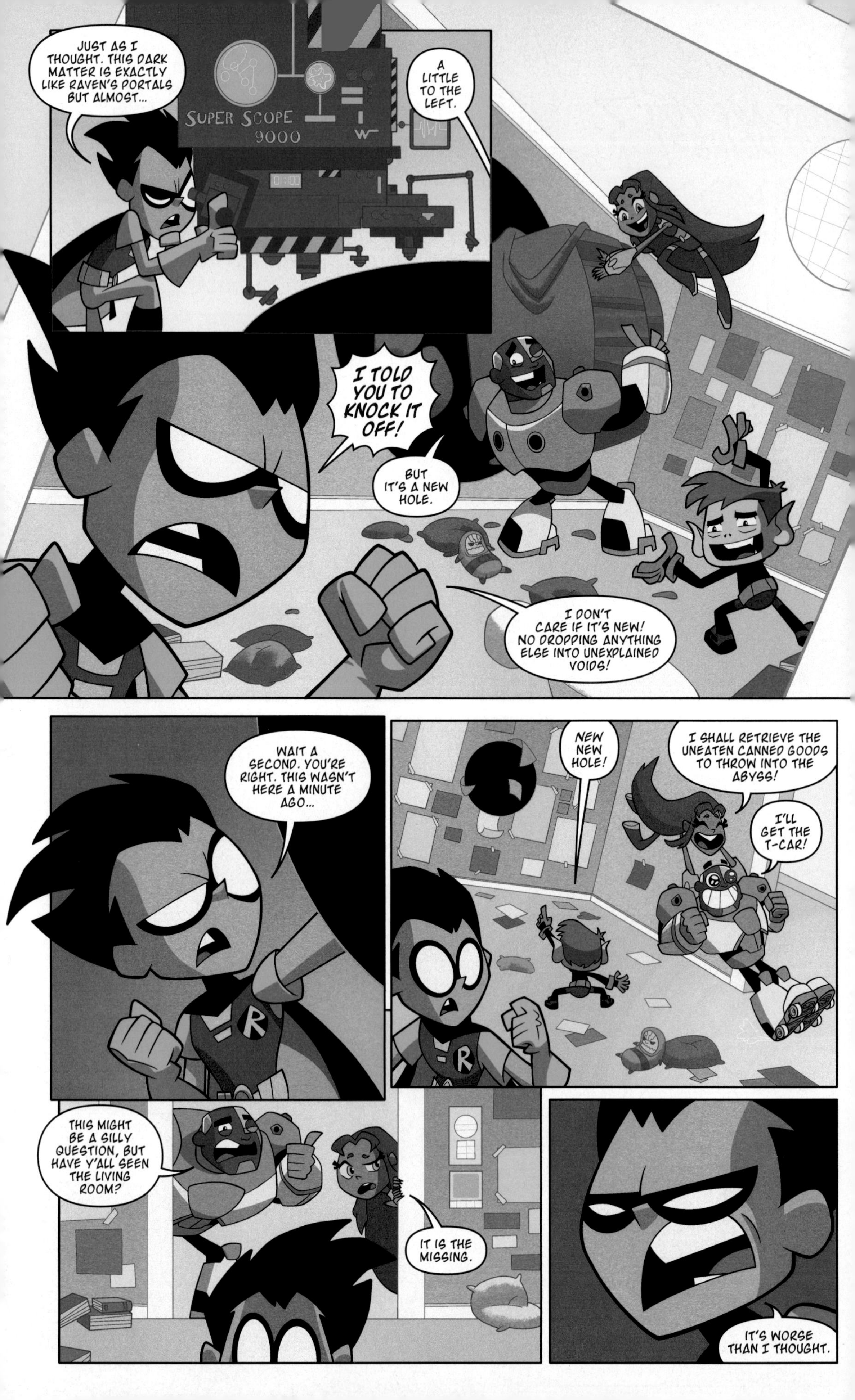

JUST AS I THOUGHT. THIS DARK MATTER IS EXACTLY LIKE RAVEN'S PORTALS BUT ALMOST...
SUPER SCOPE 9000
A LITTLE TO THE LEFT.
I TOLD YOU TO KNOCK IT OFF!
BUT IT'S A NEW HOLE.
I DON'T CARE IF IT'S NEW! NO DROPPING ANYTHING ELSE INTO UNEXPLAINED VOIDS!
WAIT A SECOND. YOU'RE RIGHT. THIS WASN'T HERE A MINUTE AGO...
NEW NEW HOLE!
I SHALL RETRIEVE THE UNEATEN CANNED GOODS TO THROW INTO THE ABYSS!
I'LL GET THE T-CAR!
THIS MIGHT BE A SILLY QUESTION, BUT HAVE Y'ALL SEEN THE LIVING ROOM?
IT IS THE MISSING.
IT'S WORSE THAN I THOUGHT.

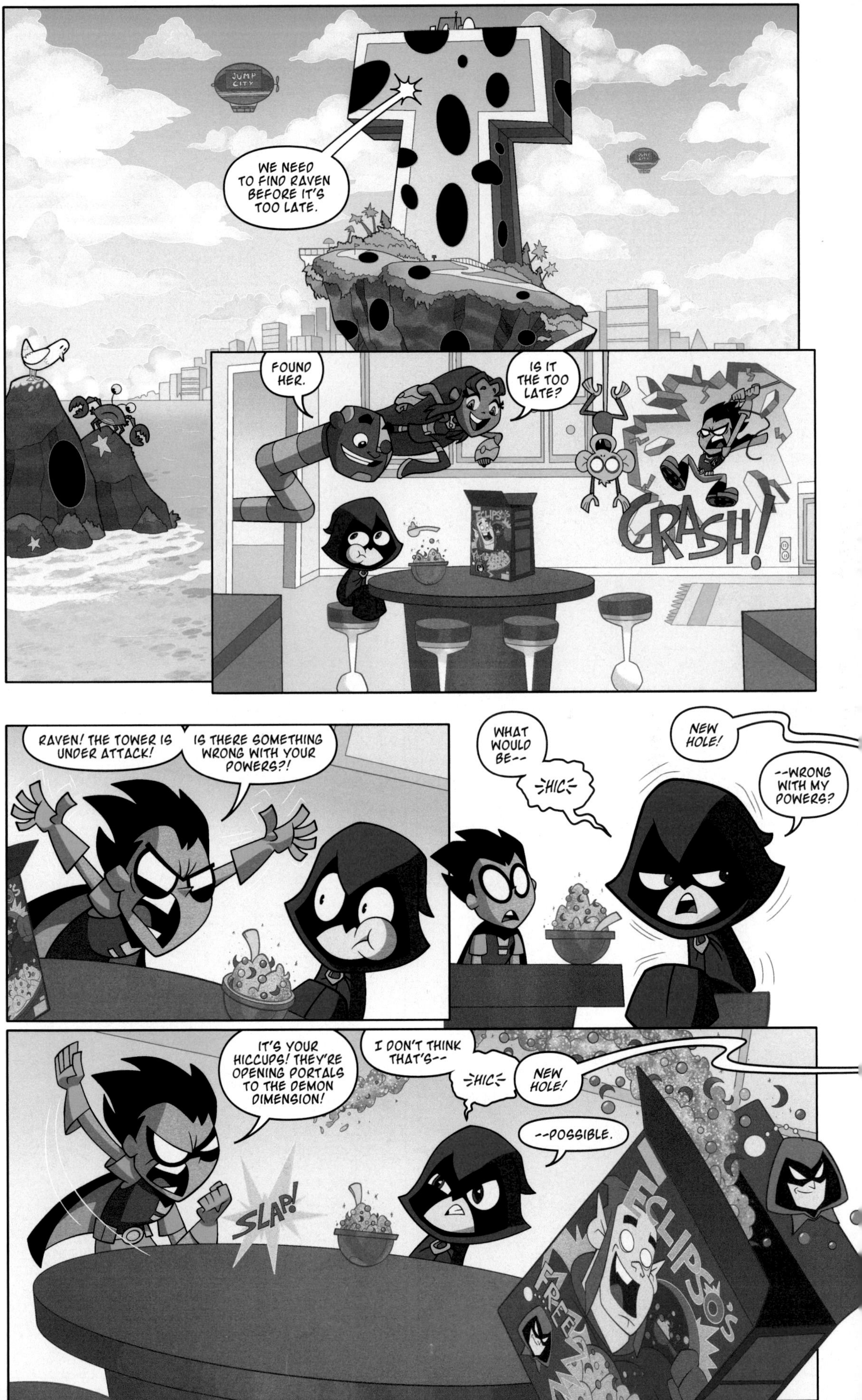
JUMP CITY
WE NEED TO FIND RAVEN BEFORE IT'S TOO LATE.
FOUND HER.
IS IT THE TOO LATE?
CRASH!
RAVEN! THE TOWER IS UNDER ATTACK!
IS THERE SOMETHING WRONG WITH YOUR POWERS?!
WHAT WOULD BE--
HIC
NEW HOLE!
--WRONG WITH MY POWERS?
IT'S YOUR HICCUPS! THEY'RE OPENING PORTALS TO THE DEMON DIMENSION!
I DON'T THINK THAT'S--
HIC
NEW HOLE!
--POSSIBLE.
SLAP!
ECLIPSO'S

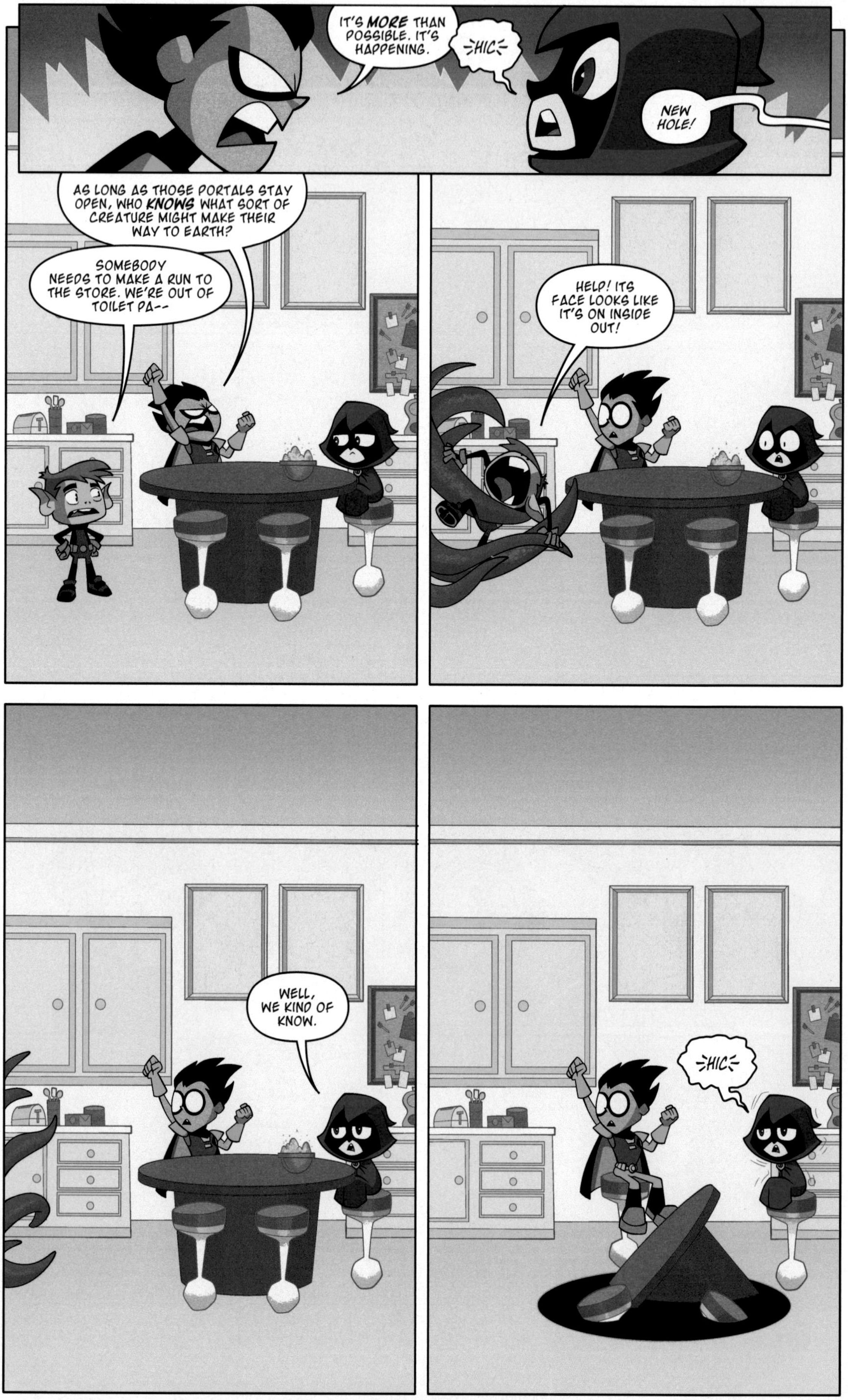
IT'S MORE THAN POSSIBLE. IT'S HAPPENING.
HIC
NEW HOLE!
AS LONG AS THOSE PORTALS STAY OPEN, WHO KNOWS WHAT SORT OF CREATURE MIGHT MAKE THEIR WAY TO EARTH?
SOMEBODY NEEDS TO MAKE A RUN TO THE STORE. WE'RE OUT OF TOILET PA--
HELP! ITS FACE LOOKS LIKE IT'S ON INSIDE OUT!
WELL, WE KIND OF KNOW.
HIC

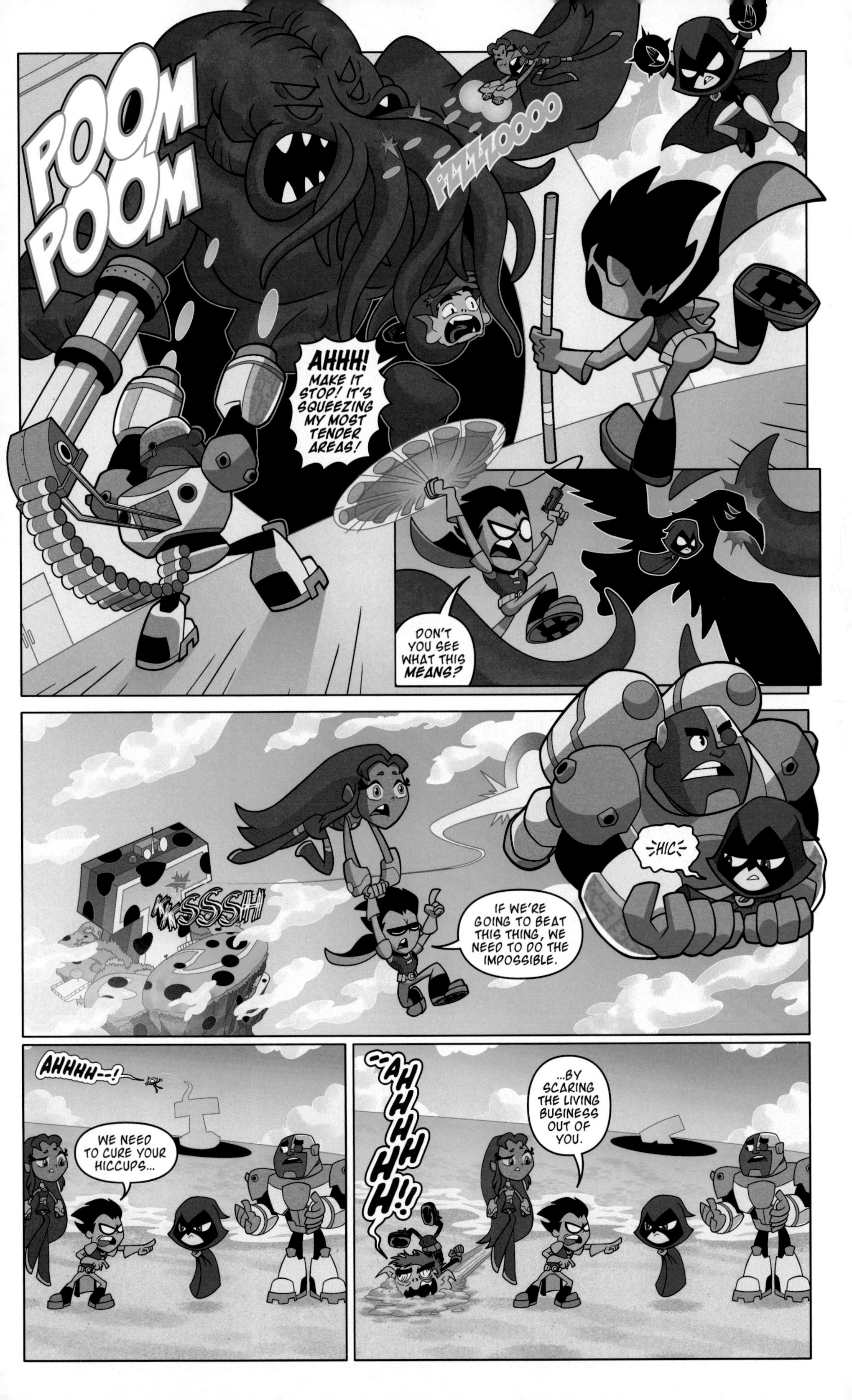
POOM POOM
FZZZZOOOO
AHHH! MAKE IT STOP! IT'S SQUEEZING MY MOST TENDER AREAS!
DON'T YOU SEE WHAT THIS MEANS?
KKSSSSH
HIC
IF WE'RE GOING TO BEAT THIS THING, WE NEED TO DO THE IMPOSSIBLE.
AHHHH--!
WE NEED TO CURE YOUR HICCUPS...
--AHHHHHHH!!
...BY SCARING THE LIVING BUSINESS OUT OF YOU.

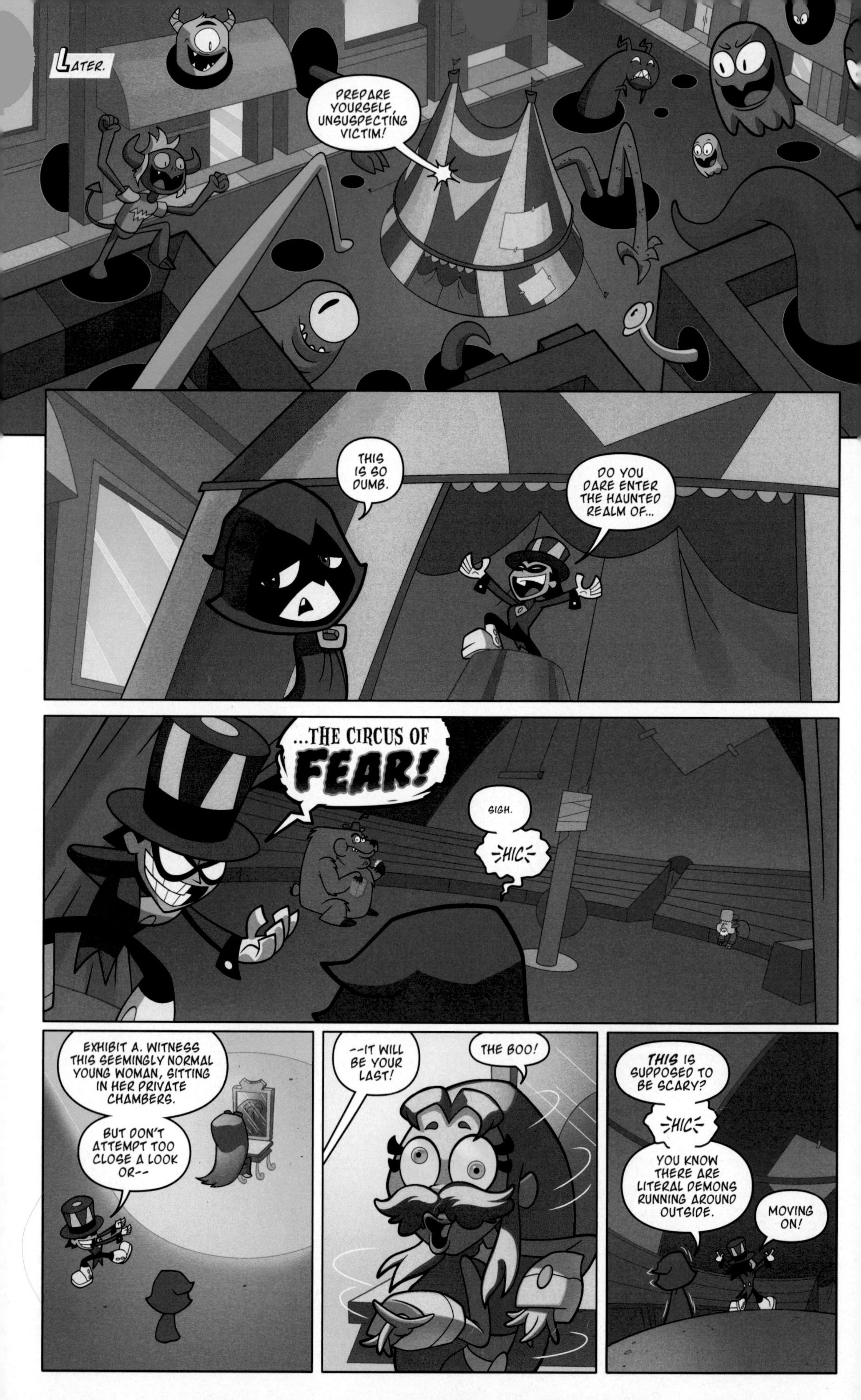
LATER.
PREPARE YOURSELF, UNSUSPECTING VICTIM!
THIS IS SO DUMB.
DO YOU DARE ENTER THE HAUNTED REALM OF...
...THE CIRCUS OF FEAR!
SIGH.
HIC
EXHIBIT A. WITNESS THIS SEEMINGLY NORMAL YOUNG WOMAN, SITTING IN HER PRIVATE CHAMBERS.
BUT DON'T ATTEMPT TOO CLOSE A LOOK OR--
--IT WILL BE YOUR LAST!
THE BOO!
THIS IS SUPPOSED TO BE SCARY?
HIC
YOU KNOW THERE ARE LITERAL DEMONS RUNNING AROUND OUTSIDE.
MOVING ON!

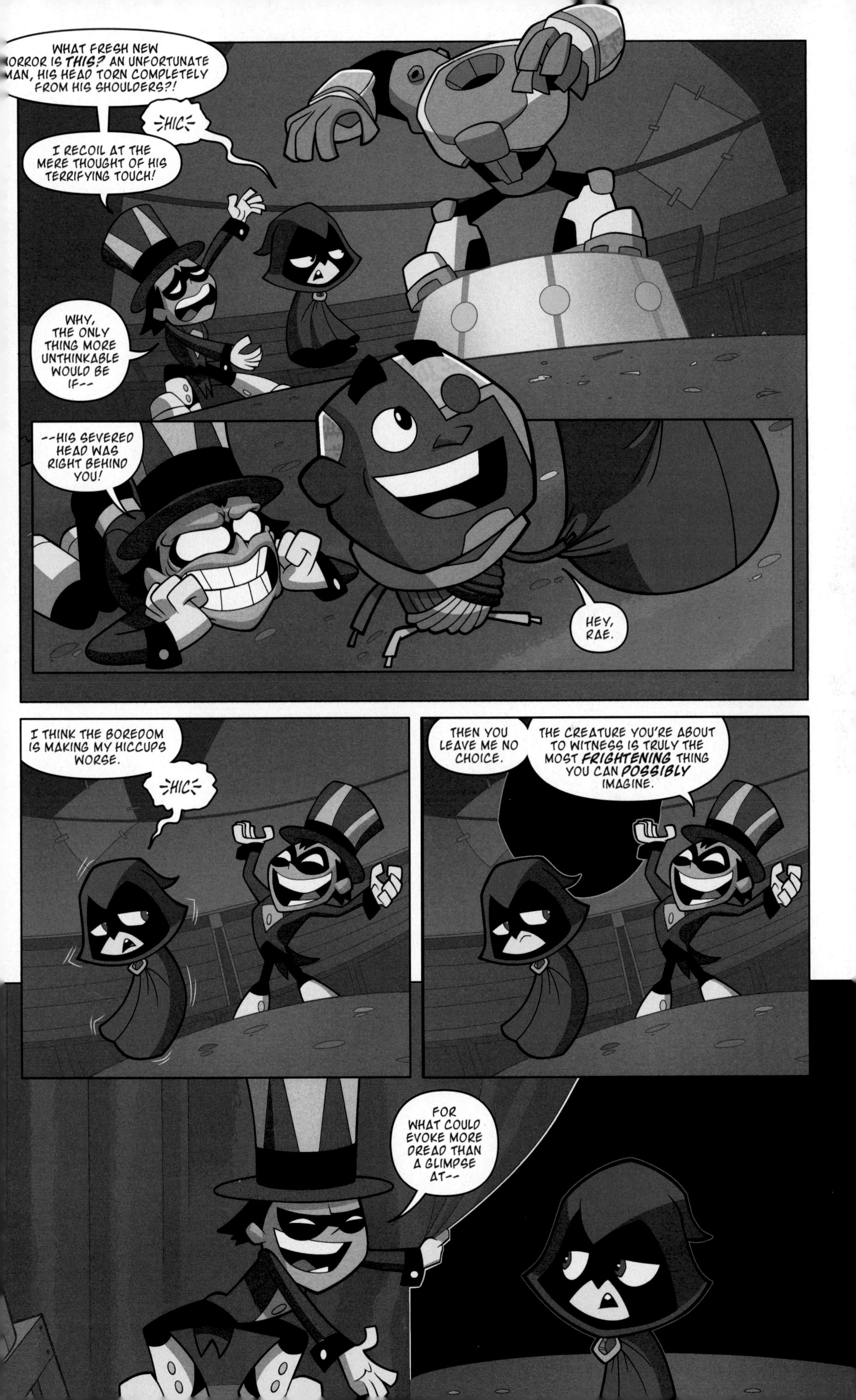
WHAT FRESH NEW HORROR IS THIS? AN UNFORTUNATE MAN, HIS HEAD TORN COMPLETELY FROM HIS SHOULDERS?!
I RECOIL AT THE MERE THOUGHT OF HIS TERRIFYING TOUCH!
HIC
WHY, THE ONLY THING MORE UNTHINKABLE WOULD BE IF--
--HIS SEVERED HEAD WAS RIGHT BEHIND YOU!
HEY, RAE.
I THINK THE BOREDOM IS MAKING MY HICCUPS WORSE.
HIC
THEN YOU LEAVE ME NO CHOICE.
THE CREATURE YOU'RE ABOUT TO WITNESS IS TRULY THE MOST FRIGHTENING THING YOU CAN POSSIBLY IMAGINE.
FOR WHAT COULD EVOKE MORE DREAD THAN A GLIMPSE AT--

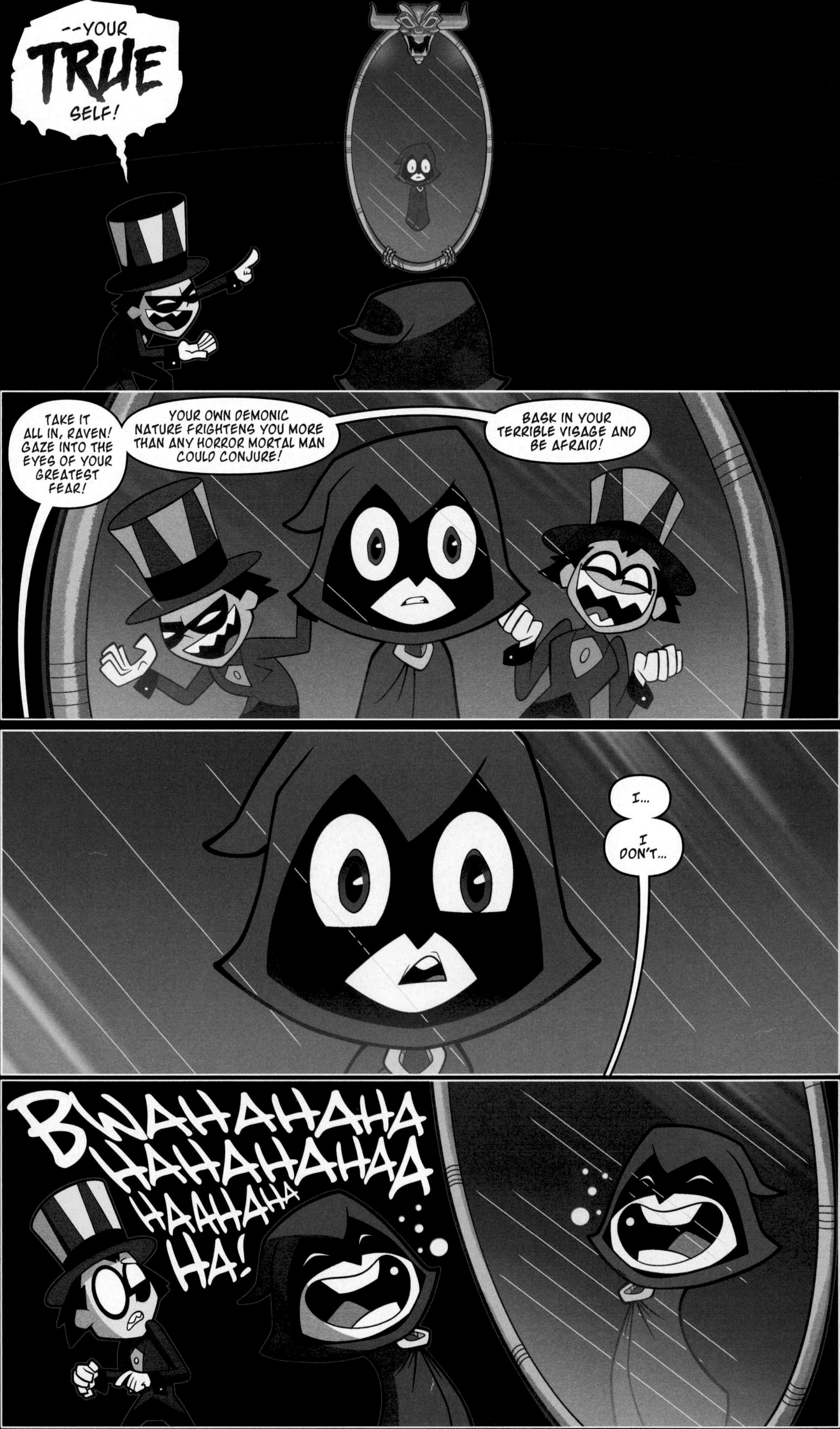
--YOUR TRUE SELF!
TAKE IT ALL IN, RAVEN! GAZE INTO THE EYES OF YOUR GREATEST FEAR!
YOUR OWN DEMONIC NATURE FRIGHTENS YOU MORE THAN ANY HORROR MORTAL MAN COULD CONJURE!
BASK IN YOUR TERRIBLE VISAGE AND BE AFRAID!
I...
I DON'T...
BWAHAHAHA HAHAHAHAHA HAAHAHA HA!

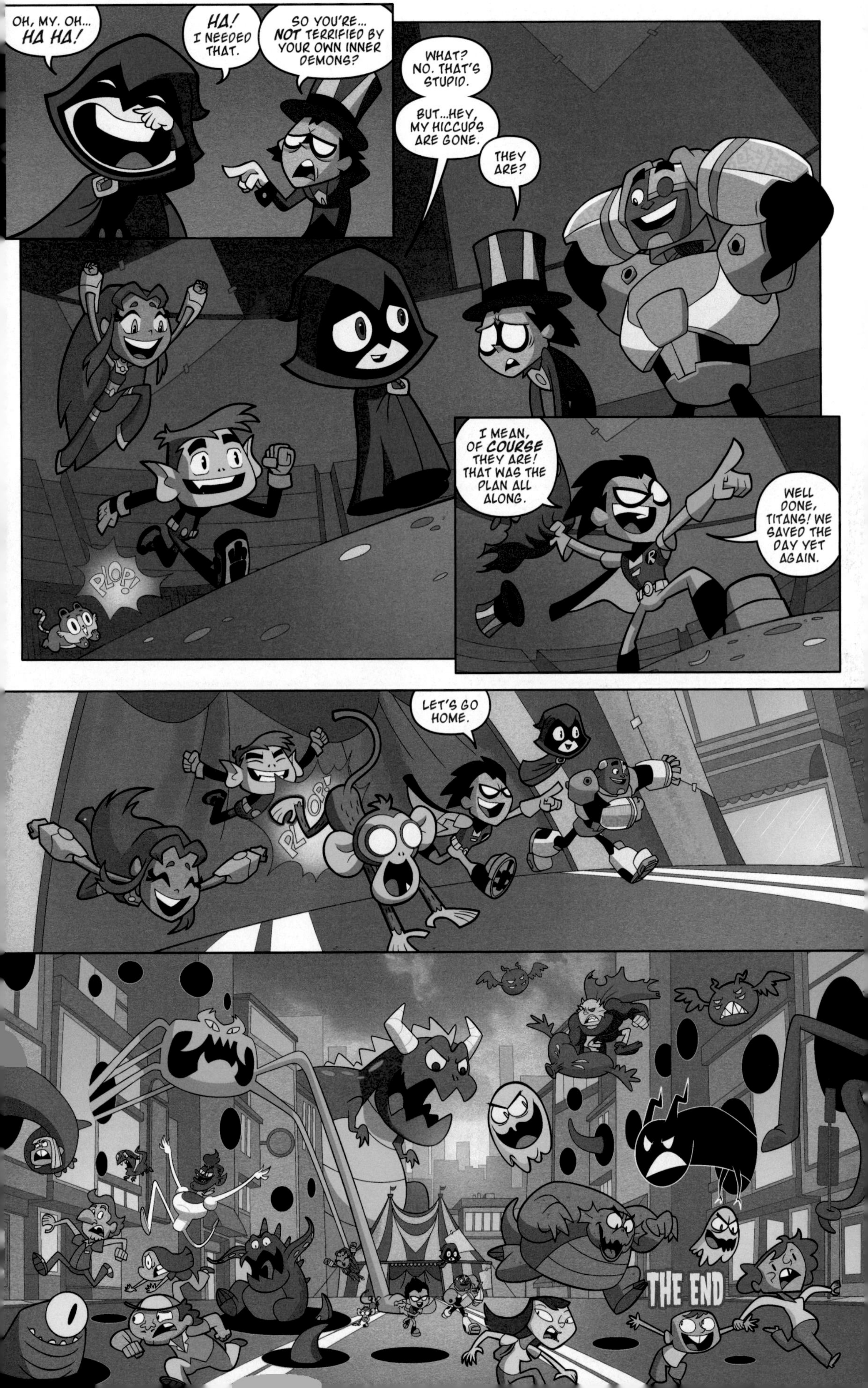
OH, MY. OH... HA HA!
HA! I NEEDED THAT.
SO YOU'RE... NOT TERRIFIED BY YOUR OWN INNER DEMONS?
WHAT? NO. THAT'S STUPID.
BUT...HEY, MY HICCUPS ARE GONE.
THEY ARE?
PLOP!
I MEAN, OF COURSE THEY ARE! THAT WAS THE PLAN ALL ALONG.
WELL DONE, TITANS! WE SAVED THE DAY YET AGAIN.
LET'S GO HOME.
PLOP!
THE END

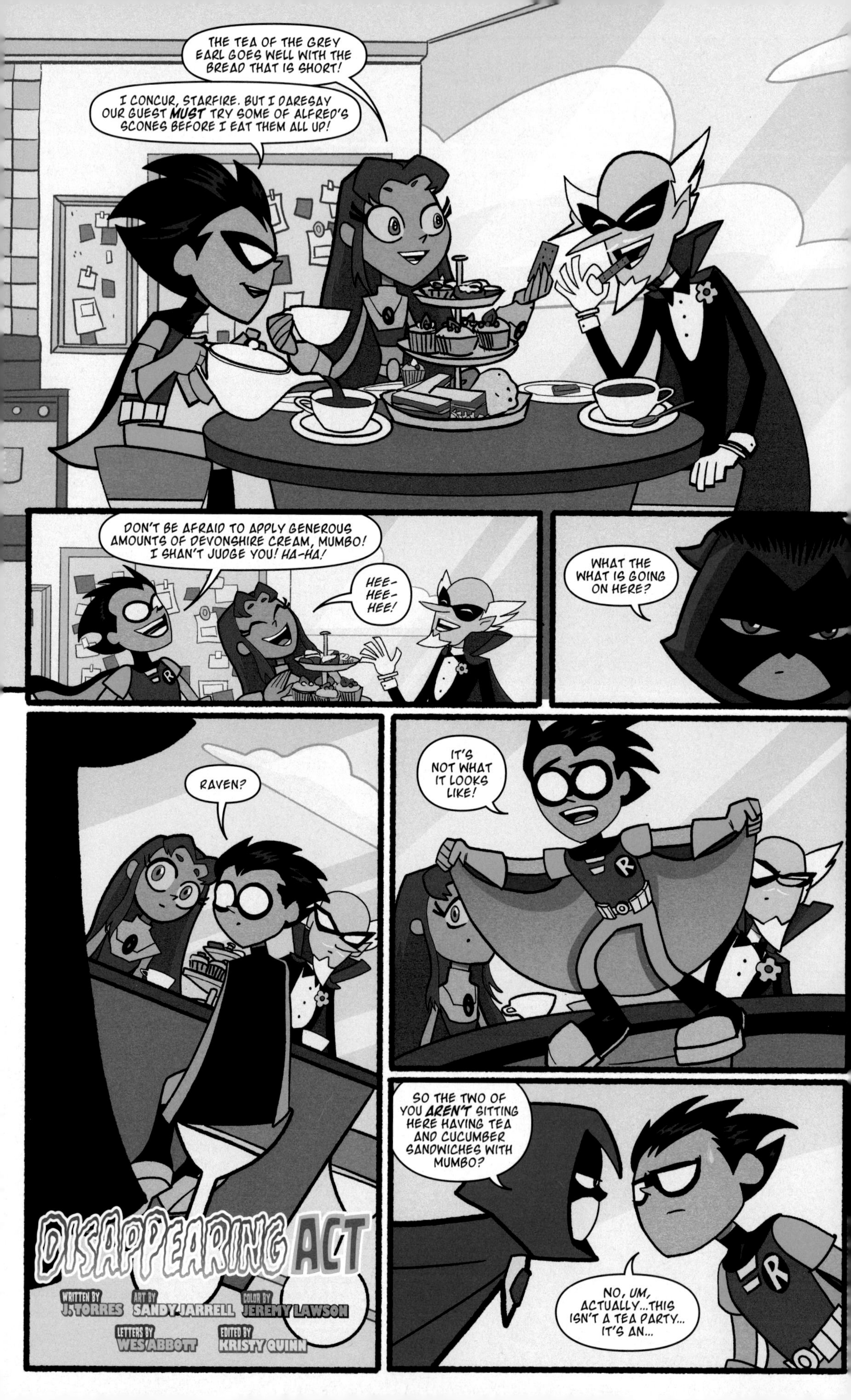
THE TEA OF THE GREY EARL GOES WELL WITH THE BREAD THAT IS SHORT!
I CONCUR, STARFIRE. BUT I DARESAY OUR GUEST MUST TRY SOME OF ALFRED'S SCONES BEFORE I EAT THEM ALL UP!
DON'T BE AFRAID TO APPLY GENEROUS AMOUNTS OF DEVONSHIRE CREAM, MUMBO! I SHAN'T JUDGE YOU! HA-HA!
HEE-HEE-HEE!
WHAT THE WHAT IS GOING ON HERE?
RAVEN?
IT'S NOT WHAT IT LOOKS LIKE!
DISAPPEARING ACT
WRITTEN BY J. TORRES
ART BY SANDY JARRELL
COLOR BY JEREMY LAWSON
LETTERS BY WES ABBOTT
EDITED BY KRISTY QUINN
SO THE TWO OF YOU AREN'T SITTING HERE HAVING TEA AND CUCUMBER SANDWICHES WITH MUMBO?
NO, UM, ACTUALLY...THIS ISN'T A TEA PARTY... IT'S AN...

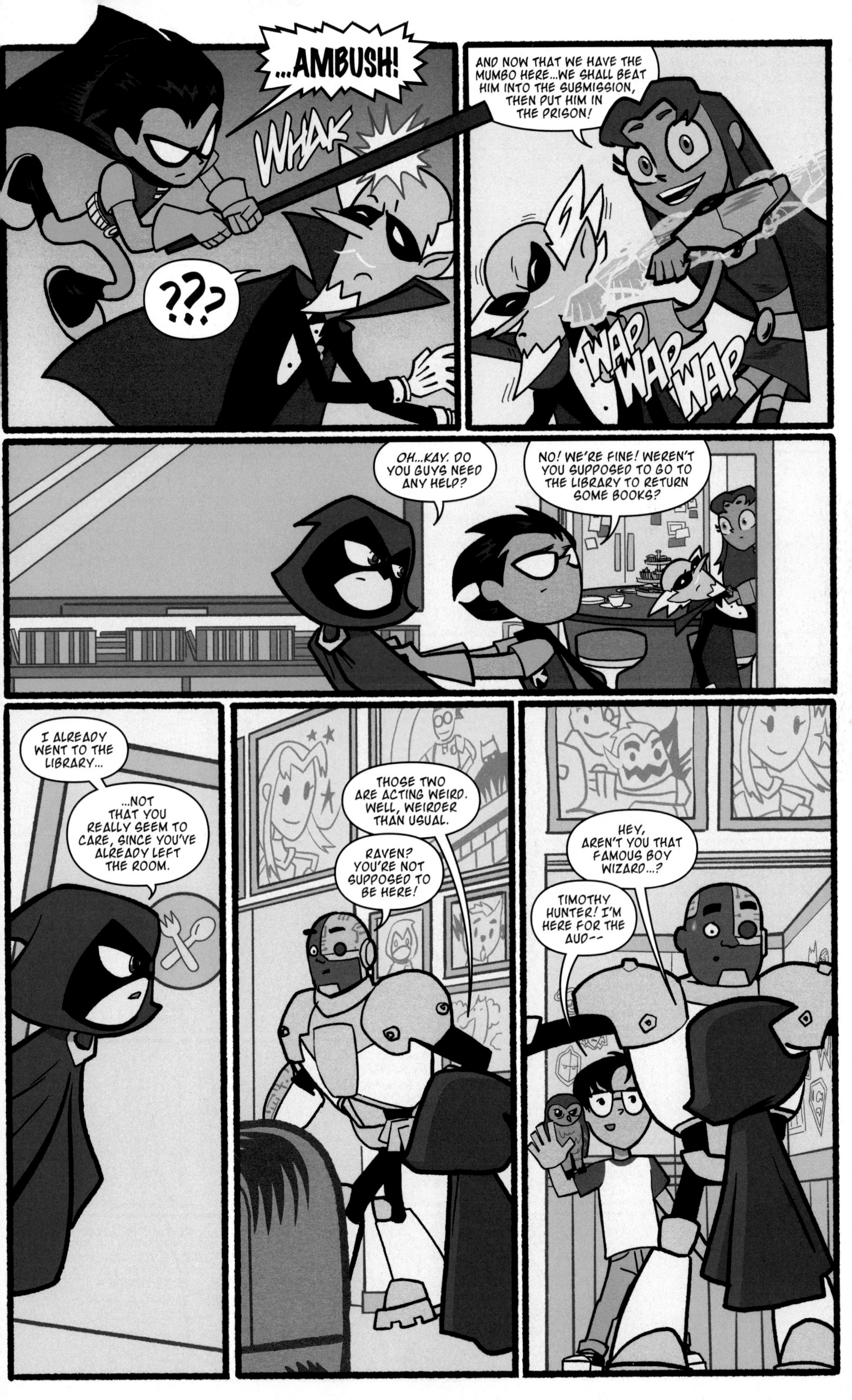
...AMBUSH!
WHAK
???
AND NOW THAT WE HAVE THE MUMBO HERE...WE SHALL BEAT HIM INTO THE SUBMISSION, THEN PUT HIM IN THE PRISON!
WAP WAP WAP
OH...KAY. DO YOU GUYS NEED ANY HELP?
NO! WE'RE FINE! WEREN'T YOU SUPPOSED TO GO TO THE LIBRARY TO RETURN SOME BOOKS?
I ALREADY WENT TO THE LIBRARY...
...NOT THAT YOU REALLY SEEM TO CARE, SINCE YOU'VE ALREADY LEFT THE ROOM.
THOSE TWO ARE ACTING WEIRD. WELL, WEIRDER THAN USUAL.
RAVEN? YOU'RE NOT SUPPOSED TO BE HERE!
HEY, AREN'T YOU THAT FAMOUS BOY WIZARD...?
TIMOTHY HUNTER! I'M HERE FOR THE AUD--

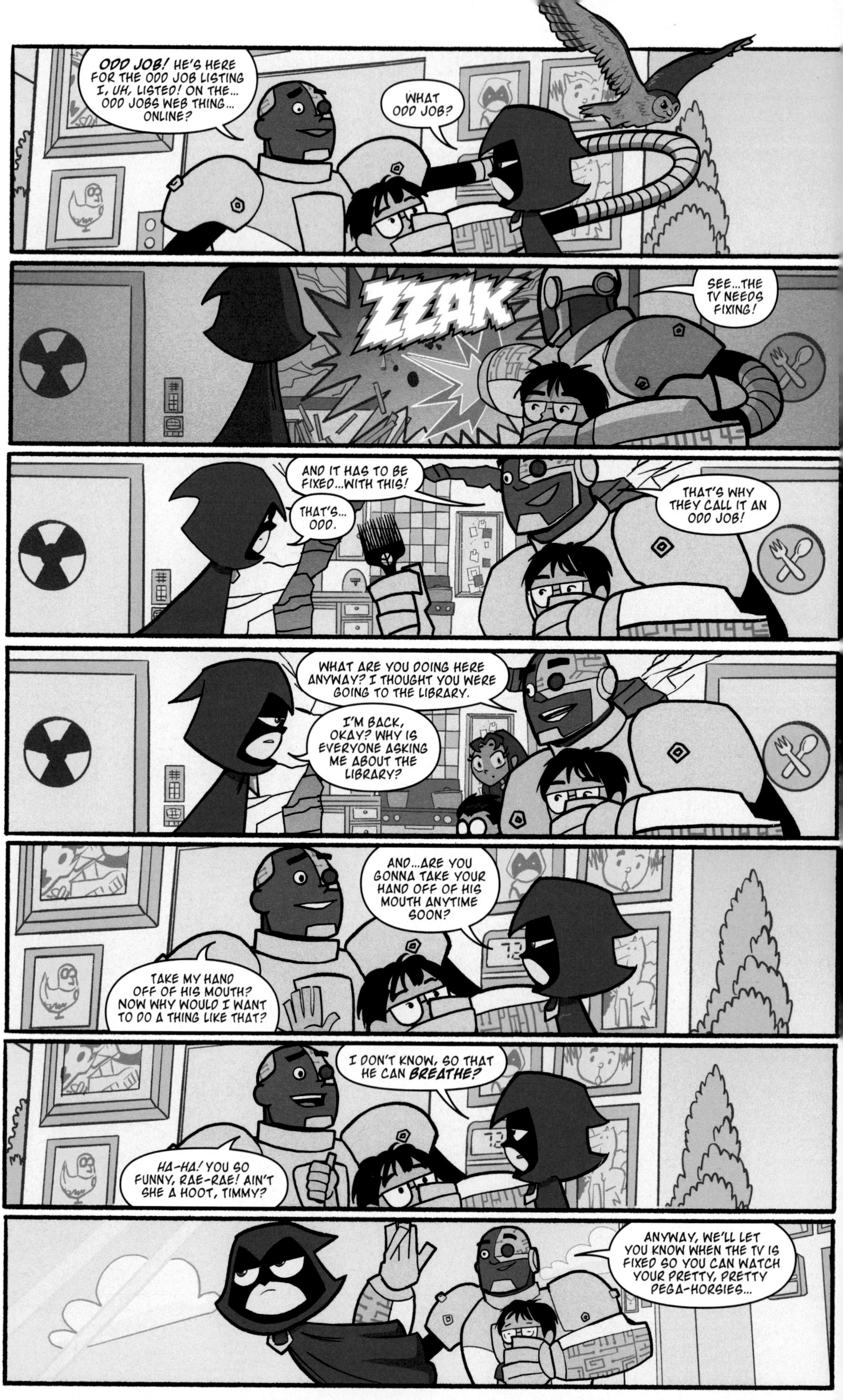
ODD JOB! HE'S HERE FOR THE ODD JOB LISTING I, UH, LISTED! ON THE... ODD JOBS WEB THING... ONLINE?
WHAT ODD JOB?
ZZAK
SEE...THE TV NEEDS FIXING!
AND IT HAS TO BE FIXED...WITH THIS!
THAT'S... ODD.
THAT'S WHY THEY CALL IT AN ODD JOB!
WHAT ARE YOU DOING HERE ANYWAY? I THOUGHT YOU WERE GOING TO THE LIBRARY.
I'M BACK, OKAY? WHY IS EVERYONE ASKING ME ABOUT THE LIBRARY?
AND...ARE YOU GONNA TAKE YOUR HAND OFF OF HIS MOUTH ANYTIME SOON?
TAKE MY HAND OFF OF HIS MOUTH? NOW WHY WOULD I WANT TO DO A THING LIKE THAT?
I DON'T KNOW, SO THAT HE CAN BREATHE?
HA-HA! YOU SO FUNNY, RAE-RAE! AIN'T SHE A HOOT, TIMMY?
ANYWAY, WE'LL LET YOU KNOW WHEN THE TV IS FIXED SO YOU CAN WATCH YOUR PRETTY, PRETTY PEGA-HORSIES...

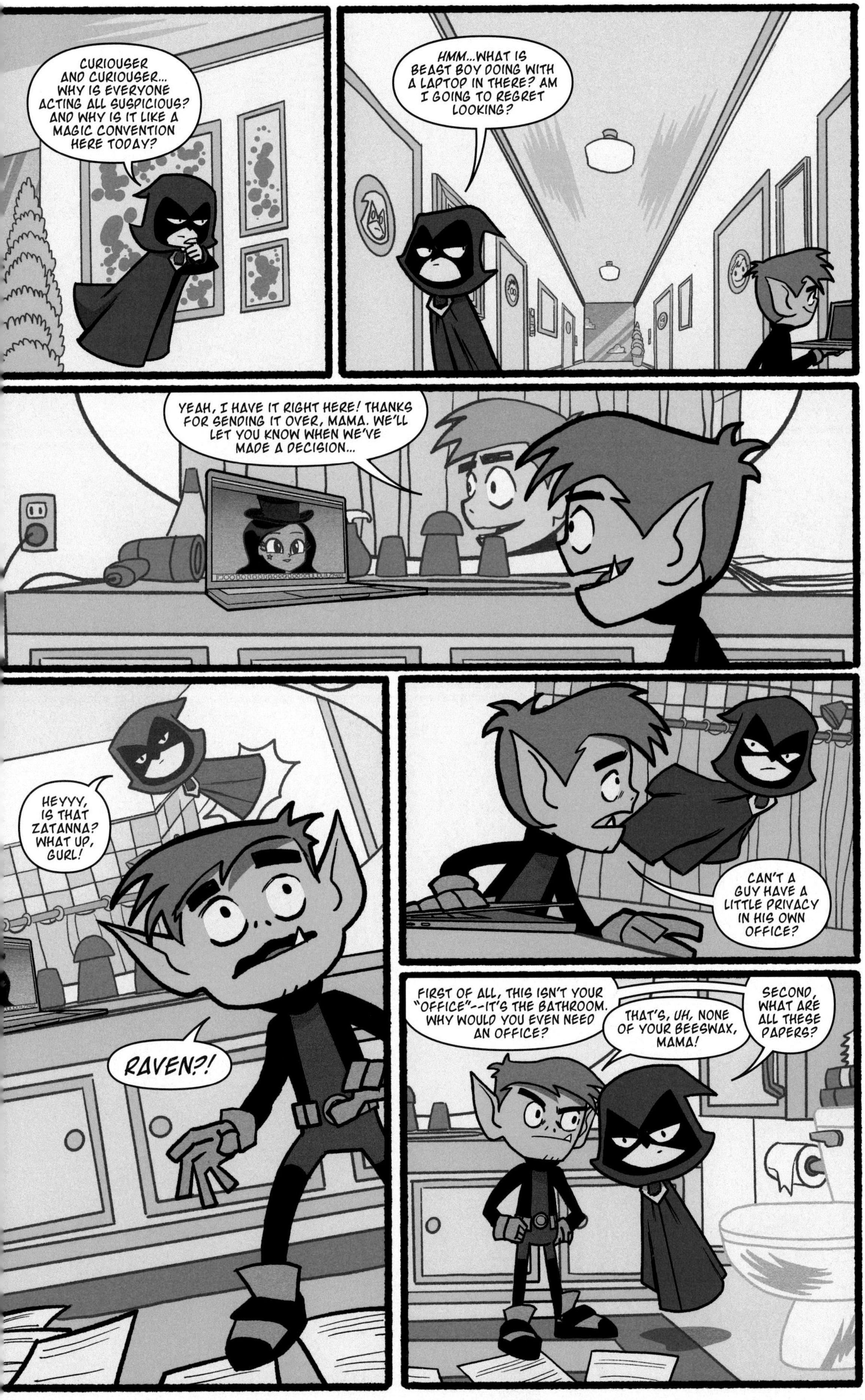
CURIOUSER AND CURIOUSER... WHY IS EVERYONE ACTING ALL SUSPICIOUS? AND WHY IS IT LIKE A MAGIC CONVENTION HERE TODAY?
HMM...WHAT IS BEAST BOY DOING WITH A LAPTOP IN THERE? AM I GOING TO REGRET LOOKING?
YEAH, I HAVE IT RIGHT HERE! THANKS FOR SENDING IT OVER, MAMA. WE'LL LET YOU KNOW WHEN WE'VE MADE A DECISION...
HEYYY, IS THAT ZATANNA? WHAT UP, GURL!
RAVEN?!
CAN'T A GUY HAVE A LITTLE PRIVACY IN HIS OWN OFFICE?
FIRST OF ALL, THIS ISN'T YOUR "OFFICE"--IT'S THE BATHROOM. WHY WOULD YOU EVEN NEED AN OFFICE?
THAT'S, UH, NONE OF YOUR BEESWAX, MAMA!
SECOND, WHAT ARE ALL THESE PAPERS?

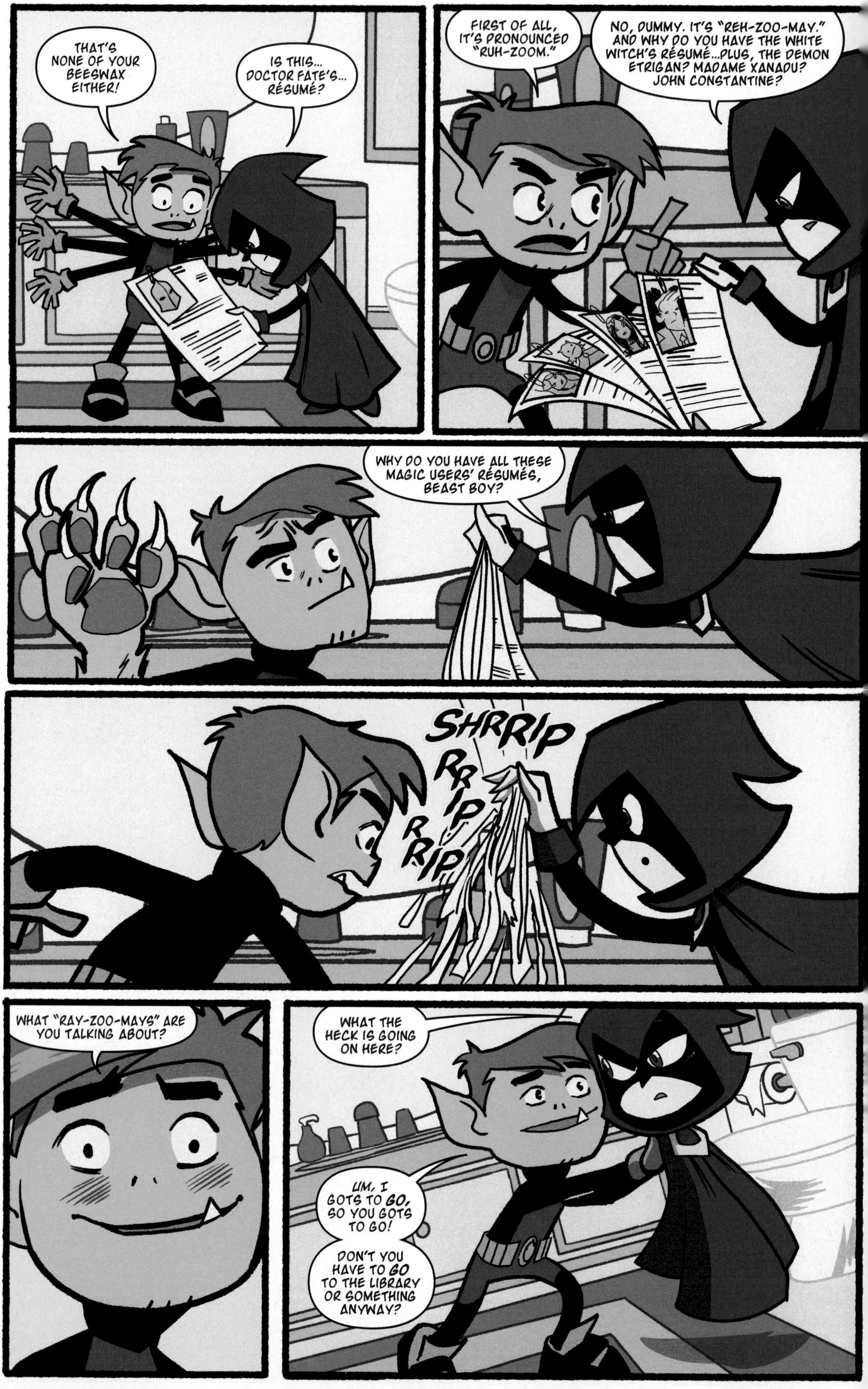

THAT'S NONE OF YOUR BEESWAX EITHER!
IS THIS... DOCTOR FATE'S... RÉSUMÉ?
FIRST OF ALL, IT'S PRONOUNCED "RUH-ZOOM."
NO, DUMMY. IT'S "REH-ZOO-MAY." AND WHY DO YOU HAVE THE WHITE WITCH'S RÉSUMÉ...PLUS, THE DEMON ETRIGAN? MADAME XANADU? JOHN CONSTANTINE?
WHY DO YOU HAVE ALL THESE MAGIC USERS' RÉSUMÉS, BEAST BOY?
SHRRIP
RRIP!
RRIP
WHAT "RAY-ZOO-MAYS" ARE YOU TALKING ABOUT?
WHAT THE HECK IS GOING ON HERE?
UM, I GOTS TO GO, SO YOU GOTS TO GO!
DON'T YOU HAVE TO GO TO THE LIBRARY OR SOMETHING ANYWAY?

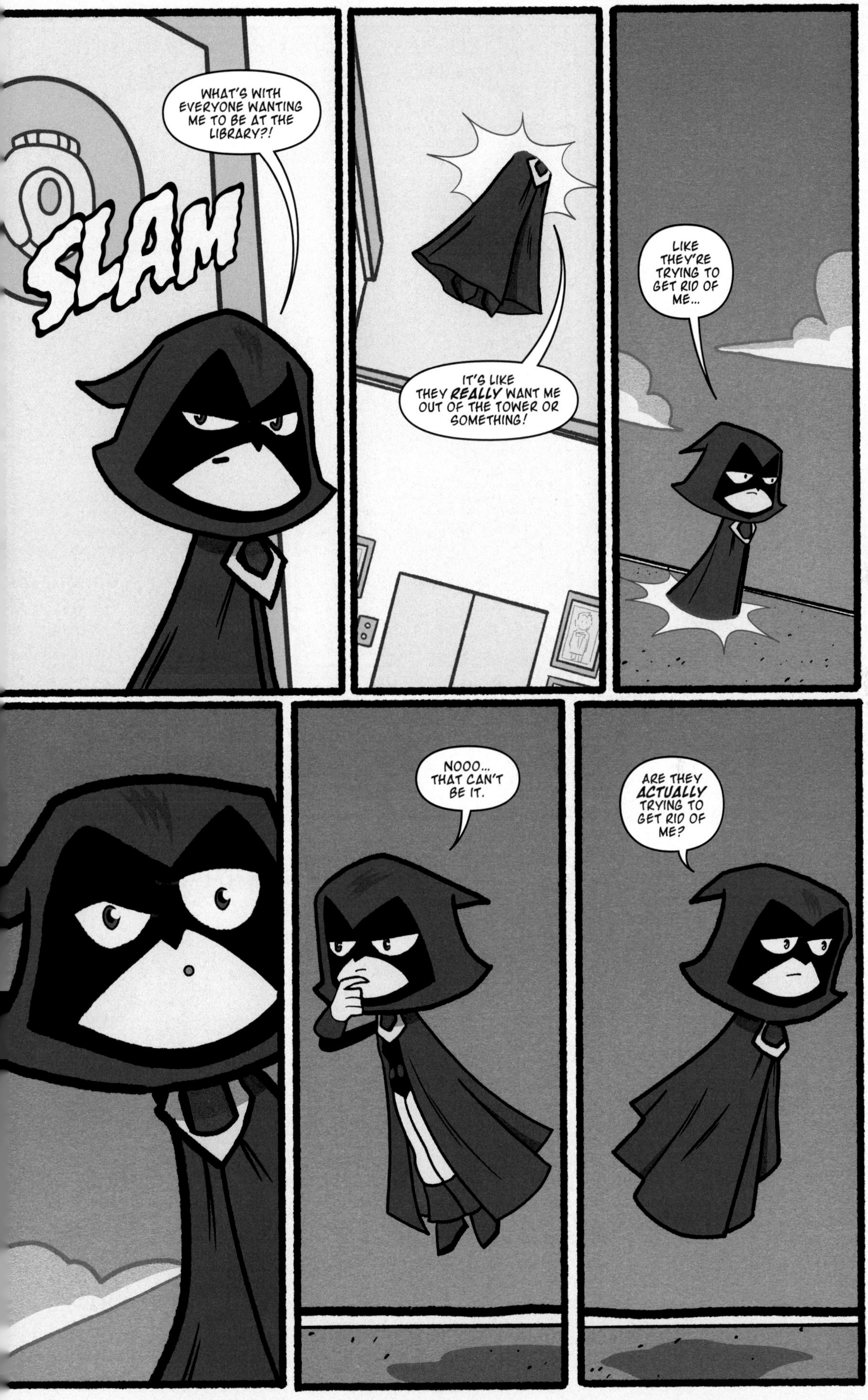
WHAT'S WITH EVERYONE WANTING ME TO BE AT THE LIBRARY?!
SLAM
IT'S LIKE THEY *REALLY* WANT ME OUT OF THE TOWER OR SOMETHING!
LIKE THEY'RE TRYING TO GET RID OF ME...
NOOO... THAT CAN'T BE IT.
ARE THEY *ACTUALLY* TRYING TO GET RID OF ME?

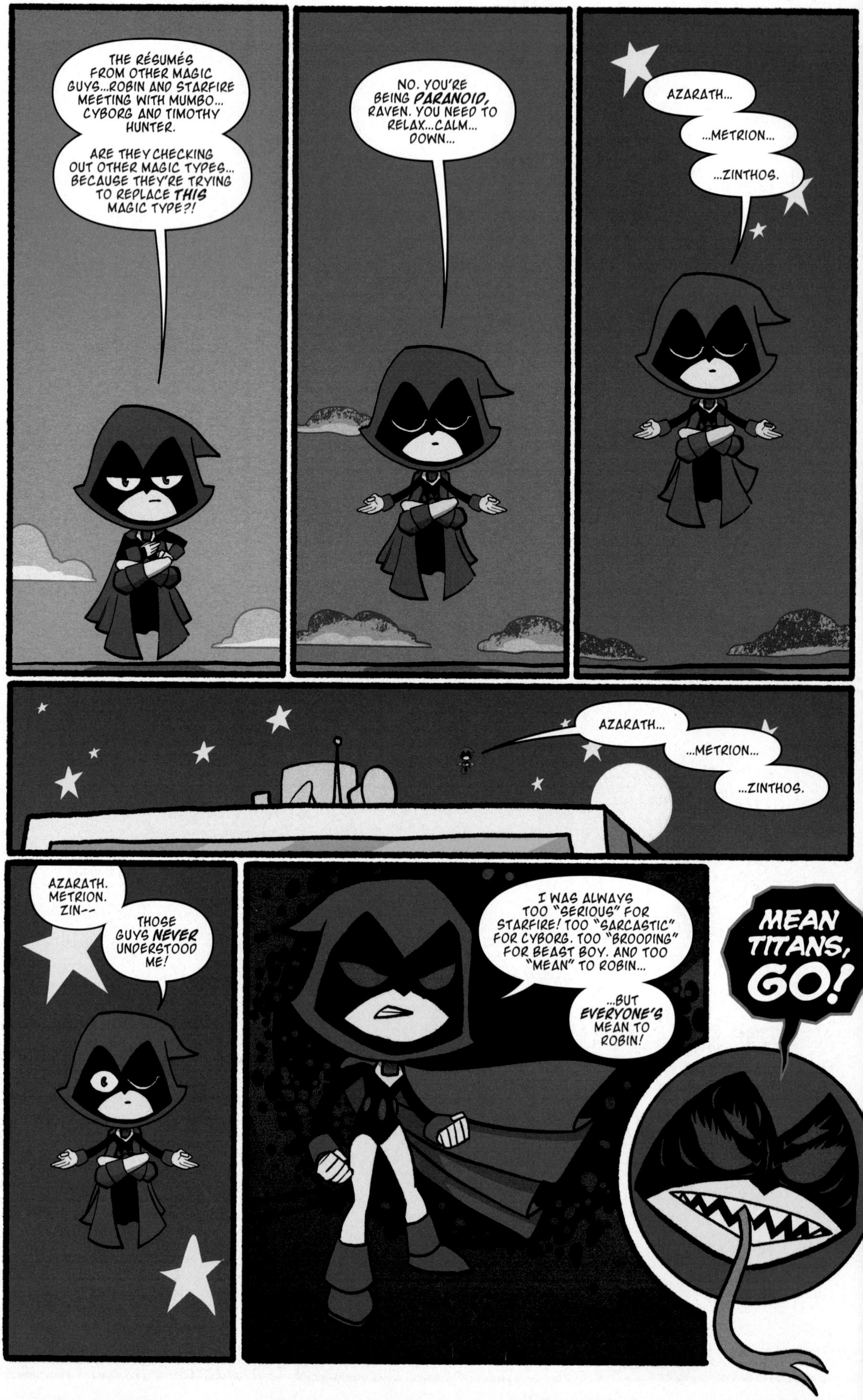
THE RÉSUMÉS FROM OTHER MAGIC GUYS...ROBIN AND STARFIRE MEETING WITH MUMBO... CYBORG AND TIMOTHY HUNTER.
ARE THEY CHECKING OUT OTHER MAGIC TYPES... BECAUSE THEY'RE TRYING TO REPLACE THIS MAGIC TYPE?!
NO. YOU'RE BEING PARANOID, RAVEN. YOU NEED TO RELAX...CALM... DOWN...
AZARATH...
...METRION...
...ZINTHOS.
AZARATH...
...METRION...
...ZINTHOS.
AZARATH. METRION. ZIN--
THOSE GUYS NEVER UNDERSTOOD ME!
I WAS ALWAYS TOO "SERIOUS" FOR STARFIRE! TOO "SARCASTIC" FOR CYBORG. TOO "BROODING" FOR BEAST BOY. AND TOO "MEAN" TO ROBIN...
...BUT EVERYONE'S MEAN TO ROBIN!
MEAN TITANS, GO!

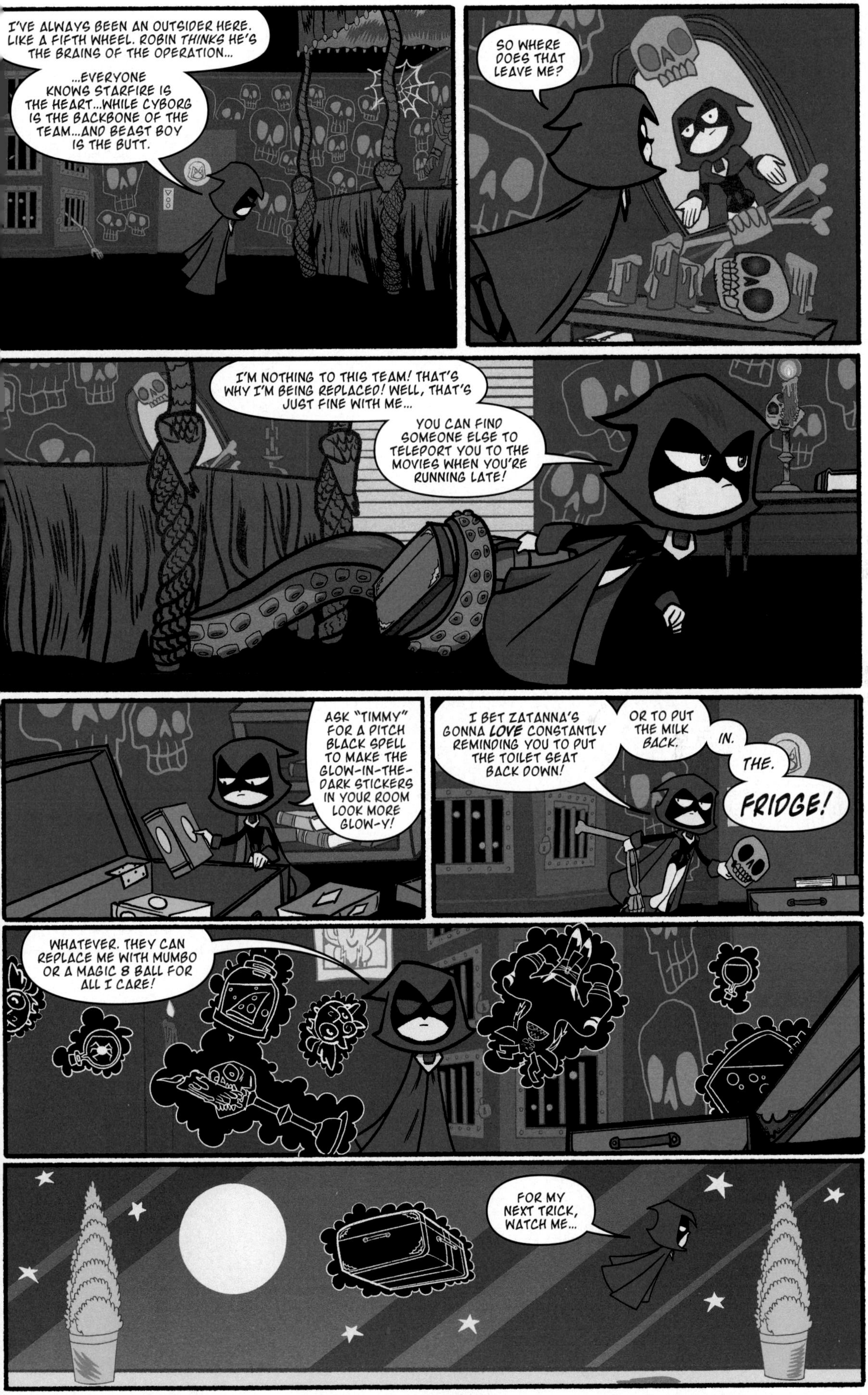

I'VE ALWAYS BEEN AN OUTSIDER HERE. LIKE A FIFTH WHEEL. ROBIN *THINKS* HE'S THE BRAINS OF THE OPERATION...
...EVERYONE KNOWS STARFIRE IS THE HEART...WHILE CYBORG IS THE BACKBONE OF THE TEAM...AND BEAST BOY IS THE BUTT.
SO WHERE DOES THAT LEAVE ME?
I'M NOTHING TO THIS TEAM! THAT'S WHY I'M BEING REPLACED! WELL, THAT'S JUST FINE WITH ME...
YOU CAN FIND SOMEONE ELSE TO TELEPORT YOU TO THE MOVIES WHEN YOU'RE RUNNING LATE!
ASK "TIMMY" FOR A PITCH BLACK SPELL TO MAKE THE GLOW-IN-THE-DARK STICKERS IN YOUR ROOM LOOK MORE GLOW-Y!
I BET ZATANNA'S GONNA **LOVE** CONSTANTLY REMINDING YOU TO PUT THE TOILET SEAT BACK DOWN!
OR TO PUT THE MILK BACK.
IN.
THE.
FRIDGE!
WHATEVER. THEY CAN REPLACE ME WITH MUMBO OR A MAGIC 8 BALL FOR ALL I CARE!
FOR MY NEXT TRICK, WATCH ME...

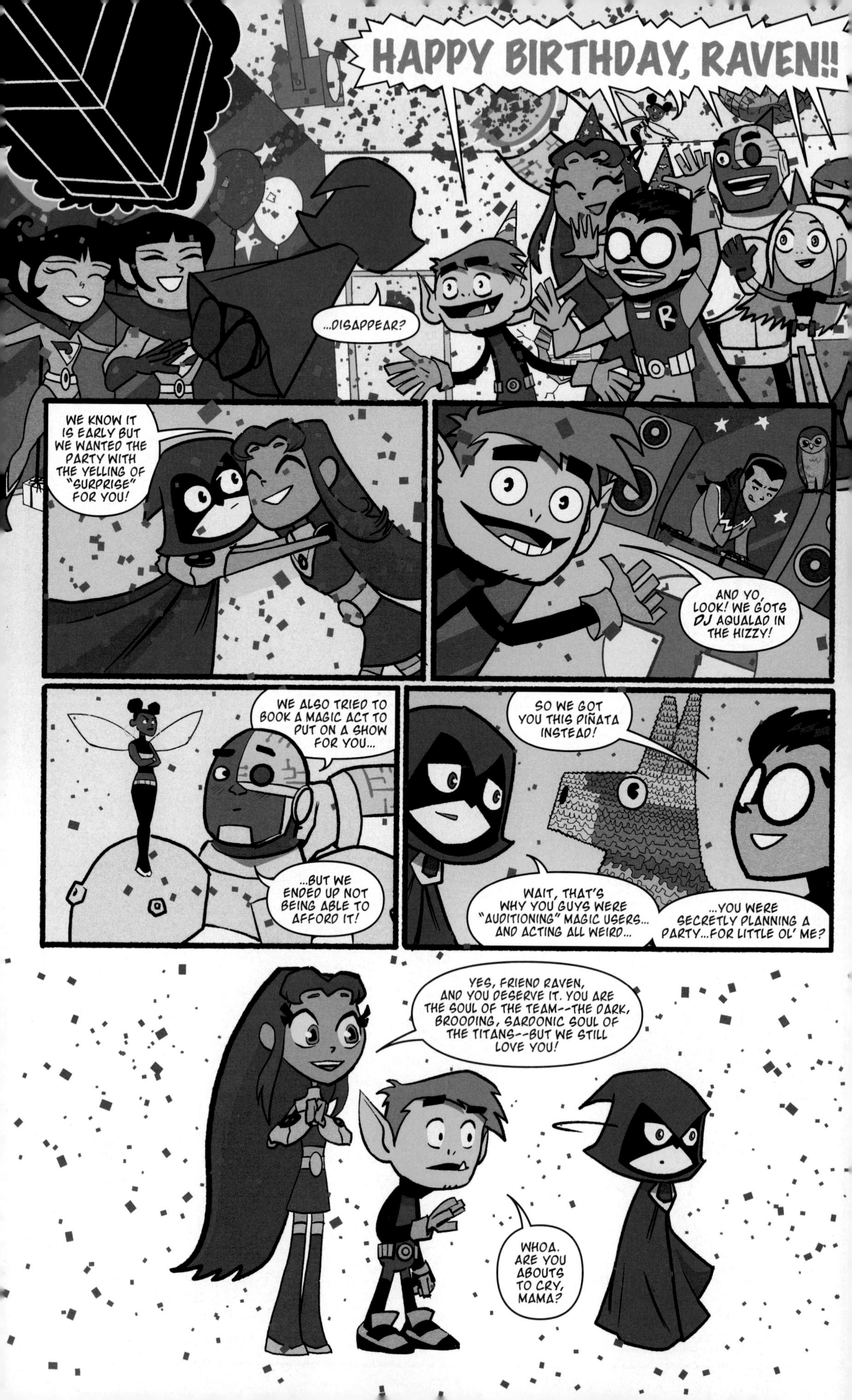
HAPPY BIRTHDAY, RAVEN!!
...DISAPPEAR?
WE KNOW IT IS EARLY BUT WE WANTED THE PARTY WITH THE YELLING OF "SURPRISE" FOR YOU!
AND YO, LOOK! WE GOTS DJ AQUALAD IN THE HIZZY!
WE ALSO TRIED TO BOOK A MAGIC ACT TO PUT ON A SHOW FOR YOU...
...BUT WE ENDED UP NOT BEING ABLE TO AFFORD IT!
SO WE GOT YOU THIS PIÑATA INSTEAD!
WAIT, THAT'S WHY YOU GUYS WERE "AUDITIONING" MAGIC USERS... AND ACTING ALL WEIRD...
...YOU WERE SECRETLY PLANNING A PARTY...FOR LITTLE OL' ME?
YES, FRIEND RAVEN, AND YOU DESERVE IT. YOU ARE THE SOUL OF THE TEAM--THE DARK, BROODING, SARDONIC SOUL OF THE TITANS--BUT WE STILL LOVE YOU!
WHOA. ARE YOU ABOUTS TO CRY, MAMA?

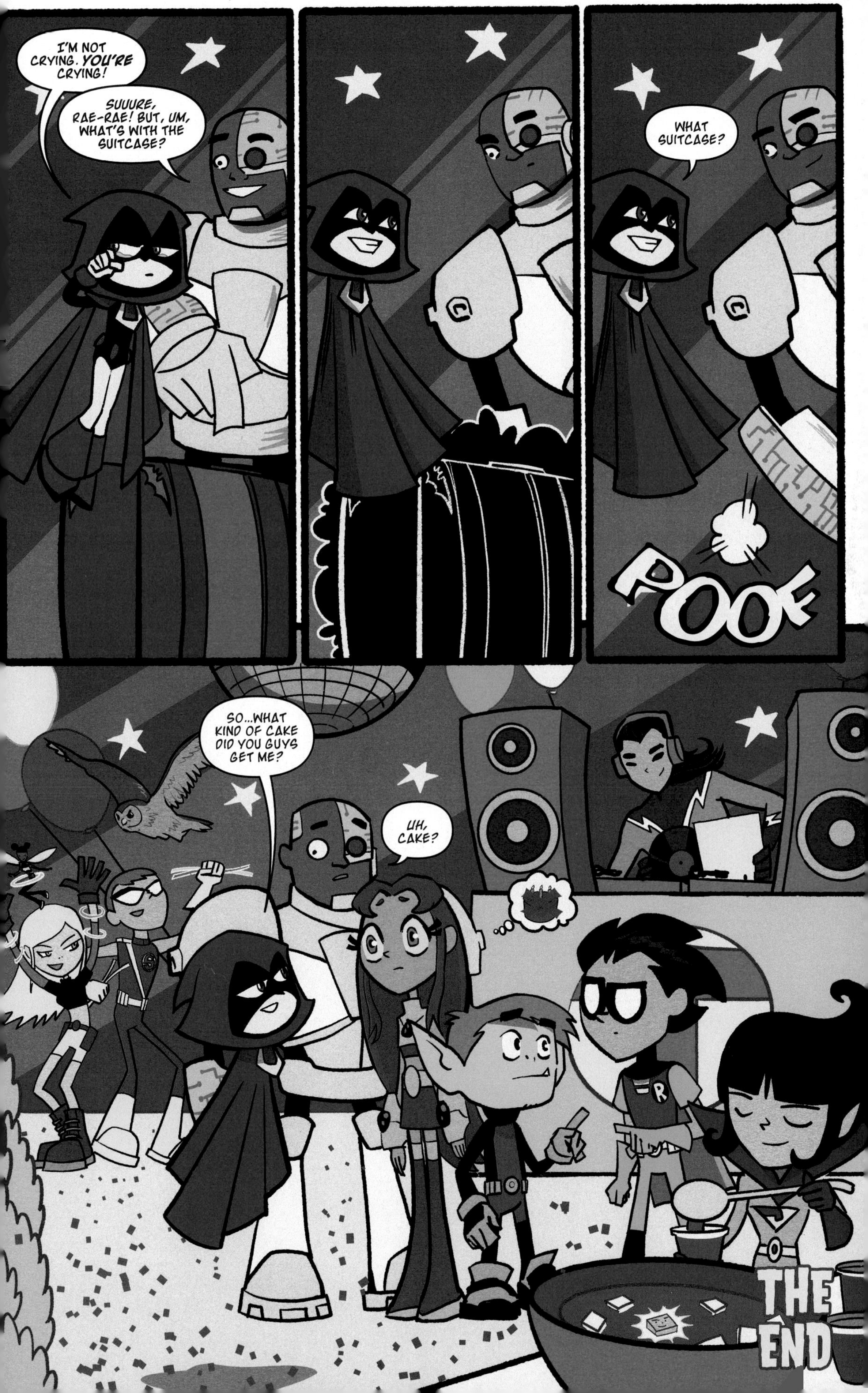
I'M NOT CRYING. YOU'RE CRYING!
SUUURE, RAE-RAE! BUT, UM, WHAT'S WITH THE SUITCASE?
WHAT SUITCASE?
POOF
SO...WHAT KIND OF CAKE DID YOU GUYS GET ME?
UH, CAKE?
THE END

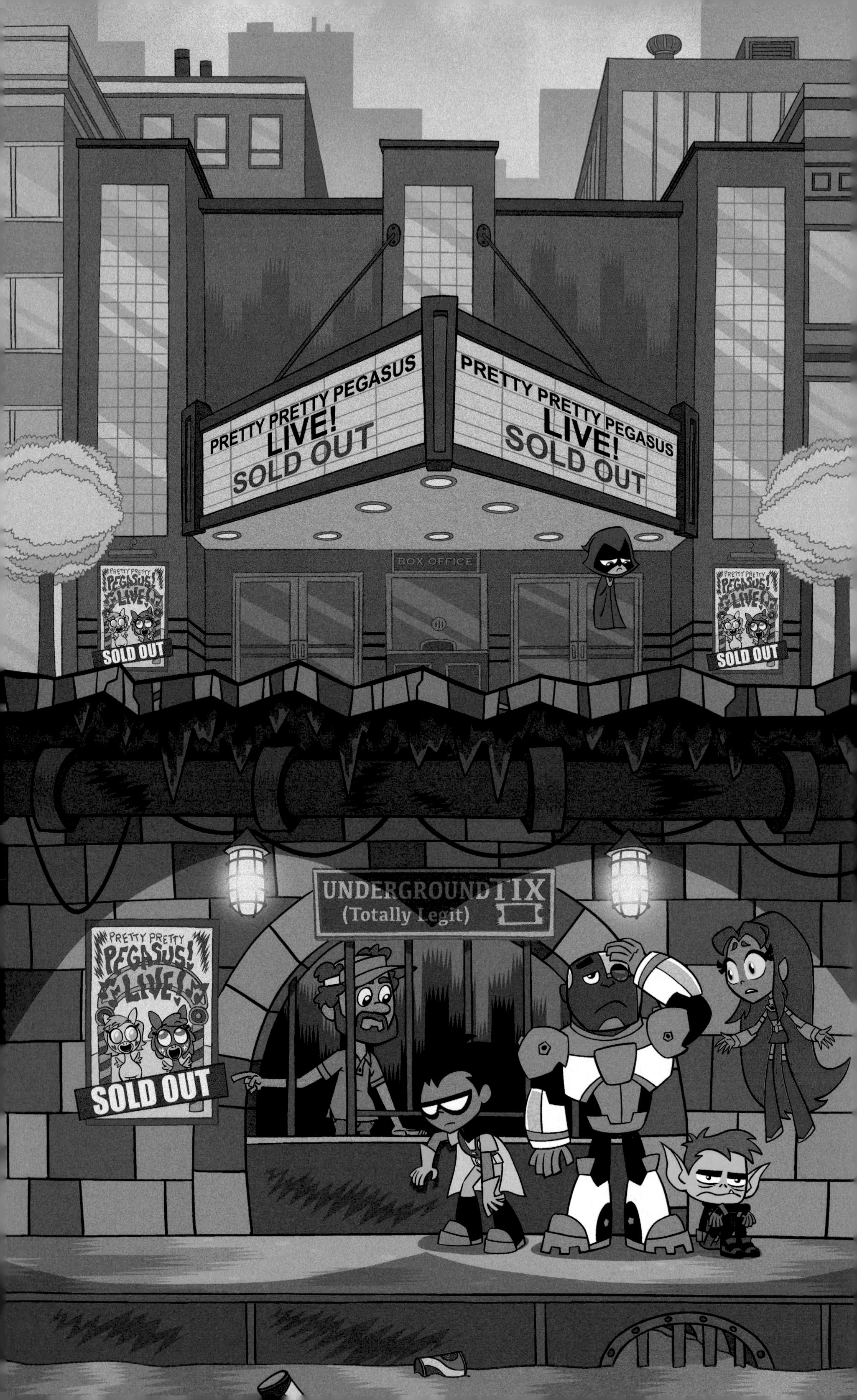
PRETTY PRETTY PEGASUS
LIVE!
SOLD OUT
PRETTY PRETTY PEGASUS
LIVE!
SOLD OUT
BOX OFFICE
PRETTY PRETTY PEGASUS! LIVE!
SOLD OUT
PRETTY PRETTY PEGASUS! LIVE!
SOLD OUT
UNDERGROUND TIX
(Totally Legit)
PRETTY PRETTY PEGASUS! LIVE!
SOLD OUT

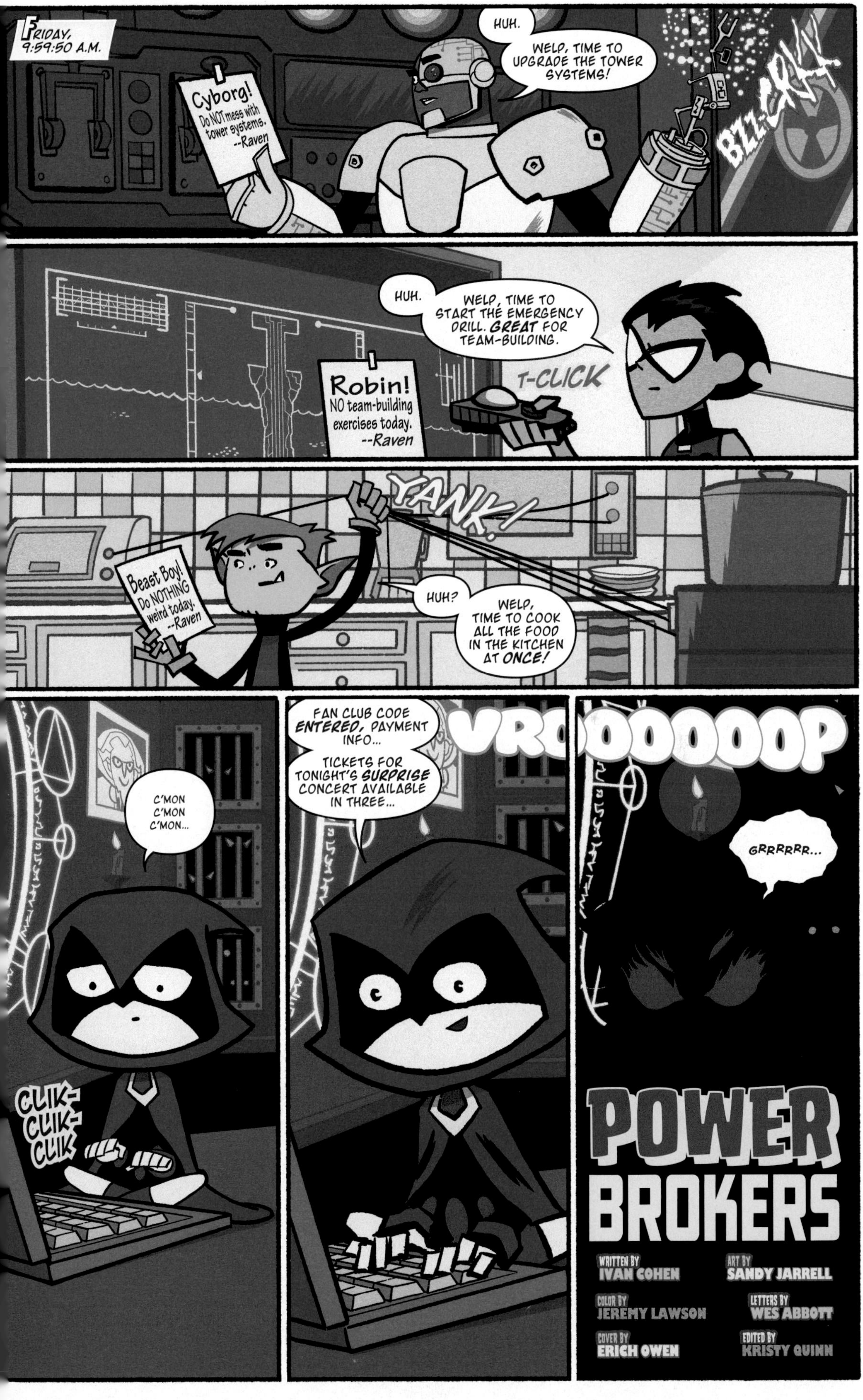
Friday, 9:59:50 A.M.
Cyborg! Do NOT mess with tower systems. --Raven
HUH.
WELP, TIME TO UPGRADE THE TOWER SYSTEMS!
BZZ-CRK!
HUH.
WELP, TIME TO START THE EMERGENCY DRILL. GREAT FOR TEAM-BUILDING.
Robin! NO team-building exercises today. --Raven
T-CLICK
YANK!
Beast Boy! Do NOTHING weird today. --Raven
HUH?
WELP, TIME TO COOK ALL THE FOOD IN THE KITCHEN AT ONCE!
C'MON C'MON C'MON...
CLIK-CLIK-CLIK
FAN CLUB CODE ENTERED, PAYMENT INFO...
TICKETS FOR TONIGHT'S SURPRISE CONCERT AVAILABLE IN THREE...
VROOOOOOOP
GRRRRRR...
POWER BROKERS
WRITTEN BY IVAN COHEN
ART BY SANDY JARRELL
COLOR BY JEREMY LAWSON
LETTERS BY WES ABBOTT
COVER BY ERICH OWEN
EDITED BY KRISTY QUINN

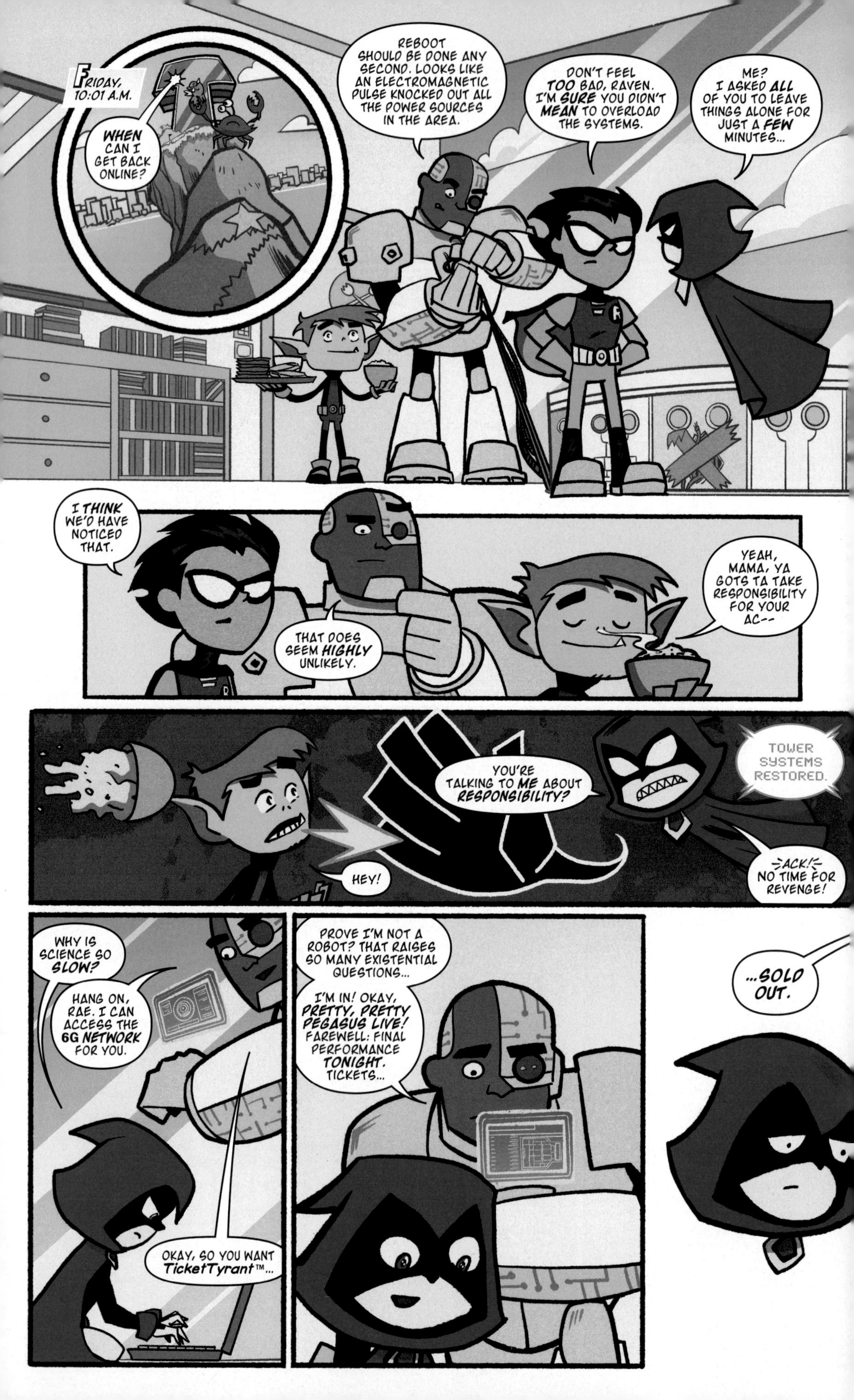
FRIDAY, 10:01 A.M.
WHEN CAN I GET BACK ONLINE?
REBOOT SHOULD BE DONE ANY SECOND. LOOKS LIKE AN ELECTROMAGNETIC PULSE KNOCKED OUT ALL THE POWER SOURCES IN THE AREA.
DON'T FEEL TOO BAD, RAVEN. I'M SURE YOU DIDN'T MEAN TO OVERLOAD THE SYSTEMS.
ME? I ASKED ALL OF YOU TO LEAVE THINGS ALONE FOR JUST A FEW MINUTES...
I THINK WE'D HAVE NOTICED THAT.
THAT DOES SEEM HIGHLY UNLIKELY.
YEAH, MAMA, YA GOTS TA TAKE RESPONSIBILITY FOR YOUR AC--
YOU'RE TALKING TO ME ABOUT RESPONSIBILITY?
TOWER SYSTEMS RESTORED.
HEY!
ACK! NO TIME FOR REVENGE!
WHY IS SCIENCE SO SLOW?
HANG ON, RAE. I CAN ACCESS THE 6G NETWORK FOR YOU.
OKAY, SO YOU WANT TicketTyrant™...
PROVE I'M NOT A ROBOT? THAT RAISES SO MANY EXISTENTIAL QUESTIONS...
I'M IN! OKAY, PRETTY, PRETTY PEGASUS LIVE! FAREWELL: FINAL PERFORMANCE TONIGHT. TICKETS...
...SOLD OUT.

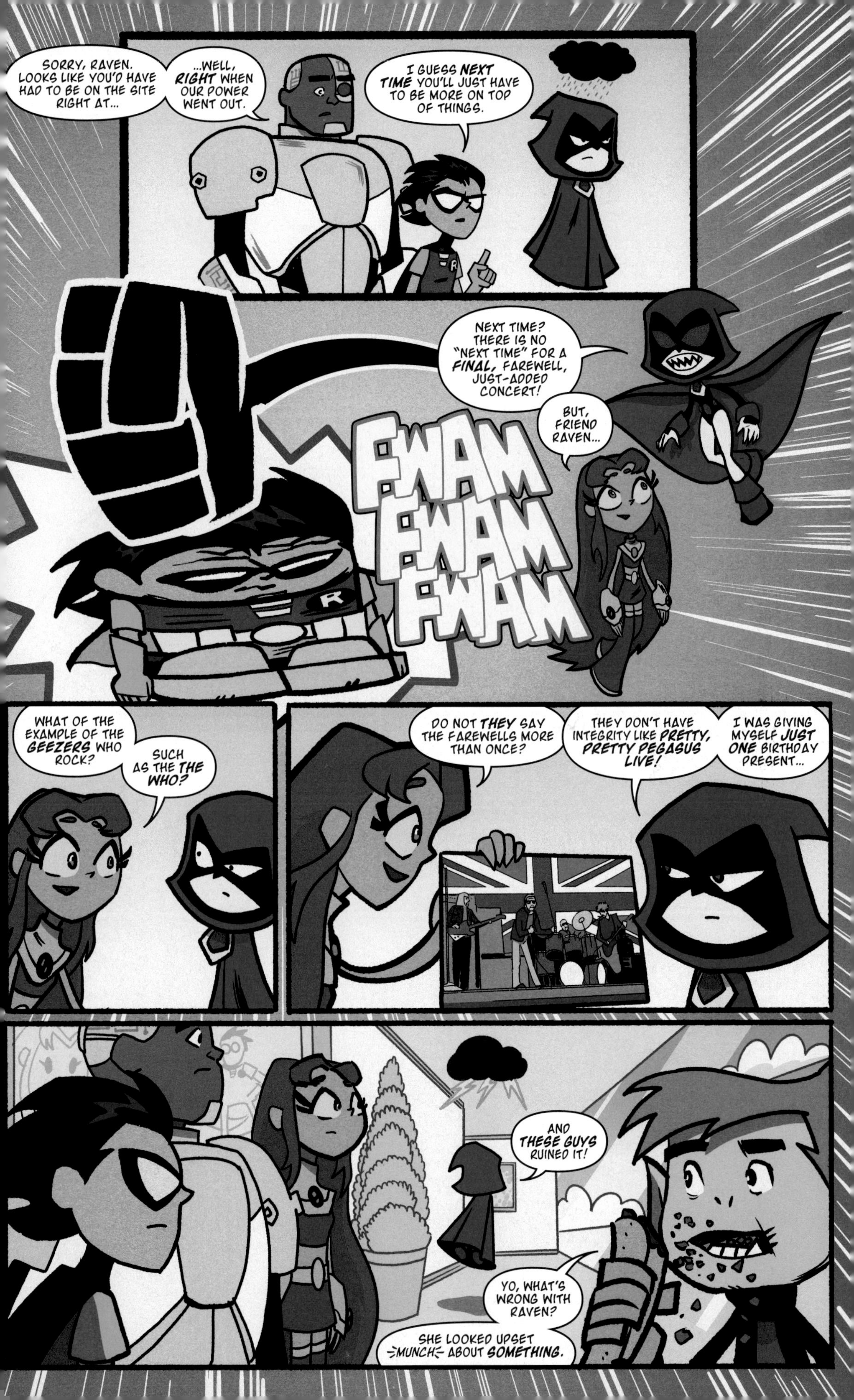
SORRY, RAVEN. LOOKS LIKE YOU'D HAVE HAD TO BE ON THE SITE RIGHT AT...
...WELL, RIGHT WHEN OUR POWER WENT OUT.
I GUESS NEXT TIME YOU'LL JUST HAVE TO BE MORE ON TOP OF THINGS.
NEXT TIME? THERE IS NO "NEXT TIME" FOR A FINAL, FAREWELL, JUST-ADDED CONCERT!
BUT, FRIEND RAVEN...
FWAM FWAM FWAM
WHAT OF THE EXAMPLE OF THE GEEZERS WHO ROCK?
SUCH AS THE THE WHO?
DO NOT THEY SAY THE FAREWELLS MORE THAN ONCE?
THEY DON'T HAVE INTEGRITY LIKE PRETTY, PRETTY PEGASUS LIVE!
I WAS GIVING MYSELF JUST ONE BIRTHDAY PRESENT...
AND THESE GUYS RUINED IT!
YO, WHAT'S WRONG WITH RAVEN?
SHE LOOKED UPSET =MUNCH= ABOUT SOMETHING.

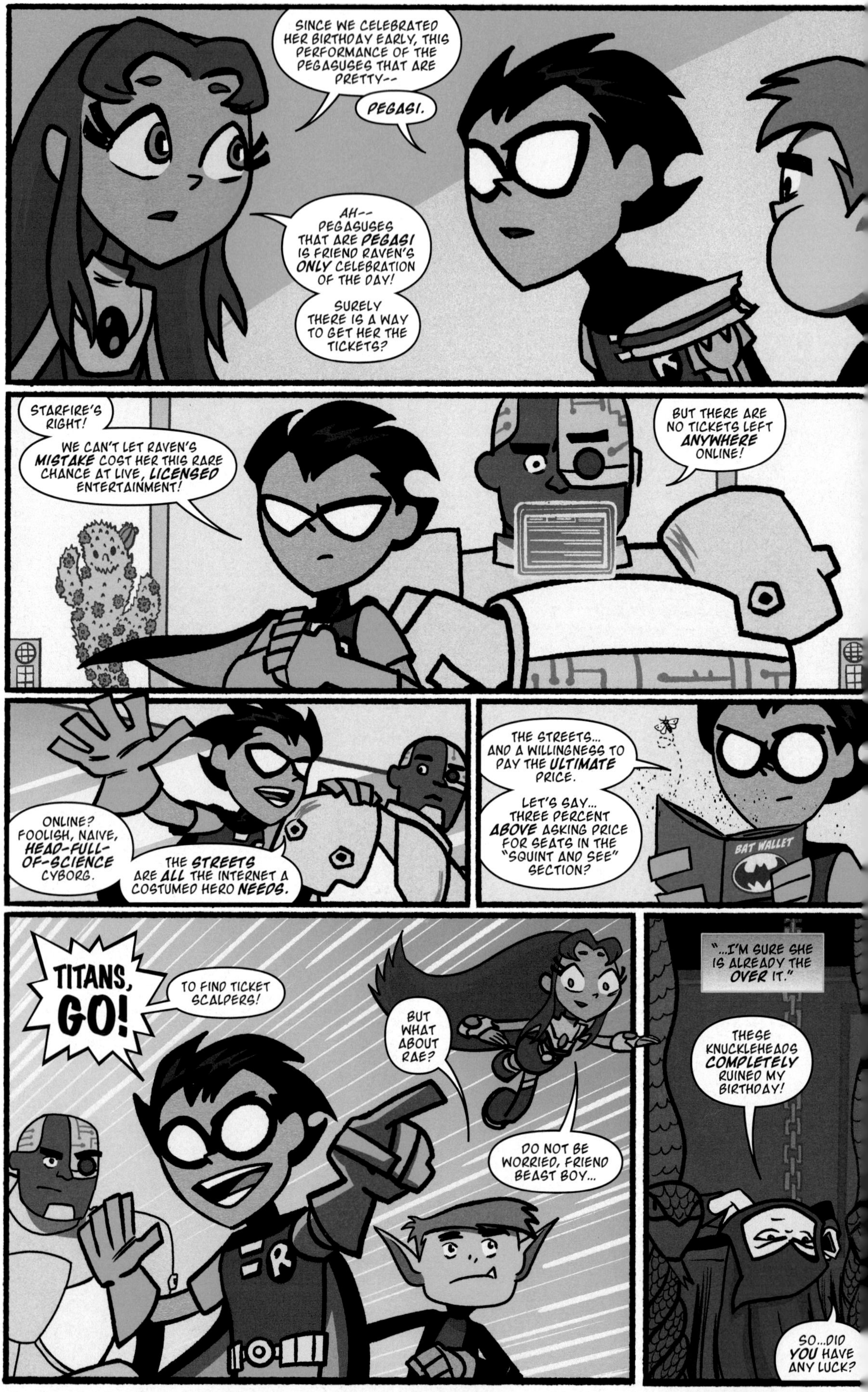

SINCE WE CELEBRATED HER BIRTHDAY EARLY, THIS PERFORMANCE OF THE PEGASUSES THAT ARE PRETTY--
PEGASI.
AH-- PEGASUSES THAT ARE PEGASI IS FRIEND RAVEN'S ONLY CELEBRATION OF THE DAY!
SURELY THERE IS A WAY TO GET HER THE TICKETS?
STARFIRE'S RIGHT!
WE CAN'T LET RAVEN'S MISTAKE COST HER THIS RARE CHANCE AT LIVE, LICENSED ENTERTAINMENT!
BUT THERE ARE NO TICKETS LEFT ANYWHERE ONLINE!
ONLINE? FOOLISH, NAIVE, HEAD-FULL-OF-SCIENCE CYBORG.
THE STREETS ARE ALL THE INTERNET A COSTUMED HERO NEEDS.
THE STREETS... AND A WILLINGNESS TO PAY THE ULTIMATE PRICE.
LET'S SAY... THREE PERCENT ABOVE ASKING PRICE FOR SEATS IN THE "SQUINT AND SEE" SECTION?
BAT WALLET
TITANS, GO!
TO FIND TICKET SCALPERS!
BUT WHAT ABOUT RAE?
DO NOT BE WORRIED, FRIEND BEAST BOY...
"...I'M SURE SHE IS ALREADY THE OVER IT."
THESE KNUCKLEHEADS COMPLETELY RUINED MY BIRTHDAY!
SO...DID YOU HAVE ANY LUCK?

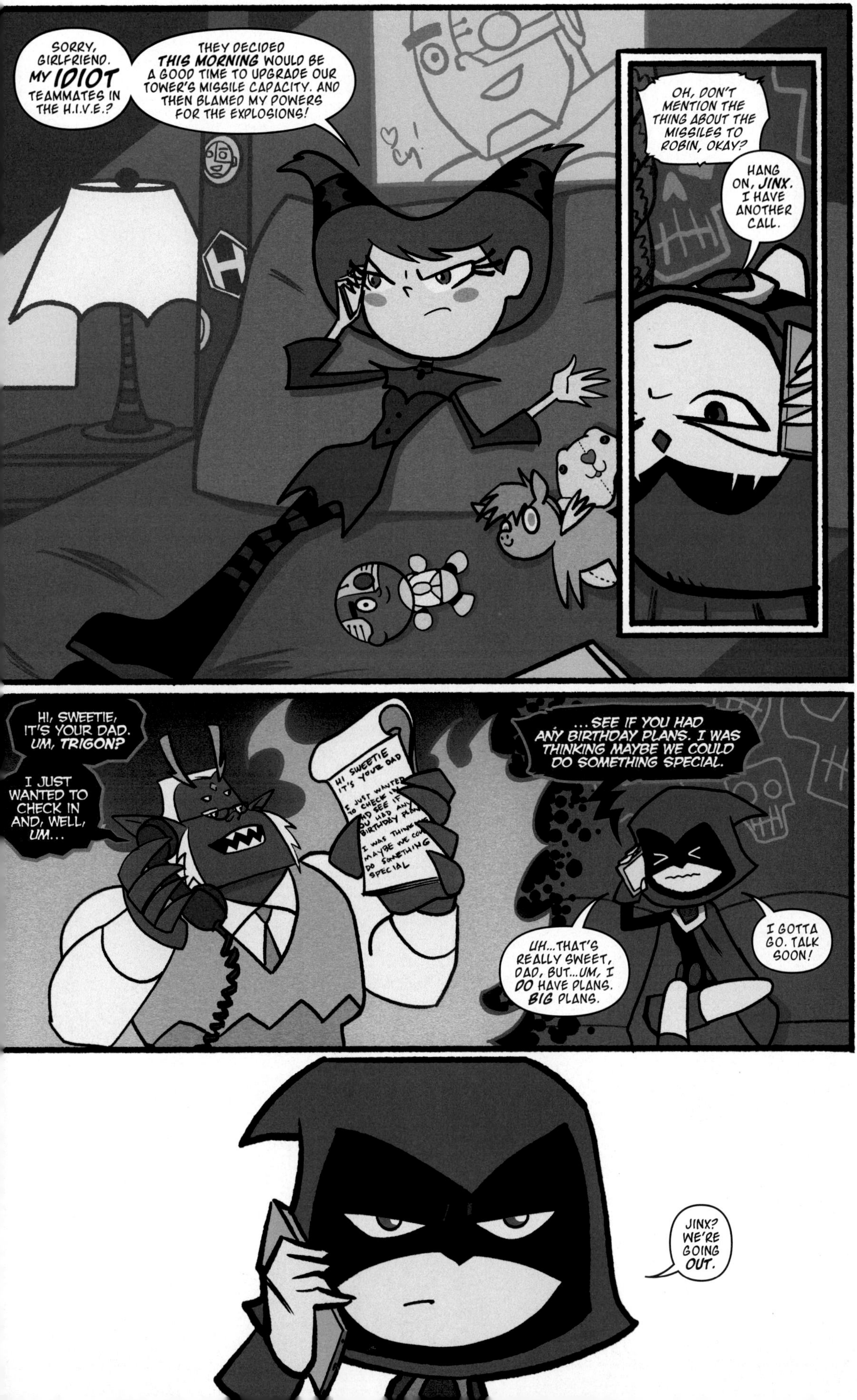
SORRY, GIRLFRIEND. MY IDIOT TEAMMATES IN THE H.I.V.E.?
THEY DECIDED THIS MORNING WOULD BE A GOOD TIME TO UPGRADE OUR TOWER'S MISSILE CAPACITY. AND THEN BLAMED MY POWERS FOR THE EXPLOSIONS!
OH, DON'T MENTION THE THING ABOUT THE MISSILES TO ROBIN, OKAY?
HANG ON, JINX. I HAVE ANOTHER CALL.
HI, SWEETIE, IT'S YOUR DAD. UM, TRIGON?
I JUST WANTED TO CHECK IN AND, WELL, UM...
HI SWEETIE IT'S YOUR DAD I JUST WANTED TO CHECK IN AND SEE IF YOU HAD ANY BIRTHDAY PLANS I WAS THINKING MAYBE WE COULD DO SOMETHING SPECIAL
...SEE IF YOU HAD ANY BIRTHDAY PLANS. I WAS THINKING MAYBE WE COULD DO SOMETHING SPECIAL.
UH...THAT'S REALLY SWEET, DAD, BUT...UM, I DO HAVE PLANS. BIG PLANS.
I GOTTA GO. TALK SOON!
JINX? WE'RE GOING OUT.

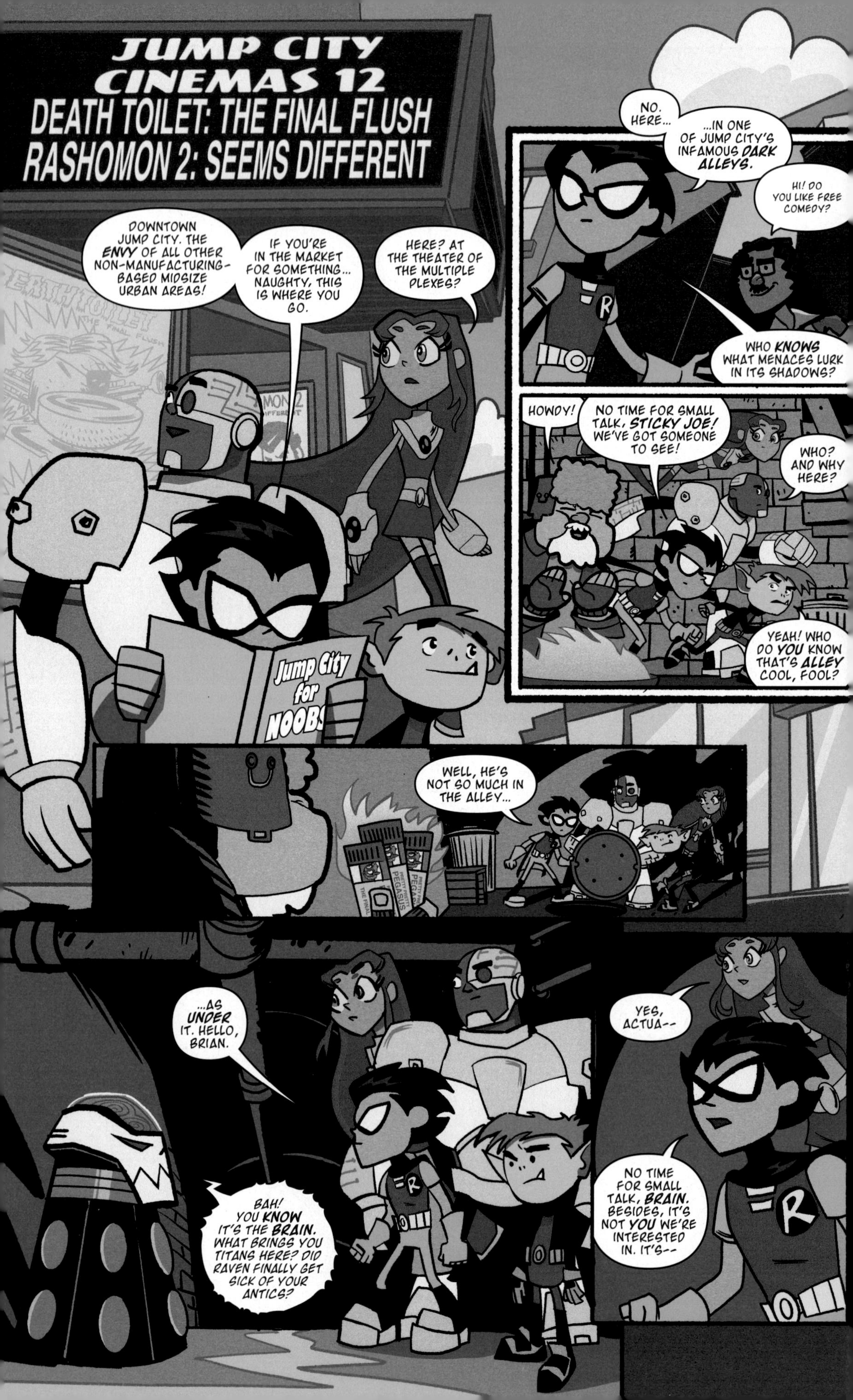
JUMP CITY CINEMAS 12
DEATH TOILET: THE FINAL FLUSH
RASHOMON 2: SEEMS DIFFERENT
DOWNTOWN JUMP CITY. THE ENVY OF ALL OTHER NON-MANUFACTURING-BASED MIDSIZE URBAN AREAS!
IF YOU'RE IN THE MARKET FOR SOMETHING... NAUGHTY, THIS IS WHERE YOU GO.
HERE? AT THE THEATER OF THE MULTIPLE PLEXES?
Jump City for NOOBS
NO. HERE...
...IN ONE OF JUMP CITY'S INFAMOUS DARK ALLEYS.
HI! DO YOU LIKE FREE COMEDY?
WHO KNOWS WHAT MENACES LURK IN ITS SHADOWS?
HOWDY!
NO TIME FOR SMALL TALK, STICKY JOE! WE'VE GOT SOMEONE TO SEE!
WHO? AND WHY HERE?
YEAH! WHO DO YOU KNOW THAT'S ALLEY COOL, FOOL?
WELL, HE'S NOT SO MUCH IN THE ALLEY...
PEGASUS
...AS UNDER IT. HELLO, BRIAN.
BAH! YOU KNOW IT'S THE BRAIN. WHAT BRINGS YOU TITANS HERE? DID RAVEN FINALLY GET SICK OF YOUR ANTICS?
YES, ACTUA--
NO TIME FOR SMALL TALK, BRAIN. BESIDES, IT'S NOT YOU WE'RE INTERESTED IN. IT'S--

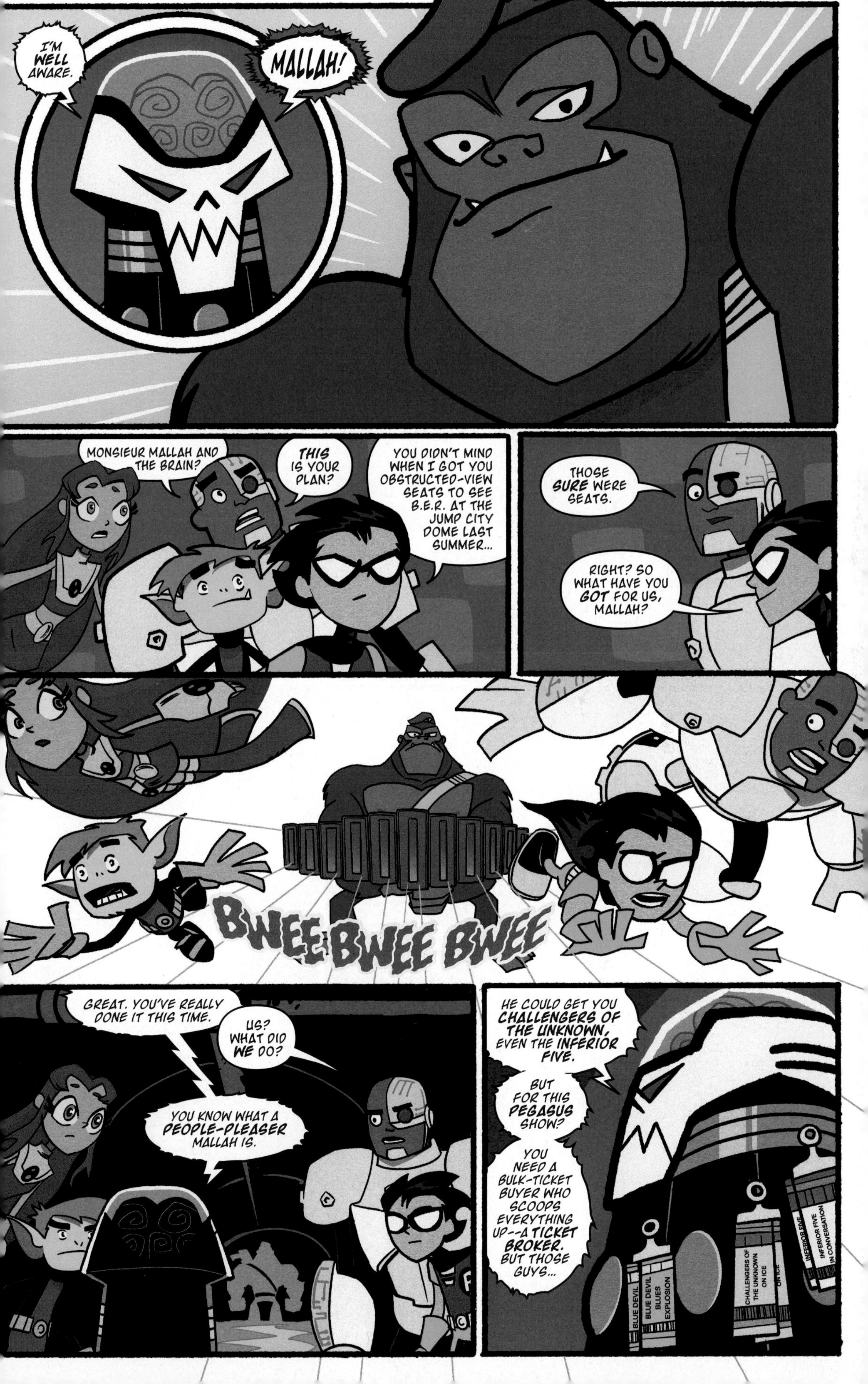

I'M WELL AWARE.
MALLAH!
MONSIEUR MALLAH AND THE BRAIN?
THIS IS YOUR PLAN?
YOU DIDN'T MIND WHEN I GOT YOU OBSTRUCTED-VIEW SEATS TO SEE B.E.R. AT THE JUMP CITY DOME LAST SUMMER...
THOSE SURE WERE SEATS.
RIGHT? SO WHAT HAVE YOU GOT FOR US, MALLAH?
BWEE BWEE BWEE
GREAT. YOU'VE REALLY DONE IT THIS TIME.
US? WHAT DID WE DO?
YOU KNOW WHAT A PEOPLE-PLEASER MALLAH IS.
HE COULD GET YOU CHALLENGERS OF THE UNKNOWN, EVEN THE INFERIOR FIVE.
BUT FOR THIS PEGASUS SHOW?
YOU NEED A BULK-TICKET BUYER WHO SCOOPS EVERYTHING UP--A TICKET BROKER. BUT THOSE GUYS...
BLUE DEVIL
BLUE DEVIL BLUES EXPLOSION
CHALLENGERS OF THE UNKNOWN ON ICE
ON ICE
INFERIOR FIVE
INFERIOR FIVE IN CONVERSATION

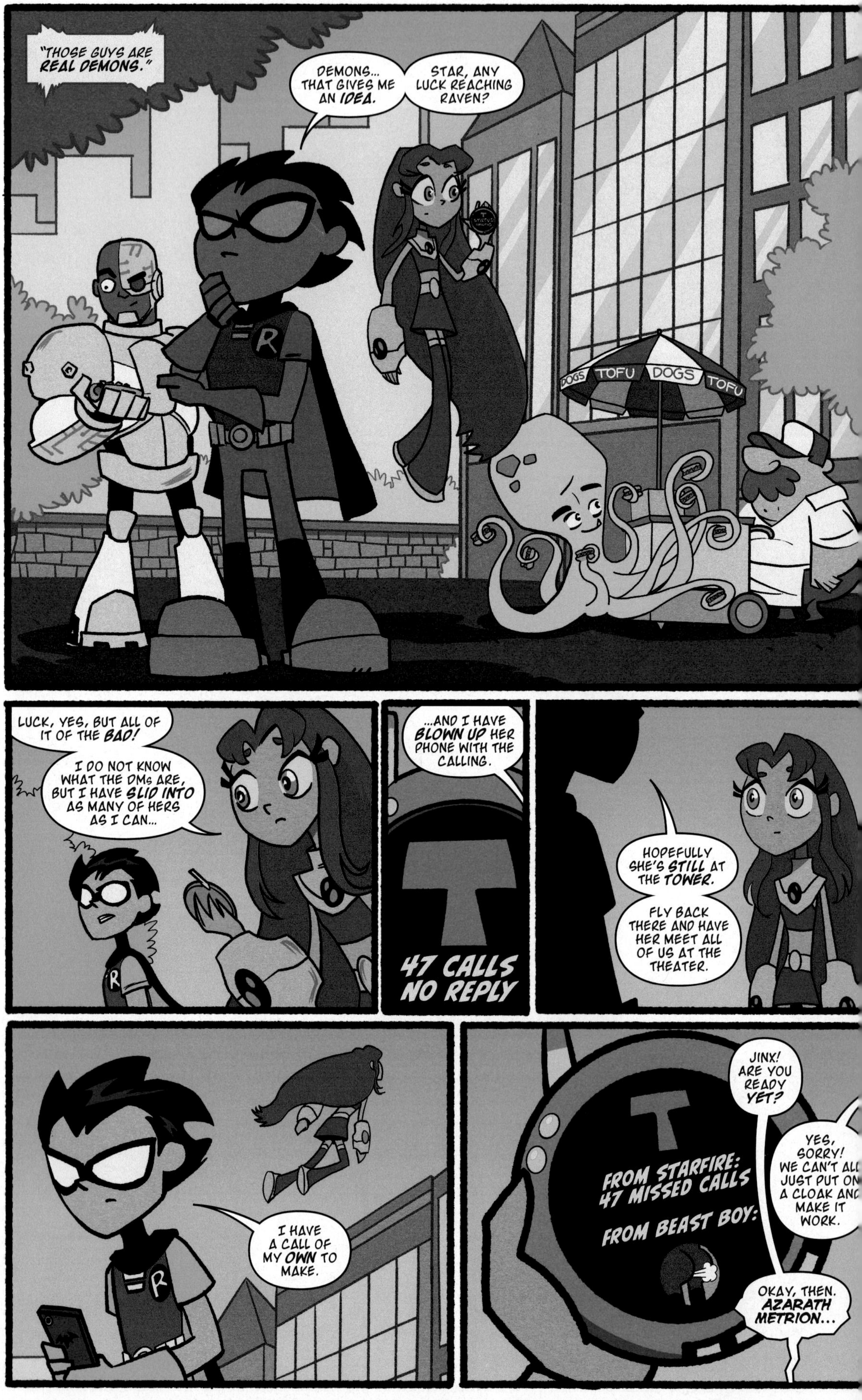
"THOSE GUYS ARE REAL DEMONS."
DEMONS... THAT GIVES ME AN IDEA.
STAR, ANY LUCK REACHING RAVEN?
TOFU DOGS TOFU DOGS TOFU
LUCK, YES, BUT ALL OF IT OF THE BAD!
I DO NOT KNOW WHAT THE DMs ARE, BUT I HAVE SLID INTO AS MANY OF HERS AS I CAN...
...AND I HAVE BLOWN UP HER PHONE WITH THE CALLING.
47 CALLS NO REPLY
HOPEFULLY SHE'S STILL AT THE TOWER.
FLY BACK THERE AND HAVE HER MEET ALL OF US AT THE THEATER.
I HAVE A CALL OF MY OWN TO MAKE.
FROM STARFIRE: 47 MISSED CALLS
FROM BEAST BOY:
JINX! ARE YOU READY YET?
YES, SORRY! WE CAN'T ALL JUST PUT ON A CLOAK AND MAKE IT WORK.
OKAY, THEN. AZARATH METRION...

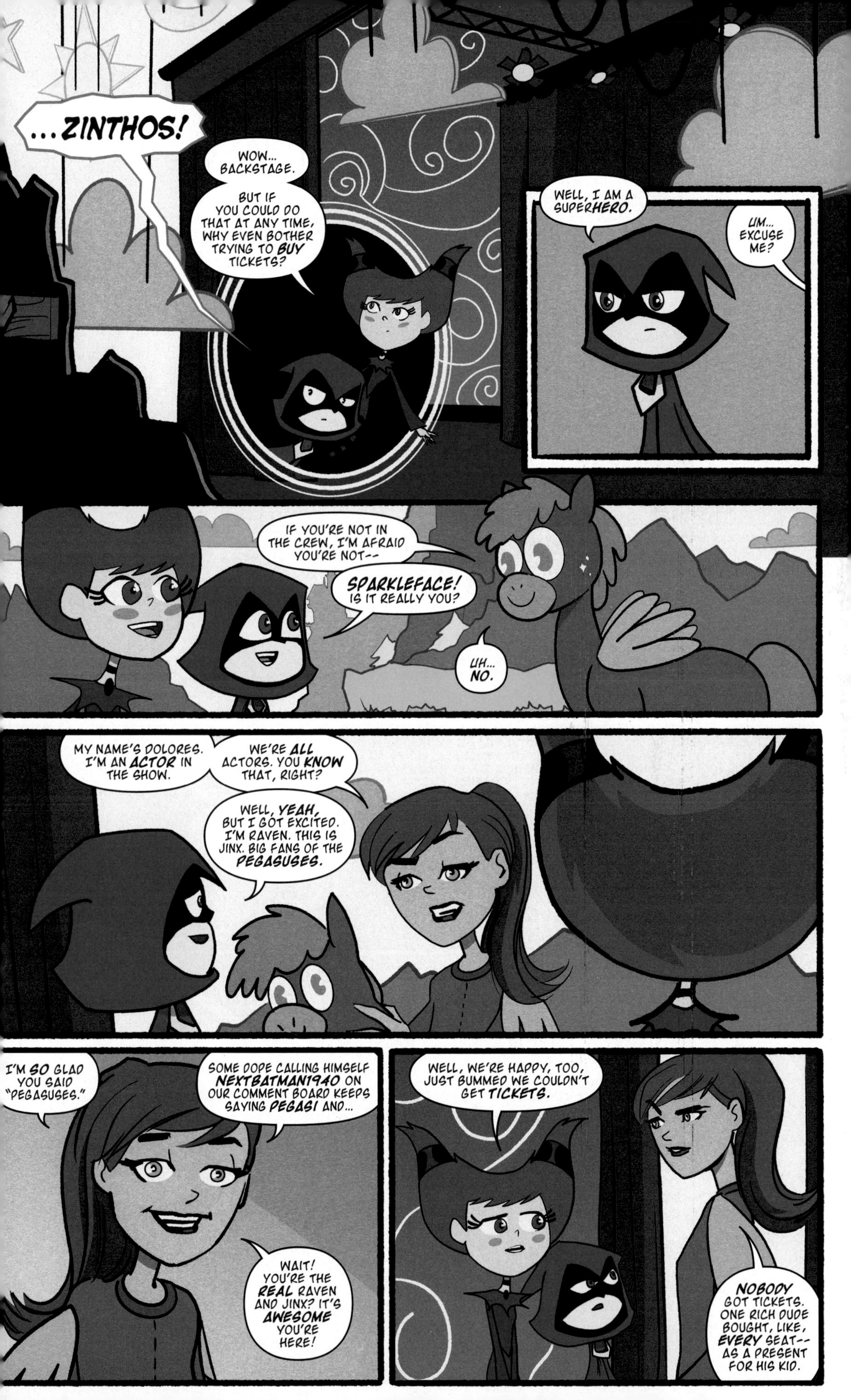
...ZINTHOS!
WOW... BACKSTAGE.
BUT IF YOU COULD DO THAT AT ANY TIME, WHY EVEN BOTHER TRYING TO BUY TICKETS?
WELL, I AM A SUPERHERO.
UM... EXCUSE ME?
IF YOU'RE NOT IN THE CREW, I'M AFRAID YOU'RE NOT--
SPARKLEFACE! IS IT REALLY YOU?
UH... NO.
MY NAME'S DOLORES. I'M AN ACTOR IN THE SHOW.
WE'RE ALL ACTORS. YOU KNOW THAT, RIGHT?
WELL, YEAH, BUT I GOT EXCITED. I'M RAVEN. THIS IS JINX. BIG FANS OF THE PEGASUSES.
I'M SO GLAD YOU SAID "PEGASUSES."
SOME DOPE CALLING HIMSELF NEXTBATMAN1940 ON OUR COMMENT BOARD KEEPS SAYING PEGASI AND...
WAIT! YOU'RE THE REAL RAVEN AND JINX? IT'S AWESOME YOU'RE HERE!
WELL, WE'RE HAPPY, TOO, JUST BUMMED WE COULDN'T GET TICKETS.
NOBODY GOT TICKETS. ONE RICH DUDE BOUGHT, LIKE, EVERY SEAT-- AS A PRESENT FOR HIS KID.

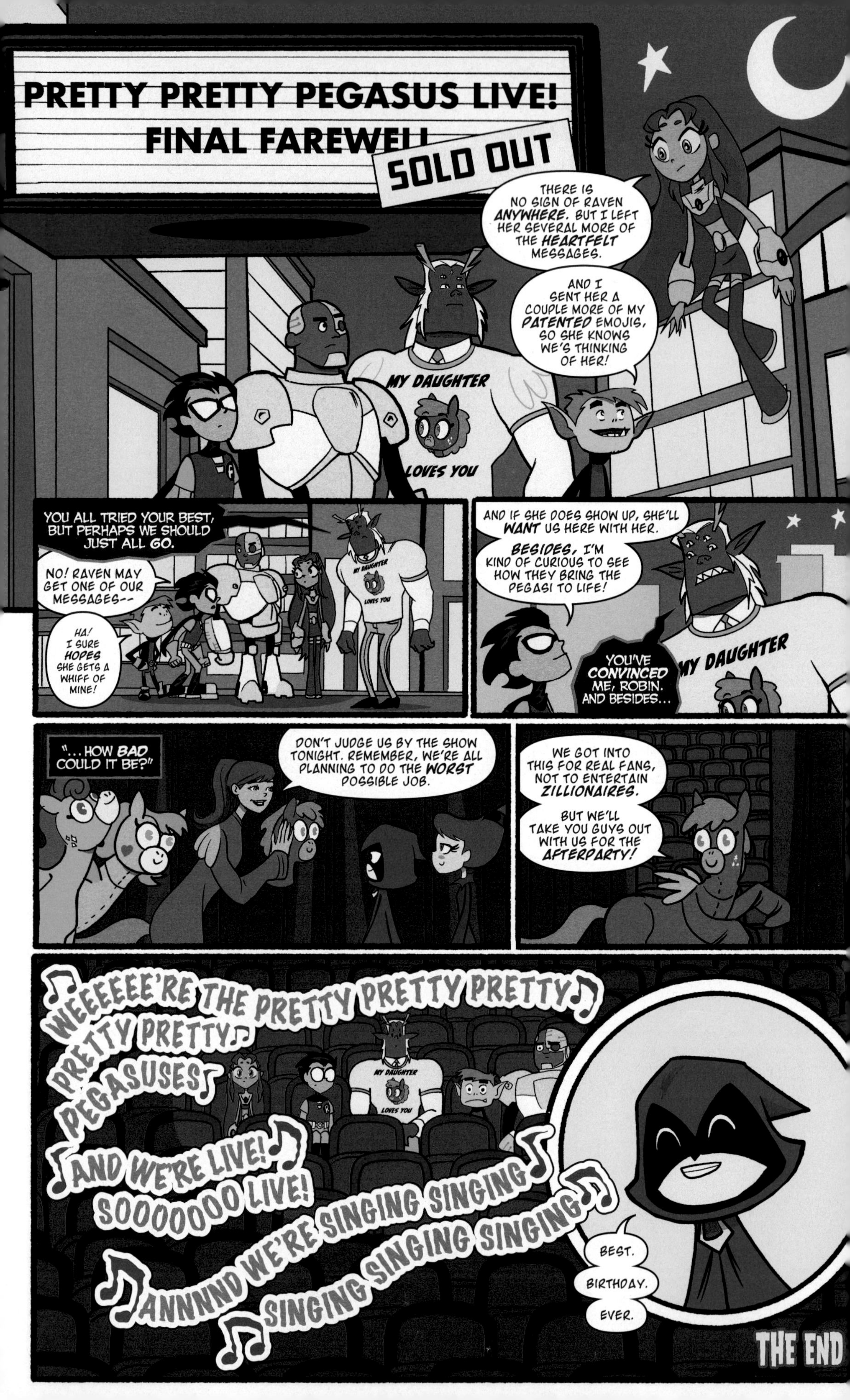
PRETTY PRETTY PEGASUS LIVE!
FINAL FAREWELL
SOLD OUT
THERE IS NO SIGN OF RAVEN ANYWHERE. BUT I LEFT HER SEVERAL MORE OF THE HEARTFELT MESSAGES.
AND I SENT HER A COUPLE MORE OF MY PATENTED EMOJIS, SO SHE KNOWS WE'S THINKING OF HER!
MY DAUGHTER
LOVES YOU
YOU ALL TRIED YOUR BEST, BUT PERHAPS WE SHOULD JUST ALL GO.
NO! RAVEN MAY GET ONE OF OUR MESSAGES--
HA! I SURE HOPES SHE GETS A WHIFF OF MINE!
AND IF SHE DOES SHOW UP, SHE'LL WANT US HERE WITH HER.
BESIDES, I'M KIND OF CURIOUS TO SEE HOW THEY BRING THE PEGASI TO LIFE!
YOU'VE CONVINCED ME, ROBIN. AND BESIDES...
"...HOW BAD COULD IT BE?"
DON'T JUDGE US BY THE SHOW TONIGHT. REMEMBER, WE'RE ALL PLANNING TO DO THE WORST POSSIBLE JOB.
WE GOT INTO THIS FOR REAL FANS, NOT TO ENTERTAIN ZILLIONAIRES.
BUT WE'LL TAKE YOU GUYS OUT WITH US FOR THE AFTERPARTY!
WEEEEEE'RE THE PRETTY PRETTY PRETTY
PRETTY PRETTY
PEGASUSES
AND WE'RE LIVE!
SOOOOOOO LIVE!
ANNNND WE'RE SINGING SINGING
SINGING SINGING SINGING
BEST.
BIRTHDAY.
EVER.
THE END

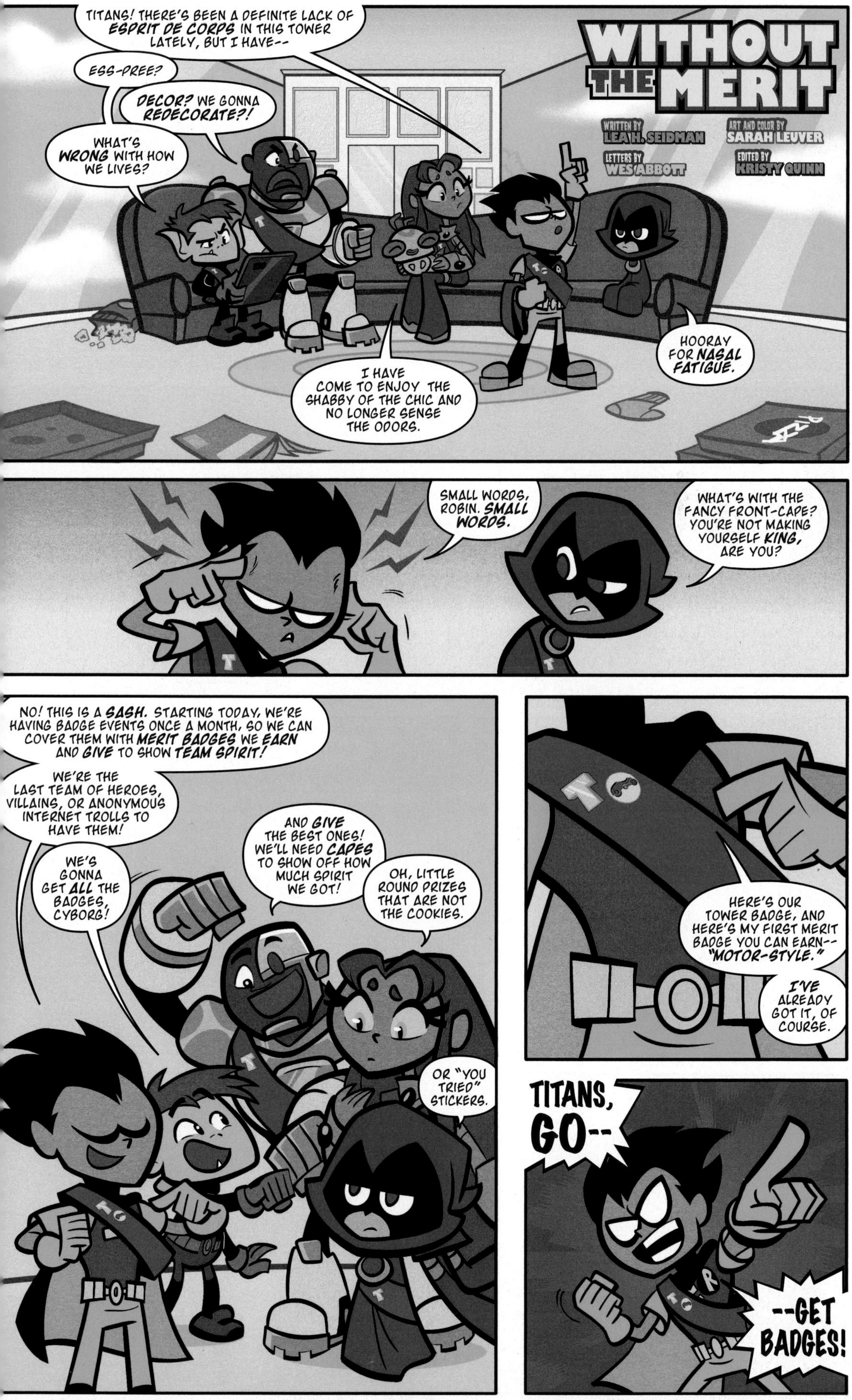
WITHOUT THE MERIT
WRITTEN BY LEA H. SEIDMAN
ART AND COLOR BY SARAH LEUVER
LETTERS BY WES ABBOTT
EDITED BY KRISTY QUINN
TITANS! THERE'S BEEN A DEFINITE LACK OF ESPRIT DE CORPS IN THIS TOWER LATELY, BUT I HAVE--
ESS-PREE?
DECOR? WE GONNA REDECORATE?!
WHAT'S WRONG WITH HOW WE LIVES?
I HAVE COME TO ENJOY THE SHABBY OF THE CHIC AND NO LONGER SENSE THE ODORS.
HOORAY FOR NASAL FATIGUE.
PIZZA
SMALL WORDS, ROBIN. SMALL WORDS.
WHAT'S WITH THE FANCY FRONT-CAPE? YOU'RE NOT MAKING YOURSELF KING, ARE YOU?
NO! THIS IS A SASH. STARTING TODAY, WE'RE HAVING BADGE EVENTS ONCE A MONTH, SO WE CAN COVER THEM WITH MERIT BADGES WE EARN AND GIVE TO SHOW TEAM SPIRIT!
WE'RE THE LAST TEAM OF HEROES, VILLAINS, OR ANONYMOUS INTERNET TROLLS TO HAVE THEM!
WE'S GONNA GET ALL THE BADGES, CYBORG!
AND GIVE THE BEST ONES! WE'LL NEED CAPES TO SHOW OFF HOW MUCH SPIRIT WE GOT!
OH, LITTLE ROUND PRIZES THAT ARE NOT THE COOKIES.
OR "YOU TRIED" STICKERS.
HERE'S OUR TOWER BADGE, AND HERE'S MY FIRST MERIT BADGE YOU CAN EARN-- "MOTOR-STYLE."
I'VE ALREADY GOT IT, OF COURSE.
TITANS, GO--
--GET BADGES!

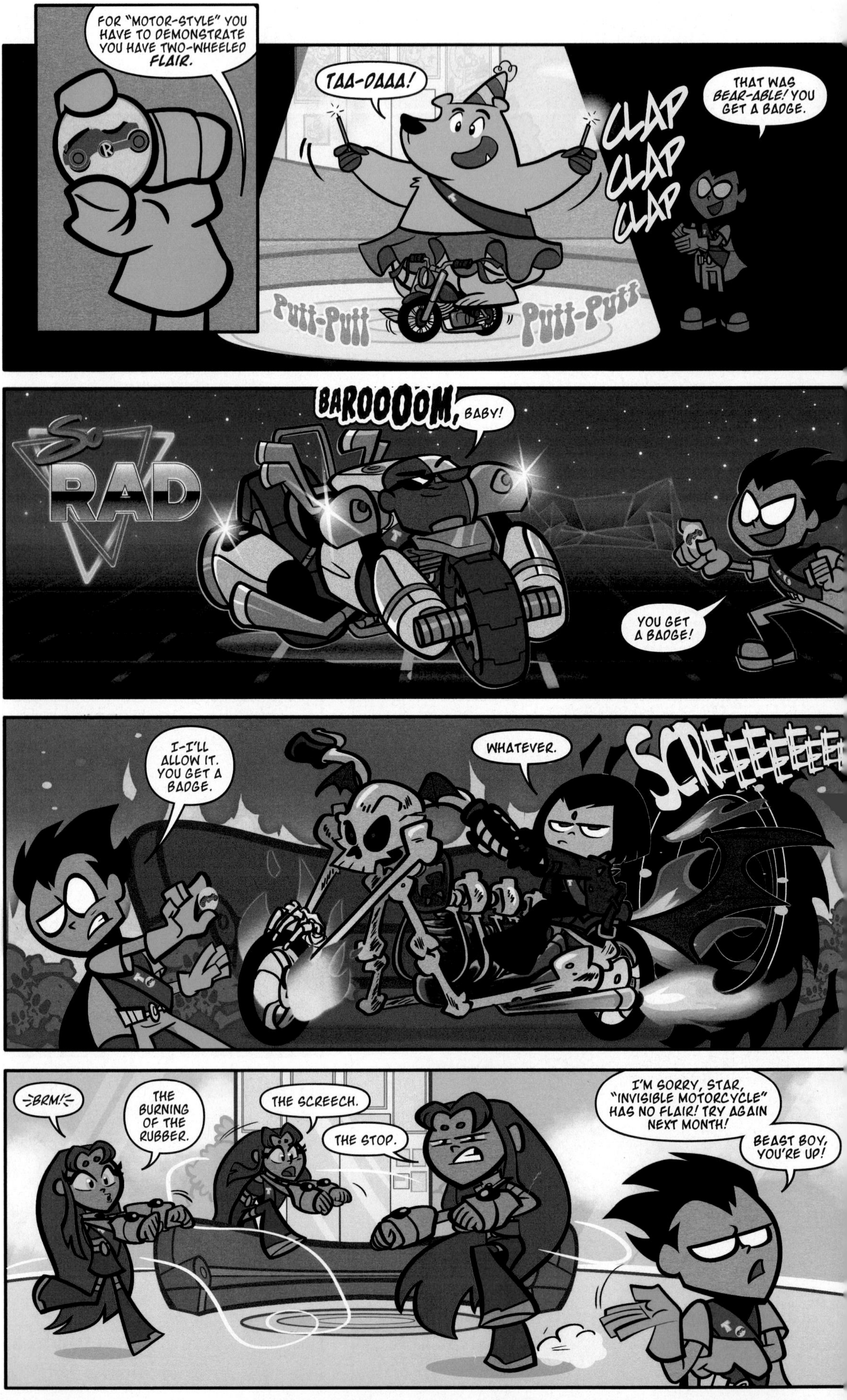
FOR "MOTOR-STYLE" YOU HAVE TO DEMONSTRATE YOU HAVE TWO-WHEELED FLAIR.
TAA-DAAA!
Putt-Putt
Putt-Putt
CLAP CLAP CLAP
THAT WAS BEAR-ABLE! YOU GET A BADGE.
So RAD
BAROOOOM, BABY!
YOU GET A BADGE!
I-I'LL ALLOW IT. YOU GET A BADGE.
WHATEVER.
BRM!
THE BURNING OF THE RUBBER.
THE SCREECH.
THE STOP.
I'M SORRY, STAR, "INVISIBLE MOTORCYCLE" HAS NO FLAIR! TRY AGAIN NEXT MONTH!
BEAST BOY, YOU'RE UP!

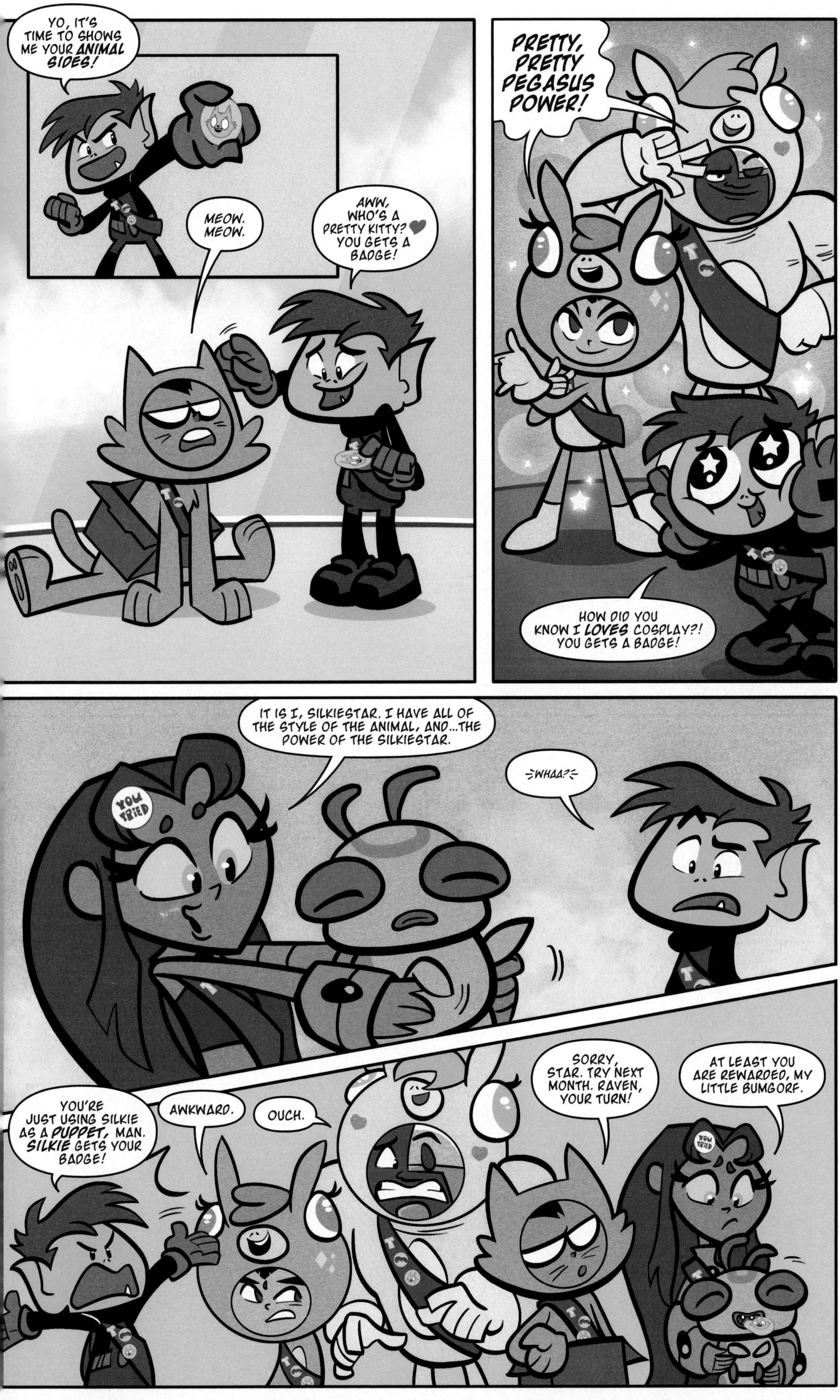
YO, IT'S TIME TO SHOWS ME YOUR ANIMAL SIDES!
MEOW. MEOW.
AWW, WHO'S A PRETTY KITTY? ♥ YOU GETS A BADGE!
PRETTY, PRETTY PEGASUS POWER!
HOW DID YOU KNOW I LOVES COSPLAY?! YOU GETS A BADGE!
IT IS I, SILKIESTAR. I HAVE ALL OF THE STYLE OF THE ANIMAL, AND...THE POWER OF THE SILKIESTAR.
WHAA?
YOU TRIED
YOU'RE JUST USING SILKIE AS A PUPPET, MAN. SILKIE GETS YOUR BADGE!
AWKWARD.
OUCH.
SORRY, STAR. TRY NEXT MONTH. RAVEN, YOUR TURN!
AT LEAST YOU ARE REWARDED, MY LITTLE BUMGORF.

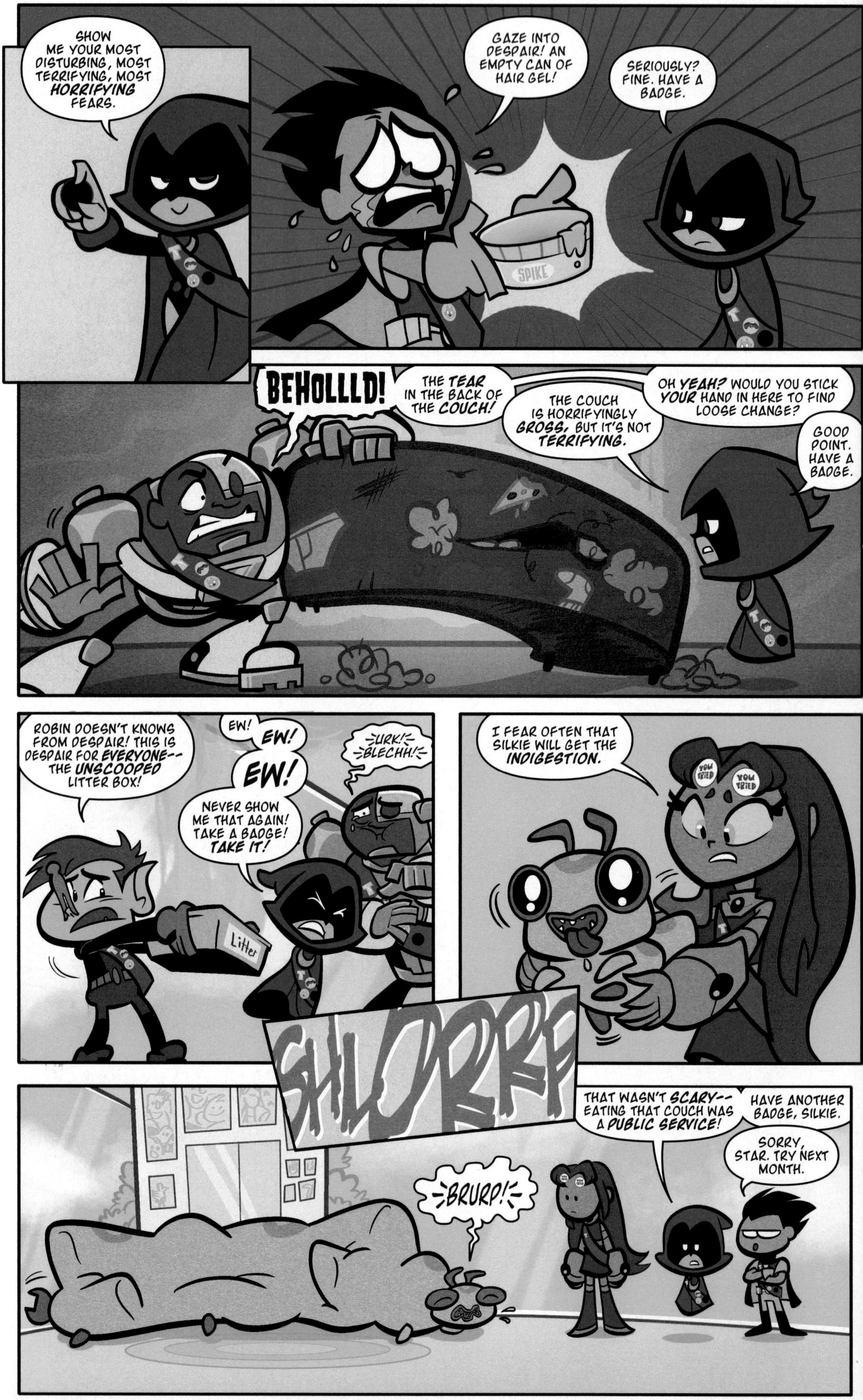
SHOW ME YOUR MOST DISTURBING, MOST TERRIFYING, MOST HORRIFYING FEARS.
GAZE INTO DESPAIR! AN EMPTY CAN OF HAIR GEL!
SPIKE
SERIOUSLY? FINE. HAVE A BADGE.
BEHOLLLD!
THE TEAR IN THE BACK OF THE COUCH!
THE COUCH IS HORRIFYINGLY GROSS, BUT IT'S NOT TERRIFYING.
OH YEAH? WOULD YOU STICK YOUR HAND IN HERE TO FIND LOOSE CHANGE?
GOOD POINT. HAVE A BADGE.
ROBIN DOESN'T KNOWS FROM DESPAIR! THIS IS DESPAIR FOR EVERYONE-- THE UNSCOOPED LITTER BOX!
EW!
EW!
EW!
URK! BLECHH!
NEVER SHOW ME THAT AGAIN! TAKE A BADGE! TAKE IT!
Litter
I FEAR OFTEN THAT SILKIE WILL GET THE INDIGESTION.
YOU TRIED
YOU TRIED
SHLORRF
BRURP!
THAT WASN'T SCARY-- EATING THAT COUCH WAS A PUBLIC SERVICE!
HAVE ANOTHER BADGE, SILKIE.
SORRY, STAR. TRY NEXT MONTH.

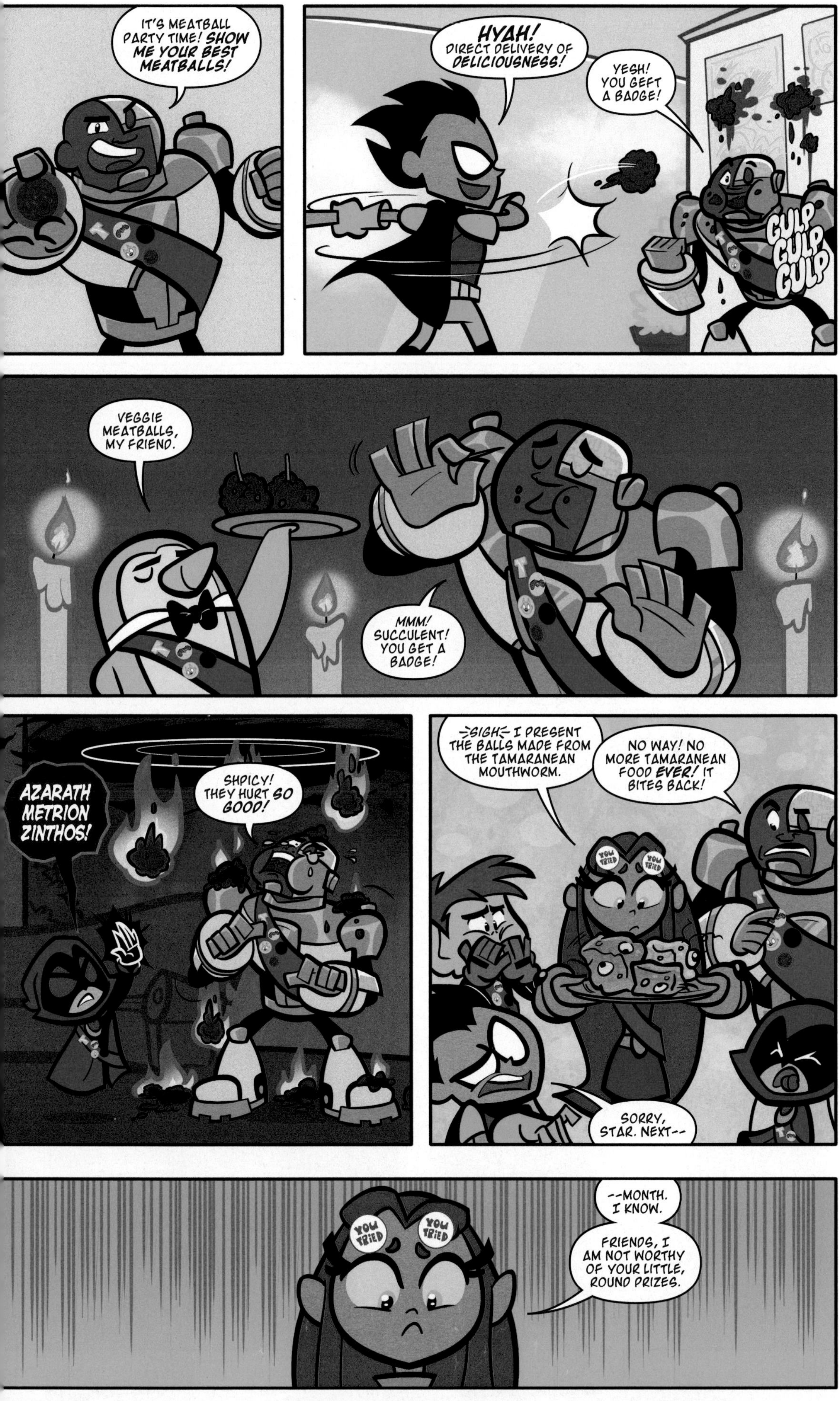

IT'S MEATBALL PARTY TIME! SHOW ME YOUR BEST MEATBALLS!
HYAH! DIRECT DELIVERY OF DELICIOUSNESS!
YESH! YOU GEFT A BADGE!
GULP GULP GULP
VEGGIE MEATBALLS, MY FRIEND.
MMM! SUCCULENT! YOU GET A BADGE!
AZARATH METRION ZINTHOS!
SHPICY! THEY HURT SO GOOD!
≈SIGH≈ I PRESENT THE BALLS MADE FROM THE TAMARANEAN MOUTHWORM.
NO WAY! NO MORE TAMARANEAN FOOD EVER! IT BITES BACK!
YOU TRIED
SORRY, STAR. NEXT--
--MONTH. I KNOW.
FRIENDS, I AM NOT WORTHY OF YOUR LITTLE, ROUND PRIZES.

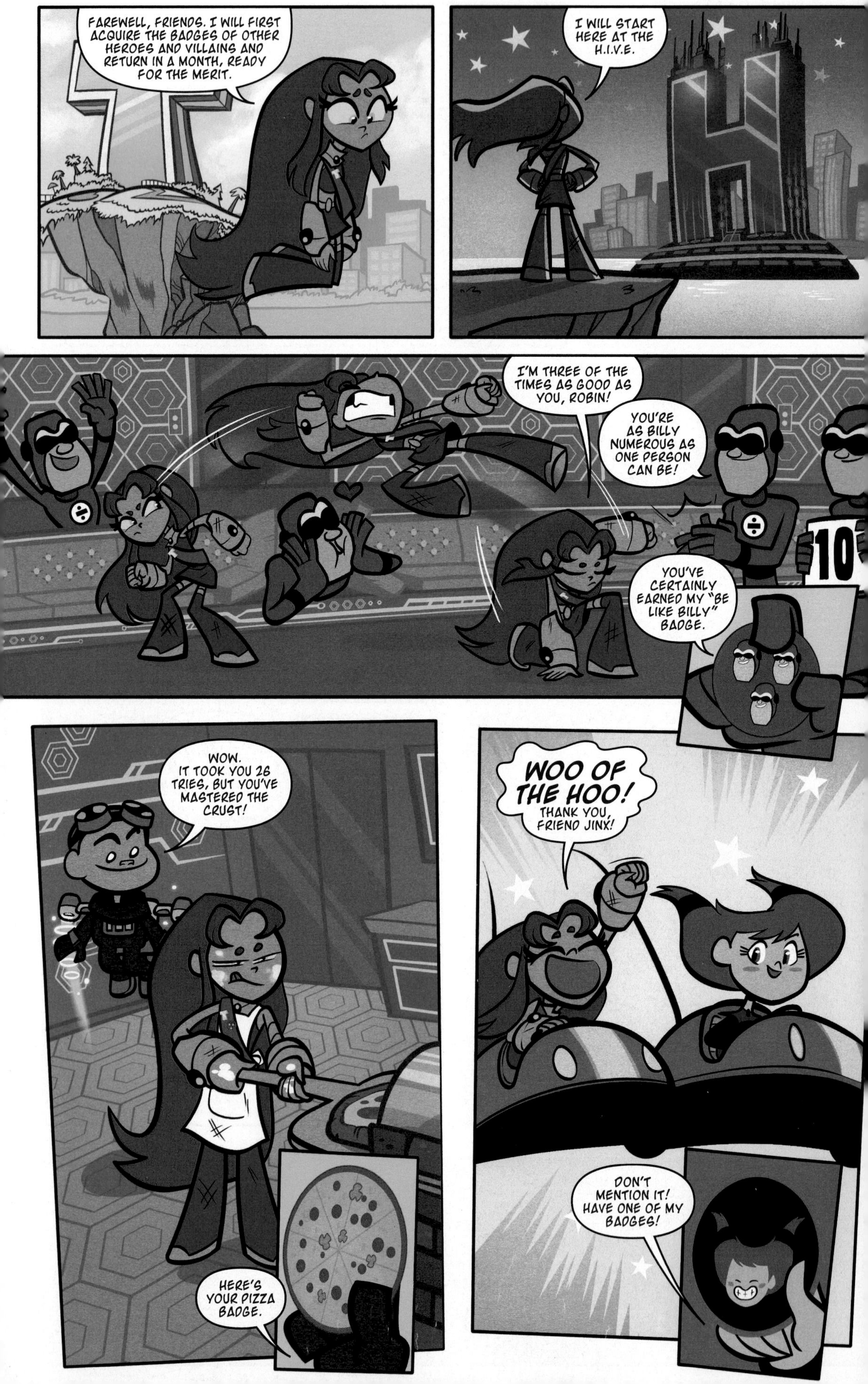

FAREWELL, FRIENDS. I WILL FIRST ACQUIRE THE BADGES OF OTHER HEROES AND VILLAINS AND RETURN IN A MONTH, READY FOR THE MERIT.
I WILL START HERE AT THE H.I.V.E.
I'M THREE OF THE TIMES AS GOOD AS YOU, ROBIN!
YOU'RE AS BILLY NUMEROUS AS ONE PERSON CAN BE!
10
YOU'VE CERTAINLY EARNED MY "BE LIKE BILLY" BADGE.
WOW. IT TOOK YOU 26 TRIES, BUT YOU'VE MASTERED THE CRUST!
HERE'S YOUR PIZZA BADGE.
WOO OF THE HOO! THANK YOU, FRIEND JINX!
DON'T MENTION IT! HAVE ONE OF MY BADGES!

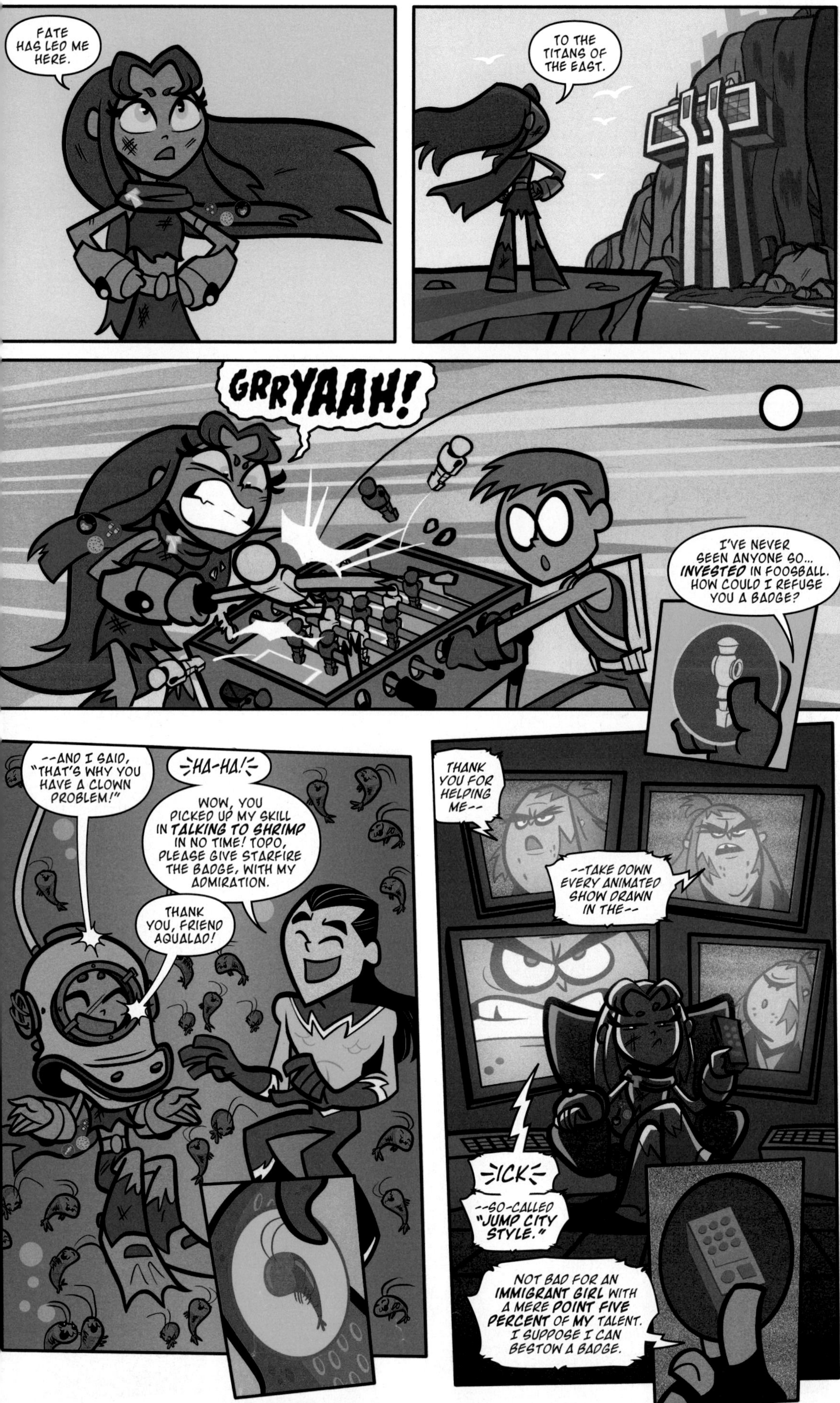
FATE HAS LED ME HERE.
TO THE TITANS OF THE EAST.
GRRYAAH!
I'VE NEVER SEEN ANYONE SO... INVESTED IN FOOSBALL. HOW COULD I REFUSE YOU A BADGE?
--AND I SAID, "THAT'S WHY YOU HAVE A CLOWN PROBLEM!"
HA-HA!
WOW, YOU PICKED UP MY SKILL IN TALKING TO SHRIMP IN NO TIME! TOPO, PLEASE GIVE STARFIRE THE BADGE, WITH MY ADMIRATION.
THANK YOU, FRIEND AQUALAD!
THANK YOU FOR HELPING ME--
--TAKE DOWN EVERY ANIMATED SHOW DRAWN IN THE--
ICK
--SO-CALLED "JUMP CITY STYLE."
NOT BAD FOR AN IMMIGRANT GIRL WITH A MERE POINT FIVE PERCENT OF MY TALENT. I SUPPOSE I CAN BESTOW A BADGE.

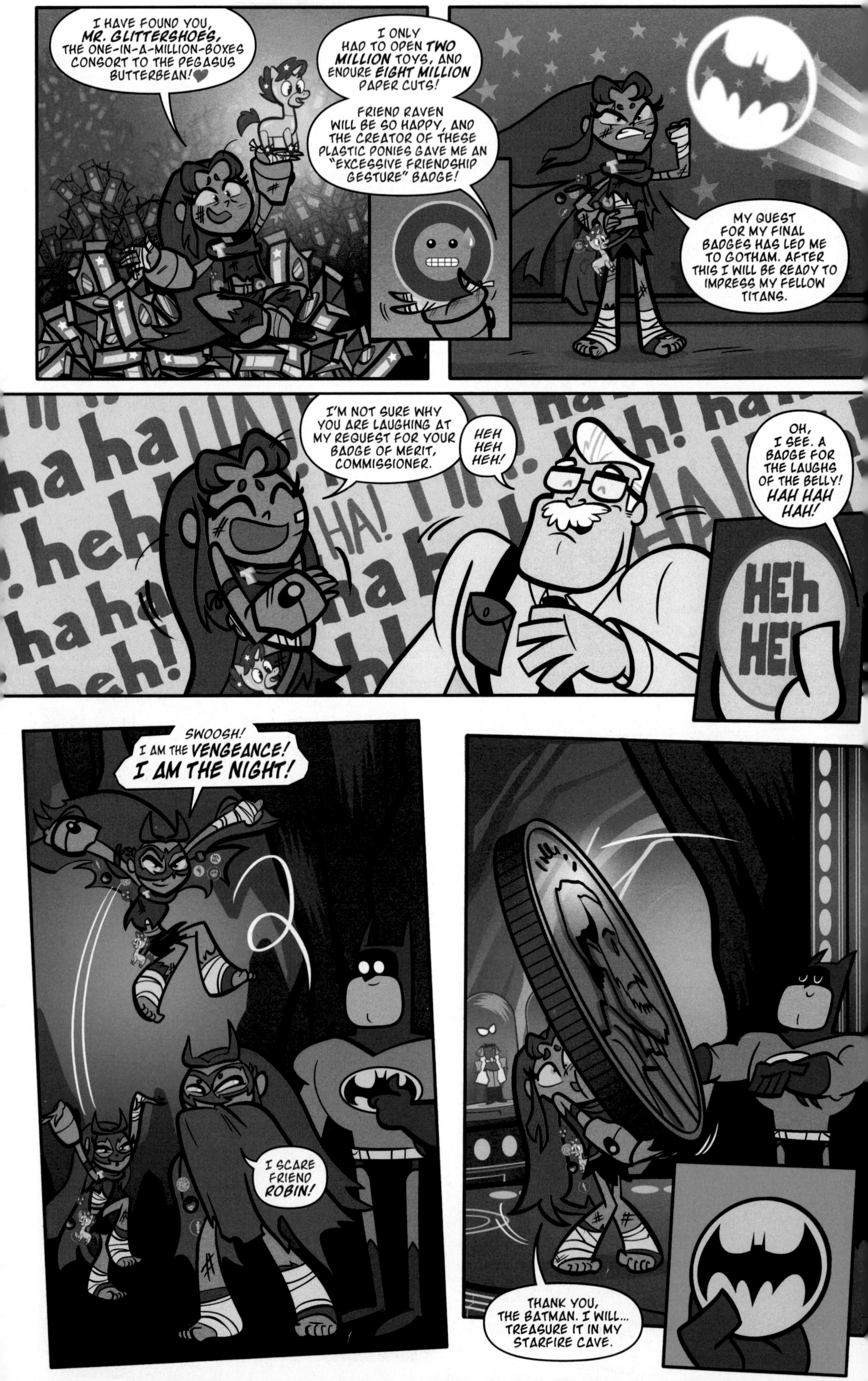
I HAVE FOUND YOU, MR. GLITTERSHOES, THE ONE-IN-A-MILLION-BOXES CONSORT TO THE PEGASUS BUTTERBEAN!
I ONLY HAD TO OPEN TWO MILLION TOYS, AND ENDURE EIGHT MILLION PAPER CUTS!
FRIEND RAVEN WILL BE SO HAPPY, AND THE CREATOR OF THESE PLASTIC PONIES GAVE ME AN "EXCESSIVE FRIENDSHIP GESTURE" BADGE!
MY QUEST FOR MY FINAL BADGES HAS LED ME TO GOTHAM. AFTER THIS I WILL BE READY TO IMPRESS MY FELLOW TITANS.
I'M NOT SURE WHY YOU ARE LAUGHING AT MY REQUEST FOR YOUR BADGE OF MERIT, COMMISSIONER.
HEH HEH HEH!
OH, I SEE. A BADGE FOR THE LAUGHS OF THE BELLY! HAH HAH HAH!
SWOOSH! I AM THE VENGEANCE! I AM THE NIGHT!
I SCARE FRIEND ROBIN!
THANK YOU, THE BATMAN. I WILL... TREASURE IT IN MY STARFIRE CAVE.

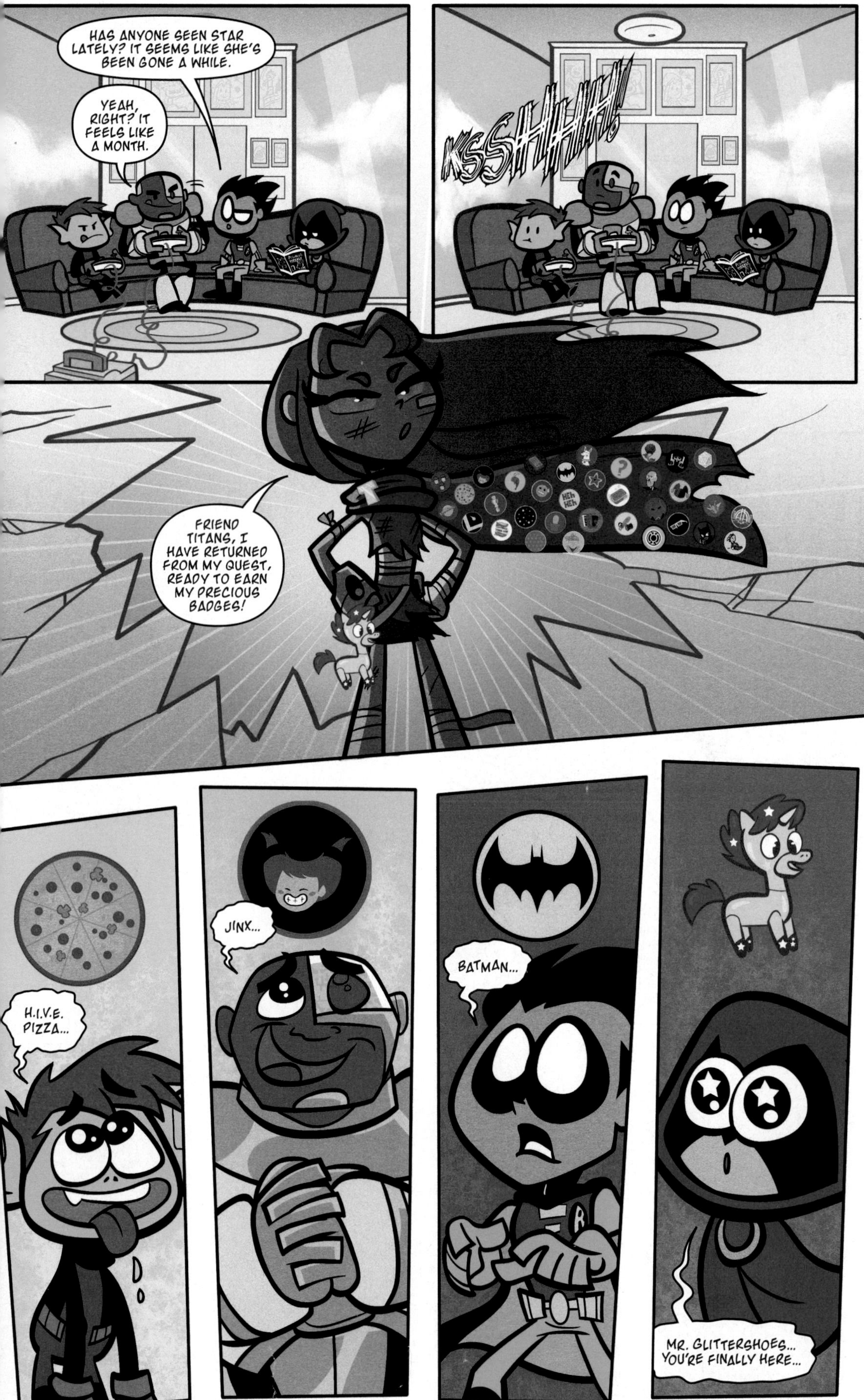

HAS ANYONE SEEN STAR LATELY? IT SEEMS LIKE SHE'S BEEN GONE A WHILE.
YEAH, RIGHT? IT FEELS LIKE A MONTH.
KSSHHHH!
FRIEND TITANS, I HAVE RETURNED FROM MY QUEST, READY TO EARN MY PRECIOUS BADGES!
H.I.V.E. PIZZA...
JINX...
BATMAN...
MR. GLITTERSHOES... YOU'RE FINALLY HERE...

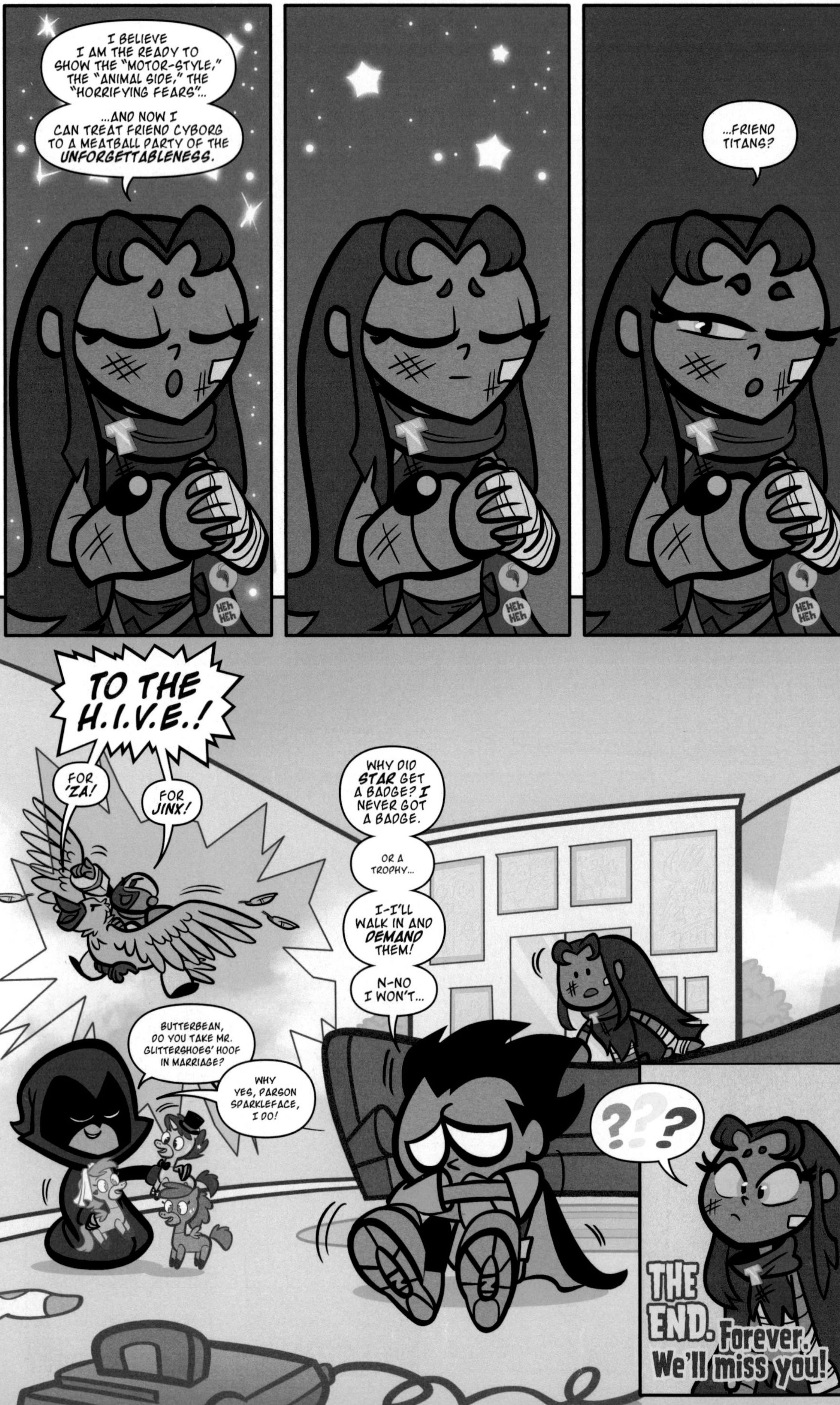
I BELIEVE I AM THE READY TO SHOW THE "MOTOR-STYLE," THE "ANIMAL SIDE," THE "HORRIFYING FEARS"...
...AND NOW I CAN TREAT FRIEND CYBORG TO A MEATBALL PARTY OF THE UNFORGETTABLENESS.
...FRIEND TITANS?
HEH HEH
TO THE H.I.V.E.!
FOR 'ZA!
FOR JINX!
WHY DID STAR GET A BADGE? I NEVER GOT A BADGE.
OR A TROPHY...
I-I'LL WALK IN AND DEMAND THEM!
N-NO I WON'T...
BUTTERBEAN, DO YOU TAKE MR. GLITTERSHOES' HOOF IN MARRIAGE?
WHY YES, PARSON SPARKLEFACE, I DO!
???
THE END. Forever. We'll miss you!